Blow my Fuse

HOLLYWOOD DEMONS #2

USA TODAY BESTSELLING AUTHOR
AUTUMN JONES LAKE

BLOW MY FUSE

Hollywood Demons #2

AUTUMN JONES LAKE

Hollywood Demons #2
Copyright © 2020 Autumn Jones Lake
All rights reserved.

Digital ISBN #: 978-1-943950-53-9
Print ISBN #: 978-1-943950-55-3
Large Print ISBN #: 978-1-943950-56-0
Audio ISBN #: 978-1-943950-57-7

Cover Model: Megan Napolitan
Cover Designer: Lori Jackson Design
Photographer: Wander Aguiar Photography
Edited by: Angela James
Proofread by: Fairest Reviews Editing Services

ALSO BY AUTUMN JONES LAKE

THE LOST KINGS MC SERIES

Slow Burn (Lost Kings MC #1)

Corrupting Cinderella (Lost Kings MC #2)

Three Kings, One Night (Lost Kings MC #2.5)

Strength From Loyalty (Lost Kings MC #3)

Tattered on My Sleeve (Lost Kings MC #4)

White Heat (Lost Kings MC #5)

Between Embers (Lost Kings MC #5.5)

More Than Miles (Lost Kings MC #6)

White Knuckles (Lost Kings MC #7)

Beyond Reckless (Lost Kings MC #8)

Beyond Reason (Lost Kings MC #9)

One Empire Night (Lost Kings MC #9.5)

After Burn (Lost Kings MC #10)

After Glow (Lost Kings MC #11)

Zero Hour (Lost Kings MC #11.5)

Zero Tolerance (Lost Kings MC #12)

Zero Regret (Lost Kings MC #13)

Zero Apologies (Lost Kings MC #14)

White Lies (Lost Kings MC #15)

Swagger and Sass (A Lost Kings MC Novella)

Rhythm of the Road (Lost Kings MC #16)

The Lost Kings MC World

Hollywood Demons Series

Kickstart My Heart

Blow My Fuse

Wheels of Fire

Standalones

Bullets & Bonfires

Warnings & Wildfires

Cards of Love: Knight of Swords

Paranormal Romance

Catnip & Cauldrons Series

Onyx Night

Onyx Shadows

Feral Escape

CHAPTER ONE

"I NEED you to go home to L.A."

As far as morning greetings go, that's probably my rudest one yet.

Mallory's still groggy, so she doesn't hold it against me. She yawns, then rolls out of bed and shuffles into the bathroom.

It's hard to be sympathetic when someone you've considered a brother lands on your bad side. Yesterday, Jacob slammed into my bad side at 180 miles-per-hour. Attempting to set Mallory up with Davey Revolver by luring her to that creep's hotel room is the lowest stunt Jacob's ever pulled and possibly my breaking point. I don't care how hard he thinks we've worked or how desperately he wants our band to finally achieve success. At the moment, I'm fresh out of compassion.

All night long I considered my options.

Kill Jacob.

Kill Davey.

Quit the band and go home.

Murder Jacob and Davey then quit the band.

One and two are currently my favorite options.

Now that I've appeased the punishment-thirsty demon inside me by considering the bloodiest options, I go over some more practical solutions.

Sending Mallory home is the best way to keep her safe. After what happened yesterday, if I have her continue on the tour, I'm only putting her in danger. Davey will be a hell of a lot sneakier next time.

As much as I'd love to march into our next band meeting and announce that I'm quitting, I can't do it. Call it pride or stubbornness, but I refuse to let Jacob's stupid stunt ruin everything I've spent the last few years working toward.

Mallory's safety is my top priority. As much as I'll miss having her by my side for the rest of the tour, I can't be selfish and have her stay. I hope she sees the situation the same way and isn't hurt or doesn't feel like I'm punishing *her* for what happened.

She's so damn cute as she toddles back to bed, yawning and blinking. I flip the covers aside, and she crawls into bed, curling up next to me.

How am I supposed to send her home and finish the tour without her by my side?

Easy, there's no other choice.

"What was that you said, now?" she mumbles.

"After yesterday, I'm worried about you finishing out the tour. I need you to fly home. Today if possible."

She takes a deep breath and lets it out slowly. "Thank you."

"You're not mad?"

"Are you kidding? If anything, I'm relieved." She shifts her gaze away from me. "I feel guilty though. I don't want to abandon you if you need me."

Christ, I love this woman so much. I reach out and cup her face with my hand, rubbing my thumb over her cheek. "You're not abandoning me at all. I want you somewhere safe, away from that asshole, while I deal with the fallout." I'm expecting some sort of payback from Revolver, and I don't want Mallory here when retribution arrives.

She bites her lip and nods. "I'll start packing up my stuff."

While she packs, I roll over, grab the hotel phone and dial downstairs, asking the operator to connect me to the airport.

After an hour of arguing and charging a ridiculous amount on my lone credit card, I have her booked on a flight home.

I can't manage her bags on the bike that I rented, so when we get downstairs, I ask the bellman to hail a cab for us.

"You okay?" I ask. Mallory has my hand in a death grip the whole way to the airport. "Are you afraid of flying so far by yourself?"

She turns and blinks tears out of her eyes. "It's not that. I hate leaving you. I hate leaving like this. I'm so sorry I messed things up for you."

I can't stand her thinking she's done something wrong when she hasn't been anything other than a loyal, supportive woman.

It hits me hard—I'd choose *her* over music in a heartbeat every day of the week. "You're not responsible for this. If they didn't have me by the balls with that contract, I'd go home with you." Davey would no doubt tie me up in lawsuits for the next few years, and I won't allow that asshole to have that kind of influence over my life.

"I would never ask you to leave. Then they win. And

you've worked too hard and for too many years to allow that dirty old man to take your career away from you."

This woman floors me. Every damn time. I expected her to be bitter, maybe pissed that I wasn't coming home with her. Something. She's everything sweet and loyal I don't deserve.

I swallow hard past the lump in my throat. "I still don't know what I'm going to do about Jacob."

"He wants to succeed at any cost. I'm sure in his mind he was doing me a favor. A win-win for everyone. He's probably shocked I didn't jump at the chance to screw Davey, and you didn't fall at his feet with gratitude." She shrugs. "I don't respect it, but I understand to a certain extent."

I'm glad she understands, because I sure as fuck don't. More than ever, I miss home. Miss my MC family. I made a mistake thinking my bandmates had the same loyalty as my MC brothers.

Back home, if a brother even joked about passing another brother's old lady around, the punishment would be severe. In this world, I'm the one who stands to be punished. By the record label, my manager, my band, as well as Bloody Revolver if they decide to kick us off the tour.

Even if I end up losing everything, I wouldn't change a thing about the way I handled it.

Still doesn't change the fact that sending her home will rip my heart in two.

CHAPTER TWO

Saying goodbye to Chaser is almost impossible. I can't release his hand, and every time I look at his beautiful face, my heart constricts with pain.

We're at the gate, and I need to board the plane, but I can't let go.

Our eyes meet, and he draws me into a tight embrace. "It's okay, little dove. I'll be home next week. You won't have time to miss me."

"I already miss you." My throat's so tight I barely get the words out. *Don't cry. Don't cry. Don't you dare cry.* I'll cry by myself on the plane where Chaser can't see me and feel any worse about this than I already know he does.

He leans down and presses his lips against mine. My hand

tunnels into his hair, holding him to me for a much deeper, longer kiss.

"Call me as soon as you're settled. I don't care how much it costs"

"I will. I'll call my agent tomorrow too, so she knows I'm back early and can set some stuff up for me."

He hesitates. "Wait until I get back, please. Or at least don't go to any auditions alone."

"I went on auditions alone before while you were away."

"Please." His simple plea can't be ignored. "I hate being so far away if something happens."

"I won't. I promise."

"I love you so much, little dove. You're my whole world."

Agony tightens its fingers around my throat. "I love you, too," I whisper.

I can't stall any longer. I have to go. With trembling fingers, I take my bag out of his hands. I turn once, before stepping into the long hallway leading to the plane. Chaser stands there, thumbs hooked in his pockets, legs wide, stoic expression in place. He nods and mouths, *"Go on. I love you."*

"Me too."

I make it onto the plane and into my seat without shedding a tear.

The gentleman in the next seat leers at me and rubs my arm. "What's a pretty girl like you doing traveling all alone?" His fingers graze the side of my breast. "Are you all right, sweetheart?"

I've had it with creeps invading my personal space. "I'm fine," I answer tartly, jerking my arm away.

I take out my Walkman and snap in a cassette. As I'm adjusting my headphones, he mutters, "Bitch" under his breath.

If not wanting to be groped makes me a bitch, then so be it.

I bet if a man were in this seat, he wouldn't have rubbed *his* arm.

When the stewardess walks by, I reach out to grab her attention.

"Is there another seat I can move to?" I tilt my head and put as much effort as possible into my get-me-away-from-this-jerk eyes.

She shifts her gaze toward the creep next to the window and nods. "Come on. There are a few empty seats on this flight. I'll set you up near the back."

Once I'm settled in my new, creep-free spot, I slip my headphones into place, rest my head against the seat and close my eyes.

The pilot makes an announcement.

The plane moves down the runway.

Sadness intertwined with pain comes in waves. Ripping out my heart and leaving it in England might have hurt less.

Fear scoots in behind the pain of leaving Chaser.

Only time will tell if our love is real or if I've been living in a fantasy.

He put everything on the line for me. Over the next few weeks, will he see it as a mistake? Resent me for making things difficult for him? Did I ruin everything he and his band have worked so hard for?

We'll survive this separation, right?

CHAPTER THREE

Chaser

RAGE BEATS against my skin from the inside, threatening to break free and pound the next person who pisses me off into oblivion.

It hurt like hell leaving Mallory at the airport. Watching her walk onto the plane? It took every ounce of strength not to run after her.

Foul is the only way to describe my mood when I walk into our band meeting later that afternoon.

"Are we calmer today?" Val asks in a neutral tone.

"No, Val. I'm not calm at all. But I'm here to do my job, so let's get to work."

Ignoring the seat she points for me to take, I flatten my back against the wall and cross my arms over my chest. Alvin stands and takes up the spot next to me. Given the circumstances, it's a bold move, and I appreciate his support.

Jacob, the coward, won't meet my eyes. Garrett lifts his chin in my direction. A big gesture for him, since he's so tightly aligned with Jacob.

"Okay. Well, then," Val says, composing herself. "I spoke to Revolver's manager last night. And the lawyers for the record company this morning. You messed up Davey's face pretty bad, but he's not pressing charges. You're still required to finish these tour dates, but Kickstart is not invited on the next leg of the tour."

Boo-fucking-hoo. As if I would've said yes after what went down yesterday. I glare at Val and then Jacob, daring them to complain about the missed opportunity.

"Did you happen to ask the suits for any advice on the sexual harassment lawsuit Mallory should slap on Davey?" I ask.

The question startles Val out of her self-imposed calm. "Hardly. All anyone has to do is look at your video or the dozens of videos of her on stage every night."

"That's just fucking great," I snarl. "Playing a part for us means she deserves to have creeps like Davey come on to her? That's what you're saying, Val?"

For a second, a brief glimmer of remorse flickers over her face. "No, I don't think she deserves that. But that's how Davey and his lawyers would make it look."

I nod, because she's right. And maybe if this wasn't so personal, I might have seen it the same way at one point in my life. Not anymore. It's becoming crystal clear to me that honor and integrity are practically non-existent in this business.

"We need you two at the arena by seven," she continues.

My mouth twists into a smirk. Can't wait to share the news. "I sent Mallory home today."

Val sighs. "I suppose that's for the best."

"Do ya?"

"Don't you think that was a decision the band should've made?" Jacob asks.

Apparently, I didn't punch this motherfucker hard enough yesterday.

I push away from the wall and slap my hands on the table, leaning over to stare him straight in the eye. "Gee, I don't know. Shouldn't *the band* have made the decision to whore out my girlfriend for a few extra tour dates?"

He slides his gaze to the floor. "I wasn't trying to whore her out."

"No? What exactly would you call it when you lure her to a room where she's alone with a half-naked old man who wants to fuck her in exchange for giving us some extra tour dates? A matchmaking arrangement?"

He lifts his hands in the air and shrugs. "A mutually beneficial agreement?"

"Have you always been this much of an asshole? Or did the little taste of fame get to you?"

He pounds his fist against the table and winces—pussy. "Did you forget all the shit we did in the early days? All the work we put in? The endless walking up and down the strip, hustling to get even the shittiest bars to let us play? The sleeping in cars? Sleeping with girls we didn't even *like* so we had a place to stay or so they'd buy us groceries? Forget that already, Chaser?"

Val winces at that last part. Since I'm not in the mood to worry about her feelings at the moment, I ignore her. "Those were choices we made for ourselves with our eyes wide open."

"Well, Mallory was given a choice, and she chose *you* over one of the biggest rock stars on the planet." Jacob's voice rises to a mocking pitch. "It must be love. Isn't that fucking sweet?"

"You jealous, bro?" I sneer.

He glares at me. "I thought it was a way to help us and her at the same time."

"If you were trying to be so helpful, why be sneaky? Why go behind my back?"

He sits there with his mouth hanging open.

"That's what I thought."

"Enough," Val says. "What Jacob did was stupid and somewhere deep down he regrets it. Are we all able to move on from this?"

She turns her glare on Jacob, clearly waiting for him to recite whatever lines she fed him before the meeting.

Finally, he glances up and meets my eyes. "I'm sorry."

He explained his utterly bullshit reasoning. I didn't buy it. So, yeah, *now* he's genuinely sorry. Honestly, his excuses aren't much different from Mallory's analysis this morning. And I don't think I was off the mark with the jealousy question.

Surprisingly, he goes one step further. "I'll apologize to Mallory when we get home. I hope she doesn't hate me too much."

I shake my head. "Nah, she has zero respect for you now, but she doesn't hate you."

He snorts. "Fair enough."

"Are we good?" Val asks.

"I still don't trust him." I shift my gaze to Val. "Or *you*. But for now, we're fine."

She coughs and looks away. "All right then." Her voice takes on a stronger edge, and she passes her gaze over each one of us. "Let's blow the roof off these last few shows. Rock those fans so hard they won't even remember who Bloody Revolver is."

Garrett stands and lifts his arms over his head. "Fuckin' A! Let's do this, motherfuckers."

After the heated talk, I finally laugh and slap Garrett on the back. Val gives me a stiff one-armed hug, and Alvin thumps my back a few times.

I'm not quite ready to hug it out with Jacob yet, but I slap his hand when he holds it up.

While I've made peace with my band—sort of—I doubt the situation with Davey Revolver will be resolved as smoothly. I'm not sure how much lower the guy can sink, but I'll definitely have to watch my back for the rest of the tour.

CHAPTER FOUR

Mallory

I DRAG myself off the plane with a heavy heart. I'm so out of it, I get lost on my way to baggage claim but finally find my way there.

"Mallory!"

My groggy eyes scan the area, finally landing on Audrey waving frantically.

"What are you doing here?" I rush over and accept her embrace.

"Chaser called and asked if I'd come get you."

"He did?" I assumed I'd find a taxi, but I appreciate his thoughtfulness. I can't imagine how big his phone bill will be when he finally checks out.

"Are you okay?" She rests her hand on my shoulder and peers into my bleary eyes.

"I'm exhausted."

"Let's grab your stuff and get out of here." She loops her arm through mine and leads me to the carousel.

Thankfully, my luggage doesn't take long to spit out of the chute.

"You're coming home with me," Audrey announces on our way to the parking lot.

Before I can protest, she holds up one hand. "I'm not at the apartment anymore. I'm renting a place on Walnut street. It's got a guest room and everything. You'll be safe there."

"Sounds perfect." I wasn't looking forward to explaining to Vickie, Holly, and Dorothy what happened in England.

"You'll tell me all about it tomorrow."

Unable to formulate any more words today, I simply nod.

The next morning, sunlight streaming through the sheer white curtains wakes me. I stretch and blink. It takes a second to remember where I am and the incidents that landed me here.

I wander into the living room, admiring Audrey's place. It's a lovely home with dark wood floors. The walls are painted in an eclectic variety of colors. Bright rugs, embroidered wall tapestries, and more gauzy curtains give it a bohemian vibe that suits Audrey much more than her previous white and beige apartment.

"Morning," she greets me when I find my way into the kitchen. "I didn't want to wake you."

"Thanks." I glance around the teal kitchen splashed with red accents. "I love the house."

"It's cute, right? Most of the time, it's nice and quiet too." She gestures toward the front door. "There's some asshole rocker a few streets over who throws loud parties, but other than that, it's good."

I chuckle because I'm familiar with asshole rockers and their loud parties.

For some reason, Audrey can't stop grinning.

"What's up with you?"

"Nothing." She sways from side to side for a second. "I'm actually renting it from one of my...from a guy I'm seeing."

"Oh?" That seems like more personal involvement than Audrey prefers. "How is that working out?" I ask casually.

"Not bad. It's no big deal. He's in real estate, so he has several properties." She snaps her mouth closed.

"What aren't you saying?"

She glances down and taps her perfectly red manicured nails against the counter. "He's kind of asked to see me exclusively." She takes a deep breath. "I mean, asked me to see him exclusively."

"And how do you feel about that?" I ask carefully, afraid I'll offend her.

"He's very kind." Her mouth twists. "But it's scary. That's really not what I ever pictured happening. I figured I'd escort until I turned thirty-five, bank some money, then run off to Paris, bum around Europe, and finally settle down in Italy. Just me and fifty or so cats."

I chuckle softly. "But?"

"I like him. A lot. He says he'll move money into an account for me, so I feel secure about my future." She pauses and quietly adds, "He says he's ready to run away to Paris with me right now."

I sit back and blink. "Whoa. That's...quite an offer."

"Yeah." She looks up at me from under her lashes. "Do you think I'm crazy for considering it?"

"Not at all." I can't help adding, "Just be careful."

She heaves out a deep breath. "Thank you." She slaps the counter, signaling the end of that conversation and diving into another. "Enough about me. Tell me what happened. Chaser couldn't talk long, and he said it was up to you if you wanted to share the details."

My lips twitch. Chaser never stops being thoughtful or worrying about my needs. Regret for leaving him settles over me again. "You know how they were opening for Bloody Revolver over there, right?"

There's a subtle shift in her expression. Her gaze darts away for a second before she nods. "I remember."

I recount the whole story for her. The amazing shows, the fun Chaser and I had exploring England, Jacob's increasing annoyance with me—how did I not see that for what it was at the time? Finally, I end with Davey's proposition, Chaser's rescue, and our decision that it was safer for me to come home than finish the tour with them.

"Wow," she breathes out, absorbing my story. "That's... intense, Mallory."

"Good word for it." I force a laugh I'm not really feeling at the moment.

"You're lucky. Chaser cares for you so much. A lot of guys would have encouraged you to...you know, take the *job*. He probably risked everything—"

"I know."

"Sorry, I wasn't trying to make you feel bad." She bites her lip and a bit of mischief glitters in her usually serious brown eyes. "If I tell you something, you have to promise not to repeat it."

Unsure of where this new direction in our conversation is headed, I shrug.

"Davey's a big...um, spender at my agency. And probably several other ones in town." She touches her chest and quickly adds. "I've never been on a date with him. But I know one of the girls he sees a lot." She tilts her head and studies me. "You guys actually look a lot alike."

"Creepy."

"Anyway, he's boring, loves to talk about himself, and his massive ego is definitely *not* in proportion to his dick."

The laughter that bursts out of me is a welcome relief. Didn't think I'd be able to laugh about this situation, well, ever. "Gross. Not surprised, but still, yuck."

She skirts the edge of the counter to join me on the other side and gives me a big hug. "I'm so happy you're here. You can stay with me until Chaser gets back if you want."

"Won't I be in the way?" I raise an eyebrow. She blushes when she gets my meaning.

"Not at all."

I have to go back to the apartment to unpack and call my agent, but for now, I accept the offer to hide out at Audrey's for a little longer.

My gaze strays to the clock.

I close my eyes and wish Chaser luck.

My body may have made it home to the states, but my heart's about to go on stage in England.

CHAPTER FIVE

Chaser

Tonight's show defines tense.

Before sound check, we had another quick, slightly-less-awkward band meeting to go over the set list.

We arrived on time and ready to go, but Bloody Revolver's sound guys fucked around for so long, none of our equipment was properly checked.

The crowd's large. Easily one of the largest we've played.

And we've been having nothing but trouble since the lights went down.

"Revolver has a fucking death wish," I growl, when my mic goes out for the second time. Jacob's wasn't working at all when we first took the stage. Fucker was screaming his ass off, and no one could hear him for about ten minutes.

The confused looks and people pointing to their ears finally clued him in to the problem. We had to stop and get someone on stage to fix it.

Basically, we look like a bunch of unprofessional dicks in front of a new-to-us audience.

Normally, my solos last anywhere from five to seven minutes, depending on the energy from the crowd and what time we have to be off stage. I usually channel my emotions into a musical journey and lose myself in the music, but tonight, I'm not feeling any of it. I power through, but my playing feels uninspired at best.

When we launch into 'Candy Jar,' I want to puke. I wish we'd cut it from the set tonight. My gaze wanders to the edge of the stage where Mallory's usually waiting, and my irritation over the whole situation rises again.

Playing has always soothed my chaotic soul, keeping my hands occupied and my mind focused. It's where I reach a peaceful state, much like riding my bike. But tonight, I can't find my center.

Maybe the guys are off-balance, too. Jacob's ragged voice lacks its usual soul. Overall, our playing's choppy and clipped. It feels too loose, and thanks to the rushed soundcheck, out of tune.

While I've noticed the crowds in the U.K. are generally more reserved than our audiences back home, tonight they're barely even paying attention, further spiking my irritation.

When our set mercifully finishes, I storm off the stage. "Fucking bullshit, Val," I shout at her as I pass by.

She hurries down the hall to catch up to me. "What did you expect?"

"I'm not rehashing this with you." I stop so fast, she almost trips against me. "Fix it."

"What do you want me to do?"

My fuse is short, threatening to blow any moment. "Your

fucking job. Call the lawyers. Remind that asshole we have a contract. Do whatever the fuck it is we pay you to do."

She huffs and runs off muttering and cursing to herself.

Still livid, I move out of the way of everyone hustling backstage and lean against the wall. I take a deep breath, close my eyes, and rest my head against the concrete. Almost done. A few more shows and I'll be on my way home to my girl.

"That's Chaser!" Someone shrieks. "That's him!"

The eager voices invade my moment and the corners of my mouth tip up.

I set my fury over the shitty show aside and search for the source of the chatter. A cluster of fans jump and wave from behind a short metal barricade.

The security guard who works for the venue holds one beefy arm out, keeping the fans at bay as I approach.

"Ease up. I want to say hello."

"It's on you, man," he grumbles and steps back a few feet.

"I love you, Chaser!" A girl thrusts a little white notebook with pink pages in my hand. Better than the underwear I was asked to sign earlier but still kind of odd.

"Thank you for coming to see us." I hand her the notebook and move to the next person. Quite a few people turned out for Kickstart; I spend the next twenty or so minutes signing everything from T-shirts to ticket stubs.

"You were amazing! I love you!" A girl screams in my face when I finally reach the end of the line.

"Thanks, sweetheart. What's your name?" I ask as I scribble my signature on the liner notes from our first cassette.

"Brenda."

"Well, Brenda, sorry the sound was so bad tonight."

The crowd eager to see me has thinned out, most of the people moving back into the main part of the club to catch Revolver's set. Not this one. She's intensely focused on me.

"It doesn't matter. I'm so happy I got to see you in person. This is just the ultimate…"

Her voice trails off and the color drains from her face. Fuck, I'm not exactly skilled in CPR if she passes out.

"Calm down. You all right?"

She nods, but her skin's still chalky and her hands shaky. "I never expected to meet you."

"You want to meet Jacob, too?" Girls always want to meet that little jackass.

Her hands flutter in front of her chest, drawing my attention to the Kickstart T-shirt she's sporting. Something about it lifts the gloom the last couple days have left on me. There has always been a reason I love music that goes beyond pussy, booze, and partying.

"Can my friend Melissa come with me? She was too nervous to say hello to you."

I flash what I've been told is a charming smile. "Am I that terrifying, Brenda?"

She blushes. "I don't think so."

I try to remain as calm and normal as possible when her friend shyly walks over, so she doesn't freak the fuck out too.

"Enjoy the show?"

She nods.

"Looking forward to seeing Bloody Revolver, Melissa?" Yeah, Davey's scum of the earth, but the fans don't need to know about our personal beef.

She shakes her head. "No, we only came to see you," she answers in a soft voice. These two don't look like our usual fans. They're certainly not groupies. Way too quiet and over-dressed. Probably still in high school. But they're sweet and genuine as I talk to them about their favorite Kickstart songs.

"'Cry it Out' is my favorite," the shier one says.

That's one I wrote most of the lyrics for and I'm surprised she mentions it since we never play it live.

"I wrote that about a girl I knew in high school." It's basically an anti-suicide ballad. We recorded it before big power ballads were all the rage, and the suits have been after us to revamp it and re-record it, so they can exploit the shit out of it—something that pisses me off every time they float the suggestion.

She nods. "I know. I read it in an interview you did."

Shit, that must've been a while ago.

Brenda takes her friend's hand and squeezes. A dozen unspoken words seem to pass between the girls.

"I listen to it a lot," Melissa says softly.

The undercurrent of what Melissa's saying hits me in the gut, and I reach out to awkwardly pat her on the back.

"I'm really glad you're here. Talking to you has been the best part of my day so far." I'm not lying either. Everything about today sucked. Saying goodbye to Mallory. Listening to Jacob's bullshit. Behaving myself when I want to punch Davey in the face a couple dozen more times. The craptacular show.

This moment puts it all in perspective.

The girls beam mega-watt smiles at me.

Maybe letting the suits exploit that very personal song isn't so bad if it means it reaches more people. If it can make more girls like Melissa feel less alone.

"So, do you want to meet the rest of the guys?" I ask.

Brenda bounces on her toes and clasps her hands in front of her face in a worshipful pose. "Yes, please. Thank you so much. That would be so totally awesome."

Hearing *totally awesome* in her crisp British accent makes me chuckle. I wrap an arm over each of their shoulders and walk them to our meet-and-greet room. It's about the size of a closet. I'm pretty sure it was a toilet at some point. Sure smells like shit. But it's what we have to work with tonight, and the girls don't seem to care.

Flashes go off, and my head snaps up, seeking the source. One of Revolver's roadies. I barely resist the urge to flip him off.

I did, after all, promise Val I'd behave tonight.

"Yo, Jacob, Alvin!" I shout to get their attention. Garrett's family was supposed to come to this show, so I assume he's off with them.

Alvin's his usual goofy self. The girls chatter a mile a minute with him. Jacob engages in some harmless flirting that makes the girls blush and stammer.

After a couple minutes, I pull Alvin aside. "Make sure they get out of here safe."

"They jailbait?"

"Probably. But be nice, please."

"You leaving?"

"Yeah, I'm done."

Satisfied Alvin will take good care of the girls, I back out a few minutes later.

A song I recognize from my own teenage years reverberates through the building. Bloody Revolver must have taken the stage. *Their* sound seems to be working fine.

Christ, if I'd known back then Davey was such a lowlife, I would've tossed his band's tape in the trash. Thank fuck, I never hung any Bloody Revolver posters up in my room.

At the front desk of the hotel, the clerk waves me over. "You have a message, sir."

I grab the paper. "Thanks."

At Audrey's for the night. Mallory.

When I spoke to Audrey earlier, she mentioned that she was living somewhere new, so I'm not worried. "Do you know when she called?"

"I don't, sir. I'm sorry."

"That's all right. Thank you."

Val's gonna kill me when we check out, and she's handed the whopping international phone bill I've racked up, but too fucking bad.

Guess she should've thought of that before she tried to sell my girlfriend to Davey Revolver.

CHAPTER SIX

Mallory

THE WEEK HOME without Chaser seems to drag, giving me a glimpse of what being in a relationship with a musician will mean long-term.

I try not to dwell on it too much.

The time difference and the expense of long-distance calls has kept our communication to a minimum.

I couldn't stay at Audrey's for too long. Eventually, I return to the apartment. Tiptoeing upstairs past the guys' place only worked for a few hours. The second I started moving around, the girls were knocking on my door.

Explaining why I was home so early was an uncomfortable conversation.

A few nights later, Holly and Vickie stop by to cheer me up. Well, that's what they *say.*

"Um, you should probably see this," Vickie says, handing over a popular tabloid. "Turn to page six."

Chaser Adams Bounces Back After Big Break-Up!

After Chaser's relationship with model Mallory Dove blew up, the guitarist for heavy metal band Kickstart finds comfort in the arms of two young groupies.

My hands shake as I scan the photos. The pictures are innocent enough. He's signing something for a girl—I assume a fan. Then there's another photo of him with his arms around two girls with worshipful expressions on their faces.

Chaser, on the other hand, looks tired. He's wearing the polite smile that doesn't quite reach his eyes.

A source close to the band says Adams rocked the young ladies all night long to get over the heartbreak of Dove storming out in the middle of their U.K. tour.

"Bullshit," I say, thrusting the magazine back at Vickie. "The 'source close to the band' is probably Davey Revolver trying to start more trouble because he didn't get his way."

"Keep reading," Vickie says, handing the magazine back to me. The twitch at the corner of her mouth suggests she's enjoying this a little too much.

Maybe pouring my heart out to them when I came home was a bad idea. But how else was I supposed to explain why I was home so early?

Sources say Adams caught Dove in a compromising position with Davey Revolver, lead singer of Bloody Revolver, who is headlining the tour. Revolver had no comment.

There's a picture underneath that paragraph of me sitting next to Davey. Chaser's been cut out of the photo, but his disembodied hand still rests on my shoulder.

The rest of the article goes on to talk about Revolver's long career, the current tour, and the band's new album.

"That asshole!"

"We tried to warn you," Vickie says. "Rockers always cheat on the road."

"Not Chaser. Davey. He couldn't get what he wanted, so he used me anyway. Look at the rest of the 'article'—it's all about him and his band." I'm fuming but don't know who to be more angry with—the tabloid, Davey Revolver, or myself.

"Maybe he's still into you, Mallory. And this is his way of reaching out," Holly says.

"Huh? Who?"

She rolls her eyes. "Davey. Honey, I can't believe you turned him down. Like, I totally get it, Chaser's way hotter, but Davey is *loaded*. This whole apartment building could fit inside one wing of his mansion."

"So what?" I grew up surrounded by wealth. No matter what items my father gave me, it never made up for the loss of my mother or the lack of his affection and attention. A man like Davey would be no different. When I outlived my usefulness, he'd replace me with a younger model.

No amount of money or "stuff" would ever fill the empty, aching little girl in me who has always longed to love and be loved.

I finally have that with Chaser. I love him whether or not he ever makes it 'big.'

"Holly's right," Vickie says. "Davey is a fantastic catch. It wouldn't hurt to see what he has to say if he reaches out to you again."

Anger simmers in my blood. "Sure. Hey, look, I'm tired. Think we can hang out tomorrow instead?" I fake a yawn to go along with the brush-off.

They're full of false, syrupy sympathy as they give me air-kisses and make me promise to call if I need anything.

I shut the door behind them and lean against it, closing my eyes. What's Chaser doing right now? Who is he with?

My gaze lands on the tabloid the girls conveniently left behind.

I love Chaser way too much to lose him.

And I know he loves me, too.

Sighing, I lock the door and toss the tabloid in the trash.

But not before giving it a second read-through.

Please don't let my blind faith in Chaser be wrong.

CHAPTER SEVEN

Chaser

"THAT FUCKING PIECE OF SHIT!" I bellow when Val cautiously explains some tabloid claims I cheated on Mallory. "Are you fucking kidding me?"

"I warned you something like this would happen if you confronted him."

So help me, I've never hit a woman in my life, but Val's begging to be the first. "What was I supposed to do? Let him nail my girlfriend?"

"Maybe there's a chance Mallory hasn't seen it. Won't see it."

I shake my head and let out a bitter laugh. "Nah, someone will make sure they show it to her soon as possible. Guarantee it." The three little nosey bitches currently watching the guys' apartment won't be able to help themselves. As soon as they see it, they'll run right up to shove it in Mallory's face under the guise of 'concern.'

"Look at it this way, it's exposure for you and the band. Your name is in the headline. You look like a young, virile, rocking stud in the picture. All press is good press."

I shoot a glare at her for the stupid stud comment. "Yeah, I hope Mallory sees it that way."

"We'll be home in a few days, and you can explain it to her."

Fuck waiting around for that, I need to talk to her *now*. But we're on the fucking road for the next two nights.

I'm a moody, irritable dick all day, every day except for the forty-five minutes we're on stage and the thirty minutes after the show that I take to meet with fans and sign everything they shove in my hands.

Once we're done, though, I'm out.

Bloody Revolver doesn't offer us their private jet on the way home—go figure.

I book the first flight I can, not wanting to wait another minute. I also didn't want to be on the same flight with Jacob. We may have worked things out to finish the tour, but I'm still pretty fucking pissed at him and don't know if I'll be able to resist the urge to toss him off the plane without a parachute once we're thirty-thousand feet in the air.

The flight's long, and it's late when I finally slide the key into the lock. Our apartment is dark. No sound, except traffic noises from outside.

Christ, I hope she didn't move out.

I drop my stuff inside the door and kick off my boots, before padding through the apartment.

I find my girl curled up on her side of the bed, so achingly beautiful I stop to watch her for a few minutes before heading into the bathroom for a quick shower.

Mallory's still asleep when I slide into bed next to her.

Needing to bask in her warmth, I gently shift closer. Not gentle enough, because she startles awake. "Chaser?"

"It's me, little dove," I whisper. "I'm home. Go back to sleep."

She rolls over and snaps on the bedside lamp. "Oh, Chaser." She tackles me, kissing and laughing at the same time. "Why didn't you tell me you were coming home, so I could meet you at the airport? Oh my God, I've missed you."

The frost that enveloped my heart the second I sent her home finally melts. "Missed you too. So much." I wrap my arms around her, holding her tight.

The weight of her soft body against mine wakes another need. To connect and claim my woman in the most primal way possible.

No woman has ever had such an effect on me. I've been dreaming of her warmth, the scent of her skin, her uneven breathing when I pleasure her.

My whole body aches for her. I slide my hands under her T-shirt and fill my hands with her soft, full breasts, rubbing my thumbs over her nipples.

"Oh." Her breathing hitches, and her eyes close.

The air around us crackles with desire.

I strip off her shirt and fit my hands into the curve of her waist, pulling her fully on top of me. My rock-hard dick snuggles up to her cotton panties. Heat pours off her as I lift my hips, rubbing against her. Showing her how much I want her.

Her fingers slowly slide through my hair, and she stares down into my eyes. "I saw the article. The pictures."

Well, doesn't that put our reunion on ice.

"Mallory." I try to sit up, but she presses her hands against my chest. She straddles me, rubbing her hot, wet center against my cock.

My jaw clenches, my fingers digging into her firm little ass cheeks.

"I know it was all lies. Probably planted by Davey." She keeps drilling me with that probing stare, searching my eyes. Not for hints of guilt. No, I think my girl wants me to understand how much *she* trusts *me*.

It's a powerful feeling, being so deeply connected to someone else. A few days apart didn't alter our soul-deep link. If anything, I feel even closer to her.

I press my palms to her cheeks. "Baby, you're the only face I see every night before I go to sleep. You're on my mind, in my heart, every day, all day."

"I know, because I feel the same way," she whispers.

"I wasn't with anyone after you left. Couldn't be." I grind my cock against her again. "You got the keys to my heart *and* my dick."

"Hmm...do I?" She kisses my chest and reaches down, palming my hard-on. "You came to bed naked?"

"Didn't want to wake you."

"I like it."

I've missed her, needed her so bad, this performance will be laughable. I'm ready to come right this second.

I reach down, pulling the thin strip of cotton between her legs to the side. Her breathing hitches, and she spreads her legs wider to take me inside her.

"Oh, fuck," I growl, as her slick heat surrounds my cock. Squeezing so fucking tight.

No random groupie will ever satisfy me. No woman can ever take Mallory's place.

She eases down, taking me in slowly. Gasps and raises up when she hits bottom. "Easy, little dove. I'm not going anywhere."

I'm home. My cock's back home where he belongs—and never wants to leave. So good. Tight. Warm. Wet.

Fuck.

My hands lock on her hips, urging her up and down. Faster. Harder. Her nails dig into my thighs as she detonates. "Ch... Chaser. I'm...uh."

"I feel you. Come for me. Ride it out. I got you." I'm not sure that's true. I'm ready to blow.

She falls down over me, pressing her forehead to mine, our breaths mingle. The sexiest whimpers pass her lips. "I love you."

Done. Pleasure rocks down my spine. The sensation so strong, every muscle in my body tenses as I release inside her.

"Come here." I pull her closer for a long, melting kiss.

"There's no one but you, Mallory."

And that's how I always want it to be.

CHAPTER EIGHT

Chaser

JET LAG IS one mean bitch.

"Babe," I groan, throwing my arm over my eyes to block out the sunlight streaming into our room. "Why are you up at this hour?"

"It's eleven o'clock." Damn, her voice is so soft and silky. Missed waking up to it every morning. I blindly swing my arm out, reaching for her.

"If you were in England, you'd be getting ready to go on stage right about now." The bed dips. Velvet fingertips brush against my skin.

I open my eyes to find her staring down at me, her hair tickling my bare chest. "You're pretty."

"Good morning." She kisses my cheek and darts away before I can grab her, stopping in the doorway.

I sit up. "Where you goin'?"

"To see my agent. She said she has something for me."

"Want me to go with you?"

"You don't have to." She hesitates. "Get some more sleep."

"I sleep any longer I'll be even more fucked up."

"What are your plans now that you're home?" she asks from the doorway.

"I feel like 'fuck you in every position possible' isn't the answer you're looking for?"

She chuckles. "Besides that."

"Alvin and I will probably get together to do some writing this week." I stand and stretch, long and slow.

"Mmm, looking good, Chaser Adams," she murmurs. Her greedy gaze sweeps over my body.

Love the sexy humming noises Mallory makes every time I show off the goods.

"Band meeting later," I add.

"I hope that goes well."

"It'll be fine." I slip on a pair of shorts, leaving the button undone. "I want to talk Valerie into booking us some time at the studio over on Vine. They have an echo chamber that's supposed to give this amazing reverb. I've always wanted to record something there."

"You're sexy when you talk all music-y." She slides her arms around my waist, molding the front of her body to mine and slipping her hands down the back of my shorts. "Am I allowed to come watch?"

"Do you *want* to after that shit show over there?"

"Oh." She steps back, taking all her warmth with her. "I didn't think about that. I was only thinking of you."

"That's perfectly fine with me."

We spent most of the night catching up. I filled her in on the truce with Jacob, hoping she didn't think I was too much of an asshole. But that's not Mallory. She's practical and understands this business better than I do sometimes. She filled me in on the girls bringing over the tabloid and how she knew it was all bullshit. As much as I love writing lyrics and words, even I can't express how much her belief in me, in *us*, means.

"Hey," I tug her close again. "Thank you."

"For what?" she asks, grabbing her purse off the doorknob.

"Believing in me."

She stops, her face softening. "I'll always believe in you." Her gaze strays to the door. "I'm running late. I'll try not to be too long."

"No, do what you gotta do. I'll unpack, maybe give my dad a call before meeting with Val."

She tilts her head. "You should. He's probably worried about you."

Emptiness rings through the apartment after she's gone. I glance at my bag. My dirty T-shirts and grungy jeans won't take long to unpack, so I might as well call Dad first.

My father answers with a gruff greeting—somewhere between "hello" and "who the fuck is this?"

"Hey, Dad."

"Shit, son. You back in the states?"

"Got in last night. Late."

"How'd it go?"

"It was an... *experience*. Rented a Triumph Bonneville for a couple days. That was fun."

"You get the hang of the driving on the other side of road thing okay?"

I snort. "We had a few dicey moments."

"We? Huh. How's Mallory?" he asks with a suspicious tone. To my knowledge, my father's never picked up a magazine that didn't have a naked lady, gun, motorcycle, or dead deer on the cover. So, I find it hard to believe he saw the article about our supposed break-up and my subsequent groupie-banging spree.

"She's fine. Sent her home a few days early."

He's silent for a few seconds. "Yeah, I think I read something about that."

I laugh, a humorless sound given the circumstances. "Since when do you read tabloids?"

"Since one of the girls sees your name in a headline, brings it to the clubhouse like her ass is on fire, and shoves it in my face."

"It was all lies. The singer of the band we were opening for turned out to be a sleaze."

"Weren't they that shitty band you used to listen to all time? Bloody Roosters?"

"Revolver. Bloody Revolver, Dad. Yes, it was a clusterfuck."

"You handle it?"

"Fuck yeah I did."

"That's what I like to hear. Mallory okay?"

There aren't many females my father gives a fuck about. Not that he's cruel. More indifferent. My mother kind of soured him on women in general. I'm pretty sure he only bothered to learn the name of one of my high school girlfriends. That he's asking about Mallory means a lot. Even with all the trouble of getting us involved with the Russians, he's accepted her. Considers her family.

"She's good, Dad."

"She buy your story?"

I grind my teeth before answering. "There was no story to sell her. It was all lies."

"Thank fuck. The girls in the photo looked underage."

"They were just fans." I pause and consider whether I should share this part. "You remember Diane?"

He's quiet for a second. "Yeah, I remember her."

"Well, one of them reminded me of her, so I spent some extra time talking to them. That's it. I think one of Davey's people took the photo and made up a story to go with it."

"Fucking assholes," he grumbles. "You want Torrin to handle him? His enforcer, Freak, didn't get that name by accident. Won't matter how much security Revolver has. Torrin's a sneaky fuck who can get to anyone."

"No, Dad." Dragging the MC into some petty rock star spat mixes my two worlds in a way I'm not comfortable with. But I appreciate my dad's support. "Mallory and I are fine. That's all I care about."

"When you coming home again?" I'm starting to wonder if he really means when are you coming home *for good*.

"We're supposed to record our new album soon." First, I need to finish working out a few more songs, and we need to find a producer but that's not stuff my dad cares to hear about.

His sigh comes through the phone loud and clear.

"Something wrong, Dad?"

"Let me know when you do plan to come home. May ask you to bring me a souvenir."

Souvenir. One of our Cali brothers nearby probably has drugs, guns, or cash they want me to bring to New York. Not exactly a thrilling prospect when most likely Mallory will be riding with me.

Since another MC had been infiltrated by the FBI a couple years ago, my father won't supply more information over the phone. "Whatever you need, Dad."

We talk for a few more minutes.

"Any club runs I'm missing out on?"

"Headed to Empire this weekend."

"Meeting up with the Lost Kings?"

"Possibly."

"Good. Say hi to Grinder for me."

"Will do."

Miss riding with my club. Would love to have Mallory on the back of my bike for a trip like that.

After we hang up, I stare at the phone for a while.

I'm too old to be homesick, right?

Mallory

My agent's cloud of puffy blonde curls are barely visible over the files piled on her desk. Even so, she radiates authority, and I jump when she barks at me. "Don't sit. Go. Now."

She thrusts some papers in my hand. "A pilot. Primetime television. Blonde with big boobs. You're perfect. If the show gets picked up for a full season, it could be huge for you." She shoos me out the door with no other information.

The role is "sexy lifeguard." Since I possess zero knowledge about lifeguarding, I keep my expectations low.

On my way to the audition, I stop at a pay phone to call Chaser and leave him a message.

Blondes of every height and bust size occupy the casting office when I arrive. I locate someone who seems to be in charge to sign-in and hand over my headshot.

"Have a seat." The girl flicks her hand in my direction without glancing up.

I scan the room for any available chair. The only spot open is in the corner next to a woman who, judging by the downcast gazes and lack of chatter in her section of the room, everyone else seems to fear.

She sweeps her gaze over me as I approach and moves a magazine off the seat next to her. "Hi, I'm Pamela Scott." She holds out her hand, tilting her head and staring at me as if her name should mean something.

"Mallory Dove." I shake her hand.

"Yeah," she narrows her eyes, "I thought you looked familiar." Her soft, southern drawl almost takes the sting out of her condescending attitude.

What should I say? Somehow, *thanks* doesn't seem appropriate.

"My boyfriend saw your picture in *L.A. Weekly.*" She places her thumb by her ear, pinky pointing toward her mouth. "He calls me up like, 'babe, you're in *L.A. Weekly.* That's so cool.'" Her gaze roams over me in such a disapproving way, I wonder if her boyfriend made it out of that conversation alive.

"How wild is that? I see the guy every day, but he confuses me for some random blonde chick on a magazine cover."

A nervous smile flickers over my lips. I can't say I'm fond of being referred to as 'some random blonde chick,' although, I guess it could be worse.

Finally, she shrugs and laughs. "He's dumber than a box of bricks, but he has a *massive* cock."

"Congratulations." How else should I respond to that statement?

I force myself to appear calm. To hide how much she intimidates me as I give her a cautious once-over.

I suppose we look somewhat similar. To be completely honest, she's like some gorgeous, exaggerated version of me. Bigger, blonder hair, fuller lips, larger breasts, smaller waist, flawless tan. I kind of wish I'd chosen a different seat now.

"So, what's your story?" she asks, focusing her laser-beam eyes on my face. "What have *you* been in?"

Feeling like I'm interviewing for a job I never applied for, I tick off my short list of accomplishments.

"Pfft. Kickstart. Oh my *Gawd*. Music videos. Why would you waste your time with a job that pays so little and gives you lousy exposure?" She leans in closer. "No one's going to take you seriously with *that* on your resume."

Are we not sitting at the same audition together? Not in the mood to be judged by this stranger, I pretend to take an interest in her job history. "What have you done?"

Her lips part and she stares at me for so long I have the urge pull out my compact and check my makeup. "I was January's Playmate of the month last year."

Sorry, Playboy *isn't on my reading list.* "Oh. That's great." My voice creeps up at the end of the word, making it sound like a question—almost sarcastic, which wasn't my intention.

She fluffs her hair and throws an imperious scowl my way. "I was Miss Louisiana. That's how I was discovered."

"Oh." I don't know a damn thing about pageants. "That must have been fun?"

"Sure." She snorts.

"Pamela Scott!"

"Wish me luck!" She pats my leg as she breezes past me.

"Good luck," I mutter.

More nervous than ever, I focus on studying my one page of lines.

CHAPTER NINE

Mallory

ONE OF MY favorite things about living with Chaser has to be the impromptu concerts I walk in on almost daily.

My mouth quirks as I open the door and find him on the couch strumming his guitar, every so often stopping to jot down a few words. Today, he's intensely focused on playing the same succession of notes over and over.

I close the door behind me as quietly as possible, not wanting to disrupt his flow.

He tips his head up anyway.

"Whatever that was sounded awfully sexy." I motion for him to continue playing.

"Yeah?" His mouth stretches into a smile, but the distance in his eyes says he's still focused on music. "It's this riff I've had in my head for a couple of years now."

"Years?"

"We have a few half-assed lyrics for it, but I haven't found the right melody." He shrugs. "Alvin said he's been working on something."

"Wow." I'm endlessly fascinated by their process and the way the guys seem to work together seamlessly, sometimes.

And other times how they want to rip out each other's throats.

"Go on." I wave my hands at him. "I didn't mean to interrupt you."

"Sit with me?"

"Sure." I perch on the edge of the chair across from him and wait.

He reaches over and resets his metronome.

"You're working with the metronome today?"

He shrugs. "It keeps me honest."

I'm not sure how to interpret that but I've noticed he only uses it on occasion; other times, he prefers to sit and play whatever comes to him.

Over and over, he works on the same chords he'd been fiddling with when I came home. Sometimes humming along. Other times with his eyes closed.

Finally, he shakes his head and sets his guitar in its case.

"How was the audition?" he asks.

I shrug. At first it had been awkward, but the director was kind and put me at ease. "They want me to come back."

"That's awesome." He stands and hugs me. "Proud of you, little dove."

"Thanks."

"We should celebrate."

"It's not that big of a deal."

"Sure, it is." He glances at his watch. "It's too early to go out now. You want to head downstairs and see what Alvin's come up with?"

"I would love that." I turn toward the door and then hesitate. "Is Jacob going to be there?"

"Don't know, honestly. Haven't seen him yet."

I stand tall, shoulders back, chin up. "Well, I'll run into him eventually, right?"

"Thank you." He approaches and grasps both my hands, holding tight. "Trust me, I made it clear how I feel about what he did."

I huff out a laugh. "I can only imagine what that means."

Downstairs, Garrett's on the couch with two girls I don't recognize and barely glances up when we come in. We find Alvin alone in the bedroom, running his fingers over a portable keyboard

He glances up and a slow smile stretches across his face when he sees us. "Hey, Mallory. Wasn't sure you'd ever associate with us again."

"I'll always make an exception for you, Alvin."

"I hope you know I had nothing to do with it." His smile turns into more of a pained expression. "It was a shitty thing to do. I let Jacob know that."

"Thank you," I whisper.

"The tabloid was all bullshit." Alvin leans toward me. "I was there that night. Chaser left those girls with me, and I walked them outside to meet their parents maybe a half hour later."

Chaser rests his hand on my back.

"I know it was lies Davey planted." I reach over and pat Alvin's leg. "But thank you."

The guys settle down to play an acoustic song I haven't heard before. Chaser sings, and, as I always suspected, his voice is the perfect combination of rich and raspy. This performance is different from any other one. I've seen glimpses of this Chaser on stage before. He plays the way he makes love. As if every word and note comes from his deep, beautiful, complex soul.

I'm so completely caught up, no—mesmerized, it feels like my world spins away when they stop playing.

"Uh-oh. That bad?" Alvin says.

"No, no! It's perfect. Beautiful. I thought you didn't like ballads?"

Chaser shrugs. "It's something different we've been playing around with."

"Just the two of you?"

"Yeah."

"Are you going to record it for the new album?"

Alvin shakes his head. "It's too far from our usual sound. Jacob doesn't like it."

"Doesn't like the sound or doesn't like Chaser singing?"

"Probably both." Alvin laughs.

I move closer to Chaser, leaning against him and running my fingers down his arm. "How come you don't play for me like this?"

"Didn't think you'd want me to," he rasps.

"You know I love your sexy voice."

Alvin clears his throat, reminding us he's still in the room.

I nod to Chaser's guitar. "That's not what you were working on upstairs, though, is it?"

"No," he grins and taps my nose. "I need to be plugged in for that."

"You two are so sweet my teeth hurt," Alvin mumbles. "Was that 'Queen of the Road' you were working on before?"

"Yeah, you said you had something for me."

"Give me a second." He pauses. "I'm gonna leave you two alone. Can you behave?" Alvin teases.

"Yes, we can—"

Chaser curls his hand behind my legs, cutting off my

indignant response. He drags me closer, and I tumble down on top of him.

"Chaser..."

He silences me with a firm, soothing kiss. Shivers dance over my skin as he traces his fingers against the backs of my legs, drawing my long peasant skirt up, up, up.

"How can you be so fucking sexy in a skirt that covers your ankles, woman?"

"Everything turns you on." I laugh as his rough fingers tickle behind my knees.

"No, everything about *you* turns me on."

Someone knocks on the bedroom door and pushes it open before we answer. Garrett sticks his head in the room. "Dude, you have your own apartment. Get out." He waggles his eyebrows in what I assume is his sly way to let us know he needs the bedroom for carnal purposes.

Sure enough, two girls giggle behind him.

Chaser places his guitar in its case and takes my hand. "We're leaving, ya perv."

The door opens wider, revealing Jacob standing behind the two girls. "Don't act like you've never done the same thing, Chaser."

Chaser growls, and Jacob glances at me. "Whoops. Didn't see you there, Mallory."

My cheeks flare hot when our eyes meet, and I quickly look away. Why should I be embarrassed about the situation Jacob caused in England? But for some reason, I can't stop the reaction. Why can't my body react by kneeing him in the groin instead?

"We'll get out of your hair." Chaser's gruff tone nixes any other conversation.

As we pass, Jacob reaches out, wrapping his fingers around my arm to stop me. I shake off his touch, and he holds his hands in the air. "Hey, I'm sorry about what happened over there," he says in a low voice, not meant to be overheard.

Chaser moves in behind me, curling an arm around my waist.

"I misjudged you. You're nothing like them." Jacob jerks his thumb over his shoulder toward the girls who just entered the bedroom. "So, I'm sorry about that."

Despite his dilated pupils and non-stop jittering, his words seem sincere.

"Thank you, Jacob." I won't tell him it's okay or let him off the hook completely, but I accept his apology.

Chaser squeezes my hip, offering his support or thanking me for making an effort to get along with his bandmate. I'm not sure.

Jacob glances up, nods at Chaser, then shoves the bedroom door open, letting it swing halfway closed behind him.

"Well," I say, taking a second to absorb the interaction, "I never expected an apology from him."

"It's the least he should do," Chaser grumbles.

"I'm willing to let it go." I'll still never fully trust Jacob. But I refuse to be the reason for any tension within the band.

Tucked into the corner of the living room, Alvin's behind his drum kit, tapping out a beat, when we enter the living room. He tips his head back and grins at us. "Let's rock it, Adams."

"I'll be right back." Chaser kisses my cheek and runs out the door. My gaze follows his legs up the stairs, and my ears pick up his footsteps as he jogs into our apartment, grabs his guitar and probably his amp, before pounding back downstairs.

"All right." Chaser tosses his notebook on the low coffee table and sets up his gear. "This is what I've got."

Alvin double taps his sticks and beats out a steady rhythm while Chaser's fingers fly over the strings in a repetitive pattern. Whatever they're doing is completely infectious, and I find myself moving along with the sound.

Chaser peeks up at me, winks and then pulls something out of his pocket. He slips it on the fingers moving up and down the neck of the guitar. He slides it over the strings, wringing every drop of sound from the simple notes.

"What'd you do? Get a slide?" A shirtless Garrett brushes past me to get to Chaser. "Do that again."

Alvin and Chaser launch into another round of the hypnotic riff, while Garrett sets up his bass. I move to the other side of the room to stay out of his way.

A few minutes later, Garrett joins in, dropping a pattern of notes around Chaser's riff.

"There she is. Queen of the road," Jacob belts out the words as he strolls into the living room. He stares at the guys for a few seconds before dropping onto the couch and closing his eyes. "Give me more."

I watch, fascinated, as they keep working through the simple chord patterns, adding and expanding to the melody. Each new layer compliments and enhances the song.

"Lines of fire leading me home," Jacob sings.

"Keep going," Chaser says without picking up his head.

"Away from the storm." Jacob's mouth stays open, but no more words come out. His hands ball into fists, and he closes his eyes again. "Fuck."

"It'll come to you," Garrett shouts.

"Hey! Where'd you guys go?" One of the girls bounces into the living room in her bra and underwear.

I'm brimming with the urge to shush her. *Can't you see they're making magic?*

"Oh cool!" the other girl shouts, running into the room and straight into her friend. The two of them grab hands and start jumping, laughing, and dancing around.

Garrett's playing grinds to a stop. "Knock it off." He jerks his head sideways. "Go wait in the bedroom if you're going to be obnoxious."

Chaser stops playing and wanders closer to me while fiddling with the tuning pegs at head of his guitar.

"I like it," I whisper.

He cocks an eyebrow. "Yeah? It still needs the right words. But we're moving in the right direction."

"They'll come to you guys." I reach up and kiss his cheek. "When the timing's right."

"Why does she get to stay?" one of the girls whines, pointing at me.

Garrett slaps the complainer's ass. "Chaser's woman knows how to behave."

Behave. What am I? An obedient dog? I don't even bother acknowledging the exchange.

The girl scurries back to the bedroom. Not for the first time, it irritates me the shitty way the guys treat the girls who hang around worshiping them. I guess since none of the girls ever complain and they keep returning for more of the same, it's not my business, but it sure doesn't make me think much of Jacob and Garrett.

A bone-jarring thud slams against the door. I jump and turn.

Chaser reaches over and flings it open. "What?"

"Keep the fucking noise down, or I'll call the cops." The gruff, threatening voice sounds like our downstairs neighbor.

"Fuck off, old man!" Alvin shouts.

"We're done for the day," Jacob says. "I need to get my dick sucked anyway."

The neighbor groans. Footsteps thunder away from the apartment while the guys laugh.

"Val said she wants to set us up with a rehearsal space." Chaser slams the door. "Might be time to take her up on it."

"Do you remember our first 'rehearsal space?'" Alvin presses his hands against his stomach and shakes with laughter.

"The rats!" Garrett and Alvin shout at the same time.

"It was a storage unit," Chaser explains to me. "But Jacob and I built loft beds so the four of us lived there for a while."

"But how? Wasn't that uncomfortable?"

"Alley was right outside whenever we needed to take a piss," Garrett explains.

"That's...lovely."

"Tell her how you broke your loft bed." Jacob slaps Chaser's arm.

"Fuck off."

"That was *you*." Garrett points to Jacob. "Genius here had a three way and the support beam snapped. He almost crushed one of our pet rats."

"Oh shit. You're right." Jacob laughs. "Me and Jack Daniels were tight back then. I forgot."

"Back then? You're like eighty-five percent Jack right this second."

"Hey," Chaser interrupts their banter. "Mallory got a callback today, we planned to go out and celebrate. Anyone up for it?"

"Fuck yeah." Alvin pumps his fist in the air. "Good job, Mal."

I chuckle at his enthusiasm over something so small. "It's not that big of a deal."

"Nope." Alvin wags his finger in my direction. "You gotta celebrate every win out here, Mallory."

"It's true," Chaser says.

Watching them work together felt like a celebration, but that seems sort of kiss-ass, so I keep the sentiment to myself.

"Val wants to meet with us tomorrow," Alvin reminds everyone. "So we can't be out too late."

"That's cool."

I catch Chaser's eye, but he doesn't seem concerned about the meeting.

So I try to follow his lead. But my forced smile does little to quell my anxiety.

CHAPTER TEN

Chaser

"How's it feel to be home?" Val asks when we're all seated in her new office.

"Nice digs, Val." Garrett bounces around in his chair. "Moving up in the world." The fucker drank everyone under the table last night but somehow has more energy than all of us combined.

"We're *all* moving up in the world." She glances at each one of us. I swear she almost seems giddy, and it takes a lot to excite Val. "Shooting Fences has asked Kickstart to open three shows for them at the Coliseum when they start their new tour."

"Holy shit!" Alvin jumps out of his seat.

"Are you fucking with us?" Jacob asks.

Shooting Fences. Now *that's* a band my father respects.

Old school rock-n-roll. I grew up listening to plenty of their albums at home and at the clubhouse.

Three shows. At the Coliseum. A place Alvin and I climbed the fence to sneak in and watch our favorite bands when we first moved to L.A.

"Are you serious?" I finally ask.

"Dead serious."

"This is huge," Jacob mutters. "Right in our backyard."

"Are you up for it?" Val asks.

"What's the catch?" After the Revolver proposition, I figure that needs to be a staple question in my vocabulary from now until the end of time.

"Yeah, what's the catch?" Alvin echoes.

Val stares me straight in the eyes. "No catch. The conversation was only about Kickstart. Apparently, Jared Stone got his hands on a bootleg of one of your U.K. shows and liked what he saw."

The lead singer of one of the biggest bands *ever* watched some shitty, underground video of one of our performances and wants us to open for him? For real?

"People are bootlegging our shows?" Jacob shouts. "That's fucking awesome!"

Val's gaze travels the length of the table, stopping to give each of us a meaningful look. "You guys can handle this, right? Opening for them right here in L.A. is a big deal. Huge. We need serious rehearsals. I'm not sure you have enough material to cover the time slot. Why don't you work on a few covers—"

"We have the material." Garrett holds up a hand, stopping Val. None of us have ever been particularly receptive to her advice when it ventures into our music.

"You could do a cover of one of *their* songs," Val persists. "A way to—"

"We'll handle it," Jacob assures her.

Well, at least we're all on the same page in *one* area.

"All right, well, I'm trying to get you a warm-up gig at the Troubadour before the shows."

"Let us get through some rehearsals, first," Jacob says.

"Okay, now the bad news." She pauses for dramatic effect. "The video for 'Candy Jar' won't be receiving any more airplay."

"What? Why?" Jacob slams his palm on the table. "MTV filmed our show at the premiere, and the video was doing great. What changed?"

Her cool gaze flicks my way for a brief second, signaling what's about to come out of her mouth. "What do you think? Davey Revolver made good on his threats. That snake has connections everywhere."

"Jesus Christ." Garrett hangs his head. "We're fucked."

A lot of money went into that video. Money that will eventually come out of the band's bottom line.

"It's not the end of the world," Val assures us. "I have a friend I talked to. They *might* be able to sneak it on at some obscure times. Like 1:00 a.m. to 3:00 a.m."

Jacob sits back and laughs. "Joke's on Davey, then. That's when our core audience is awake. The video will get its legs back, Val."

Thank fuck. I expected Jacob to be a lot more petulant about the whole situation. Maybe throw more blame my way. Either he actually learned his lesson—which I doubt—or he's afraid of another ass-kicking. Both suit me fine.

"We'll see." Val swipes her palms together, washing away the bad news. "No matter what, we push forward. New album." Her gaze slides to me. "Don't bite my head off but the record label wants to know if you'll reconsider re-recording 'Cry it Out.' I told them—"

"Yeah, let's do it." Even with all the chaos swirling around us, I haven't stopped thinking about the two fans I talked to in England.

"Yes?" Her eyebrows seem to have permanently fused with the top of her forehead. Can't blame her. I've been a real dick about this in the past. "Really? You're sure?"

"Yeah, let's do it. No cheesy fucking bullshit video, though." All this time I couldn't stand thinking of such a personal song exploited for money. Instead, I should've considered all the people it might reach who need the reminder that they're not alone.

"Fuck yeah!" Jacob thrusts his fist in the air. "That needs to be our *first* single from the new album."

"Let's not get ahead of ourselves. Ballads are usually the second single," Val cautions.

Let the exploitation begin.

"This is great news." Val squeezes her hands together and tips her head back like she's thanking her favorite deity for my reasonableness today. "Fabulous."

After her quick prayer to the gods of beleaguered band managers everywhere, Val has a few more points to go over before setting us free. "Do you still have your hearts set on working with Mark Cutter for the new album?"

"Yeah." Jacob glances at each of us. "Right?"

We all nod. The four of us spent a lot of time researching who we wanted to produce our next album. We decided it had to be someone with a strong, solid reputation who could help us shed the fluffy image smeared all over us from "Candy Jar."

Val shakes her head. "Cutter's a slippery one. Only works with a few bands a year." She spears Jacob with a pointed look. "He won't put up with any bullshit. Although," she taps her fingers against the desk as she mulls it over, "he *has* produced the last five albums Vicious Vandals released. Working with the four of *you* would be a vacation after those guys."

The work Cutter's done with Vicious Vandals is one of the main reasons we want to work with him so bad. I have faith in Val. The woman loves a challenge.

"All right, I'll keep working on Cutter. You guys focus on blowing the roof off the Shooting Fences gigs."

After that, we're set free. The guys are already discussing where to celebrate our *good* news.

"Chaser," Val says in a low voice.

"I'll catch up." I nod to Alvin and shut the door behind him. "What's on your mind, Val?"

I return to my seat, and she moves into the chair directly across from me. "How is everything? How's Mallory?"

"Mallory's fine." *Like you give a shit.*

"Is she still willing to star in the next video?"

"As far as I know, yes."

She blows out a breath. "Good. So, you two are..."

"We're solid, Val."

"She's more than welcome to attend the Shooting Fences gigs. But she won't be asked to come on during 'Candy Jar.'"

The pleasant buzz I had going from the good news bursts. Val's treading on dangerous territory with that comment. "You realize she never wanted to do that, right? *You* came up with that bright idea. It made Mallory uncomfortable, but she did it for me. To help the band. Don't act like she was trying to use Kickstart to further *her* career because we both know that's bullshit."

Fuck, if anything, I'm starting to wonder if Mallory's association with Kickstart will *hurt* her career. Plenty of tabloids have only referred to her as the "'Candy Jar' girl" or "Chaser Adams's girlfriend" or worse, "the busty blonde model" since news of our relationship went public.

"It was good exposure for her," Val says with a straight face.

"Yeah, it's been great."

She winces at the venom in my voice.

"Are we done?"

"The record company suggested something simple for the next video." She taps her fingers on the table, completely avoiding my question. "Show how versatile you are. Everyone has you pigeon-holed as glam metal, but you're rugged, too. I suggested footage of the four of you riding Harleys through downtown or something."

"Great. Except, Jacob knows dick about bikes."

She grins. "One of you will take pity on him and let him ride bitch, won't you?"

Finally, I laugh. "Not me."

After saying goodbye to Val, I find Alvin, Garrett and Jacob sitting and flipping through magazines out in the lobby. "You waiting around for me?"

"Who else, wanker?" Garrett says.

"You in trouble with Val?" Jacob asks.

"Nope."

"Good." Jacob turns and slaps Garrett's shoulder. "We should all go down to The Palace and celebrate. Wishing Well is playing tonight. We can fuck Brent's girlfriend while he's onstage." The two idiots double over laughing.

I roll my eyes in Alvin's direction, and he smirks.

When he doesn't get the reactions he's seeking from Alvin or me, Jacob straightens up. "Seriously, we *should* celebrate. This is a big deal."

"Val didn't say so, but I think we need to keep this quiet for now." I glance around the empty lobby. Even the chair behind the reception desk is vacant. Still, I keep my voice down. "A lot of time between now and those shows for something to go wrong."

"Good point." Jacob shrugs. "We're fresh off a successful U.K. tour. That's enough reason to go out and celebrate."

None of us mention the "Candy Jar" video being sunk. I'm not as bent out of shape as I should be about it, and I suspect the guys aren't either. The video's cheesy as fuck and not at all what we want to be known for.

So, fuck Davey Revolver. As far as I'm concerned, he did us a favor.

"Shooting Fences." Alvin grins at me and slings his arm around my shoulders. "Did you think we'd ever open for them?"

Sure, I've had all the same daydreams every wanna be rock star has when they land in L.A. But to have it actually happen? "Hell no."

"You need to call your dad and let him know. He'll be so stoked."

"I will. You planning to call your folks?"

"They won't care." He rubs his palms together, and his eyes gleam. "I can't stop picturing Revolver being all pleased with himself for getting our video yanked." He chokes on a laugh. "Then hearing we're opening for Shooting Fences. Stupid fucker."

"Hey." My serious tone stops him, and he raises an eyebrow. So the other two don't overhear me, I pull Alvin in for a hug. "Thanks for having my back. With everything."

"Always, brother." He slaps my shoulder a few times. "You know that."

He casts a look down the street where Jacob and Garrett are yelling and carrying on. "We need to stick together."

The implication in his words is plain.

While today we had good news, no one knows what tomorrow will bring.

One thing is certain. The road only gets harder from here.

CHAPTER ELEVEN

Chaser

"WHERE'S MY GIRL?"

No one answers, but as I close our apartment door, the sound of running water reaches me.

Perfect.

I'm about to sneak into the bathroom and join Mallory in the shower when the water shuts off.

Damn.

I knock, and Mallory yelps. "Chaser?"

"It's me." I open the door. "I wanted to soap up your back."

She finishes wrapping a bright pink towel around her torso and flashes a smile. "How was your band meeting?"

What band meeting? Every thought in my head evaporated the second I laid eyes on her. "Drop your towel."

"What? No."

"I want to see you."

"You've seen me. Many times." She turns and wipes the steam off the mirror over the sink. "How was it?"

I creep up behind her while she starts running a wide comb through her thick, wet hair. "Things went well." I slip my hands under her towel, running them up her smooth legs to finally grip her hips and pull her against me.

"Chaser." She sets the comb down on the edge of the sink and closes her eyes.

With a quick yank, her towel opens, and I cup her breasts. "Were you getting nice and clean for me? So I could dirty you up when I got home?"

A wry smile twists her lips. "How did you guess?"

I brush her hair aside and kiss her shoulder. "Never get enough of you."

She hums a happy, sexy noise. "You know I feel the same way, Chaser, right?"

"Perch your cute little butt on the sink for me."

She turns and stares up at me. "Why?"

"So I can lick your pussy and suck on your clit until you come all over my face."

Her cheeks turn my favorite shade of pink. "Chaser."

"You asked."

"Your honesty is so..."

"Raw? Savage? Primal?"

"All of the above."

She presses her palms against the counter and boosts herself onto the edge of the sink.

"Good girl. Spread your legs."

I drop down onto the fluffy, pale-pink rug, Mallory added to the bathroom during her last decorating spree, and prepare to worship at my favorite altar.

"Take your shirt off." She reaches down and tugs at the collar of my T-shirt.

I flick my gaze up. "Why?"

"Because I said so."

I grip the fabric and yank it up over my head, tossing it in the direction of the hamper. "Better?"

"Much."

I shuffle closer and slip my arms under her thighs, resting my hands on her stomach. She shifts and plants her feet on my shoulders. "Thata girl. My shoulders are your footrests. Don't forget it." I turn and kiss her ankle, and she laughs softly. I press a kiss to her other ankle and flick my tongue over her calves.

Bending forward, I sweep my tongue through her slit. "Fucking heaven," I mumble against her slick flesh. I stop and suck at her clit, and she bucks her hips, grinding hard against my face.

I groan even louder.

"Chaser!" she shrieks and gasps. Her fingers dig into my forearms, but I don't let up. A tube of toothpaste, a cup, and a razor all go crashing to the floor as she scrambles for something to hold onto. Reaching out blind, I grab one of her hands and set it on my head. Immediately, she curls her fingers in my hair and tugs.

"Good girl," I encourage. Love how loud and uninhibited my girl's gotten. "Show me how much you love a good tongue-fucking." I dive in again. Licking and teasing until she's frantic. I keep my hands on her hips, pinning her down, sucking harder.

"Please," she begs. "Please let me come." Her body trembles. "I'm so close."

I release her hip and slide two fingers inside her, while working my tongue against her clit.

"There!" She explodes, grinding and bucking against me. The hottest fucking sounds in the world.

I reach down, pry my belt loose with one hand and unbutton my jeans.

"Chaser!" Her butt slips on the counter, and she tips forward.

"I got you." I grab her around the waist and pull her down on top of me. My back hits the bathroom floor with a thump. Mallory wastes no time unzipping my jeans the rest of the way, grabbing my cock and sliding home.

"Fuck," I groan, squeezing my eyes shut. "I didn't say you could have that yet."

"What are you going to do about it?" she challenges.

I grip her hips tighter, holding her down while I thrust up. We're wild and frantic in the tiny space until I finally slam my head against the wall one too many times.

"Fuck this." I power up, lifting us off the floor while somehow keeping her impaled on my cock, and shuffle our way into the bedroom.

She lets out the wildest laugh-moans the entire way, fueling me to get there faster.

We fall onto the mattress, and I cover her body with my own.

She presses her palms against my cheeks and stares up at me. "I love you."

"Love you, too." I kiss the tip of her nose. "Wrap your legs around me."

That's all it takes. Five seconds later, I'm groaning against her neck, biting her shoulder and seeing fucking stars.

She keeps kissing my cheek, along my jaw, and running her fingers through my hair.

When my brain can function again, I press a kiss to her lips, then flop down on the bed next to her. "Come here," I whisper, flapping my hand in the air.

"Aw, Chaser," she teases. "Are you all worn out from a little hard work?"

"Little? Woman, not many men could lift you off the floor and carry you in here without missing a beat."

"I wouldn't know." She chuckles and rests her head against my chest. "And you're the only man I care about."

And thank fuck for that.

"Good." I wrap my arm around her and pat her ass.

"So, your band meeting must have gone well?"

I reach down and hike her thigh over my leg. "I think so. I forgot all about it once I caught you coming out of the shower."

She swats my chest. "I'm serious."

"So am I."

"You're impossible." She moves to roll away from me, but I hold her tight.

"Yeah, it went well. Val got us dates opening for Shooting Fences at the Coliseum."

"Oh my God! Are you serious? That's...that's huge!"

"Yup."

She squeezes her eyes shut. "Thank God. I was so worried Davey would screw things up for you guys."

"Hey." I rub my thumb over her cheek until she opens her eyes and peers up at me. "Even if he did, I wouldn't change a thing about how we handled him."

"Neither would I. That doesn't mean I haven't been worried."

I close my eyes and say a quick thanks to whatever forces in the universe brought this woman into my life.

"Val wants to know if you're still up for doing our next video."

"Of course I am. She can't scare me off that easily." She runs her hand over my chest. "Do *you* still want me to?"

I take a deep breath and think over how to phrase my answer. "As long as you're sure it's not going to have a negative impact on your career."

"Why? Your video is what *launched* my career."

"Yeah, but you're getting more serious auditions now. I don't want you labeled as some band dude's girlfriend."

"You're not 'some band dude.'"

"You know what I mean. Just talk it over with your agent and make sure it's still good for you."

"Okay," she whispers. "Thank you, Chaser."

I twist my fingers in a lock of her hair, winding it into a curl before setting it free. "The video won't have any firehoses this time. Val says we're going 'simple and rugged.' Whatever the fuck that's supposed to mean."

"That sounds much better. Not just for me but for you guys. Something stripped down and simple might help set you apart from everyone else."

"She had bad news, too. MTV yanked the 'Candy Jar' video. Davey's revenge on us I guess."

She covers her mouth with her hand. "Will you be mad if I say I'm not torn up over that?"

"Nope." I sit up and kiss her forehead. "Not even a little."

Mallory

"Let's wash up." Chaser turns and glances at the clock. "We were supposed to meet the guys about half an hour ago. They want to go out and celebrate."

"Do you want me to join you?"

He stares at me as if I'd just asked if the world was flat. "Yes, I want you with me." One corner of his mouth lifts. "I got distracted by your very fine form coming out of the shower all wet and sexy."

We clean up quickly, and he holds my blow dryer while I try to fix my still-damp, messy hair into something somewhat presentable.

I catch his eye in the mirror. "You think anyone would believe the great Chaser Adams helps me dry my hair?"

"If they knew I have the privilege of doing it while staring at your naked body, they would."

As much criticism as I've taken on everything from my nose (not button enough) to my breasts (too big and somehow also too small) to my ankles (too bird-like) since I arrived in Hollywood, it's impossible to be self-conscious when Chaser constantly lavishes me with compliments.

I signal for him to shut off the dryer, finish curling my bangs, and shoo him out, so I can spray a cloud of Extra Super Hold AquaNet over my head.

"What should I wear?" I ask when I find him in the bedroom.

"Sweater?" He grazes his chin with the edge of his hand. "Something that comes up to here?"

"You're hilarious."

He drops his hand and shrugs. "You have anything white? You look pretty in white."

"Hmmm..." I poke through my dresser drawer, pulling out white underwear and a strapless bra, tossing them on the bed before heading over to the closet. "I was given this after a catalog shoot, but I wasn't sure where it would be appropriate to wear."

I pull out the white, stretchy dress with plunging neckline and glittering crystals sewn into the fabric. It fit like a second skin and made me feel sexy when I wore it for photographs on a closed set. I'd be too uncomfortable wearing it in public without Chaser by my side.

He narrows his eyes as he studies the dress. "Is it a...halter top?"

"No, it's a dress. The material's stretchy."

When I finally get it on and everything into place, I do a

quick twirl for him. "It looks like the top *half* of Marilyn Monroe's dress from that movie."

I press my hands to the top of my thighs and lean over, imitating the famous pose from *Some Like It Hot* while also checking to make sure my boobs won't pop free. "Well, at least if I find myself bending over while standing on a subway grate at some point tonight, my skirt won't fly up."

"Funny girl. You bend over in that thing, you'll flash your ass to the world, and I'll be gouging out the eyeballs of every man who takes a peek." As if he didn't just threaten to maim half of Hollywood, he holds up a pair of jeans. "I'm dressing up too. Freshly laundered gray jeans and Chucks."

"Fancy."

"Thought you'd approve."

I grab a pair of silver heels and a small silver clutch from the top shelf of my closet.

Someone bangs on our front door.

Chaser glances up. "Probably the guys."

"I'll answer it. Finish getting dressed," I call over my shoulder.

Alvin and Garrett's voices come through clearly, but I still stop and check the peephole before opening the door.

"Wow." Garrett whistles and allows his gaze to roam over me for a few seconds longer than comfortable. "I guess you're coming out with us, Mallory?"

"Well, uh, Chaser said..." I step back for them to come inside.

Alvin shakes his head and mouths "ignore him" behind Garrett's back. "You look lovely."

"Thank you, Alvin."

"Yes, she's coming with us." Chaser's warning tone can't be mistaken. He strides into the room, shirtless and still buckling his belt. "What's your problem, Garrett?"

"Nothing, we've been waiting. You said you'd be right down."

Chaser's mouth quirks as he catches my eye. "Yeah, had to take care of something first."

My cheeks heat up, but I can't tear my gaze away from him.

"We *know*," Jacob shouts, strolling through the doorway. He nods at me. "Could hear her shrieking like a banshee a block away."

The heat from my face spreads down my neck. "W-what?"

Garrett doubles over laughing, while Alvin just shakes his head.

"We thought it was an earthquake at first." Jacob points at the ceiling. "Except all the noises and shaking were coming from above."

Chaser's expression darkens, but he casually slips on his shirt and moves closer to me, curling his arm around my waist. "I know you're unfamiliar with the concept, but those are the sounds a satisfied woman makes."

Frowning, I shift my gaze Chaser's way. *How is that helpful?*

Jacob doesn't seem to detect the threat in Chaser's tone. I've always assumed Jacob was the kind of kid who needed to be electrocuted a few times before he'd stop sticking his fingers in the electrical socket.

"Well, maybe next time, you should invite us up for a little education." Jacob smirks.

Garrett and Alvin fall silent.

"What did you say?" Chaser's low, threatening tone wipes the smile off Jacob's face.

"I'm just fucking with you." Jacob lifts his chin at me. "Mal knows I'm kidding, right?"

Sure, this is the face of a person who's in on the joke.

"Stop being a dick, Jacob." Alvin moves between Chaser and Jacob. "Are we going or not?"

"Yeah, let's go." Jacob jerks his head toward the door. "Although Garrett and I talked about checking out Seven Sins instead of The Palace."

Chaser stops moving. "I thought you wanted to have a laugh at Wishing Well?"

"I don't mind," I whisper to Chaser. "It's fine." Sure, Seven Sins is a strip club. And more than one person has suggested I apply for a job there since I arrived in Hollywood. According to Vickie, the girls are stunning, and it's where most of the local bands find their future wives.

"Worried Bongo will offer Mallory a job?" Jacob punctuates his obnoxious question with a laugh.

"Let's just go to The Palace like we planned," Alvin pleads. "Rich is always asking us to stop by. You know he'll set us up with a private table, free food, and drinks. Seven Sins ain't giving us shit for free."

"Good point," Garrett says. "Free gets my vote."

While Alvin diffused the situation for now, I'm still not reassured as we head out into the night.

CHAPTER TWELVE

MALLORY

By the time we make it to The Palace, my feet are killing me. The line to get inside runs down the block. I glance down at my sleek silver heels and say a quick prayer for my pinched toes.

"I can't believe anyone lines up to see these poseurs," Jacob grumbles.

The hunk of muscle manning the door scans the crowd. He stops on our party of five and waves us up front.

"Good to see you." He high-fives Chaser. "Wish *you guys* were on stage tonight," he adds in a lower voice.

"When it's time to hire a bodyguard, the job is yours, Robbie." Garrett slaps the bouncer on the back.

"Fuck that. I'll do it for free right now. You going on tour soon?"

The guys glance at each other. "We have a few things lined up."

"You know where to find me." He tips his head and nods. "Evening, Miss Mallory. You're lovely as always."

"Thank you, Robbie."

He raises his hand and whistles, sending hand signals to someone inside. "Go on. They'll set up a table for you."

Jacob and Garrett head straight for the bar.

"Don't let them get too fucked up," Chaser says to Alvin.

"Mallory!"

I search the crowd for whoever called my name. My gaze lands on the girl I'd met at the audition the other day.

Thankfully, the club's too loud for anyone to overhear my groan.

"Hey, Pamela!" I raise my hand and wave back.

She struts over, wearing what appears to be a painted-on silver mini-dress that barely covers her crotch. A tall, shirtless, tattooed man is glued to her side. She drops the man's hand to lean in and air kiss both of my cheeks. "I thought that was you."

I paste on a fake smile and force some polite enthusiasm into my voice. "Good to see you again."

Pamela runs what I can only describe as a predatory gaze over Chaser, then tugs the man at her side forward. "This is my boyfriend—"

"Andrew Lane," Chaser sticks out his hand. "Big fan. Vicious Vandals at the Troubadour was the first show my buddy and I saw when we moved out here. You're a beast on the drums."

"Chaser Adams." Andrew shakes Chaser's hand with violent enthusiasm. "Been watching the rise of Kickstart. I dig your style, man. You're like one of the last genuine bands on the strip these days. You have some amazing riffs."

I've never witnessed Chaser tongue-tied or starstruck before, but it takes him a few seconds to mutter a quick, "Thank you."

Obviously, this guy's band is a big enough deal to make Chaser drop his usual air of cool.

"Mallory Dove." Andrew's gaze slides over my body. "'The Candy Jar' girl." His deep, silky voice can easily be heard above all the noise. "*You* could be Pammy's little sister." He rubs his hand over his chin while he continues his slow eye-fondle.

I really wish I'd worn a sweater like Chaser first suggested. "Uh...

Her raises one suggestive eyebrow. "Have *you* been to one of our shows?"

I cast a nervous glance Chaser's way. I don't want to insult this guy I just met who Chaser seems to have a lot of respect for. While I've *heard* of Vicious Vandals, it's not like I'd go out of my way to see them live or anything. Or be able to pick their drummer out of a crowd.

Andrew's eyes linger on my face. "Nah, I definitely would've remembered *you*."

"Not yet," I answer lamely. "Sorry. I haven't been out here long."

"That's cool." Andrew waves his hand in the air, like it's no big deal, which at least helps me feel less stupid.

Truthfully, as handsome as he is, Andrew's personality reminds me of a goofy puppy. Although, as I run my gaze over his tall, lean, muscled, heavily inked frame, which he clearly enjoys showing off, I can't stop thinking about what Pamela said about *other* parts of his anatomy.

"We definitely need to catch Kickstart's next show." Pamela smiles up at her boyfriend sweetly. "Since they're basically the new and improved Vicious Vandals."

Touché. Inside, I'm laughing at her comeback for Andrew's earlier dig.

Andrew smirks at her.

Wait a second? Didn't she make fun of me for starring in a music video? And here she is dating a rocker herself.

"Well, we're meeting people." Pamela touches my shoulder. "I heard you got a call back too, so I'll definitely see you soon."

Goodie. Can't wait.

She slants a look Chaser's way. "I'm sure I'll see you again soon too."

"Later," Andrew calls over his shoulder.

Jacob and Garrett leave the bar, tripping over themselves to get to us. Alvin follows behind, shaking his head.

"How do you know Pamela Scott?" Jacob's dumbfounded face would make me laugh if I wasn't so rattled by running into my doppelganger.

"We met at an audition."

"You're auditioning with Pamela Scott?" His eyebrows crawl all the way up his forehead.

His shock is a bit insulting. "What exactly do you think I do all day, Jacob?"

"Curl your hair. Try on clothes." He shrugs. "Fuck Chaser?"

"Knock it off, dick," Chaser growls.

"What? It's a compliment."

"When we met, she made a point to tell me about her boyfriend's massive cock." I smile at him sweetly. "So, I don't think you have a shot with her, Jacob."

Garrett rolls his eyes. "As if the whole world hasn't already seen Andrew Lane's massive dick."

Jacob grabs the button of his jeans. "You saying I got a small dick? Because I assure you—"

"Keep your pants on, asshole. No one wants to measure your sad little noodle." Chaser glances in Pamela and Andrew's direction. "Even if you're smuggling a tree trunk down there, she's way out of your league."

I cast a stink-eye Chaser's way, but he doesn't seem to notice.

"That's what you should do next." Jacob leers at me. "*Playboy*. You'd make a great centerfold—"

"She's not doing *Playboy*. Shut the fuck up," Chaser growls.

While I have no interest in posing nude, for some reason, Chaser's proclamation rubs me wrong.

There's no time to protest it, though. The five of us are waved over to a roomy booth in the back of the club where we have privacy but still have a great view of the stage.

Chaser pulls me into his lap and kisses my neck. "You okay?"

I'm not spilling all my insecurities in the middle of our celebratory night, but I need to get one thing off my chest. "I find it amusing she made fun of me for being in Kickstart's video, then eyed *you* like you were a hamburger."

Chaser tips his head back. One corner of his mouth pulls up. "I'm at least a T-bone steak, don't you think?"

I bare my teeth at him and let out a growly noise. He swoops in and captures my lips in a kiss. The club's loud, but our heavy breathing and beating hearts are the only sounds I'm aware of for a few precious minutes. Chaser slides one of his hands over my bare thigh, stopping to play with the hem of my dress.

"Mind if we join you?"

Slightly dazed from Chaser's drugging kiss, I slowly open my eyes and lift my gaze.

Andrew's grinning face stares down at us. Pamela's less enthusiastic expression makes me sit up straighter and yank my dress over my thighs.

"Yeah, totally," Jacob says, sliding over on the opposite side.

Andrew and Pamela don't move.

"Uh, sure." Chaser nudges me out of his lap and stands to

let them slide into the booth. Somehow, I end up wedged between Andrew and Chaser.

"So, Pammy says you're both up for the same part?" Andrew asks me.

Surprised he cares, I shrug. "I guess."

Alvin reaches over to shake Andrew's hand. "Really cool to hang with you, man. Chaser and I used our last couple bucks to see Vicious Vandals when we moved out here."

Andrew chuckles. "He mentioned it. That's rad. I'm so stoked your band's like headed right to the top." He shoots his fist high in the air, in case we're not sure where *the top* is located.

He has to be the first rocker I've met out here who doesn't seem threatened by his "competition." In fact, he spends a lot of time talking with the guys about different concerts, managers to avoid, and lots of other general business advice. It turns out Andrew Lane can talk. A lot.

The guys eat up every word. Even Chaser, who usually seems indifferent in these settings.

Pamela and I sort of look at each other and sigh.

Andrew takes a breath and glances over. "You two should sit closer, so we're not boring you to death."

Maybe with our seating arrangements, it's the most logical move, but I'm totally unprepared for Andrew to put his hands on my hips, lift me up, and physically move me into the empty space next to him.

Nervous, I laugh and try to ignore the way he briefly stops long enough for my butt to brush over his lap.

Please dear God let that be a tree trunk in his pants and not his dick grazing my ass cheeks.

I land on the seat next to Pamela with a bounce. She flashes an almost apologetic smile and pats my leg. "Lord help us when they start talking music. Andrew never shuts up."

Since I could listen to Chaser talk about music all day, I can't help asking her, "How long have you guys been together?"

"A year?" She wrinkles her nose. "Maybe longer? It was after my *Playboy* spread for sure."

"Eighteen months," Andrew corrects without looking at us. He leans over the table toward Jacob. "The second I saw her in *Playboy*, I called my manager and begged him to track her down. That's what *Playboy* and *Penthouse* are for." He thrusts his hands in front of him and mimes flipping through a magazine or phone book. "Girlfriend catalog for rock stars."

Gross.

While Garrett, Jacob, and even Alvin hang on every word, I cast a look Chaser's way. His less-than-impressed expression is probably the only thing stopping me from crawling under the table to get away from this conversation.

"Dude!" Andrew's eyes widen, and he sits back with a dramatic thump against the booth. "Kickstart needs to go on the road with us! It would be totally rad to have you open for us on our next tour."

"Oh shit, we'd be down for that," Jacob says without so much as flicking a glance to any of his bandmates.

I glance over at Pamela. "Guess we'll be seeing a lot more of each other."

Chaser

Conflicted doesn't cover what I'm feeling tonight.

I wasn't lying about being a fan of Vicious Vandals. In fact, Alvin and I spent a lot of time studying their rise to success when we first moved out here. I have mad respect for their dedication and business sense. Hanging with Andrew Lane in the middle of The Palace like it's no big deal is probably one of the cooler things to happen to Kickstart.

But when he touched Mallory, he came damn close to finishing out the night with bloody stumps where his hands used to be.

Vicious Vandals breaks up after drummer's hands are ripped off and used to beat him to death.

Wouldn't that be a sensational headline for *L.A. Weekly.*

The lights dim and people scream.

I can't believe I'm about to willingly subject myself to a Wishing Well show.

"They're such a bunch of fucking poseurs." Andrew leans up against me and shouts in my ear.

"You see Christine?" Jacob asks, twisting around in his seat to search the bar.

Andrew shakes with laughter, slams his fists against the table and stomps his feet, bouncing up and down like an excitable toddler. "Oh, man! They opened for us at the Whiskey years ago, and I totally titty-fucked the shit out of her while they were on stage."

Jacob leans over to high-five him.

A lesson I should've learned with Davey Revolver—never meet your heroes. They're bound to disappoint you. Or in Andrew's case, disgust me.

On stage, Brent runs out in his full-length black leather trench coat, screeching into the microphone and aiming his glossy pink pout at the ladies clamoring to get to him.

"Pammy used to fuck Brent, so she *loves* to shake her ass at his shows to remind him of what he's missing." Andrew turns. "Right, babe?"

She answers with her middle finger, which is pretty damn funny coming from such a pretty girl.

Andrew sets his elbow on the table and points to the stage, while leaning in closer to me. "Now, Danny Desmond's fucking talented."

"Yeah, he's a good guitar player." As much as Wishing Well's music makes my ears bleed, I can admit Desmond has skills. Why he wastes his talent playing shitty party pop metal, I've never understood.

"I don't know why he puts up with the whole big hair, makeup, sparkly white leather outfits bullshit. He's better than that."

The observation's amusing coming from a guy who used to wear just as much, if not more, makeup on stage when he started out.

Andrew bumps my shoulder again. "Yeah, yeah, I know. I'm a big fucking hypocrite because we did the big hair and makeup too. But that was back in '82 when no one else was doing it, you know? Now, it's everywhere. No one's original anymore."

At least he's self-aware. "Gotcha."

He takes one of his massive hands and thumps me on the back a few times. "You're pretty rad, Chaser. You always look like such a grumpy, scary asshole up on stage, but you're all right."

When has he seen us play and why didn't anyone tell us? "Thanks."

"Is it a chick thing?" he asks in a lower voice. Still loud enough to be heard by half the bar but it seems to be his best attempt at volume modulation. "Chicks always want to tame the scary dude." He shifts his hand under the table and grabs his crotch. "I get 'em because they all wanna find out if the legend of the monster in my pants is true."

"Thanks for the visual."

He bounces with more laughter and slaps my shoulder. "Aw, fuck yeah, you're cool!" He leans over the table to grab the other guys' attention. "Hey, why don't you all come back to my place?" He juts his chin toward the stage. "Fuck this bullshit.

Vinny's coming over. We can all jam together. It'll be fucking *rad*."

Vinnie as in Vinnie Price? Vicious Vandals' guitar player? Maybe that last thump from Andrew gave me a stroke. Am I hallucinating or are we about to hang out and jam with half of one of our favorite bands?

"That okay with you, babe?" he asks Pamela.

"Whatever you want."

Once it's decided we're all coming home with him, he can't sit still another second. I have to scoot out of the booth fast or else it's clear Andrew has no problem crawling over my lap. He slaps a hundred-dollar bill on the table, even though all we'd ordered so far was a pitcher of beer.

"Let's go! Let's go!" he chants at about a hundred miles an hour, while clapping his hands like he's training a bunch of rogue puppies.

Keeping one eye on Andrew, Mallory slides out of the booth, carefully pulling her dress down and taking my hand.

Whatever material Pamela's dress is made of sticks to the vinyl booth, but I don't think that has anything to do with the way she very deliberately stops and spreads her legs before standing, making it clear to everyone in a five foot radius that underwear had *not* been part of her wardrobe choice this evening.

For fuck's sake, I'm only human, and it's *right there*.

Completely unfazed that she just flashed her pussy to everyone on this side of the bar, she grabs her purse and hurries to catch up with Andrew.

"I could've happily gone the rest of my life without knowing she's not a natural blonde," Mallory mutters. She narrows her eyes and clasps her hand over my jaw. "Close your mouth before you drool on yourself."

I shake her off. "Sorry, I wasn't expecting *that*."

Jacob blinks and sways on his feet. "Dude, beers with Andrew Lane *and* Pamela Scott flashed her pussy at us. We've died and gone to heaven."

"Or hell," Mallory mutters.

CHAPTER THIRTEEN

MALLORY

"Are you sure you're okay with this?" Chaser asks as we head back to our place to get his bike.

Okay, probably isn't the right word, but I don't want to ruin such an exciting moment for Chaser. "It isn't every day you're invited over to one of your idol's houses."

"Idol might be a stretch."

Sure.

"Let me run upstairs and change."

He follows me but seems jittery. "Are you sure *you* want to go over there?" I ask.

"Yeah. It'll be fun."

It takes almost an hour to get to Andrew's house in Hollywood Hills. The driveway's packed, and music permeates everything on the quiet little street.

"I bet the neighbors *love* him," I whisper.

Chaser takes my hand and squeezes. "We won't stay long."

"I'm fine." I glance at the house. "Just don't leave me alone with—"

"I won't."

Andrew's living room is set up like a stage. That's the only way to describe the scene. He has two full drum kits, a white baby grand piano, mic stands, a keyboard, and a row of guitars. Some sort of music equipment strewn in every corner of the room. Gold albums and lots of portraits of naked women decorate the walls.

Another black-haired, shirtless rocker is busy hammering out notes on his guitar but pauses to nod at us when we walk inside.

Andrew stops bashing his drums and stands. Commanding as a king, he points his drumsticks at us and yells, "Chaser Adams meet Vinnie Price. Vinnie, that's Chaser and his chick."

Chaser's jaw twitches.

Vinnie holds out his hand. "Cool to finally meet you." He glances my way.

Chaser nudges me. "This is my girlfriend, Mallory."

"'Candy Jar' girl. Right. Hey, Mallory." Vinnie sort of half-waves at me instead of shaking my hand, which suits me fine. "I hope you don't get too bored. Pam headed straight upstairs when I arrived." He leans in and adds in a lower voice. "She hates our all-night jam sessions."

"Nah, I got her this huge fucking gas-powered vibrator. She's *busy*," Andrew yells. "It's cool."

I blink and stare at one of the few blank spaces on the wall, wishing I could erase that information from my brain.

"Asshole!" A black, patent leather boot flies out of the stairwell, thunking against Andrew's head. He laughs and tosses it over his shoulder.

Even in flannel pants, a tight T-shirt, and no makeup, Pamela is disgustingly beautiful. She waves her perfectly manicured middle finger in Andrew's direction. "He's kidding."

"Help yourself!" Andrew yells, pointing a drumstick toward the coffee table.

My gaze follows the direction of his sticks to five Tupperware containers set out on the table. The lid of the middle container is off, and I'm pretty sure that's a sandbox worth of cocaine I'm staring at. In my lifetime, I've seen baggies, I've seen bricks, I've seen vials of the white powder, but I have never seen anyone store it in Tupperware.

I mean, I guess if you're storing it in such large quantities, freshness *is* a concern.

Pamela drops down on the floor cross-legged and carefully chops up a few lines. When she's finished, she hands me a silver straw.

"I'm fine, thanks."

Andrew races over, scoops the straw out of Pamela's hand and hoovers up everything she just laid out.

Well, that explains so much.

"Help yourself," Vinnie says to Chaser, waving his arm at a row of guitars in stands against the wall. "We weren't sure if you'd bring your own."

"First three are mine!" Andrew calls over his shoulder. "Use whatever you want."

Pamela leans into her boyfriend, and they spend a few minutes *licking* each other before she snorts a few lines of her own.

I shift my gaze to Chaser, but he seems to miss that my eyes are screaming *get me away from these crazy people* and flashes me a thumbs up.

Vinnie plays a few notes I recognize as one of Kickstart's songs. "'Hammer to the Heart' is a killer riff," he shouts to Chaser.

Chaser watches Vinnie with round eyes and slack jaw, telegraphing how shocked he is that Vinnie knows *any* of the notes to one of his songs.

Vinnie plays it a few times, stumbling over the same section of notes. Finally, he stops. "Tricky fucker, though."

"Uh." Chaser hefts one of the guitars in his arms and demonstrates. "Yeah, there's a skip from D while still hitting the B string."

"Oh, *fuuuck*. Very fucking cool, bro." Vinnie slaps Chaser's shoulder and tries the riff again on his guitar.

Andrew races back to his drums and joins in.

"Jesus H. Christ, they can be at this until eight in the morning." Pamela rolls her eyes.

"It's fun watching them." As weird as the night continues to be, I can only imagine how exciting it must be for Chaser to play with one of his favorite bands.

"God," she drawls in the most condescending tone ever. "You *are* new at this, aren't you?"

"Have you dated other musicians?"

"A few. They're all the same. Big kids with big egos."

"And big dicks!" Andrew yells.

"He misses nothing, huh?" I say quietly to Pamela.

"That's an understatement."

Except for the excessive licking, there doesn't seem to be a lot of love between the two of them. Although, every once in a while, Andrew will stop playing, yell, "Hey baby," and blow a kiss her way. She reaches up to catch every single one.

It's sweet in a totally strange way.

The guys launch into a classic rock song, each of them interpreting it in their own unique style, culminating in a cacophony loud enough to rattle the windows.

"Who's your agent?" Pamela shouts.

"Marilyn Stewart."

"Oh, she's good from what I hear."

"So far."

"I started with Plume Talent, but they're mostly modeling gigs, and I think I want to focus on acting."

"Have you been on a lot of auditions?"

"Not really. I've been taking acting classes with Vera Walters, though, trying to prepare myself. Where do you study?"

When I first arrived in Hollywood, acting lessons were suggested, but since I landed parts right away, I sort of skipped it. Now that I've been to more serious auditions, maybe it's time to buckle down. Feeling foolish and unprofessional, I admit, "I haven't found a class yet."

"Oh, you should come with me! You have to audition to get into her classes, but Vera's great. You'll love her."

Somehow, whether I want to or not, I feel like Pamela and I will be spending a lot of time together in the near future.

Chaser

Mallory's half-asleep when we finally wind down.

"Yo, I got plenty of room." Andrew points to the stairs. "Guest room, first door on the left is all yours if you want to stay." He turns his sticks toward Jacob, Garrett, and Alvin. "You wanna ride my couches, that's cool. Got plenty of 'em."

"That okay?" I whisper to Mallory.

"Sure." She yawns.

I wrap my arm around her, pulling her tight to my side as we say goodnight to everyone.

Upstairs, I close and lock the bedroom door behind us. "Sure you're okay with this?"

Without answering, she pokes around the room, searching behind the television and mirror.

"Babe, what are you doing?"

"Andrew strikes me as the kind of guy who would have hidden cameras set up," she whispers.

"Can't disagree with you on that one," I whisper back.

She chuckles softly and unbuttons her jeans.

"Let me do that."

"I'm leaving everything else on," she warns.

Once we're settled under the covers, she cuddles up and rests her head on my chest. "Did you have fun?"

"Fun?" How do I answer her question? Andrew's a big personality. Jamming with a band I admire was pretty damn cool, though. "It was an experience. My mind's a little blown."

The bedroom door bursts open, bouncing off the wall with a sharp bang.

Mallory and I shoot straight up.

Andrew grins at us. "Are ya fuckin'?"

I'm too stunned to answer or yell for him to get out. Shocked from the intrusion *and* the fact that he's wearing nothing but what appears to be a black leather *thong*. The material seems to be having trouble containing him. Why is everyone flashing their crotch tonight? Pamela's pussy earlier had been one thing. But I'm in no way interested in getting an eyeful of Andrew Lane's log and berries.

"What the fuck, man?" I bite out.

"Oh." Andrew grins. "Door doesn't lock." He crosses his arms over his chest and leans against the wall. "Sooo, why aren't ya fuckin'?"

"Because we knew a crazy person was going to bust in on us?" Mallory must sense I'm about ready to answer with my fists.

"Ha!" Andrew claps his hands and points at me. "You two are totally rad. Night!"

"What the fuuuuck was that?" I groan and stare at the door. "Maybe we should go home."

Mallory eyes the door. "He might follow us."

Neither of us settle back down right away. I keep my eyes trained on the door, concerned it will burst open any second, and this time, Andrew *will* be naked.

A shriek echoes down the hallway. Loud moans and steady banging follow.

"Should we barge in on them?" Mallory shakes with laughter. "Maybe critique their skills?"

"No. They'd probably enjoy that."

"Party time!" someone yells.

My body tenses, waiting for another intrusion, but the footsteps pound away from our door.

"Jesus Christ," I mutter. "Come here." I pull Mallory closer and bury my face against her hair.

The chaos continues into the early morning hours.

I don't remember signing up for the circus; yet, here we are.

The bits of sleep I manage to capture fall in between moments of questioning the whole night.

I can't decide if meeting Andrew and Vinnie is the beginning of something great for the band.

Or the end of everything.

CHAPTER FOURTEEN

MALLORY

"You didn't get the part."

One thing my agent is known for is her directness.

Still, sometimes I'd like to have bad news broken to me gently. I don't have to ask *which* part. It's the one I've been calling and pestering her about every day since the audition.

"They went with Pamela Scott. But from what I heard, it was a close call."

Pamela Scott. Why couldn't it have been anyone else in the world?

"Close. Great." I hang my head, wishing I'd stayed in bed this morning.

"Hey," Marilyn snaps. "Out of four hundred girls, they narrowed it down to *you* and Pamela Scott. I'd stay that's fucking amazing, kid."

Well, when she puts it that way. "I guess so."

"It's close to pilot season, you'll be running yourself ragged all over Hollywood soon enough."

"What else?"

She flicks a piece of paper at me. "Commercials. Coffee. Pancake syrup. You're perfect for both."

"Thanks."

It wasn't meant to be. It's okay. I try to reassure myself on the way out of Marilyn's office. Outside, I stare at the street for a few seconds. My gaze finally lands on my bank branch, and suddenly, I know exactly how to cheer myself up.

Unfortunately, guilt takes a stroll to the bank with me.

At the time we had to send the money back to my father's associates, Chaser never asked questions, and I never volunteered that I'd hung onto quite a few extra thousand dollars.

In my mind, it's our emergency fund. I haven't touched a penny.

Until today.

When the bank attendant walks away, leaving me to view my safety deposit box in privacy, I pull out a stack of bills and swiftly count out enough for what I want.

Outside there's a pay phone and I dial Audrey's number from memory. It never occurred to me how I was going to get where I want *and* lug the items home. "Are you busy today?"

"Not until later. What's up?"

"Would you mind giving me a ride?"

She's there in half an hour. "Nice car. When did this happen?" I slide into the shiny red Corvette and snap my seatbelt into place.

"It was a present."

"From Paris guy?"

She flips the blinker on and pulls into traffic. "Yes. He's seriously wearing me down."

I glance around at the buttery-smooth tan interior. "I don't blame you. But I'm going to be sad if you run away to Paris."

"We might stick around."

"We, huh?"

"God, I can't believe I said that." She blows out a frustrated breath. "Where are am I taking you?"

I recite the directions, and she chuckles.

"Do you want me to wait in the car?" she asks when we pull up in front of the shop.

"You don't have to."

Her pager beeps, and she twists around, searching the street. "You see a pay phone?"

I point one out up ahead, and she shoos me out of the car. "Go on. This is Douglas, I don't want him to worry."

"Oooo...Paris guy has a name?"

"Yes, he has a name." She's smiling too hard to be as exasperated as she wants me to believe.

The little bells over the door jingle as I enter the store. Julius is behind the counter and lights up when he sees me. "Chaser's girl! What can I help you with? I don't suppose you're here to take lessons?"

"Nope." I point to the Gibson Cherry Sunburst guitar Chaser had been so in love with on our last visit. "I'm here for her."

He flashes an indulgent smile. "Sweetheart, maybe you didn't look at the price tag last time." Even though he's clearly humoring me, he takes the guitar down and sets it on the counter between us.

"You take cash, right?"

A little more interest enters his expression. He flips over the price tag, and I nod at him. "Can you sell me a case for it too?" I glance around the store. "What else does Chaser need to go with it?"

"Wait here." He pushes a set of black curtains aside, behind the counter I'd never noticed, and disappears. A few minutes later, he returns with a black case and sets it on the counter. Shiny red velvet lines the inside, and Julius carefully places the guitar inside. "Chaser's a picky one. Better off letting him come in and choose his own accoutrements. He should have enough to get started."

"Thank you."

He rings up the guitar and watches me with an amused expression, probably figuring I'm going to be shocked at the total and back out of the deal. Amusement turns to delight when I calmly count out several neat stacks of hundred-dollar bills.

"You a drug dealer?" he asks.

"No. I'm an actress." *And a thief.*

"Damn, girlie. Beauty and generosity, Chaser's a lucky man."

"He's been very good to me, he works hard, and I want him to have it."

"He better appreciate you. If not, you come see me and I'll kick his behind."

I chuckle as I lift the heavy case. No wonder Chaser has such sculpted arms. Lugging his equipment around all the time is an effective workout.

"Let me help you," Julius offers.

"Mallory!" Audrey hustles inside the shop. "What on earth? I figured you were picking up some strings or something."

"Nope." I heft the case in my arms. "Thank you, Julius."

It takes us a few seconds, but Audrey and I end up wedging the case behind our seats.

"Don't get into an accident. That case will decapitate us," I warn.

"Not funny. I can't believe you bought him a guitar. Doesn't he already have like ten?"

"This one is special."

"Wow. I mean, even a cheap guitar can't be that cheap."

"I don't know what one is supposed to cost. But I know he's had his eye on *that* one for a while and I want him to have it."

She reaches over and pats my leg. "I'm sure he's going to love it."

"I hope so."

Chaser's supposed to be at rehearsals until three, but his bike is parked at the curb in front of our building. "Dammit," I mutter. "I wanted to surprise him."

"Honey, I think he'll be plenty surprised." She glances at the building. "You should probably put insurance on it in case someone steals it in this neighborhood."

Shoot, I hadn't thought of that. "The guys keep things so filthy downstairs; I think anyone's afraid to venture up to our floor. They're like an extra layer of security."

She wrinkles her nose instead of laughing. "Do you want me to ask Douglas if he has any rentals?"

"Maybe." I glance at our building again. "I know Chaser likes being near the band, so they can get together to write or play stuff when the mood strikes them."

"Well, I'd give you and maybe Chaser a reference but not the rest of them."

I lean over and kiss her cheek. "Can't blame you there."

The band must have decided to rehearse here today. The steady grind of one of the songs they've been working on for days punctures the atmosphere as soon as I open the door to our building. My lips twitch. Every time I hear it, they've added some new element.

How the hell am I going to sneak by the guys' apartment? If the door's closed, I should be fine. If they left the door open, I might be able to pass without them noticing, if they're really into their session.

I lug the case up the stairs, careful not to bump it into anything. As I approach the door to their apartment, the music comes to a sudden stop. Loud voices pierce the quiet hallway. I cock my head. Sounds like their usual sharp banter over a lyric or riff. Should keep them occupied for a few minutes.

I tiptoe past their door and up the stairs as fast as possible, without making too much noise.

Phew.

I'm sweating by the time I step inside the apartment. I set the guitar on the couch. It looks so much bigger in our tiny apartment. Where the heck am I going to hide it?

Figuring it can wait, I switch on the box fan in the window, stopping to bend over and stick my face in the breeze for a few seconds.

"Now, that's hot," Chaser says.

"What?" I jump and turn, my heart beating frantically. "I thought you were downstairs working with the guys?" My gaze darts to the couch where any second Chaser will notice the big, black guitar case.

"Yeah, but I heard someone up here and came to check. Why didn't you stop by?"

"Practice sounded good, I didn't want to interrupt you."

He crosses the room and fits his hands to my waist, pulling me forward. "You can always interrupt me," he murmurs before sweeping a kiss over my lips.

With a sigh, I melt into him and slip my arms around his neck. "I thought you'd be at the rehearsal space?"

"Nah, we just started jamming and never made it out of here."

"Why doesn't that surprise me?" I lean up and kiss him again.

"We got stuck, but I'm suddenly feeling very inspired."

"I feel that."

He scoops me up in his arms and turns toward the bedroom. "Aren't the guys waiting for you to come back?"

"Fuck 'em."

Well, I suppose this is one way to keep his attention away from the couch. I draw his head down for a kiss, but he stops moving.

"What's that?"

"Uh." I struggle to right myself, so he'll set me down. "Nothing."

"Pretty big for nothing." He lowers me until my feet touch the floor. "You taking up guitar lessons or something?"

I blow out a frustrated breath. "No, it's a present for *you*. I was trying to surprise you though."

"You bought me a present?"

"Why is that so hard to believe?"

"My birthday isn't for a few more months."

"I wanted you to have it *now*."

He approaches the case slowly, a sly smile forming on his lips. "What'd you get me?" His playful tone and expression erase my disappointment. The surprise might not have gone the way I envisioned, but he clearly doesn't suspect it's his dream guitar inside.

I slide around to the other side and set my hand on the case. "I had a whole scenario in mind where I meet you at the door wearing nothing but stockings and heels while standing behind the case."

"Want me to leave and come back?"

"No, open it."

He unsnaps the locks and slowly lifts the lid, revealing the shiny Gibson inside. "Oh fuck me." He brings his fist to his mouth, biting down on his index finger. A gesture I've only witnessed him do once or twice. "Mallory, you didn't."

I step closer, resting my hand on his arm. "I'm so proud of you. I wanted you to have it to play the Shooting Fences shows."

"Even if Julius gave you the greatest deal in the world, this cost a fortune. I can't accept this from you."

"Why not?"

He opens his arms wide and turns in a half-circle. "Look where I have you living. If I had *this* kind of money, you'd be in an apartment worthy of you."

"As long as we're together, I don't care where we live. It's good for you to be close to the guys, so you can play whenever inspiration strikes." I stare down at the guitar between us. "I want you to understand how much I love you and believe in you every time you play it. It's my gift to you, and you'll hurt my feelings if you reject it."

"Mallory." He groans. "Where did you get the money for it?" A note of dread colors his question. Chaser's too smart not to sense the answer.

"Do you really want to know?"

He closes his eyes and shakes his head. The corners of his mouth twitch. "I *knew* you hung onto more of your father's money than you let on."

I shrug. "Not my fault they can't count."

"What about your father? You think he won't know how much he's really missing?"

That had occurred to me, but if he hasn't said anything by now, I figure he won't. I shrug.

"Sneaky girl."

"I *have* been naughty, haven't I?"

"Very."

The heat in Chaser's eyes says I don't have long to express why buying him the guitar was so important.

"To me, this is an investment in *our* future." I reach down and caress the wood body. "I've had 'Queen of the Road' in my head since you guys were playing it the other day."

Chaser reverently pulls it out and gives the strings an experimental strum. "Yeah?"

"Maybe this will help you finish it."

He leans down and presses a soft kiss against my lips. "Thank you. You don't know how much this means to me."

"Promise me you'll keep it."

"Till the day I die, little dove."

The serious sentiment sends a crackle of pain through my heart.

His brow wrinkles. "What's wrong?"

"I'm pretty sure," I bite my lip, afraid to even say the words, "if you die, I won't be far behind."

CHAPTER FIFTEEN

MALLORY

As the Shooting Fences shows draw closer, Chaser's been asking me to join them at rehearsal more often.

"Are you sure I'm allowed to visit the rehearsal space again?" I ask for probably the tenth time this morning.

So far, the guys haven't seemed to mind, but I figure they'll only tolerate my presence for so long.

"Fuck yeah. I'm more inspired when you're there."

Just when I think the man can't make me swoon any harder.

"Are you sure you won't be too bored?" he asks.

"Nope." Today, I have a script in my bag to keep me busy.

Although, once the guys get into their session, it's almost impossible to tear myself away from watching them and concentrate on anything else.

"You're bringing it?" I nod to the Gibson case, excited Chaser's finally going to use the guitar I gave him. He's only played it at home. Almost as if it's a newborn he's worried to introduce to the big, bad world.

"Yeah, I thought it might help." He kisses my cheek. "Come on, Alvin's waiting downstairs."

I end up in the back seat wedged between the drums and guitar case, praying no one clips the little car on the way there.

Garrett's car is parked by the entrance of the squatty square building, and we find him alone inside the room reserved for Kickstart's practice sessions.

"Jacob isn't here? What the fuck?" Chaser growls, setting his guitar case down. "We don't have a lot of time to waste."

Garrett lifts his head and rubs his hand over his throat. "He's trying to rest his vocal cords. I'm not sure he'll be here at all today. He's shitting bricks that he's gonna blow 'em out before the shows."

"Fuck."

Is that possible? Although I've witnessed some of the lengthy vocal warm-ups he performs before a show, I've never given Jacob's contribution a lot of thought. It makes sense, though. His voice is an instrument that needs to be cared for like everyone else's. Maybe more so since he can't swap out or buy new vocal cords.

"I'm here, fuckers." Jacob slumps into the room. Jacket collar up and sunglasses obscuring most of his face.

"You all right?" Chaser asks, lifting his chin at the cup in Jacob's hand.

Jacob curls the cup closer to his chest. "It's tea."

"I didn't ask."

After some back and forth, Jacob climbs on top of the desk next to me. He sits cross-legged and sets a notepad on his lap.

Chaser and Alvin launch into the now familiar riff of "Queen of the Road," playing it a few times before Garrett joins them.

Jacob watches, swaying side to side for a few minutes, before closing his eyes and opening his mouth.

"There she is."

"Queen of the Road."

"Two wheels of fire."

"Leading me home."

Jacob stops and takes a quick sip of tea.

"Tell me to stay!" Alvin shouts.

"If you think I belong!" Garrett adds.

"Good," Jacob mutters, quickly scribbling down the lines in his notebook.

Over his shoulder, I notice him marking an A next to the line Alvin contributed and a G next to Garrett's. For some reason, I find that funny.

"Ahead there's a storm," Chaser sings.

The guys keep playing, but no one belts out another line.

A few words pop into my head, and I blurt them out before thinking it through. "I need your fire to keep me warm."

"Nice!" Alvin yells.

Jacob slants a look my way.

Guess I was supposed to keep quiet. But then he scribbles down the two lines, marking Chaser's with a "C" and mine with an "M."

"I like that," he mutters.

Chaser winks and blows me a kiss. He closes his eyes and begins a beautiful solo using the slide again.

The guys work steadily, without stopping for a couple of hours. Everything magically seems to come together. Every note and word perfect, until Jacob's last, final haunting line.

"Queen of the road, take me home."

Excitement propels me out of my spot. Jumping and clapping. "That was beautiful! Perfect!"

"Not perfect." Jacob scribbles down a few notes without looking at us. "But it's getting there."

Chaser sweeps me into his arms, spinning us in a half circle. "Knew you'd bring us luck," he whispers.

"I'm sorry I interrupted," I whisper back. "I got caught up in the—"

He silences me with a quick kiss. "Don't apologize. I love that you jumped in. It's a good line too. It worked." He sets me down. "I always wanted to write something with you one day."

"With me? Why?"

"You're clever and put words together in an interesting way."

That can't be true. I sure can't put any words together at the moment.

"Whoa, when'd you buy the Starburst? How?" Jacob asks almost knocking me out of the way to ogle Chaser's guitar.

"Mallory gave it to me," Chaser says. "You just noticed it now?"

Jacob jerks his chin my way. "Who'd you blow to get the money for that?"

I don't have a chance to respond. Chaser slaps his palm against Jacob's chest hard, shoving him back a few feet. "Watch your fucking mouth."

"I'm just saying, if Mallory's got that kind of money—"

"It's none of your business." Chaser thumps Jacob's chest once more to emphasize his warning.

"Jesus, calm down."

"That was sweet, Mallory," Garrett says, inspecting the instrument. "He's had his eye on it forever."

I shrug, uncomfortable having them questioning the personal gift. Somehow in my excitement to buy it for Chaser, I never considered it would pique the guys' curiosity.

"We still have a lot more work to get through," Alvin

reminds everyone. "We need to interview some of those producers Val lined up for us in case Cutter doesn't pan out."

"I don't want to work with anyone but Mark Cutter." Jacob thrusts his chin in the air and crosses his arms over his chest. Clearly as far as he's concerned, this isn't open for discussion.

"Well, I suggest you get your shit together, and act like a professional, so *he* wants to work with *us*," Chaser says.

"Maybe Andrew can put in a word?" Alvin suggests. "Vandals haven't worked with anyone else since *Serves You Right*. He must be tight with Cutter."

I touch Chaser's shoulder. "I might run into Pamela tomorrow. Do you want me to suggest we all get together or something?"

"You want to suggest something to Pamela Scott, suggest she call *me*." Jacob puts his hand up to his ear. "Massive cock or not, with the amount of coke Andrew does, I doubt he can raise that log for long."

"Andrew said to call him if we needed anything." Chaser runs his hand over the back of his neck, ignoring Jacob. "I don't know how serious he was, though. Fuck, I wonder if he even remembers what happened the other night?"

"Not bloody likely," Garrett scoffs.

The band's time is up, so we head back to the apartment.

"What are you going to do if you can't get this producer?" I ask when Alvin, Chaser, and I are alone in the car.

"Val has some talented people lined up," Alvin says. "Jacob may need to readjust that attitude of his."

"Cutter hasn't said no, yet," Chaser adds.

Alvin quirks an eyebrow. "Refusing to return our manager's calls might be as good as a *no*."

I want to tell them to not give up so quickly, but there's a strong possibility Alvin's right.

We trudge upstairs to our apartment and open the door as

our answering machine clicks on, and the caller starts to leave their message.

I recognize the obnoxious, overgrown, teenager's enthusiastic voice immediately.

Chaser and I both stop and stare at each other. Talk about uncanny timing.

"*Call me back, fucker! I have a proposition for you. It's going to be totally rad!*"

CHAPTER SIXTEEN

CHASER

Favors always come with strings attached. Something I learned a long time ago. My father's not a fan of owing anyone anything and that's been the example I followed for most of my life.

Andrew asked me if I'd help *him* write a song for his band's new album.

Once I recovered from the shock, I couldn't say yes fast enough. Figured it would be good exposure for me, *and* this way, Andrew would owe me a favor. Something simple, like say, introducing me to Mark Cutter and maybe convincing the guy to produce Kickstart's next album.

I should've considered the consequences of this plan more thoroughly.

Andrew's a fucking nutjob.

I grew up around some questionable bikers and lord knows the band and I have our ups and downs.

But Andrew? This dude is all up and no down.

No off button or filter either.

I don't know if he's always been this way or if it's the massive amounts of coke he's constantly shoveling up his nose, but working with him is like trying to wrangle a squirrel on angel dust.

"Here! Here! Try this with the bridge." Andrew plays a succession of notes on the piano.

I listen carefully, pick it up and follow along.

As nuts as he is, he's more talented than I realized. Sure, he's a fantastic drummer in a successful rock band. But it turns out, that doesn't scratch the surface. Over the last few days, I've discovered he can pick up and play *any* instrument with ease.

He also has the most voracious appetite for cocaine of any human being I've ever met. And he *never* stops talking. About any and every topic that pops into his overworked brain, but especially sex.

"Is Mallory a firecracker in bed? I bet she's a firecracker. She has that prim, proper vibe but—"

I hold up a hand to stop him. "Mallory is off-limits. Can we go back to this?" I tap my pencil on the papers scattered over the table in front of us.

"Yeah." He works for about ten seconds straight before opening his mouth again. "So, like, you don't fuck girls when you're out on the road?"

"I've already done plenty of that." I don't bother adding that it got old a long time ago and that the thought of being with anyone but Mallory makes my skin crawl. Those aren't sentiments Andrew can wrap his mind around.

"Dammmn, dude. Mallory must be awe-*some*."

"What did I say about her?" Boundaries. Someone obviously needs to set some with this fucker.

"Right." He holds up one hand like he's swearing a boy scout oath. "Off-limits. But, dude, you're what, like twenty-two? Are you out of your mind? I was knee-deep in as much pussy as possible at your age." He smirks. "Still am."

"Good for you."

He claps his hand on my shoulder and attempts a serious expression. "Listen, I feel it's my mission, from like, Satan, to guide you in matters of the flesh, son."

I shrug him off. "I already have a father. Actually, you sound a lot like him."

"He must be cool as fuck."

"That he is." I snicker to myself, picturing my father spending more than two seconds in Andrew's company. He'd probably shoot him. "He's also alone."

"So, you're scared to be alone? Dude, I'm *never* alone. I can call—"

"I'm not scared to be alone, you dick." How do you explain such a difficult concept to a man who apparently has the brainpower of a two-year old?

"I love you, man." He squeezes his eyes shut and grins like an idiot. "No one else has the balls to call me a dick to my face. Even when I'm being a total asshole."

"Happens often, huh?"

"See?" He cracks up and slaps my shoulder again. "Okay, give me that riff again."

Thank fuck.

The band is counting on me to get Andrew to talk Mark Cutter into producing our next album. It's the only reason I've been able to tolerate these insane collaboration sessions without killing Andrew. Although, I'm starting to have my doubts about this plan.

He claims he works best at night, which means I'm up into the wee hours working with him in the soundproof studio he has in his basement.

"Dude, I wish you guys lived closer. We could be at this all the time."

I shudder at the thought. "It'll be a while before we can afford a house in your neighborhood."

"I feel ya. It happened fast for us, but at the time, it seemed so slow. We lived in all these downright gnarly places in the beginning." He pulls a pouty face and glances around his living room. "Soon as we all had cash, we got our big, expensive houses and never saw each other anymore."

Can't imagine why.

"I mean Vinnie and I hang all the time. Kyle and Boner, I never see those dudes unless we're in the studio or on the road."

Jesus, is he going to cry on me? That might be worse than the night I spent listening to him explain in excruciating detail every single position he's ever fucked his girlfriend.

"Just, like, hang onto these early moments. You're all young and hungry now. Living in the gutter. Everything's exciting. Soon, Kickstart's gonna explode. I feel it in my bones."

Fuck, he makes it hard to hate him when he's always complimenting the band and offering advice or help. "Thanks."

"But, you'll wake up and miss how it used to be. Trust and believe, brother."

Suuuuure.

"Appreciate you saying that, Andrew."

"Mallory seems cool too. Like, she never gets pissed when you're jamming late and stuff?"

"No," I answer carefully, in case he thinks I'm giving him the green light to dig for more information. That I refuse to share intimate details about Mallory continues to vex him.

"You don't care if she lands a part where she has to kiss some dude?"

Well, fuck me. I honestly never thought about that. Not that I don't think Mallory's talented and will probably find success before I do, but shit. After Jacob made out with her in the "Candy Jar" video, how did that never occur to me?

"Guess it depends on the role. I trust her judgment."

"Aw, dude. What if she, like, has to fuck some director to get a part or something?"

"*That* she wouldn't do. And I already beat the fuck out of the last couple of pervs who tried."

"Whoa." His eyes bug out. "Really? That's hardcore."

"No, it's what needed to be done." Surprised Andrew hadn't heard about the Revolver situation since I'm learning the music business runs in incestuous circles with the latest gossip everyone's favorite topic.

"Pammy would totally fuck for a part." He scratches his head. "I'm pretty sure she blew the guy for the lifeguard gig. Like, it's business, though, so it's cool."

"You think it's 'cool' and 'just business' to let some asshole degrade the woman you supposedly care about? That's fucked up."

"Sex is currency." He shrugs. "She doesn't give me shit about what happens on the road."

Not really comfortable being placed in this strange lecturing role I seem to find myself in, I shake my head. "Whatever works for you two."

"You'd really be mad if Mallory..." He waves his hand instead of continuing the question.

"I don't have to worry about it, because that's not the way she wants to succeed."

"Bro, I think you're in for a heartbreak. Every woman is the same." He slaps my arm. "How'd you two meet, anyway?"

"On our video for 'Candy Jar.'"

He closes his eyes and bounces up and down, rocking the piano bench from side to side. "Oh fuck! She was *so hot* in that tiny wet tank top!"

I grit my teeth.

"That song's awesome by the way."

Situation avoided. For a second, I thought I was going to have to punch him after all. "Thanks."

"I mean it's totally cheese-anthem-pop-metal that I bet the suits made you write because it had commercial appeal, but you guys fucking rocked it."

Not at all insulted by his honest interpretation, I bust out laughing. "Nailed it. And thanks."

A few hours later, Andrew's used up every ounce of my goodwill. I'm exhausted and dying to crawl into bed. Hell, I'd crawl in the gutter right now, as long as Andrew's not there.

"You're falling asleep on me!" he shouts in my face.

I blink and stare at him.

He pushes a mirror with three small precision-cut lines of coke on it under my nose. "This'll help."

"I'm good."

"Bro, come on. We still have a few hours."

A few more hours of this?

Well-aware of all the ingredients suppliers sometimes add to stretch their product, I stare at the powder. "What's it cut with?"

"It's pure. I swear."

It's not like I haven't experimented in the past. On long runs in my prospecting days, a few lines made all the difference between getting there on time and getting an ass-kicking.

It wasn't a big deal then and it won't be now.

"That's my boy!" Andrew slaps my shoulder as I snort the first line.

Fuck, that's unpleasant. Wherever he obtained this batch, it's a speedy, lightning bolt to the brain.

Fired up and flying high, we're back to work in no time. Unfortunately, coke messes with my rhythm, and I can't seem to play a note. Embarrassing and inconvenient but Andrew doesn't seem to mind. Instead, we lob ideas back and forth for the next few hours.

For now, he may have sucked me into his ocean of crazy, but I'm thoroughly confident I won't drown in the undertow.

CHAPTER SEVENTEEN

MALLORY

"Are you sure you're okay with this?" I ask Chaser one last time, as we head up Audrey's front sidewalk.

He closes his red-rimmed eyes and tips his head back to soak up the last rays of sunshine. "It's good to be out. I could use a quiet night for once."

"You and Andrew have been working hard."

Chaser grunts in response.

"Are you sure you wouldn't rather have more rehearsal time?"

"Yes." His patience seems thin, and the evening hasn't even started.

The hurt on my face must be evident because he stops and brushes his knuckles against my cheek. "All I've been doing is worrying about the Shooting Fences gigs. A night off with non-musicians is a welcome relief."

I lean up and kiss his cheek. "Thank you."

"Nice place." He scans the quiet, narrow street. "I get so turned around in the Hills, but I think Andrew's house is a few streets above here."

"Yikes." I pull a wide-eyed silly face. "He's not going to pop out of the bushes in his leather thong, is he?" I duck down, pretending to search under the ornamental shrubs decorating the walkway.

He actually chuckles. "Why else do you think I pulled my bike up to the garage, where it can't be seen from the road?"

"Good thinking."

"Come here." He curls his arm around my shoulders and pulls me in close. "I'm sorry I've been a moody prick lately."

"I know you're stressed. I only want to help."

"You already do. More than you know." He leans down to brush his lips against mine.

"I have a guest room if you'd rather not go at it on my sidewalk," Audrey calls out, putting an end to our make-out session.

"We're coming." I pull the bottle of wine out of my purse. "We have gifts too."

"Hey." Audrey hugs me when I reach her. "Long time, girl."

"Things have been nuts." It's still no excuse for not visiting Audrey.

"Hey, Chaser." After accepting a quick hug from him, she takes a few steps back and reaches for the older distinguished gentleman at her side. "This is my...this is Doug."

"Hi, I've heard such nice things about you," I gush, shaking his hand.

"Same." He shines a genuine, warm smile at Chaser and me.

"Nice to meet you." Chaser shakes his hand quickly.

"Let me take that." Audrey grabs the bottle out of my hands and scurries off to the kitchen. "Dinner's almost ready. Will you help me set the table, Mallory?"

"Sure."

I thought Chaser would be uncomfortable. I can't imagine he has a lot to talk about with a forty-something real estate tycoon, but he settles into one of the dining room chairs to discuss football with Doug.

"I didn't know Chaser knew anything about football," I whisper to Audrey as we watch them from the kitchen.

"All men do." She waves one hand at them. "It's like a secret language so they always have something to talk about when they congregate somewhere."

I chuckle and follow her into the dining room. The evening flows naturally. Audrey's lasagna is to die for and reminds me of how infrequently I bother to cook anymore.

"Chaser's band is opening for Shooting Fences at the Coliseum," Audrey announces. "This weekend, right?"

Chaser nods like it's no big deal. "Three shows."

"I heard they sold out fast," Doug says.

Too humble to brag about the sold-out shows, Chaser shrugs. "I can get you tickets if you want to go."

Audrey and Doug share such a couple-y look that my heart does a happy tap dance. "That would be wonderful," Doug says. "If it's not too much trouble."

"Saturday?" Chaser grins. "Let us get one show under our belts before you see us."

"That works."

"The band's staying at the Golden Sands, next to the arena for the weekend. Maybe we can meet for lunch and I'll get you set up with tickets and passes."

"Sure."

"This is huge, Chaser." Audrey tips her wineglass in his direction. "I think the first time I saw Kickstart play was in front of maybe fifteen people."

He chuckles. "That seems like a lifetime ago."

The rest of the evening is quiet and pleasant. A far cry from the usual chaos that always seems to invade our lives these days. It makes me long for a fraction of the slice of peace Audrey seems to have carved out for herself.

It's still early when we leave her house.

"You want to go down to the beach?" Chaser asks.

"That sounds perfect." Anything to avoid going back to our noisy, smelly apartment for a little longer.

Since there's nowhere else I'd rather be than the back of Chaser's bike, the traffic doesn't bother me as much as it usually would. Eventually, we wind our way down a secluded lane that opens up to a rocky beach.

Chaser stops the bike next to a cluster of trees. The crashing ocean replaces the rumble of the engine. I tilt my head back and inhale the salty night air.

With only the moonlight to guide our way, we traipse through the sand to a cluster of rocks.

"This looks like a good spot." Chaser slaps his hand against the side of a rock almost as tall as he is.

"For you, maybe. How am I going to climb up there?"

He effortlessly bounds up onto a lower rock and makes his way to the top of the taller one, then extends his hand to me.

The flat top is narrower than it looked from below. "You have to cuddle up close to me," Chaser says.

He drops down and pulls me into his lap. Resting my head on his chest, I tip my head back so I can see his face.

"Did you have a good time?" I ask. The mood surrounding him seems so sullen.

"It felt like having dinner with...parents or something." His lips quirk. "Not *my* parents, obviously."

"I know what you mean. I'm happy for her. He seems really kind."

"It's hard not to like the guy. As long as he treats her well, that's all that matters."

I hum a happy noise and press my cheek against his chest. His heart thumps a steady rhythm, mixing with the crashing waves beating against the sand.

"This is nice," he rumbles. "We need more of this."

At the longing in his voice, I lift my head. "I was thinking the same thing."

"I'm sorry things have been so shitty lately."

I raise my hand, allowing my fingers to skate over his bristly cheek. "I'm with you for the long haul, Chaser. Our road will be bumpy from time-to-time. As long as we have each other, we'll survive anything."

He ducks his head, burying his face against my shoulder. "I love you so much," he murmurs.

I sense there's more, but he remains quiet after his declaration.

"Is everything okay, Chaser?"

"This collaboration with Andrew's been more work and less fun than I expected."

"You're no stranger to hard work."

"It's not that." He stares out at the sea for a few minutes.

"Have you asked him about Mark Cutter?"

"I mentioned it once."

"And?"

He tips his head down and raises an eyebrow. "You've met Andrew. He can't focus on anything for more than five seconds."

"It's probably all the cocaine."

Chaser shifts and lowers his gaze.

"Are you sure everything's all right?" I ask again.

He takes a while to answer. "It will be."

CHAPTER EIGHTEEN

MALLORY

"Miss Dove, we're pleased to inform you..."

I stare at the answering machine as I replay the message over and over.

I got the part.

And no one's here to share the news.

This certainly takes the sting out of losing the lifeguard role on *Shallow End* to Pamela. Not that I'm salty about the loss. Or jealous that the show got picked up for a whole season.

I hurry over to Marilyn's to share the news before she leaves for the day.

"I just heard," she says. "Good girl. I'm proud of you. You'll nail it."

At first, I'm not sure what to think when I show up and they explain I'll be playing a "wholesome mom." That wasn't the part I'd read at the audition.

"So," the director explains her vision. "You're home with

the kids all day. The only time that's yours is that fifteen-minute window in the morning before everyone gets up and demands your attention to enjoy your cup of coffee. Got it?"

Since I have zero experience with any of that, I feel like a fraud for plastering a big smile on my face. "Got it!"

"Perfect. Take one!"

My mug is actually empty, so the acting challenges begin right away.

"Come on!" The director encourages between takes. "Your husband's a selfish little boy only aware of his own needs and problems. That coffee is your only joy in life."

Well, that got depressing fast.

The last take I stare longingly into my coffee the moment my fake children run screaming into the kitchen.

"There!" The director stands and waves her arms in the air. "Cut! That's the one. Excellent job, honey."

"Thank you," I gush, not used to so much feedback about my performances.

Chaser's waiting for me outside and I race over to him, eager to share my news.

"How'd it go?"

"Incredible."

He picks me up and swings me around. "That's my girl."

"I played a mom who practically orgasms over her morning coffee."

"I can't wait to see that."

CHAPTER NINETEEN

CHASER

All my chill vanishes the second we pull into the arena's parking lot. Whatever nothing-ruffles-me, rock star persona I've managed to develop over the last couple of years dissolves with the fumes pouring out of Alvin's tailpipe.

Thousands of people fill the arena's parking lot, waiting to rush past the chain link gates. Mallory clings to my arm, her nervous gaze taking in our surroundings.

Backstage at the Coliseum, it's everything I expected and more. Guys in black T-shirts yell at more guys in black T-shirts while moving equipment. Amps wheel by, suits stand in clusters smoking cigars, laughter from random groupies trills through the air. Noisy, crowded, chaos everywhere.

We've even been assigned our own dressing room, decked out with a mini-buffet of cold cuts and cut up vegetables. I don't dare eat a bite. Spewing on stage isn't on my list of rock star experiences I want to have before I die.

"Are you ready?" Val asks me for the tenth time in less than ten minutes. Our usually cool manager seems to be as nervous as the rest of us.

"I'm okay."

"Are your parents coming, Jacob?" she asks.

They live not too far from here, so it's not a stretch that they'd attend their son's big show. Unfortunately, they won't make an appearance. Who am I kidding? Make that *fortunately*. They've never supported Jacob's rock stardom aspirations.

Jacob growls at her and stalks out of the dressing room, slamming the door behind him.

"Keep him away from the liquor." Val points at our newly hired security guard, Robbie. "He's going to be a godsend," she mutters after Robbie tears after Jacob.

"Tired of wrangling us on your own, Val?"

She stares at me for a few seconds. "With great success comes great responsibility."

Val's not usually one to spout off one-liners of wisdom. "For you or us?" I ask.

"Both."

Not sure what to make of that, I drop onto the cracked leather couch and fiddle with the Gibson.

Soundcheck had gone smoothly. We haven't met the guys from Shooting Fences yet, but Valerie assures us they're still thrilled to have Kickstart opening for them.

Jacob returns a few minutes later with Robbie on his tail.

"I need to do my warm-ups," Jacob announces.

I sweep my arms open wide. The floor's all his.

"I can't do it with an audience. You know that."

Actually, this is a new hang-up of his. Normally, I'd razz him, but tonight's too important to all of us to give him grief. Instead, I hold out my hand to Mallory. "Let's go check things out."

Placing my hands on her hips, I guide her into the jam-packed hallway ahead of me. My gaze drops to the orange, red, and pink straps of her dress. The material clings to her body in a maze of knots down her back, giving her the appearance of a flickering flame as we move through the crowd.

"You're beautiful," I whisper in her ear.

"Thank you." Her shaky hands smooth down the sides of her dress. "I don't know why I'm so nervous tonight. It's not *me* going on stage."

Maybe not, but Mallory's been to almost all of our rehearsals this week and has been as excited and enthusiastic as all of us.

"Is Jacob going to be okay?" she asks when we're a good distance from the dressing room.

"He'll pull it together before we go on." At least I hope he will.

Alvin's side stage, watching the crew set up Shooting Fence's elaborate set. When they're finished, they toss some black curtains in front of the whole thing. The guys we hired to be our roadies for this weekend will put together our more modest backdrop.

I clap Alvin on the back, and he jumps about ten feet in the air. Guess we're all on edge tonight.

"You all right, bro?"

"Yeah, you sneaky motherfucker." He clutches his chest with one hand. "You trying to give me a heart attack?" His gaze slides to Mallory, and the panic slowly leaves his expression. "Damn, *you're* the heart attack."

"At ease, soldier." I smack his shoulder, and he laughs.

"Chaser!"

I briefly close my eyes when I recognize the voice.

"Why is Cokefiend McMassivePenis here?" Alvin asks

through the phony smile plastered on his face. "Hey, Andrew!" He waves.

"Great, call him over," I mutter.

"Like he's not headed our way."

Andrew bounds over to us with the gait of a giraffe mixed with the eagerness of a golden retriever. In his never-ending quest to annoy the shit out of me, he stops to gawk at Mallory.

"I'm not even going to say how hot you are because it won't do you justice." He darts a guilty look my way. "And Chaser might kill me."

"Hey, Andrew." Mallory smiles up at him.

"Are you guys so stoked?" he asks, grinning like someone who doesn't have to go on stage in front of seventeen thousand people in two hours.

"Getting there." My gaze drops to his T-shirt. His *Kickstart* T-shirt. "What are you wearing, bro?"

He tugs at the material and stares down at it like he's just as shocked as I am, then grins. "There's a photographer from HIT around; I thought it'd make a cool photo." He gestures to the four of us. "One big happy."

"Thanks." Now I feel shitty for being annoyed with him.

"Oh! I brought a friend I want to introduce you to." He turns, searching the area behind him. "Give me a minute."

"You think it's one of Pamela's Playmate friends?" Alvin asks with hopefully raised eyebrows.

"No," I answer as Andrew curls his arm around the shoulders of an older man in a plaid shirt and points him in our direction. "Hold onto your shit," I say to Alvin.

Grinning and pointing at his friend, Andrew returns. "This is the man! No one better to work with. Not just in L.A. but the entire world! Mark Cutter, these are the dudes I told you about. Chaser's a musical wizard. That piece I brought you? *This* is the genius who helped me arrange it."

Am I having a stroke?

It has to be well over a hundred degrees back here.

Maybe I'm hallucinating.

Am I finally meeting Mark Cutter?

I tune back into the introductions while Andrew's praising Alvin's skin-bashing abilities as, "The best drummer since *me*."

"And Mallory's the coolest chick around," he finishes.

"Hi, Mr. Cutter," Mallory leans forward to shake his hand, filling the gap since Alvin and I both seem to have lost control of our manners and motor functions.

"Mr. Cutter, it's an honor to meet you." I finally pull my head out of my ass and shake the man's hand. Alvin does the same, then gives me a subtle elbow bump.

"Andrew insisted I get my ass down here to see Kickstart live." In a lower voice, he adds, "he mentioned you might be looking for someone to produce your next record?"

"Y-Yes," Alvin stutters. "Yes, sir. We are."

"Where's Jacob?" Andrew asks. "And Garrett?"

"Jacob's doing his vocal warm-ups. Not sure where Garrett disappeared to."

"Getting head?" Andrew asks with a straight face. "That always calms me down before a big show."

Mark side-eyes him, and Andrew shrugs. "What? It does."

If this man has put up with Andrew's tornado of crazy for so many years, producing Kickstart will be a warm, gentle breeze.

"Vinnie's here too somewhere," Andrew says, searching the area behind him again.

Great, more people to watch me choke tonight.

"I need to speak to Jared," Mark says, excusing himself. "Looking forward to sitting down with you, Chaser, Alvin." He nods to both of us. "Nice to meet you, Mallory."

He rests a hand on Andrew's shoulder and pulls him closer, saying a few things against his ear before walking away.

Andrew turns to us, thrusts his hips forward and gives us two thumbs up. "Mark's the best. I mean, he'll totally papa bear you in the studio. And you can't get away with any shit under his watch. But he'll also squeeze out your best work."

"Thank you."

He slaps me on the back. "No problem."

Mallory's completely giddy and wide-eyed, but she waits until Andrew stalks off in search of the bar, before grabbing my arm and bouncing up and down. "Oh. My. God," she mouths. "Are you excited?" She stops her little happy dance and her mouth pulls down. "Is Valerie going to freak?"

I exchange a glance with Alvin. Val has been frustrated with her inability to get to Cutter. Figuring nothing would come of it, I hadn't shared with her that I'd asked Andrew for the introduction.

"Maybe."

"Nah, she knows how it is." Alvin doesn't seem as convinced as he's trying to sound. "She'll be happy if we finally get our asses in the studio."

I hope he's right.

CHAPTER TWENTY

Chaser

This isn't our finest performance.

I doubt anyone else notices, but as usual, I can't help picking apart every single detail.

"Anyone want to hear something new we've been working on?" Jacob shouts into his microphone. Most of his banter tonight has been short and sounded more rehearsed than his usual, easy flowing style.

The crowd responds with a bellowing, "yes!"

My earlier solo had been brief and mechanical. It's time to redeem myself.

I turn to watch Alvin count off the opening beats to "Queen of the Road." He executes a signature twirl of his drumstick, but this time, instead of crashing against his cymbal, the stick sails across the stage, thwacking into the back of Garrett's head.

He turns and scowls at Alvin.

"Fuck, sorry!" Alvin shouts without missing a beat.

One of the roadies races out and grabs the stick, quickly tossing it into the crowd where a bunch of eager fans dive after it.

When we launch into the chorus, the crowd actually sings along. Something none of us expected since we've never played it live before.

I glance over at Mallory. Hands clasped under her chin, she's watching with tears in her eyes and mouths, "I love you."

This solo comes from somewhere else. Like some cosmic force is using my fingers to play each note.

The screams from the audience for more thunder against the stage.

People start chanting, "Candy Jar!" at us, and for the first time since the Bloody Revolver tour, I'm actually eager to play it.

Not even Andrew standing behind my girl and watching her smile up at him sours my mood. Although, I briefly wonder how much Julius will charge me to fix my guitar if I slam it into Andrew's face a couple dozen times.

A wave of people rush the stage, pushing the metal barrier a few feet. Security works to push them back, but one girl manages to break free and scampers onto the stage to hug Jacob and scream, "I love you!" in his face.

She wraps her skinny little arms around his waist and hangs on tight while Robbie tries to pry her off the stage. Jacob sings through the mauling, breaking into laughter a few times.

A red, lacy bra lands at my feet. I pause long enough to pick it up and toss it to Garrett, who hangs it on the end of his bass. My gaze scans the crowd, landing on a topless girl sitting on her boyfriend's shoulders. She points at Garrett and cups her tits, indicating—I think—that the bra was meant for *me*. Not sure what she wants me to do with that, I shrug and nod at her and keep on playing.

The crowd's still screaming their heads off when we finish. The four of us meet in the middle of the stage to put our arms around each other and bow.

Robbie tosses a towel my way as I pass by.

Mallory's waiting for me, and I push past people to get her into my arms, lifting her in the air. I crash my lips against hers, and she presses my face between her hands, kissing me back just as hard.

"That was incredible," she whispers against my lips in between kisses.

My heart's still pounding from the show, and I realize I'm dangerously close to hiking up Mallory's dress and fucking her in front of everyone backstage. Reluctantly, I set her down, but she keeps her arms looped around my neck.

"I hope Cutter didn't stick around to watch that," I mutter.

"Why? You were amazing."

I shrug, still bothered by the choppy start to our set.

"You're too hard on yourself." Mallory slides her hands down my sweaty chest while peering up at me from under her lashes. "You should be hard on *me* instead."

"Done." I sling my arm around her shoulders and turn her toward the hallway. Surely, there's an empty room or broom closet around here somewhere.

We're thwarted by Valerie herding all of us into our dressing room.

"Fuck!" Jacob throws his towel at the couch and chugs a bottle of water. "That was insane!"

Alvin's still jumping up and down. "Did you see that reaction?"

Garrett's more reserved. "Still have a few rough edges to smooth out." He shoots a glare at Alvin. "And maybe degrease your fingers."

"I was sweating my balls off up there, bro."

"Guys, I have never been prouder," Val gushes. "You were born to play crowds this big."

She gives each of us a hug, landing on Jacob last. She pats his cheek. "You sounded good."

"I'm dying. I behaved all day. I need a drink." Jacob wipes his towel over his sweaty forehead and gives her one of his pleading puppy faces.

"We have two more shows," I remind him. "You can't afford to get shit-faced tonight."

"Did you see that crowd?" He points in the direction of the stage. "We need to celebrate."

Shit. What's the better option here? Let him have a mini-celebration tonight or risk him drowning in a vat of Jack Daniels Sunday after we've finished all three shows?

"We'll discuss it in a minute," Val says, pushing Jacob toward the couch. "Sit." Her eyes gleam. "I heard Mark Cutter's here tonight."

"Uh," I raise my hand. "Alvin and I met him earlier."

Poor Valerie completely deflates. "Why didn't you say something?"

"Yeah, why the fuck didn't you tell us?" Jacob adds.

"Well, *you* were busy with your diva act in here." I gesture at Garrett. "And no one knew where *you* were until two minutes before we went on stage. Andrew brought him and introduced us."

"I knew working with that crackhead would pay off!" Jacob high-fives me. "You're the man, Chaser."

"Good job." Val squints. "What did he say?"

"He was looking forward to sitting down with us." Val knows I wouldn't try to undermine her on purpose. Hasn't she been busting my balls about "networking more" for years now? "Andrew talked us up quite a bit."

"Good." She nods again. "Good, that's better coming from another musician Cutter already has a relationship with than coming from your manager. Good."

If she says *good* one more time, it's going to be clear we're anything but.

CHAPTER TWENTY-ONE

MALLORY

"One down, two to go." Val points to Jacob. "For the love of all things holy, stay sober tonight. Fuck your way through that wall of groupies waiting out there, but you have two more shows to nail, and I need you at your best."

"I'll be fine." Jacob pats her on the back and sips his water.

"Well, I'm going to go watch Shooting Fences." Val glances at each one of us. "Anyone joining me?"

"When do we get to meet them?" Alvin asks.

The already tense smile on Val's face fades away. "Well, uh, about that..."

"What?" Jacob sits forward and frowns at Val.

"It's nothing personal. They're happy you're here."

"But?" Garrett prompts.

"Well, remember last year when it was all over MTV and in every magazine how they took all that time off to get sober?"

"Everyone knows that," Chaser says. "So?"

Val flaps her hands in the air, and my stomach drops. "Kickstart's developed a bit of a party reputation." She drops her gaze. "Their sobriety coach doesn't want you anywhere near them."

Ouch. If I wasn't a witness to the constant partying going on in the guys' apartment, I'd be offended on Kickstart's behalf.

Chaser glares in Jacob's direction.

Jacob shrugs. "Hypocrites."

"Sobriety coach?" Garrett scoffs. "What the fuck is that?"

"Exactly what it sounds like," Val snaps. "They spent an assload of money to get clean, and the record company isn't taking chances. They sent someone out on the road to keep them away from all chemical temptations."

"That's the least rock-n-roll thing I've ever heard of." Jacob slaps his leg and doubles over.

"They're professionals who want to maintain their career," Val counters. "Jared almost died of an overdose." Her prickly demeanor softens. "Please, prove them wrong. Behave this weekend."

"Whatever." Jacob shoos her away.

"We'll be there in a few," Chaser promises her.

I nudge him with my elbow. I thought we had other plans.

"Well, that was awkward as fuck," Alvin mutters as soon as Val leaves.

"Andrew fucking Lane actually came through." Garrett lightly punches Chaser's shoulder. "Good job."

"Val can't even get the guy to return her phone call." Jacob shakes his head. "But Andrew delivered him on a silver platter."

"It was cool of him, for sure," Chaser says. "But Val's been working her ass off for us for years."

Garrett and Jacob share a look that isn't missed by Chaser. "What?"

"Working her ass off? She couldn't even defend us to some pansy sobriety coach," Jacob argues.

Chaser just stares at him.

"Forget that. Who cares what those old farts think." Garrett plops down on the couch and stretches his arms across the back. "Thom Woodworth approached us about managing the band."

"When?"

"Earlier." He smirks at Chaser. "You're not the only one keeping secrets."

"I wasn't keeping secrets." Chaser blows out a breath. "Val's done a lot for us. We wouldn't be here tonight if she hadn't gotten us these shows."

"Agreed," Alvin says.

Garrett holds up his hands in surrender. "Agreed."

Music reverberates through the building.

"Sounds like Shooting Fences has started." Alvin takes a swig of the brown liquid in his glass. "You going to watch?"

"Yeah." Chaser grabs a shirt and ballcap, slipping on both before leading me outside.

It's even more crowded in the hallway now, although the bulk of people seem to be up ahead, watching the band. A few girls rush over to Chaser and ask him to sign various items.

While I'm standing to the side, trying to stay out of the way, something rough skims over a spot on my back left bare by my dress. "He must be riding high," Andrew says from behind me.

I jump and turn, shaking off his fingers.

He smiles down at me and touches his leather jacket. "Are you cold?"

"I'm fine. It's hot back here."

He sweeps his gaze over me. "Yes. It is."

My jaw drops, but before I come up with a response, shrill screams pierce the air.

"Andrew Lane! Oh my God!" One of the girls Chaser had been signing an autograph for rushes toward us.

"Fuck," Andrew mutters. "I should've waited."

He genuinely seems stressed to intrude on Chaser's moment, which erases my annoyance over our encounter.

I stay put while Andrew swaggers over and steers the rogue fan Chaser's way. "Wasn't this dude friggin' amazing tonight?" he asks, slinging an arm over Chaser's shoulders.

"Yes!"

Andrew signs a bunch of stuff and tolerates a lot of photos before a big guy waddles over and interrupts. "Andrew, they're looking for you."

"Thanks, dude." He slaps the guy's shoulder.

"Ladies, if you'll excuse us." Andrew motions for me to join him and Chaser.

"Where are we going?" Chaser asks.

"That photographer I told you about is here."

"Do you want me to grab Alvin and the others?" I ask, tripping over my heels to keep up with Andrew's long-legged pace.

"I sent Benny to fetch them."

Even though Andrew's not playing tonight, he somehow managed to procure a room for himself backstage. Vinnie and a woman with a camera around her neck are chatting when we enter.

"Oh, wow. Chaser Adams." She rushes over. "Judy Herlands. Big fan of yours. Great performance tonight."

"Thank you." Chaser shakes her hand.

"Mallory Dove, right?" Judy extends her hand to me. "So great to meet you."

"Uh, thank you."

"Judy's with *HIT Magazine,*" Andrew explains.

"Well, I just started..." She blushes and taps her camera.

"Yeah, so we thought it would be cool if she got like shots of us hanging together backstage." Andrew's so excited, I'm expecting him to blast through the roof any second now. "Something different than their usual pieces to help Judy stand out at her new job."

She blushes, and, once again, I'm struck by how thoughtful Andrew can be at times.

"Our readers love stories about friendships between their favorite bands." Judy gestures toward me. "And rock star romances are always huge, of course."

"Sure," I mumble still overwhelmed.

Benny knocks and pushes the door open to announce the rest of Kickstart has arrived.

"What's up, brother!" Andrew high-fives Jacob. "Killer show!"

"You watched?" Jacob asks.

"Damn right! You dudes rocked the house!"

Poor Judy's wide-eyed and pale. Maybe this is too much rock star friendship for her fragile fangirl heart to handle.

"Do they hang out a lot?" she asks me.

"Chaser is working on a project with Andrew, so they've been playing together quite a bit recently."

"Wow. Can we expect a Kickstart/Vicious Vandals collaboration soon, guys?" she asks.

"You'll have to wait and see." Andrew winks at her.

We pose for some photos while she peppers the guys with questions.

Eventually, everyone winds down, and after throwing a warning scowl at Andrew, Vinnie walks Judy out.

"That was cool. Thanks, bro." Garrett shakes Andrew's hand.

"No problem." Andrew's gaze slides to Chaser. "Did Chaser tell you Mark Cutter might be interested in working with you? He had to leave before your set, but he's planning to come see you play Sunday night."

"Holy shit?" Jacob punches his fist in the air. "Seriously?"

Andrew bobs his head up and down. "My thanks for letting me borrow Chaser."

Chaser huffs out a laugh.

"You nodding out on me, bro?" Andrew reaches into his pocket. "I got something for you."

"I'm good." Chaser holds up his hands and takes a step back.

"You sure?" Andrew waves a baggie of white powder at him. "It's the same stuff from Col—"

"I said, I'm fine." Chaser curls his arm around me. "Let's go catch the rest of the show."

"Are you upset?" I ask when we're alone.

"No, I just think it's rude for us not to watch the band who invited us to open for them."

"Andrew does have a way of making everything about him, huh?" I tease.

"Yeah, but he's so nice about it—"

"You can't be mad?"

"Something like that."

"Hold up!" Alvin calls.

We stop and turn, waiting for him to reach us.

Alvin swipes at his nose and lifts his gaze to Chaser. "They're *skiing.* After what Val said, I don't even want to be in the vicinity."

"Jesus Christ." Chaser scowls in the direction of the room we just vacated. "I thought Jacob needed vocal rest?"

"He's a big boy." Alvin shrugs. "Let's go watch the show."

"We don't need more rumors spreading."

Alvin follows Chaser's gaze. "Andrew doesn't need the bad press either. It'll be fine."

Somehow, I don't think it's that simple. Secrets have a way of coming to light at the worst possible time.

But it's not my decision to make. So when Chaser takes my hand, I follow.

CHAPTER TWENTY-TWO

CHASER

A loud thump, followed by shrill laughter, wakes me out of a dead sleep.

"What's going on?" Mallory mumbles.

"I don't know. Stay here."

I'd lost track of Garrett and Jacob after the show last night. Andrew had disappeared too. Although, judging from the sounds in the hallway, he didn't go far.

"Woooo!" someone screams.

Thuds and bangs echo up and down the hallway.

I open the door as Jacob races by in his underwear, followed by Andrew in his black leather thong.

"What the fuck? It's five in the morning."

"Chaser! We were looking all over for you." Andrew wraps his hand around my arm and tries to yank me into the hallway.

"I was sleeping."

"Oh, fuck! Run! Security's coming." Jacob races past us, then backpedals.

"No you don't. Go hide in your own room."

Behind me, the phone rings, and I slam the door shut, locking it.

"Fuckers."

"It's Val," Mallory calls out.

I snatch the phone out of her hand. "What?"

"Please tell me Jacob isn't responsible for all that noise?"

"And Andrew."

"You need to stop him. The hotel's going to throw all of us out if they get any more complaints."

"Jesus Christ, Val."

"Robbie's on his way up."

"Great." I slam the phone down and search the floor for my jeans.

"What's going on?" Mallory asks.

"Jacob's going to get us all thrown out."

She tosses the covers back. "I'll help—"

"No. Stay here."

She watches me for a few seconds before agreeing.

I throw on a T-shirt and stalk into the hallway, running into Robbie. "Where'd they go?" he asks.

"That way."

Alvin runs around the corner, tripping and then catching himself. "They're going up on the roof. Hurry."

"What?"

Robbie and I race after him into the stairwell and jog the eight or nine flights up to the door that opens to the roof.

"Woooo!"

"Sounds like Andrew," I mutter. He's not my responsibility, though, Jacob is.

My bare feet scratch over the rough roof top tiles. Orange

flickering light guides our way to Andrew, Jacob, and Garrett roasting marshmallows over a small black, charcoal grill.

"You started a fire up here?" Alvin asks.

Andrew glances up and grins when he sees us. "I paid a guy to let us borrow the rooftop grill. Isn't that rad?"

One day I want to start a game where I punch Andrew in the face every time the word *rad* comes out of his mouth.

Jacob salutes me with a bottle of whiskey, sloshing enough around for flames to shoot up.

"Easy, Jacob." Andrew claps him on the back. "Don't want to burn the marshmallows."

Yeah, that's what we should be worried about.

"Why isn't Pammy here with you?" Jacob slurs. "She's hot."

"She has to be on set *early*," Andrew whines the last word. "No fun, that girl, sometimes." Andrew waves the long metal rod with three blackened, oozing marshmallows skewered to the end in my direction. "Back me up, Chase-man. These days all these chicks wanna have a 'career,' right? Real men don't give a fuck if a woman's got some corporate gig—"

From the corner, Garrett giggles. "What corporate chick's trying to bang *you*?"

"You'd be surprised," Andrew says, not offended in the least. "They wanna go to college or have an acting career, when all I want is someone who looks pretty cooking my damn dinner."

"With big tits," Jacob adds.

I gaze up at the stars for a second. If he wasn't absolutely fucking crazy, Andrew would fit in perfectly with lots of bikers I know.

When I don't agree with him right away, he pokes me with the sticky end of his skewer. "Right, Chaser?"

I slap the hot metal away. "That sounded like a whole lot of words for, 'I don't know how to find a clit' to me."

"Nah," Alvin chimes in. "Sounded more like, 'I've never given a woman an orgasm.'"

"Fuck both of ya!" Andrew throws his arms open wide, accidentally flinging his marshmallows to the side. "Bring me a woman right now. Any woman. I'll strum her clitty to orgasm in five seconds flat."

Jacob points his bottle at Andrew. "Is Pammy a screamer? I feel like she's a screamer."

Andrew scratches his chin, settling in for what I'm sure will be a lengthy story about Pamela's octave range.

Before he opens his mouth, I remind Jacob, "You were supposed to keep the partying to a minimum this weekend."

"Chill the fuck out, Chaser," Garrett slurs. "You're not the boss of us."

Since he's regressed to the same arguments an eight-year-old would use, it's a safe bet Garrett's already killed a bottle on his own.

"Every rock star knows true binge-drinking is an artform." Jacob flaps his arms in the air, leaning too close to the edge of the building for my comfort. "And I am motherfucking Michelangelo!"

"Preach, brotha!" Andrew reaches up to high-five Jacob, sending him teetering closer to the edge.

This is fucking ridiculous. I elbow Andrew out of the way.

"That's great." I loop my arm around Jacob's waist and drag him off the ledge. "Let's go downstairs. The hotel's ready to throw us out."

"No!" Jacob protests. "We're having fun."

"I think you've had enough fun."

"I won't let them throw you out, Chaser," Andrew pleads. "Don't go."

"Bro, we have two more shows to get through," I remind him.

Jacob tips his bottle back, drains the contents, and tosses it against the brick wall, where it shatters. "Need to find another one."

"I bet Robbie has a fresh bottle waiting for you in your room."

He stares at me with glassy eyes then scowls past me at Robbie. "Nu-uh, Val told him to keep me away from booze." Jacob's mouth pulls into a goofy grin, and he points at Andrew. "But Andrew hooked us up!"

Andrew pinches his fingers together. "He may have had a little bit of coke too."

"That's great. Very helpful. Thanks, Andrew."

"We were celebrating your awesome show tonight."

"I got you covered, Jacob," Robbie says. "Come on back downstairs."

Hopefully, Jacob passes out; otherwise, I'm prepared to *knock* him out.

The next afternoon, Mallory and I are headed back to our room after finishing lunch with Audrey and Doug when Jacob finally makes an appearance.

"Are you all right, Jacob?" Mallory asks.

He peers at her over his sunglasses. "Where's the coffee?"

"We'll have some sent up," Mallory promises. "You don't look too good."

"You're looking foxy, Mallory." He grins at her.

"Still high, bro?" I ask.

"Come on," Mallory steers him into our room and goes over to the phone to order room service.

"What the fuck, Jacob?" I look him up and down. "We have

to be on stage in a couple of hours and you smell like warmed-over death."

"We might have to cancel."

I stand there and absorb the shock of his suggestion. We've *never* canceled a show. No matter how shitfaced we've been in the past, we always pulled ourselves together so that our shows never suffered.

"Jacob, last night was one of our best and biggest performances, and you want to blow off tonight's show?" He has to be out of his damn mind.

"It fucking sucked and you know it," he rasps.

"What?"

"Dude, I choked. I was awkward and could barely get any words out. I know you noticed."

"We were all a little nervous, Jacob. My first solo wasn't great. But come on, think of the reaction we got for 'Queen of the Road.' How many times have we seen a band perform a new song just to have the crowd stand around and scratch their heads?"

He flashes a hint of a smile. "That's true."

I glance up, and Mallory flashes ten fingers at me, then points to the door.

"Coffee's on its way."

Jacob brushes his fingers against his throat. "I don't know how much longer this can last."

"What are you talking about?"

He tilts his head, watching me from the corner of his eye. "I'm not like you. My daddy didn't send me to professional lessons. I've been opening my mouth and screaming since the beginning."

Half-truth, but now isn't the time to call him out. His parents sent him for lessons, then declared he wasn't good enough and stopped paying for them. It's how he learned the same vocal warm-ups he still uses today. "Use some of the money we're making to take the lessons now."

"I can't change my signature style. It's gotten us this far."

"You can change if you think it will save your voice." I bite the inside of my cheek, debating my next words. "The coke and alcohol don't help."

"Give me a break. That's got nothing to do with my voice." How deep his denial runs.

"Like fuck it doesn't." I gesture toward the door. "You ran up and down the hallway screaming at the top of your lungs last night. That can't be good for your vocal cords."

He scratches the side of his head. "No, I didn't."

"Yeah. You did. I found you up on the roof. We had to drag you downstairs kicking and screaming. Robbie tied you to the bed, so you wouldn't get loose again."

Instead of, oh, I don't know, being fucking horrified, he doubles over laughing. "Oh, fuck. That's some funny shit. I thought I hooked up with some kinky chick, but it was Robbie."

"It wasn't funny at all, dude. The hotel was going to kick all of us out."

Jacob finally pulls himself together about an hour before we go on stage. And by *pull together,* I mean, has dropped the pity party and graduated to pissing me off.

"Who's the old dude? That Mallory's dad?" Jacob lifts his chin in Audrey and Doug's direction. "You trying to set him up with Audrey?"

"Knock it off. That's Audrey's boyfriend. He's a nice guy." Square and out of place at a rock concert, sure. That doesn't mean I want anyone to hassle him.

"Her *boyfriend?* Does he know?" Jacob wiggles his eyebrows like a jackass.

"I don't know, so keep your mouth shut and don't be a dick."

"Whatever." He shrugs. "Good for her. It's a lot more respectable to straight up fuck for money than fuck with a bunch of hidden expectations." He aims a glare down the hallway. I follow his line of sight to Holly.

"What's wrong now?"

"Nothing. I told her I didn't want her to come tonight, yet she procured tickets and passes from somewhere."

I hold up my hands. "Wasn't me."

"No, it was probably Jane. She keeps insisting Holly and I are made for each other." He finishes that last part in a high-pitched voice and clasps his hands under his chin.

"Aw, where is Janey?" I tease.

"Stay away from my baby sister."

"But I haven't seen her in forever." I cast a lecherous look around the area just to piss him off. Legend has it, Jane had a crush on me when she was younger. I never encouraged her and stayed far the fuck away, but after the bullshit I put up with last night, I feel entitled to torment Jacob.

He slaps my chest. "She thinks you and Mallory are a cute couple."

"I'm flattered." I glance around again. "Seriously, though. Did she show up? Make sure Robbie looks out for her if she's only here with Holly."

"Nah, I doubt my parents let her come."

"Let her? Isn't she like nineteen now?"

He shrugs. "They pay for everything."

"Try not to be too mean to Holly. She and Mallory are still friends."

"What do you want to do, double date?"

"Fuck no." I slap him on the shoulder.

Valerie approaches like we're two poisonous snakes on the loose. "How do we feel about tonight, boys?"

Jacob and I share a look. "Good," we answer at the same time.

Val blows out a relieved breath. "Thank God. You scared the shit out of me last night, Jacob."

"Scared? Why? Sounds like I had a blast."

Please let us survive these next two shows.

CHAPTER TWENTY-THREE

CHASER

The final show is the best one yet.

"I could do ten more of these!" Garrett shouts, pumping his fist in the air, as we file into our dressing room.

"Glad you can. I'm wiped," Jacob rasps. He falls onto the couch and closes his eyes.

To his credit, after last night's show, he went straight to bed and stayed there.

There's a knock at our door, and since Valerie's closest, she opens it. Her slack-jawed expression and the way she slowly opens the door pulls me to my feet.

Mark Cutter walks in and introduces himself to Val.

"Sorry, I haven't been able to get back to you, but I'm here to discuss Kickstart now," he says.

"Come on in. They're just relaxing after the show."

"Good stuff up there tonight," Mark says, taking the chair across from Jacob.

"Thanks." I perch on the edge of the couch and glance over at Mallory who seems to be trying to blend in with the wallpaper.

"So, Andrew swears you guys are more than the 'Candy Jar' fluff piece," Cutter says, digging right in.

I knew that fucking song would haunt us.

"Absolutely." Jacob sits forward, all business now. "Chaser and I wrote it as a joke in like a half hour. But it took off from there."

"Pretty successful for a joke. If that's what you two can do in a half hour, I'm eager to see what you can do with more."

"We have a pretty extensive list of material we're considering for our new album," Garrett says.

Extensive is a bit of a stretch, but we've collected enough for a full-length album and a few B sides.

"Is 'Queen of the Road' one of them?"

"Yes," I answer carefully, not really in the mood for him to say it's crap.

"Complex tune. Has an interesting feel to it. Different." Cutter nods. "Who's the main songwriter?"

We all look at each other. "Everyone contributes," I say.

"The big definitive riffs are Chaser," Alvin explains. "We all help with the lyrics, but Jacob and Chaser write the bulk of it."

"That's fair," Jacob agrees.

"We collaborate best when we're all together," I explain. "I'll bring a riff and a handful of lyrics to the guys sometimes. Alvin helps me stretch it out. Garrett layers on the melody around it. Jacob listens in and works out lyrics to fit the piece."

"Teamwork. Good." Cutter squeezes his chin between his thumb and index finger. "Here's the thing, 'Candy Jar' is your only song that's charted."

"Uh, 'Hammer to the Heart' also made the Top 100," Alvin points out.

Sure, it only made it to number ninety-eight. Still counts.

"Right." Cutter wags his finger at all four of us. "Now, that's a good one. Very original. Your label should've given you more support on it."

"That's kind of what we want to get back to," Jacob says. "That grittier, raw, real life, intense feeling in our music."

"Excellent. So, I think you know I'm a busy man. I've got a few bands I regularly work with. When it's time to get in the studio, we're all in, and there's no fucking around." He glances at Jacob then me. "Everyone gets their ass into the studio on time and works together or I walk."

I shift my gaze Jacob's way, since he's the only one who's ever had an issue with time management. "That's what we're looking for."

"My time is too valuable to waste," Cutter continues. "Kickstart doesn't have enough history for me to take the risk."

Fuck. Fuck. Fuck. My stomach rockets into my boots.

"So, here's what I propose," he says slowly, like someone should be taking notes. "Round up all the material you're considering for the new album and narrow it down to your four best. Not what you think I want to hear. The songs that best represent the essence of who Kickstart is as a band."

We're all hanging on to his every word.

"Book some studio time and make me a demo of those songs. That'll show me that you're serious. If I like what I hear, we'll work together. Andrew says you're going out on the road with them, so get the demo done before you leave. By the time you're back, I'll have you on my schedule and ready to go. That way, you can work out the pieces on the road. Toss what isn't working. Improve the songs that are."

Damn, that doesn't align with the timeline the record label wants for us to put out the next album.

"The label wants them to re-record a new version of 'Cry it Out,' do you want that too?" Valerie asks.

"No. New stuff," he answers, without looking at her. "You want to add 'Cry it Out' when we go into the studio, that's fine. Right now, I want your energy focused on new stuff."

After he leaves, we sit and stare at the door.

"Shit." Garrett runs his fingers through his hair. "Fuck."

"Why so deflated?" Val claps her hands together. "Cheer up. This is great news."

"Great?" Jacob can't hide his irritation. "He's making us interview."

"It's not uncommon." Val places her hands on her hips and stares us down. "You heard all the rules he laid out? He did that because he *wants* to work with Kickstart. He *wants* you to nail this. Don't let him down."

"Who's paying for the studio time?" Jacob asks.

"Who cares? We'll find the money." I can't believe that's what he's worried about.

"Easy for you to say when your girlfriend's apparently loaded," he grumbles.

I knew letting him see the guitar Mallory bought me would bite me in the ass eventually.

"Settle down." Val glares at both of us. "The record company will cover it. As long as you get it done quickly, I don't think it will be an issue. They want you to put something out soon."

"Do it fast but make it good. That's a lot of pressure." Jacob's scratchy voice rubs some guilt in. He needs to be on vocal rest after this weekend.

Alvin's kept quiet for as long as he can. "What the fuck else have we been working for if not this?" His wild hand gestures punctuate the frustration in his thunderous voice. "We've been rehearsing the new songs. I can think of five off the top of my head right now we could give him."

"Easy, Chipmunk," Jacob rasps.

"Fuck you, Jacob. Don't ruin this because you're afraid of success."

"I'm not ruining shit."

"All right." I stand up and hold out my hands like a boxing ref trying to push my two bandmates into their corners. "Val's right. This is a good sign. We rocked this weekend. We're all exhausted from back to back shows of this caliber. Let's take the next couple days to regroup." I glance at Jacob. "You killed it this weekend, now it's time to rest your voice."

Jacob nods and mouths a quick, "Sorry" to Alvin.

"I'll do what I can to find a studio and have you set up by Wednesday," Val promises. "By the way, what's this talk about a Vicious Vandals tour?"

"Something Andrew's hinted at. Nothing's solid yet."

"Well, keep me in the loop. Maybe I can talk the label into an actual tour bus for you this time."

"Holy shit." Jacob high-fives Garrett. "A tour with Vicious Vandals will be sick! Those guys know how to *party*."

Even though this weekend was a success, I can't help feeling like, sooner or later, I'll find myself on another rooftop trying to coax half my band off the ledge.

CHAPTER TWENTY-FOUR

MALLORY

This is a joke.

My agent claims a fairly well-known producer wants to meet with me. She'll only whisper his name in person, so I have to go all the way down to her office. Supposedly, he saw me in the coffee commercial and has the perfect part for me. In an established television series.

The punchline? The meeting is supposed to take place at the Beverly Hills Hotel.

It all feels a little too familiar to how I was set up with Davey Revolver in England. When I expressed my concerns to Marilyn, because yes, I'd had to explain that whole debacle to her, she assured me these kinds of informal meetings happen all the time. I don't really buy it, but I also don't want to pass up the meeting if there's a chance it's legitimate.

"Are you fucking kidding?" The absolute look of horror and

disbelief on Chaser's face after I explain the situation would almost be comical if we weren't talking about my career.

"Trust me, I said the same thing."

He scrubs his hands over his face. "You're not going alone."

"Thank you." I didn't realize how much I'd been hoping he would say that until the words came out of his mouth.

His eyebrows shoot up as if he'd expected me to argue with him. But, nope. I'm relieved.

"What time?"

Here's the part that makes it even better. "Eight o'clock tonight."

"You fucking kidding me? Is it an audition or a date?"

"Will it cut into your session with Andrew?"

"That's not what I'm worried about." He waves his hand in the air. "We're almost done, anyway."

Chaser's been working long hours with Andrew, coming home later and later every night. The lack of sleep has made him edgy and irritable, so I can't wait until they're finished.

Chaser tugs on my hand, pulling me along. "Come on, let's get you to your audition."

Oh, how I love him for saying "audition" with a straight face.

We arrive at the hotel, and I walk up to the restaurant where our meeting is supposed to be held. The maître d' sends me to the front desk. Chaser follows me, shaking his head.

"Hello, my name is Mallory Dove, I'm supposed to have a meeting with Mr. Woods at 8 o'clock."

"Oh, yes." The smile slides off the clerk's face, and his gaze bounces between Chaser and me. "He asked you to meet him in his suite first."

Behind me, Chaser grumbles, "You've got to be kidding."

The clerk leans across the desk and in a lowered voice, says, "I would take your bodyguard with you, miss."

Does it ever end?

"What did he say?" Chaser asks, as we head toward the elevator.

"Nothing."

That answer's not good enough for Chaser, of course. As soon as we're enclosed in the elevator, he turns me to face him. "What did he say?"

"He said my bodyguard should go with me."

Chaser nods thoughtfully. "Figured."

As we approach the suite door, Chaser takes a position behind me. Music drifts into the hallway. Something slow, soft, and romantic. I hesitate before knocking.

A young man opens the door and smiles down at me. The smile fades when his gaze lands on Chaser. "Miss Dove, your friend will have to wait with me while you meet with Mr. Woods."

He opens the door wider, apparently expecting me to agree. Chaser settles his hand on the small of my back, reassuring me I'm not going anywhere without him.

"Is she here?" A masculine voice calls out a few seconds before an older gentleman steps into the living room in his bathrobe.

I briefly close my eyes and shake my head.

I knew it.

"Who the hell are you?" he demands, glaring at Chaser.

"Her bodyguard," Chaser answers in an even voice.

Anger twist the director's face. "What is this? Are you hoping for an audition too? I'm fresh out of parts for grungy hitmen."

"I'm here for Miss Dove's protection." Chaser's solemn tone makes it clear he has no plans to leave and no interest in auditioning.

My heart swells with love for Chaser. For trying so hard to

maintain an illusion of professionalism, when this whole thing reeks. He's keeping his cool for me. I know he'd prefer to handle this by throwing a few punches.

Mr. Woods continues to glare at Chaser. But Chaser's in full junkyard dog mode tonight and doesn't back down.

"Mr. Woods, do you have some lines you'd like me to read," I ask to break the tension.

"Well, I, yes." He throws one more exasperated look in Chaser's direction. "Let me grab the script."

He returns with one sheet of paper. I scan it and grit my teeth. The role is for "massage therapist" and judging by the lines on this sheet, he plans to take off his robe and have me rub oil all over him at some point.

Not happening. *So not happening.*

"I'm sorry," I say, handing the paper back. I keep my chin up and voice even. Plenty of time for tears later. "I don't think this role is a good fit for me."

He stares at me dumbfounded. I guess no one's ever said *no* to him before. Well, sign me up to be the first. I'll be damned if I'm spending my night rubbing some flabby old man for him to get his rocks off. I doubt there's even an actual role to go with this "audition."

The assistant stares at us with his mouth slightly open.

Chaser steers me toward the door.

In the hallway, I shake my head, feeling dejected and embarrassed. A complete foolish failure.

"Sorry, babe," Chaser says, rubbing his hand over my back.

"I need a new agent."

"I don't think that will make a difference," Chaser mutters.

"Probably not."

"You okay?" he asks once we're inside the elevator.

I shake my head. "I'm tired of this. What would've happened if you hadn't come with me?"

His jaw clenches, and he looks away. "If this band thing doesn't work out, maybe I need to start up a security company for young starlets."

I huff out a sad little laugh. "Obviously, it's a needed service."

"Hey," he says, gently curving his hands over my shoulders and looking me in the eye. "No more auditions unless I can go with you, okay? Even calls—"

"If I ever land another role. I'm sure I'll be blacklisted and branded 'difficult to work with' any day now."

"Mallory, look at me. I refuse to believe someone as talented as you won't find work."

His faith in me means everything. "Thank you."

"You're my tough girl." He traces his knuckles over my cheek. "When your life was turned upside down, what did you do?"

I lift an eyebrow. "Stole a bunch of money and ran from my father's goons?"

He doesn't crack a smile. "No. You took a chance and followed your dream. It took guts to come out here the way you did. Lots of people say they're going to chase their dreams but few ever have the courage to do it."

"You did."

"We're not talking about me."

I tap his chest. "I think *that's* why people call you Chaser. Not the other reason."

The corners of his mouth lift. "I like your version better."

"Call your agent," Chaser reminds me the next morning.

Not a conversation I'm looking forward to, but Chaser's

persistent. He'll keep "reminding" me until I do, so I might as well get it over with.

"Mallory, did you walk out of the meeting?" she says as soon as her secretary puts me through.

"He moved the meeting to his hotel *room*, Marilyn. That's not what I agreed to. He met me in his bathrobe and wanted me to give him a rub down."

"Oh, honey. He's just a little eccentric. No one's ever complained about him before. You probably misunderstood."

Misunderstood my ass.

"The film is about a massage parlor." She huffs. "What's he supposed to ask you to do, tap dance?"

I don't appreciate her subtly pushing the blame on me. As if I'm stupid or paranoid.

"Well, it's not the role for me," I insist.

"Okay." Her heavy sigh almost has me apologizing, but I keep my mouth shut. "I may have something else for you, but you're going to have be a grown up and do the audition."

She hangs up before I have a chance to protest.

"You can't trust any of them," Chaser says after I slam the phone down and explain the conversation. "Her loyalty is supposed to be to *you,* but she needs to stay on good terms with guys like that to find work for her *other* clients."

"*You're* the only one I trust out here." While I say "out here," I really mean *anywhere.* In my whole life, I think Chaser is the only person I've ever trusted completely. It's scary to put that much trust in someone not to hurt or betray you.

He rubs his knuckles over my cheek. "You're the only woman I've ever trusted."

Maybe for someone else that would be a red flag, but since his mother left him at such a young age, I understand why he'd be guarded.

I want to be worthy of his trust. "I'll always have your back, Chaser."

"I know, little dove."

He's already sacrificed a lot to protect me. I want to have his back as much as he has mine.

To be there for him no matter what life throws at us.

CHAPTER TWENTY-FIVE

CHASER

"For fuck's sake, Jacob, it's almost midnight," I grumble. "Get your shit together."

The fucker has the nerve to roll his eyes. He's been insufferable since we started recording the songs Mark Cutter requested.

First, it took him a week to agree to the songs he wanted to present to Cutter.

Every day since, he's either shown up late or shows up drunk. Sometimes, if we're really lucky, he's both.

"What's your problem, man? You know I create better in the midnight hours." He flaps his hands in the air like a deranged bird and spins in a circle. "We all do. Always have."

Great, guess tonight he's *high* instead of drunk.

Plus, that's not actually true. Usually, the four of us in a room together, no matter what time of day, jump starts our creativity. Especially when our record company is paying for studio time and breathing down our necks. We've always worked well under pressure.

"Listen," Garrett says, trying to be the voice of reason since it's obvious I'm about five seconds from choking Jacob. "Maybe we should go. Let you have some solitude to lay down your vocals."

"No, no, no. I need you guys here. We're supposed to record together. Our sound requires it."

Everyone groans. The rest of us have been here since noon. Jacob didn't bother to show up until after seven. I'm the only one who has to be up at six to take Mallory for a casting call.

"Are you good with the lyrics now?" I ask.

"I don't know. I might mess with that one verse."

"Jesus Christ," I grumble, shaking my head. I'm going to kill this motherfucker tonight. I stalk out of the room and down the hallway.

"What's the problem, Chaser?" our sound engineer Joe asks.

"Nothing. We've just been at this all fucking day and haven't gotten dick accomplished."

He shrugs. "It happens. All you creative genius types are a pain in the ass."

"Yeah, well, I have to be up early."

"You shouldn't be working right now. Didn't the record company give you an advance?"

Yeah, we'd each been handed fat checks. Not got-it-made money but definitely both-feet-out-of-the-gutter money. Most of it I plan to spend on buying Mallory a car.

"I'm not working. I'm pissed, though. We've been at this twelve hours a day for multiple days and have fuck-all to show for it."

He cocks his head as if he doesn't believe that's the whole story.

"And my girlfriend has an audition in the morning I need to take her to."

"Ah, I understand. Now *that* I can help you out with."

Not sure how he plans to help me out. Don't have a chance to ask either. "Chaser! Let's go. He's ready!" Alvin shouts.

Seems all of a sudden Jacob's feeling "inspired" and ready to do his fucking job.

I get my third, or is it fourth, wind and get to work.

For the next four hours, we play steadily, and by four a.m., we actually have something close to a finished song.

I'm ready to fall down. Alvin and Garrett aren't looking much better. Jacob's the only one hopped up and ready to keep going.

"Can't, bro. We got someone else coming in and need the space. It's yours again after two," Joe informs us.

Jacob pouts, but can't argue with him.

On my way out, Joe hands me a small vial. "That should help get you through the day," he says.

Normally, I'd answer with a "no thanks." Working with Andrew had gotten me way more familiar with cocaine than I ever planned. I started to develop an unhealthy appetite for the shit.

I've been around enough coke in my life to know it's something I should avoid. Christ, I can practically ski in the stuff back home. Snorting the family business up my nose always seemed like a dangerous habit to get into.

Yet, here I am thousands of miles from home and so damn tired.

A little pick-me-up for a few days won't hurt. I did it before and everything turned out fine. I can do it again. Then I'll never touch the stuff. "Thanks."

I shove the tiny container in my pocket and head home to my girl.

CHAPTER TWENTY-SIX

MALLORY

"Wake me fifteen minutes before you're ready to leave," Chaser mumbles as he crawls into bed with me.

I crack open one eye and stare at the clock. I need to be up in less than two hours. I hate like hell waking him up when he just got home. But he'll be more upset if I go without him.

"Okay," I whisper, but he's already asleep.

I wake about a minute before my alarm's about to go off. I flick the switch and take a look at Chaser's peaceful expression one more time before getting ready.

The scent of coffee lures him into the kitchen fifteen minutes later.

"I was going to let you sleep a little longer," I say, handing him a cup.

He yawns and scratches his hand over his stomach, drawing my attention to the trail of dark hair disappearing under his unbuttoned jeans. God, he's a beautiful, beautiful man.

"How'd it go last night?"

"Shitty until about midnight when Jacob finally found his *inspiration*."

From what I've overheard the guys saying, Jacob has been increasingly difficult during the recording process, so this doesn't surprise me.

We hurry through our morning routine. Chaser is sluggish, until right before we leave, when he ducks into the bathroom for a few seconds.

"All right, babe. Let's go," he barks, slapping me on the ass.

"Hey," I squeal. "Save that for when I actually get the part."

He leans down and growls in my ear. "You bet I will."

We're playful like that all the way downstairs.

At the audition, he walks me inside.

Once he's convinced it's legit, he nods. "I'll be waiting right outside if you need me."

I reach up and give him a quick kiss. "Thank you."

I'm really not sure what I would do without him.

CHAPTER TWENTY-SEVEN

CHASER

In a matter of weeks, my passion for jamming with my band has been replaced with a passion for cramming tons of powder up my nose.

We were only supposed to be in the studio for a couple of days. Not a lot of time to record an album, but plenty of time to record the demos we need to give Cutter.

With Jacob showing up late and high almost every day, our schedule keeps getting pushed back. There's a ton of pressure from the label to finish a new album, get it mixed, and get it into stores. None of which can happen until we get these demos done.

"Should we look for someone besides Cutter?" Alvin asks while we're waiting for Jacob to finish his time taking a "steam bath" to help his throat.

"Why? If he can't get his shit together now, how's he going to be when we're actually recording the album?"

"Good point." Alvin stubs out his cigarette and stares at the control board. "We're so close."

That's what makes it all the more frustrating.

Val isn't thrilled with us, either. We're making her look bad. Like she can't control us—which she never could, I don't know why anyone thought otherwise.

While we're slowly grinding out the demos, Mallory's career rockets ahead, leaving me burning both ends. I'm still not letting her go to appointments by herself. No fucking way.

This means I'm shoving increasingly larger quantities of powder up my nose just to function. I try not to dwell on what a cranky asshole it's turning me into.

It's only temporary.

"Can you talk to him, Garrett?"

"Bro, I tried. Maybe we should pack it in for the day and try again tomorrow. He's not feeling it today."

"None of us are *feeling it* right now, but we need to stop screwing off and get this done." I'm really sick of all the excuses Garrett makes for Jacob.

To top off our shitty afternoon, Andrew stops by the studio, not looking much better than the rest of us.

He motions for me to follow him into the parking lot out back where he lights a cigarette and paces over the crumbling asphalt. "How's Mallory?"

Did he really come all the way down here to ask about my girlfriend? "She's fine. Why?"

He shrugs. "Haven't seen you two in a while. Was wondering if you split."

"Fuck no. Not happening."

"Cool." He takes a long drag and blows out a thick stream of smoke. "So, what's going on, Chaser?"

"With?"

"Dude, I went out on a limb." He waves his cigarette at the

studio. "Talked you up to Cutter. You wait much longer and you won't be able to finish an album before we go on tour."

I hold out my arms, palms to the sky. "I'm trying. We've got three songs ready to go." I really don't want to throw Jacob into the fire, but Andrew has a point. He stuck his neck out for us and we're making him look bad.

"That's good." He stops pacing. "Be straight with me. Is it Jacob?"

I shake my head and look away. "Don't—"

"That's cool. I respect that. I don't know what to tell you. If it was your bass player, I'd say swap him out. But it's nearly impossible to replace your lead singer. Fuck knows we tried with Kyle," he mutters.

Shit, there's a piece of gossip I've never read in *L.A. Weekly*.

"I appreciate everything you've done for us. I didn't see this coming."

"Don't sweat it. I've been there. Biggest thing is that you guys get yourselves ready for the tour. I need you rock solid. Our fan bases overlap. It won't be like opening up for Bloody Revolver or Shooting Fences where half the audience is old enough to be your parents."

"Uh—"

"I'm being real with you. In two or three years, I want to see you where *we* are right now. Headlining your own tour and taking out some other young, hungry band on the road."

My paranoid danger barometer's pinging like crazy at Andrew's calm, rational demeanor. "Thanks."

"Now," he flicks his cigarette away and shoves his hands in his pockets, "the real reason I'm here."

"Oh, it wasn't to give me the dad speech?"

"No, fuckhead." He hands me a baggie of coke, as if we're not standing outside in the fading evening sun.

"Uh, what am I supposed to do with this?"

"One last party?" He stabs his fingers through his hair. "I'm taking off for Hawaii to get cleaned up before the tour."

I blink at him.

"Don't act so shocked. I can't play night after night if I'm fucked out of my mind. I'll exile myself to my little beach villa for a few weeks. A personal trainer comes in every day to whoop my ass. Pammy's joining me to tend to my *other* needs. By the time we're ready to get out on the road, I'll be in fighting form."

Well, shit. Guess that explains the mystery of how they've managed so many successful tours and albums.

He holds his fist in front of my face. "Trust and believe. There are two things you don't fuck with, Chaser. Recording time and tour time." He lifts one finger and then the other. "The rest of your life is yours to fuck up as you see fit."

"Mind. Blown." I touch my forehead and make an explosion noise that cracks him up.

"Touring is the best natural high. You won't miss being fucked up when you're playing stadiums."

Since I've never been into coke this much before in my life, it's hard to form an opinion on the matter.

He pulls me in for a quick hug and slaps my back. "Make me proud, Chaser."

I watch him fold his large and lanky frame into his black Ferrari before staring at the present he left.

How many times over the last month have I told myself I'd snorted my last line?

Disgusted with myself, I shove the baggie of coke in my pocket, already picturing taking it into the bathroom and cutting a few pristine lines.

CHAPTER TWENTY-EIGHT

CHASER

I can't afford to take off to Hawaii like Andrew, but I promise myself that as soon as the band makes it through this rough spot, I'll stop the coke. I have to before I go on tour.

I'll make up all the late nights and shitty moods to Mallory by taking her someplace nice for a few days.

At least that's the mantra I keep repeating.

For some reason, I'm confident that I'm different than every other drug addict I've ever known.

What I conveniently forgot was, if coke doesn't eventually make you crazy, it has plenty of other nasty side effects.

No matter how many lies I tell myself: I'm only using a little. I'll only use it for just a little longer. I'll be done with it for good once we finish the demos, I keep craving more and more. Lucky for me, the music business makes it easy to score whenever I want.

Hell, most of the time I don't even have to pay for it.

Someone shoves a baggie, vial, or eight ball in my hands just because I'm Chaser Adams—up and coming rock god.

When I'm not high out of my mind, my craving for coke pisses me the fuck off, since I've always considered myself rather disciplined.

"Chaser, what's wrong? You seem really distant lately," Mallory says.

I'm supposed to be catching up on sleep. Except, I can't sleep because I'm fucking high. Feeling no pain.

Feeling nothing actually.

"Everything's fine. Or it will be once Jacob stops fucking around so we can finish and get ready for the tour."

As fucked up as I am, I've contributed all my parts. I'm even writing crazy amounts of new stuff. Whether it's any good or not, really isn't the point. Alvin and I have plenty of time to jam at the studio while we wait for Jacob to get his shit together. Some days Garrett joins us.

She hesitates. "Are you sure that's all that's bothering you?"

"Yes, I'm sure. Stop badgering me."

"Badgering you?" She frowns and takes a step back. "I'm worried about you."

Fuck, I hate myself right now.

"You're doing too much," she continues. "Do you want me to stop auditioning until you're done?"

No fucking way do I want to be the reason she puts her career on hold. That damn coffee commercial where she looked like the hottest Suzie-homemaker ever ended up airing nationally. She's somewhat in demand right now. And I'm going to slow her down just because I need her to babysit me? Fuck no.

"No, babe. We're almost done." Thank fuck that's the truth.

We need to get down one more track. We finished number three last night. Or was it this morning? Doesn't matter.

"Chaser," she says in a soft lets-be-reasonable voice, "You can't keep this up forever. I can go to auditions by myself. I promise not to go to any hotels or anything sketchy."

"No."

"This is ridiculous!" she explodes. Mallory doesn't have much of a temper, so it's a sign of just how frayed her nerves are thanks to my bullshit. "You're leaving to go on tour for three months. What am I supposed to do then? Sit home and stare at the wall?"

I hadn't really thought that far ahead. Most of my thoughts revolve around music, Mallory, or scoring more coke. Beyond that, I can't spare the extra brain power.

"You'll come with me."

She raises her hands to the sky, completely exasperated. "Chaser, we both know that's not going to work."

All my drug-addled brain hears is, *we aren't going to work out.*

"Why? You planning to see someone else while I'm away?"

"Oh my God. Are you serious right now? After everything, how can you even ask me that?"

"You're hot." My shoulders jerk up, like her dating another man is no big deal, instead of my worst fucking nightmare. "Every guy who meets you wants to fuck you."

"That's ridiculous."

"Andrew wants to fuck you. Jesus Christ, he never *stops* asking about you."

She pauses. "Really? Why?"

Something about her question only agitates me more. "*Why?* What do you mean, *why?* You want to fuck him, too?"

Tears of what I think are frustration, fill her eyes. But my girl is tough, she lifts her chin defiantly. "I'm not going to dignify that with an answer. You're acting paranoid. Talk to me. What's going on?"

But I can't be honest.

How can I be honest with her when I've reached a point where I don't even recognize my own face in the mirror?

Besides, knowing there's cocaine in my pocket this very second cements the wall between us. Every day, I lie to her in a thousand different ways.

So, I look her in the eye and tell her the biggest lie of them all.

"Everything is fine."

CHAPTER TWENTY-NINE

MALLORY

Something has to give.

We can't keep going on like this.

Chaser's a mess.

He thinks I can't tell. That I'm too stupid to know what he's up to. But seriously, unless he's developed some sort of bladder issue, no one his age needs to spend so much time in the bathroom.

"Chaser," I say, brushing my fingers over his shoulder. "Are we meeting the guys tonight? Or are you all mine?"

His nostrils flare at the question and a sensual smile curls his lips. We may be falling apart everywhere else, but he's more focused on sex than ever. It's frequent and intense. Long, marathon sessions of hot, relentless jackhammer sex.

But for me, there's always something missing lately.

He fixes his gaze on me, and I almost cry. By his dilated

pupils and blank expression, I might as well be talking to the wall.

"Nah, let's stay in. I've seen them way too much lately."

He takes my hand and pulls me into his lap, slipping his fingers up under my shorts. "I can think of a few things to keep us occupied."

"I'm sure you can."

He doesn't react to the sarcasm. I doubt it even registered.

"Give me a minute." He stalks off to the bathroom, and I take a deep breath.

When he returns, I stand and face him.

Enough is enough.

"You don't have to keep hiding it. You're not fooling me. Might as well just snort it up out here," I say, pointing to the coffee table.

He stares at me with wide eyes.

"Do you think I'm stupid, Chaser?"

"No."

I burst into frustrated and guilty tears. How did we end up here?

"Hey," he says, wrapping his arms around me. "What's wrong?"

"This is all my fault. You weren't using before you knew me. If I didn't cause you so many problems, this wouldn't be happening."

"Nothing's wrong. I'm fine, Mallory."

"Stop lying. You're not fine."

"Everything's under control," he insists.

"You don't always have to be the man in charge. For once, let me help you."

"I'm fine," he growls again. "Drop it."

Nope. He's not getting off that easy. "I will *not* drop it. Please talk to me."

He places his hands on my shoulders. "I have it handled, Mallory. I'm fine," he says in a gentler but no less stubborn tone.

Music from downstairs thumps, loud and insistent, shaking the walls. I groan and roll my eyes. "I'm sick of living here."

"I'll go down and tell them to cool it," he says, taking a step away.

"No, it's okay. Stay here." God only knows he's probably going to get more coke. While my main concern will always be Chaser, it hasn't escaped my notice that the whole band is falling apart.

"Be right back." He kisses my cheek.

Twenty minutes later, he's still gone.

Fed up, I decide to go find him.

What am I going to do if Chaser won't get help? Leave him?

I can't picture life without him in my world.

It's too hard to admit to myself that the man I'm living with isn't the man I fell in love with.

As usual, the party has spilled into the hallway and up the stairs.

Occasionally, Kickstart's hangers-on realize Chaser lives right upstairs and try to crash our apartment. One of many reasons I want to find a new place.

Eager to make sure he's okay, I practically trip over people in my hurry to get downstairs.

And I almost die when I step inside the apartment.

CHAPTER THIRTY

CHASER

I was in the middle of...something.

Came downstairs for a reason. Fuck if I know what it was now.

Found Jacob dazed in the bathtub with a needle in his arm. That's new. Explains why he's been so much more out of it lately.

Want no part of that shit. Unless they're inking some badass designs in my skin, needles freak me the fuck out.

Since Jacob's unconscious, I relieve him of the coke in his pocket—obviously he won't be needing any. A rush of excitement burns through me as I lay out a few lines on the back of the toilet.

The burning thrum clears my head, so I snort another line.

My heart drums a frantic beat, warning me I've had enough.

"What're you doing here?" Garrett asks from behind me. I

wipe my face and stuff the baggie with the last bit of powder in my back pocket.

I point to Jacob. "This new?"

He crosses his arms over his chest and leans on the door frame "You really think you're one to talk?"

While he has a point, I'm still feeling superior for some reason. "I wouldn't touch that shit."

Garrett shrugs. "We worked hard this week. Leave him be."

I assume that's code for Garrett's dancing with Mr. Brownstone too these days. Fucking fantastic.

"I'll take care of him." Garrett jerks his head toward the living room. "Go enjoy the party." He all but shoves me out of the bathroom, closing the door behind him.

Like a five-year-old, playing the most messed up game of hide-and-seek ever, I bang on the walls, calling out for Alvin.

"Where are ya, Chipmunk?"

Finally, I find him in the bedroom smoking a joint and getting a blow job from a naked, curvy redhead.

"Sorry, mate! Carry on!" I shout.

He salutes me and I slam the door.

Living room. Music's so damn loud. Isn't that why I came down here?

I push through people who I don't recognize and don't care to talk to, seeking the way out. Who the fuck are all these people and where did they come from?

"*Chaser! How's the album?*"

"*Chaser! When's the next video?*"

"*Chaser! Are you really touring with Vicious Vandals?*"

I mumble out a few answers but keep moving.

"Hey, Chaser!" Holly jumps in front of me.

"'Sup, Holly? Haven't seen you in a while."

Her mouth twists, and she glares in the direction of the bathroom. "I've been busy. Seeing someone."

Jacob never claimed she was more than a house sitter and occasional fuck, so I'm not sure what she's so pissed about.

"Where's Mallory?"

I point to the ceiling. "Home."

"Aw, she's such a party pooper." Holly pouts.

Who over the age of ten still says that?

She wraps her fingers around my arm and drags me over to the couch. "We need to catch up. How's the new album going? Are you shooting another video? Need any extras for it?"

"Whoa. Slow down."

"I've always liked you, Chaser." She traces a line over my cheek and down my neck. It tickles, but that's not the reason I shake her off.

My heart pounds a dangerous warning. This isn't why I came down here. My girl's upstairs waiting for me.

I push Holly out of my lap. "I gotta go."

"Can I come with?"

"No."

She hooks her fingers in my belt and tugs. "Come on. Let's go use the bedroom."

"Alvin's getting a blow job."

She giggles and cups me through my jeans. "That's kind of what I had in mind."

The apartment door's wide open. Doesn't close anymore after someone kicked it in at one of the more recent parties. Anyone can find their way inside.

I shove her hand away.

"Not interested."

"Come on," she pleads, staring up at me with desperate let-me-suck-your-dick eyes.

I swear I have no interest in Holly, but her hand's back and the way she keeps rubbing me...my body responds and my coked-fueled brain forgets why this is such a bad idea.

"Get off me, Holly," I mumble.

There's a gasp from the doorway.

Ignoring everything around us, Holly slides her fingers to my belt buckle.

"Are you kidding me?" Mallory's enraged voice breaks through my cloud of indifference.

She storms into the room, so furious, she grabs Holly's hair and yanks her away from me, throwing her to the floor.

Holly screeches and grabs her scalp, but Mallory's done with her and focuses her rage on me.

"What the *fuck* is wrong with you? You said you'd be right back and you're down here—"

"Nothing happened." My protest sounds weak as fuck, even to me.

"Mallory—" Holly starts.

My girl whips her head around to stare down her friend. "You, shut the fuck up and stay away from us." She turns and focuses her glare on me. "And *you*. If you don't get your ass upstairs right now, I'm gone."

"Where?" *Yeah, that's what should be coming out of my mouth right now.*

"Wherever the fuck I want!" she screams.

Shit, I've never seen Mallory so pissed.

It's kind of hot.

The party around us ground to a halt the second Mallory flung Holly to the carpet. People stare, enjoying the show, filing away every detail for future gossip.

And I don't even care.

I'm too busy staring at Mallory. My gaze slides over her body, taking in the tight tank top her tits are practically spilling out of.

I might be high as a kite, but I'm also horny as hell now. I wrap my arms around Mallory, lift her, and carry her upstairs.

"Put me down!" she screams and thrashes against me the entire way.

Maybe I'm a sick bastard, but it only gets me more excited.

I kick the door to our apartment closed and carry her into the bedroom where I drop her on the mattress.

She lunges off the bed, reaching for the door, but I'm quicker and block her exit.

"If you think I'm having sex with you after what I walked in on, you're out of your fucking mind," she fumes.

"We didn't do anything. I told her to get off me. I was leaving when you walked in."

She's not buying any of my lame excuses and continues trying to light me on fire with her blazing blue eyes. "That's not what it looked like."

"What'd you want me to do?"

"Maybe not let her touch your dick," she fires back.

"How? Slap your friend?"

"She's not my friend anymore."

I grip her chin, tipping her head back. "I'm sorry."

All the fight drains out of her, and she shakes her head. "I can't do this, Chaser. I've never doubted you before."

"Mallory."

"I won't live like that."

"Like what, little dove?"

"Wondering what you're doing every second you're out of my sight. I don't want to be that woman."

"You don't have to worry."

"Then what was *that*?"

"I..." My mind's racing, spinning out of control, but I have no words to defend myself.

"It's the drugs, Chaser," she says softly. "It has to stop."

"Okay." After this shitshow of a night, it's time to cut back.

"No more," she warns.

"I'll handle it."

She grinds her teeth.

"I'm sorry," I whisper, backing her up to the bed.

She drops her gaze and shakes her head. "You just want to get laid."

"True." I'm ready to pin her to the wall and pound the fuck out of her. "But I *am* sorry." Also true.

She wraps her arms around my neck and stares up at me. "I love you, and I don't want to be without you. But I won't...I won't tolerate you cheating on me. What would have happened if I hadn't shown up?"

I swallow hard, my head clearing, realizing how close I came to fucking up what we have because I was too high to get away from a girl I don't even like.

Losing Mallory would be the biggest mistake of my life. It's a bullshit excuse, but I never would've been in that situation if I wasn't high.

I can't admit I have a problem, though. Not to Mallory.

I bend down and kiss her. "Don't leave me," I whisper against her lips. "Please."

"Don't give me a reason to." Her arms tighten around my neck, dragging me to her. We tumble onto the bed, and I strip off her shorts while she wiggles out of her top.

"I've never been so angry, Chaser," she admits while she works my belt loose and shoves my jeans down over my hips. "You're lucky I didn't have a knife, because I probably would've stabbed you."

"God, you're so fucking hot," I mumble against her mouth.

"It's not funny."

"I'm not laughing, little dove." I'd deserve a blade to the chest if I ever let her down.

She digs her nails into my ass and parts her legs. My cock

grazes her entrance. Wet. Hot. So fucking wet. I can't wait to sink inside her.

Huh.

I reach down to stroke my dick a few times.

"Chaser?"

I squeeze my eyes shut, trying to concentrate. "Give me a minute." Christ, I was a hard as a fucking rock seconds ago.

I grab her tits, squeezing and kneading her flesh. Rolling my rough fingers over her nipples until she gasps and squirms under me.

Nothing.

"Chaser?"

My mind and body are ready to go. My girl's primed and begging for it.

My damn dick is a sad, flaccid noodle.

This is a first.

Is this sexual karma? I let another woman put her hands on me, and now I can't perform?

I need another line.

Blood's still pounding through my ears from the three fat lines I snorted earlier. Why isn't any of it making its way to my damn dick?

Fuck!

Guys back home joke about the horrible phenomenon they refer to as "coke dick" all the time. I've always been convinced it's why my father has no issue selling the shit, but never touched it himself.

I've only been doing it for a short time.

I don't use enough for this to happen.

Do I?

I wrap my hand around my sad cock, trying to stroke it back to a happy state.

Nothing.

Apparently, I do.

Unacceptable.

Stunned and disgusted with myself, I fall down next to her.

"What's wrong? Are you mad at me?" Mallory asks.

Jesus, fuck no, I can't have her thinking that. "No, babe. It's not you."

It's me.

What have I done?

CHAPTER THIRTY-ONE

MALLORY

Last night was a nightmare, right?

Chaser made up some excuses, got me off with his hands and then went to sleep.

At least I thought he went to sleep.

I wake up alone in our bed.

That can't be good.

Worried, he's doing God knows what, I jump out of bed and hurry into the living room.

And breathe a sigh of relief.

He's sitting on the couch, writing in his song notebook.

"Hey." My voice barely above a whisper.

He tips his head up and gives me a pained smile. "Morning."

"How long have you been up?" I ask.

"Never slept."

My face must fall because he hurries to add. "I haven't left the apartment."

We stare at each other. His haunted eyes and beautiful face twist me up inside. He looks exhausted, broken, and remorseful. I love him so much but have no idea how to help him.

Finally, we break our staring contest, and he beckons me closer. "I need to talk to you."

Cautious, I approach with slow steps. Is he going to end things? Tell me he's moving out? Ask me to move out?

He reaches out and takes my hands, drawing me closer. "I need to go home."

"What? Why? When?"

He presses a finger against my lips. "You were right. I have a problem. I can't kick it here. The only way I can do it is if I go home for at least a few weeks." He cocks his head and stares at me. "Will you come with me?"

Sweet, sweet relief washes over me. "Oh my God, yes! Of course, I will!" I shout like it's a damn marriage proposal.

His eyes widen, and he sits back. "Really? You're not pissed?"

"Oh, I'm still mad about last night—"

"No, what about work, Mallory?"

The man I love is admitting he has a problem and asking for my help. There's no way I would ever say no to him.

"I'll tell my agent I'll be out of town for a few weeks." I press my palms to his face. His cheeks scratch my hands with about a week's worth of stubble. "You're more important to me."

He closes his eyes and blows out a long breath. "Thank you."

"Besides," I drop my head, "I feel guilty."

"Hey." He tips my chin up. "This isn't your fault. I thought I was smarter than everyone else, and it was no big deal. That is absolutely, one-hundred percent on me. I know it's not fair of me to ask, but I can't get better without you."

Chaser's a proud man. I know how hard it probably is to admit he needs help. "You don't have to do it alone."

"Christ." He shakes his head. "My father's gonna kick my ass."

It's mean, but I can't help laughing. "I think a good old-fashioned ass-kicking is exactly what you need."

Chaser

I wish I wasn't high. Maybe it's a good thing, though. Because if I could actually feel anything, I might cry with relief that Mallory isn't going to kick me to the curb after last night. And I think I've humiliated myself enough in the past twenty-four hours.

After Mallory fell asleep, I watched her until the sun peeked around the edges of the curtains. Even as I came down from my high, love for her filled me. I can't lose her. I won't.

Then I rolled over and snorted a line.

That's when I knew it was time to go home.

"Come here." I pull her closer for a kiss, and she ducks her head. Panic races through my fucked-up brain. "Mallory?"

"Did you make the arrangements yet?" Her big blue eyes shine with hope.

"What? No. I wanted to talk to you first."

"What if I said no?"

"Don't fuck with me, Mallory," I growl.

"I'm not. I genuinely want to know what you would have done."

What's the right answer here? I'm not sure what she's looking for, so I go with the truth. "Then, I guess I would've had to go home without you and hope you were still waiting for me when I returned."

Apparently, that was what she wanted to hear. She grabs my face and kisses the fuck out of me.

"What's that for?"

"You can't take care of anyone else if you can't take care of yourself."

"You're still coming with me, though, right?"

She laughs and bobs her head up and down, like I'm crazy for suggesting otherwise. "Yes, Chaser. You can't shake me that easily."

I can't book us on a flight to Buffalo until the next morning.

The wait is hell. An hour seems to take forever to crawl by. How am I supposed to survive the next twenty-four without losing my mind?

No matter how hard I try to concentrate, that dog shit feeling clings to me. My mind won't stop fantasizing about running downstairs to scrounge up some coke. Fuck knows the one thing that will make this so much harder to kick is how easy it is to score around here.

The need isn't even physical. It's more of a mental craving and that pisses me off even more.

Finally, I snap. I can't take another second. "I have to go downstairs and let the guys know I'm leaving." I jump up, already running for the door.

"Do you need me to go with you?" Mallory asks.

That's the last thing I need.

Because there's a pretty good chance I'll score enough coke to get me through the next day and a half.

The thought disgusts me.

All along I'd been convinced quitting wouldn't be an issue. Right up until I actually try to quit. I've never felt weaker. And I don't need Mallory to witness how low I've sunk.

CHAPTER THIRTY-TWO

CHASER

Jacob's still unconscious in the bathtub when I make it downstairs. Can't worry about him right now. Like Mallory said, I can't help anyone else until I get myself sorted.

"You sure he's still breathing?" I ask Alvin. Out of all of us, he's the responsible one who would check shit like that.

He peers into the bathroom and shrugs. "Stuck a mirror under his nose earlier. He's alive."

How did we slam into rock bottom in such a short amount of time?

"I'm fine," Jacob groans. "Get the fuck out and let me sleep."

Thank fuck. As much as Jacob pisses me off, I don't want the fucker to die.

I find my way out to the living room.

"What's wrong, Chaser? You look ready to jump out of your skin," Garrett says.

No reason to draw this out. Or ask for permission. "I'm going home for a few weeks."

Garrett sits back and runs his hands through his hair, but doesn't say a word.

Alvin pins me with a stern look. "We're not done with the demo for Cutter. The longer we make him wait, the greater the chance he refuses to work with us."

"For now, we're done." I throw my hand out toward the bathroom. "We would've delivered the songs to Cutter weeks ago if it wasn't for Jacob fucking around."

"What's going on?" Garrett asks.

"I'm too fucked up, and I need to get clean." No point in lying to my bandmates. It's not like they haven't witnessed my decline firsthand. Maybe if they know I'm getting my shit together, it will encourage them to do the same.

Hell, I can dream, right?

Garrett shakes his head and walks out of the room.

"Why now?" Alvin asks.

I lean in. "Bro, this is messing with me way too much. All the stuff I've been writing lately is shallow and shitty. I either can't sleep or I sleep too damn much." I lower my voice. "Can't keep my dick up long enough to fuck my girl. That's the final straw. The lowest I'm willing to go."

The son of a bitch roars with laughter.

"It's not funny."

"No," he says, turning serious again. "It's not."

"Will you check on our place while we're gone?" I point at him. "And do not use it as another party pad."

The corners of his mouth tip up. "Nah, if anything, I'll probably use it to get away from these two fiends."

"You gotta look after Jacob. G's got no spine when it comes to him. I'm sorry, I'm dumping it on you, but I'm no good to any of you in this condition."

"No, I get it." He rubs his hand over the back of his neck. "You tell Val yet?"

"Fuck. No, I just decided this morning."

He claps his hand over my shoulder and squeezes. "I'll go with you to break the news."

Before leaving, I need to pop upstairs and let Mallory know where I'm going. After last night, if I disappear on her right now, no matter the reason, she might not be here when I return.

"Everything okay?" The suspicious way she eyes me up and down stings.

"I'll be back in a few hours."

She works her jaw from side to side, clearly not pleased, but hesitant to argue with me in front of Alvin.

"What are you doing with your bike?" Alvin asks.

"Shit." My body twitches as I search the apartment. Like a parking spot's going to magically appear in my living room.

"We'll look for a place to store it," Alvin assures me. "Come on."

"What do you need me to do?" Mallory asks.

"Pack a bag. Make your phone calls."

"All right." A feral expression I'm not used to seeing on Mallory's face turns her features hard. No nonsense. She comes closer and grabs a fistful of my T-shirt, yanking me to her. "Don't fuck around today, Chaser." She lowers her voice. "I'm not kidding. Do what you need to do and get your ass back here."

Fuck, she's fucking hot.

"Alvin, give us a minute." I hold up one finger and nudge Mallory backward.

"Oh, no." She digs in her heels and won't budge. "You haven't earned any pussy yet. Get going."

I groan. There's nothing hotter than the word *pussy* coming out of my girl's proper-princess mouth. "You worried I'll let you down again?" I whisper in her ear.

"No." She kisses my cheek. "I'm trying to keep you focused." Her face softens, and she runs the back of her hand over my cheek. "Trust me, as soon as we're back in New York, I'm going to fuck you silly."

Blood thunders through my veins, and I pull her closer, pressing a searing kiss to her lips. "Well, now I've got something to look forward to."

Goals. Everyone needs them.

CHAPTER THIRTY-THREE

CHASER

Being out with Alvin while we run our errands gives me too much time to plan and scheme.

The addict side of me has apparently grown a pair and decided if I'm going home to get clean, I should go out with a *bang*.

To say Val's pissed about me leaving is an understatement. Since I'm not explaining my addiction or dick situation to her, I keep our conversation as vague as possible.

Unfortunately, Val can see right through my wall of cool. "Are you using? I can get you into a program here. You don't need to go all the way to New York to get sober."

"It's none of your business."

"Chaser, everything about the band is my business."

I keep my lips sealed.

"This is the worst possible time for you to disappear. That demo needs to be done. Yesterday."

A begging, pleading, reasonable-toned Val is downright unnerving.

"Trust me, I'm just as worried about it as you are. But you and I both know right now what we're missing are Jacob's vocals."

She sighs. "Tell me what's really going on with him?"

Should I tell Val? Probably. But while I strongly suspect he's added shooting smack to his drug repertoire, I don't know for certain. Besides, ratting people out isn't in my nature. "You'll have to talk to him about it."

"Give me something, Chaser."

"I've got nothing to give right now, Val. That's the truth."

"Mallory's going home with you?"

"Yeah."

"Jesus Christ, you're going to ruin both your careers in one shot."

Fury rises in my throat. I slap my hand on her desk and stand. In what's left of my rational mind, I know I'm only pissed because she voiced my worst fear. "We're done here. I'll check in with you once a week and let you know when I'm back in town."

"How mad is she?" Alvin asks as I stomp down the hallway. People actually leap out of my way. Office doors shut with a bang. Guess I must be a scary bastard today.

"Give me a second." I hold up one hand to Alvin and reverse course.

Val's assistant jumps when I rest my elbows on her desk and lean over. I give her a wink and a crooked smile. She hands out coke like Halloween candy. I'm pretty sure it's part of her job description. Another reason Val trying to talk me into rehab pisses me off so much.

The exchange takes a few seconds.

A minute later, I'm in the bathroom inhaling two fat lines.

Ah, breakfast of champions.

"Seriously?" Alvin takes one disgusted look at me when I meet him outside.

"I didn't say I was quitting *today*." I practically rip the passenger side door out of his hands and throw myself into the car. "Step off my nuts."

He slams the door in my face.

The rest of the day consists of finding a storage facility for my bike, snorting lines, and a fog of paranoia.

Every cop I see *must* be the one who will pull us over, stopping me from making it home to Mallory.

"Dude, chill the fuck out," Alvin snaps after I tell him to slow down for the millionth time. "Christ."

"I gotta get home."

"No shit." Under his breath he mutters, "Poor fucking Mallory."

The guilt tumbles over me like a pile of bricks. "Shut up and drive."

Mallory's not impressed with my condition when we return to the apartment.

"Sorry," Alvin says, holding up his hands while he backs out the door. "I tried."

"Not your fault." She gives me the stink-eye. "He's a sneaky prick."

I grin at her. "I love you."

Once we're alone, she crosses her arms over her chest and walks around me in a circle.

"Live it up now, big boy. You're not bringing drugs on the plane. I can't risk you getting arrested."

Shit. Hadn't thought of that.

Can I make it through the long flight without being fucked up? I planned to wean myself off it once we got to New York. Not quit cold turkey right this second.

The thought of going without for so long shoves me into panic mode. In my coked-out mind, it makes perfect sense to snort as much as possible *right this second*. As if my body will hang onto the high for the trip home.

At this point, I have nothing to hide from Mallory. So, I plop down on the living room floor to fret about the drug-free flight home and snort a few thick lines.

While she listens to all the crazy babble flying out of my high-as-fuck mouth, I try not to notice the tears streaming down her cheeks.

CHAPTER THIRTY-FOUR

CHASER

We made it home.

Barely.

The trip home was worse than I anticipated. I'm dying to get my hands on some coke.

Dad knows what's up as soon as he takes a look at me.

"Mallory, can you go check on Chaser's room?" he asks her in a casual tone that would ordinarily set off my danger radar. "It should be ready—"

"Sure." She pats me on the back before taking off. She may or may not mumble "good luck" as she races down the hall to get away from us.

My father points to his office. "Get in there and sit your ass down."

Once I'm seated, he walks around me in a circle, disapproval rolling off him in waves.

I struggle not to twitch while he assesses my condition.

Finally, he drops into his chair on the other side of his desk.

"Jesus Christ, son. You look like a bag of shit. What the fuck you get yourself into?"

This sucks so fucking bad. No way do I want to admit to my father—the strongest motherfucker I've ever known—that I've developed a problem.

Unfortunately, the sad reality is that I need his help to get sober. Time to set aside whatever remains of my pride.

"You using?" he asks.

I blow out a long breath before answering. "Yeah."

"At least you're not trying to deny it." He cocks his head and stares me down. I barely resist the urge to flinch under his harsh scrutiny. "You're smarter than that. What the fuck happened?"

I work my jaw from side to side. Truth is, my excuses are weak, and my father has a low tolerance for bullshit. "I started using a little here and there to keep up with everything."

"Yeah, and?"

Nothing's ever easy with this man. He's gonna yank every last embarrassing detail out if it kills me. "Now, I'm too strung out to function."

"What does that mean?"

"Just what I said." I close my eyes for a second. Verbal sparring with my father won't help my situation. "I need to lay low and get my head on straight."

And that's as detailed as I'm gonna get.

Miraculously, my vague answers satisfy him. He sits back and stares at me for a few seconds. "Proud of you, son."

"You're proud I'm a cokehead?"

"No, you dumb fuck. But you're here. You did the hardest part—admitting there's a problem. Now, you're gonna man up and fix it." He gives me a rare smile. "You'll be okay."

"Thanks."

"What about Mallory?"

"She never touches the stuff."

"Figured that. Her ass is too juicy to be snorting that shit."

"Watch it, old man," I growl, pissed I gave him the reaction he was trying to provoke with that comment.

He grins. "Where's she at with *you*?"

"Uh, fed up and about to leave my stupid ass."

The merriment slides off his face. "She came with you, so it can't be that bad."

"I think she feels like it's her fault."

"Is it?"

"No." I need to shut down that line of thinking right now. I won't have him blaming my weaknesses on Mallory.

He holds up his hands. "Just askin'."

"I'm a big boy. Fully capable of fucking up my life all on my own."

"Yes, you are." He taps his fingers against the desk for a few minutes. "She plannin' to visit her dad while she's here?"

"We never discussed it."

"Sit tight for a day or two. I'll get someone in to clean up the house. You two can stay there, so you're not putting up with this while trying to get yourself sorted." He indicates the clubhouse, not that we keep drugs—or anything incriminating stored here in case we're ever raided by the government—here, but it's still not a quiet or sober environment.

"I'm not going to some circle-jerking rehab."

"No shit, asshole. Last thing I need is you sittin' around crying to a bunch of druggies about how your mean old dad didn't love you enough as a boy."

He lets out a deep belly laugh as I shake my head.

"Seriously, I'll set you two up." He pauses and stares at the phone for a beat. "If you can't do it on your own, we'll find someone we can trust—"

"I can do it." I can't imagine anything worse than talking this out with a stranger. "Thanks, though. Appreciate it."

"Focus on getting clear-headed. You're too smart to end up with a limp dick and swiss cheese for brains."

The irony of his statement is a punch to the balls.

CHAPTER THIRTY-FIVE

CHASER

Vivid nightmares of little shadowy monsters chasing me down glowing red hallways startles me awake. The panicky need-to-escape feeling clings to me even after I shoot up and out of bed.

No walls of fire. No monsters.

Mallory's sigh anchors me in the moment. I'm at the clubhouse. Not hell.

No matter how strong you think you are, there's no magic bullet cure for addiction. Back in L.A., coming home seemed to be my perfect remedy. I naively assumed removing myself from all the readily available coke would do the trick. Home would provide a refuge for me to re-center and recharge.

Reality is a bitch-slap to the face.

Unpleasant doesn't begin to describe the sensations crawling through my body.

My teeth click together, and a chill radiates through my chest, even though I'm still sweating from the nightmare.

Careful not to wake Mallory, I search through my bag for some clean clothes. Keeping my eyes on her, I dress slowly.

She whimpers, and I freeze.

After a few seconds, she turns over.

Maybe I'm not the only one having nightmares.

I watch her for awhile, but she seems peaceful now.

Sunlight's barely peeking through the blankets nailed up over the window. Yesterday was a long, rough journey. She should be out for a couple more hours.

Enough time for me to get myself sorted.

The lock snicks into place behind me as I step into the hallway. I pause, listening for signs the noise woke Mallory.

Nothing.

All clear.

Most of the doors I pass in the hallway are shut. Snores and... *other* sounds filter past the aging hard wood.

"Where you headed?" My father's gravelly voice cuts through the mostly silent clubhouse.

Peering through the hazy glow cast by the neon signs over the bar, I make out his form, lounging on one of the couches against the far wall. A girl's stretched out on the lumpy cushions with her head in his lap. She seems familiar, but I can't place her.

Did I go to high school with her?

Doesn't matter.

"Out," I answer.

"Where?"

"To clear my head."

He curls two fingers, motioning me closer.

Fuck, just what I don't need. The way I'm feeling right now, I won't stand up to an interrogation.

I'm about two feet away when he asks, "Where?"

"Don't know."

"You walking?"

Good point.

"Keys for the truck are in my office."

"Thanks."

The weight of his stare follows me, but I keep moving. One foot in front of the other.

I grab the keys off his desk and force myself to take a breath.

Need some fresh air to cure my restlessness. I'll take a drive. Doesn't have to be anything more than that.

"Shouldn't you get some sleep, old man?" I ask when I return to the common area.

"I slept."

"And now you're sitting here in the dark like a fuckin' owl?"

He grumbles and waves off the question. "Mallory okay?"

"She's asleep."

"I'm gonna look for a car for her to use while you're here. Know what she'd like?"

That's a shift in conversation I didn't expect. "Why?"

He nods to the keys in my hands. "She can't drive that beat up thing."

"No, I mean where does she need to go?"

He tilts his head and levels one of his penetrating '*are you stupid*" stares at me. "No need to make her feel like a hostage. Here, she's got plenty of people to give her a ride, but once you settle into the house, what's she supposed to do?"

"We're not *settling into the house*. We need to be back in L.A."

He continues staring a hole through me.

I don't know why I'm bothering to argue. My father's gonna do whatever the fuck he wants.

And I really need to get out of here.

"I don't think she's picky." I try to adopt a more humble tone. "Thanks for thinking of that, Dad."

His suspicious father stare doesn't relent. "Jay said something came into the garage that might work. You want to come down and look at it with me?"

"Yeah, sure. Later, though."

He narrows his eyes.

I blink.

He doesn't.

A bead of sweat rolls down the side of my face.

"Well, I'll be back." I turn and hustle away.

"Stay out of trouble," he calls after me.

I wave at him over my shoulder and push through the front door, relieved to escape into the chilly first flush of morning.

As much as I resent my father's warning, I needed to hear it.

Too bad, I still get in the truck and head to downtown Kodack. I suppose it would've been easier to break into our warehouse and "borrow" what I need, but I'd never steal from my club.

Nope. I'll roll into the city and purchase my coke like every other addict. Even if I were an active member, I wouldn't want to use any Devil Demons MC contacts for this particular endeavor. Which means, it takes a while to locate a trustworthy looking fellow who isn't offended when I only want to purchase a quarter gram. Bad sign. Whatever I'm about to buy has probably been stepped on so much, it'll be more cornstarch than cocaine. Maybe that's a good thing. I can wean myself off the shit instead of this insanity of stopping cold.

"See you tomorrow." He grins at me.

"Nah, I'm good. Thanks."

Tomorrow. Fuck that. This is all I need. A little bit to get through this first day and then I'll be fine.

No more after today.

CHAPTER THIRTY-SIX

MALLORY

For the third day in a row, I wake up alone.

Maybe it's time to book a flight back to L.A.

I promised Chaser I'd help him through this.

Except he won't let me help him. So far, he's disappeared every day and returned high. I can't decide whether I'm annoyed that he thinks I'm too stupid to notice or flattered he's making an effort to pretend everything is normal.

We barely speak. I'm afraid if I open my mouth, I'll start screaming and never stop. This has to be the lowest point in our relationship. While I'm aware our lives can't always be sparkles and rainbows, it doesn't mean I enjoy him lying and sneaking around.

On the outside, I smile and help out around the clubhouse as much as possible.

Inside, I'm boiling over with fury.

Underneath my anger, I'm scared.

What's he doing all day? Is he in danger? Who's he with?

Worst of all, what if Chaser can't beat his addiction?

How long do I stay here and help someone who doesn't want to be helped?

After breakfast, Stump summons me into his office.

"Chaser's not here." I stall. Being alone with Stump still scares me.

"I ain't looking for him. You and me need to talk." Clearly people don't often say *no* to Stump. Guess that explains where Chaser gets his bossiness from.

Feeling like a naughty kid in trouble, I follow Stump through the clubhouse into his office.

He motions for me to take the seat across from his desk. "How you doing, princess?" he asks after he settles into his chair.

"Okay."

Kicking back, he thumps his boot-clad feet on the edge of the desk and clasps his hands behind his head. "I want you to be straight with me. This isn't a protect-your-man sort of chat we're about to engage in here."

"Uh, what do you want me to say?"

"Where you at with my son?"

"What do you mean? I left work behind to help him get better." I stare him straight in the eye without flinching. "I'm here." I'm tempted to add "but not for long if your son keeps lying to me."

He seems relieved, so I guess he believes me. "Good. That's what he needs."

No, what your son needs is a kick in the ass.

Now that he's figured out where I stand, he turns more businesslike. "What's he been up to?"

"He doesn't tell me." I hate tattling on Chaser, but I also think being honest with Stump benefits Chaser in the long run.

And frankly, I'm beyond pissed Chaser dragged me here only to ditch me and score drugs every day. "He's still getting high. He's careful not to do it in front of me, but I can tell."

"Fucker," he grumbles. He shakes his head and stares at the closed office door. "You two need your own space. I'm having the house cleaned up, so it's more suitable."

I'm not sure what he means by *suitable*. From what I remember, their home was lovely. Maybe a bit dated but still several steps up from where we live in L.A. "You don't have to go to extra trouble for us, sir. We have money—"

He tips his head down and lifts his hand in a "stop" gesture. "Don't need your money, girl. What I'm asking isn't fair to you. You two ain't been together that long. Fuck, he hasn't even put a ring on your finger yet. You don't owe him shit. Yet, you're here."

"I—"

"Don't interrupt me." He waits to see if I'm going to open my mouth again, so I keep it shut. "Nothing in this world I respect more than loyalty. Need it in this life." He taps his pen on the desk a few times. "How long's he been doin' coke?"

"I...I'm not sure. I think he started when they went into the recording studio."

"All right. So not too long. I'm hoping he can kick this on his own. Not relishing the thought of dragging his ass to cokeheads anonymous or some other bullshit."

I snort out a laugh, because I can't picture it either.

"You two still...?" He waves his hand in the air, and for such a blunt man, I can't understand what he's hinting at.

Oh.

"I don't think that's your business, sir."

His eyes close briefly, and he shakes his head. "Everything is my business, girlie. You'll learn." He waits for a few seconds then sighs. "By your silence, I'm gonna assume there's trouble in that department."

"It's just because of the drugs," I grumble, smoothing my skirt over my legs. And the fact that I'd rather punch Chaser than kiss him right about now.

"You two plannin' to have kids?"

My head snaps up. "Excuse me?"

He curls his arms together and makes a rocking motion. "Babies. You plannin' to make some with my son?"

"Uh, that's also not your business."

"You don't listen very well."

"Oh, I heard you, Mr. Adams. I just don't agree that our sex life or reproductive plans are any of your business."

He cracks a smile, then full-out laughs. "Shit, I can see why he likes you so damn much." He waves his hand at me. "Settle down. Just thinking a kid on the way might help him stay straight."

Completely insulted and embarrassed, my cheeks burn, but I fight through the discomfort to sit forward to make my point clear. "I hardly think now's the time to bring a baby into our lives. Not when everything's so...unstable. Seems unfair to do to a child, don't you think?"

He raises an eyebrow, but I keep right on going.

"A baby's not supposed to *solve* problems. I'd rather wait until our child's going to have two functioning adults to care for him or her."

Done with my speech, I sit back and force myself not to break eye contact with the stunned MC president.

As we continue staring each other down, he twirls a pen through his fingers without looking at it once. After a few too many beats, he laughs again. "I don't know if I've ever met a woman who didn't want to trap a man by gettin' knocked up."

"What's that supposed to mean?"

"Exactly what I said. I'll assume he's earning some money with his music." He flicks his hand in the air in a dismissive way I don't care for. "He stands to earn well with the club when he eventually takes over. If he ever comes home."

"I'm sorry. I've never thought of him that way. And honestly, I'm not exactly in a hurry to be tied down with a kid myself." I pick at a bit of lint on my corduroy skirt. "Before everything got messed up, we had a lot of fun in England. Did Chaser tell you he rented a bike for us over there? We can't really do that with a baby strapped to the back."

"Ah, you've got a little wanderlust in you too, huh?"

"I get it from my mother." I don't elaborate, and he doesn't ask for more details.

"All right," he says, once again shifting gears. "I'm gonna set you two up and help you get him through this."

I feel a "but" coming on.

"But in return, I need you to do something for me."

There it is.

"What do you need, sir?" I work as much respect as I can into my voice to ease the tension in the room. I think I've smarted off to him enough for one day.

"You been in touch with your father?"

"No. He told me not to contact him." While that's true, guilt presses down on me. I haven't given him a lot of thought while I've been off in California.

"Well, he's...concerned about you. I'd like you to pay him a visit once Chaser's well enough to go with you for protection."

"Wait. Concerned about me? How? Why do you know this?"

"Who do you think smoothed things over when his guys wanted their money back? I made it clear to him and everyone else, you were under our protection—meaning coming after you again would be a declaration of *war*. You're smart enough to understand men like your father and his associates don't appreciate that too much."

Oh dear. I never, ever considered that Stump might have put himself or his club in that much danger because of me.

"You seem like a bit of a romantic, Mallory, so I'll lay it out for you—we got ourselves a little Romeo and Juliet thing going on."

"That's a tragedy, not a romance," I mumble.

He chuckles. "Whatever. Point is, I need you to pay your father a visit and let him know you're okay. That you're with Chaser *willingly*. You're happy." He runs his gaze over me, and I wrap my sweater around me tighter. "You look healthy. Tell him whatever he needs to hear to be convinced his darling princess is being taken care of properly."

Darling princess my ass. "I can do that."

"Good girl." He cocks his head. "I'd leave Chaser's coke problem out of the discussion."

"I haven't talked about it with anyone except him and now you."

He raises an eyebrow as if he's impressed with my discretion. His low opinion of me is starting to grate on my nerves.

"Stump, forgive me for asking, but do you think this little of every woman or just me?"

He lets out a loud belly laugh. "Haven't known a lot of females who could be trusted in my life, Mallory. It's nothing personal. If it makes you feel better, I like you."

"Could've fooled me."

He chuckles once more, then turns serious again. "I don't want you to call the prison or alert them that you're going to make a visit. I'll set things up when you're ready. Chaser will go in with you, but at least two of my guys are gonna tag along as escorts."

A tremor of fear rolls through me. "Why? What are you afraid of?"

His gaze shifts to the left for just a second. Enough for me to suspect he's lying when he says, "Nothing, sweetheart. Only a precaution."

CHAPTER THIRTY-SEVEN

MALLORY

Once we've finished the serious talk, Stump's expression settles into something almost resembling friendly. "You got a few minutes?"

Wary, but unable to lie, I shrug. Other than catching up on soap operas and fretting about all the auditions I'm missing, my schedule is wide open. "Nothing but time."

He shakes his head and mutters something about choking the fuck out of Chaser, which I pretend to ignore.

"Come on." He motions for me to follow him. Feeling like a hound about to be banished to the doghouse, I follow Stump through the clubhouse and outside.

His boots crunch over the gravel as I hurry to keep up with his long strides.

Finally, he stops next to a blue Nissan Stanza. He reaches into his pocket, pulls out a key, and holds it out to me.

"What's this?" I ask.

"What's it look like?"

I glance at the key and back to the car. "Whose is it?"

"Yours while you're here."

"Mine?"

His brow creases. "You sleep-deprived or somethin'? What's so confusing?"

"Why are you giving me a car?"

He throws his arms open wide. "We're out in the middle of fuckin' nowhere. Don't want you to feel trapped."

My eyes water. "You got me a car?"

"Don't get too worked up. It's nothing special, Mallory." He slaps his hand on the roof. "Five years old. Got about a hundred thousand miles on it, but it's clean and runs well."

"Thank you," I whisper.

"I'm sure you're used to fancier vehicles."

If by *fancier* he means a driver tasked with taking me everywhere when I lived at home, then, yes. My father hired someone to teach me to drive just long enough to pass the driver's test and get my license. Then he never let me touch one of his precious cars again.

Maybe he always suspected I wanted to run away.

Stump hooks his fingers in the handle, opening the door for me. I slide into the soft velour seat and run my hands over the steering wheel.

"You know how to drive stick?" Stump leans into the open door.

My gaze lands on the shifter. "No."

"Eh," he grumbles. "Figured."

He stomps around to the other side and yanks open the passenger door, throwing himself into the seat. "Came into the garage. Didn't have a lot to choose from," he explains.

"I love it." I run my hand over the shiny silver knobs of the console. "Especially the tape player."

He snorts. "You sound like Chaser when he was younger. Little shit used to bitch up a storm if he couldn't listen to his crap in the car. His mom put up with it, I..." He stares out the window at the clubhouse, without finishing the thought.

Say something, Mallory. Anything.

I flip the visor down. "Oh, it has a mirror too. That's handy."

Stump chuckles and slams his door shut. "Start it up."

"I..." Good grief, it's not like I don't know where the key goes. I jab the key into the ignition and twist. The engine catches. The car lurches and stalls.

Stump grins at me. "Next time, push the clutch in."

"What?" I peer down, spying three pedals.

"Far left's your clutch." He fiddles with the stick. "Put it in neutral. Clutch down. Foot on the brake."

It takes a few tries, but I get the hang of it and spend the next couple of minutes driving around the parking lot. Stump must be getting dizzy from circling the clubhouse. He points to the road.

"Let's see if you can get it up to third."

"What? No, I'm not ready for that."

"It's not a busy road. Besides, we need to test you on some hills."

"Hills? Why?"

The corners of his mouth pull up. Not a good sign.

He directs me to the neighborhood where Chaser took me the last time we visited. I lurch and grind my way there, only stalling once. I circle the cul-de-sac, and Stump stares at his house as we pass. There's a van in the driveway and sheets of ripped-up carpet in the yard.

"Good," he mutters. "Should be ready for you two in a couple of days."

"You don't have to go to so much trouble. The house was lovely."

"Eh." He waves his hand in the air. "Needs freshening up."

Who am I to tell him what to do with his house? I just hate for him to go to all this trouble when we're not staying long.

"Turn right." He points, in case I don't know right from left, I guess.

The neighborhood's full of houses similar to Stump's. He tells me to keep going straight. Right up a steep hill. Before I crest the hill, he places his hand over mine on the shifter. "Stop."

"Here? Why?" I jam the clutch down and press my other foot to the brake, while wiggling the shifter into neutral. "Now what?"

"Go."

As soon as I take my foot off the brake, the car rolls back. Scared, I slam my foot on the gas and release the clutch too soon. The car stalls.

And I'm still rolling backward.

In between roars of laughter, Stump yells at me to, "Brake! Brake!"

"Shit," I mutter, twisting the key.

Heart pounding, cheeks burning, I try again.

And again. The engine's screaming by the time I finally get the right balance between clutch and gas.

"Drive around the block," Stump orders.

He has me stop in the same spot.

I don't stall the car this time, but it does roll back quite a way before I move forward.

"Again."

I loop around the block.

A hundred and seventeen—give or take—tries later, Stump's finally satisfied. "Good girl," he praises.

"The neighbors are going to think we're nuts."

"Fuck 'em." He waves at the open road in front of us. "Drive."

"Where?"

He guides me downtown to a shopping area and has me pull in front of a little record store. "Let's get you some music for the car."

"Uh, okay."

He smiles when I remember to pull the parking brake up. "Not too bad for your first time driving stick."

"Thanks," I mumble.

He opens the door to the record store for me and waves at me to hurry.

The cassettes are in the back, and he nods for me to go ahead. "I need to speak with the owner."

While this is certainly the strangest morning I've had since we came home, it's also the best one. I find myself smiling for the first time in days as I peruse the store's collection of cassettes. I gravitate toward the Ks in the Hard Rock section and squeal when my fingers brush over *Kickstart: Throttle Down.* I pull that cassette out and continue to the V section. Vicious Vandals has at least four albums in their catalog. Impressive. I slide one out of its slot and laugh at the picture on the front. The whole band's wearing mean, scary faces and Andrew's shirtless, of course. I check the dates and decide to buy their most recent one. The W section has one lone Wishing Well tape, and I stick out my tongue at it.

Stump's waiting for me at the register. I'm expecting him to laugh at my choices, but he seems more sad than amused. He glares at me when I reach for my purse, so I watch as he hands the cashier a twenty.

"Thank you," I say outside.

"Chaser used to spend hours here." Stump turns and gives

the building another look, before motioning for me to get in the car. "At least you're decisive."

More like heartbroken.

"Can you find your way back to the clubhouse?" Stump asks.

"Uh, I think so."

"Show me."

I mentally go over the streets and landmarks we passed on the way here.

"I'll get you a map, but I want you to know how to get to the clubhouse without it." He taps the ashtray, which I now notice is filled with quarters. "In case you ever need to stop and use a payphone."

Touched by his thoughtfulness, I thank him.

"Go on." A sigh follows his gruff order.

I manage to find my way to the road that leads to the clubhouse, only to almost miss the driveway. Stump grins as I shift into reverse and back up a few feet to make the turn. "Good job."

More bikes line the side of the clubhouse than were there when we left this morning. Stump searches the lot and asks me to park next to the garage. When I shut the engine off, he takes the keys from my hand. "Listen to me, Mallory." He waits until he's sure he has my full attention. "What we talked about this morning stays between you and me. Anyone asks you what Chaser's up to, tell them it's club business and you don't know anything about it."

Under his intense stare, I mutter, "Of course."

"Good girl." He pats my arm and opens his door while I turn over his words. "Oh," he turns and hands me the keys again. "One more thing. This car is *yours*. No one drives it, but you or me. Chaser asks to borrow the keys, you tell him no."

"I—"

"Tell him no and then come tell me. Can you do that?"

"Okay."

Done giving me orders, Stump hauls himself out of the car.

Two young guys I don't recognize are hanging out by the front door.

"Prospect!"

Both snap to attention at Stump's harsh voice. "Yes, pr...er, Yes, sir."

Stump rests his hand on my shoulder. "This is my son's old lady. She needs something, you get it for her. We clear?"

Their scared gazes only stray from Stump long enough to give me a quick scan. "Yes, sir."

I'd protest, but I know better than to contradict Stump in front of anyone. Or at all.

A battered, green Ford pick-up truck rattles into the lot and parks next to my car. Stump's eyes widen for a fraction of a second. The corners of his mouth curl up. Not sure I should stick around for whatever sinister business he has in mind, I open my mouth to excuse myself.

He snaps his fingers at me before I can sneak away. "Come here, Mallory. Someone I want you to meet."

"Uh, okay."

"What's with the cage?" Stump calls to the man who steps out of the truck.

"Hey, Prez." He jerks his head toward the truck. "Hauled all that old carpet and shit to the dump."

"Good. Got another job for you." Stump pushes me forward. "Mallory, this is Tally, the club's Treasurer."

Tally has a head of curly brown hair, brown eyes, and a warm smile. He holds out his hand to me. "Hey, Mallory. We've met in passing, I think."

Unsure of what Stump has in mind, I shake Tally's outstretched hand. "Yes, I think so."

"Good." Stump rubs his hands together. "Now that you're acquainted, Tally, I need you take Mallory down to Abbott's and let her pick out some furniture for the house."

Tally opens his mouth, but I beat him to it. "I don't—"

"Just the living room and master bedroom for now," Stump cuts me off. His voice softens. "You can do that for me, right, sweetheart?"

"Uh, I guess."

"Carpet too." He lifts his chin at Tally, who's still standing there with his mouth open. "Have them put it on my account."

Done handing out tasks, Stump turns and marches into the clubhouse, leaving Tally and I staring after him.

Well, this is awkward.

A nervous smile twitches over my lips. "I'm sorry."

"It's no problem." He stretches his arm toward the truck and bows. "My chariot awaits."

I don't know him well enough to decipher if that's supposed to be comedy or sarcasm. The poor guy probably had better things to do with his afternoon than take me shopping.

Climbing into the cab of the truck in my skirt is awkward, but I think I manage not to flash my butt. Tally slams the door once I'm inside. I take in the faded dashboard, gravel dotted floor mats and cracked vinyl seats.

"Work truck," Tally says as he hops in the other side. "You mind if we swing by the house first and get some measurements?"

"No, of course not."

The awkwardness is thick enough to slice with a steak knife. Finally, Tally breaks the silence.

"How long you guys staying?"

"Not sure yet."

"What's Chaser up to?"

I shrug. "Club business, I guess."

He *hmms* and nods.

"I wish Stump wouldn't go to so much trouble. Unless he's fixing up the house for himself."

"Doubt it. More like Prez is hoping to fill it with some grandbabies."

"Ugh." I've never known so many men with baby fever.

He chuckles. "Not your thing?"

"Not for another ten years at least."

He flicks his gaze over me again. "Not my business."

"Finally," I mutter.

"Prez can be real direct, huh?"

That's one way to put it.

CHAPTER THIRTY-EIGHT

CHASER

The coke I'm able to scrounge up here is so diluted, I've been back to the same dealer more than once. At least *potency* is the excuse I use for why I'm too weak to get myself under control.

Feeling marginally functional this afternoon, I step into our room, expecting to find Mallory. Not that I want to face her when I'm fucked up. Again.

My quick sigh of relief when the room's empty is cut off by a meaty hand around my throat.

I can't even make a sound when my back smashes into the wall. My skull makes a nice cracking thud against the wood, though.

The bedroom door slams shut.

"Where ya been, son?" My father's liverwurst and onion breath washes over me, and I try not to gag.

I cough, sputter, and attempt to pry his fingers away from my windpipe.

"That hurt?" His eyes glint with rage from about a millimeter away.

I blink once for yes.

"Tryin' to help you out, since you seem to have a death wish."

He finally releases me, and I slide to the floor, landing on my ass like a sad sack of rotten potatoes. Black spots dance behind my eyes while I fight to catch my breath.

"Get up," my father barks.

Still coughing, I stumble over to the bed and drop down. "What the fuck?" I rasp.

"Well, I tried the nice dad approach. That didn't seem to work. Now, it's tough love time."

"When have you ever been *nice dad*?"

"You're about to find out how *not* nice dad I can be, you little fuck."

"You gonna shoot me next?"

"If I have to."

Maybe I shouldn't have put that suggestion in his head.

"Where you been?" Before I open my mouth, he shoves his index finger about an inch from my nose. "And don't fucking lie."

"Out."

He pulls his revolver free from the holster under his leather cut. "Out, huh?" he mutters as he flips open the cylinder and gives it a spin.

Russian roulette has never been my father's game. The gun's probably loaded. "Downtown."

"Doing what?"

"Seems you have some suspicions."

"Who's supplying you?"

"I didn't steal from the club, Dad."

"At this point, I'd rather you did." He stares at the gun

for a few seconds before tucking it away. Thank fuck. I wouldn't put it past the old man to fire a bullet into me. "Where?"

"Some dealer downtown."

He stares at me.

"I didn't ask for credentials." I snort out a humorless laugh. "Real diluted product, though. Can't be good for the club's reputation."

"You think you're funny?"

I hold up one hand, in case he decides to go for the gun again. "Just saying."

"You remember a couple months ago when you asked the club to protect your girl?"

I slowly lift my gaze. "What's Mallory got to do with this?"

"Well, for starters, I went and poked my fingers into a nest of sleeping vipers. Last thing I need is word spreading that my son's a fucking cokehead."

"Please, that's the least of what they're into."

"That really the answer you want to go with?"

Answering him with this amount of disrespect isn't helping either of us. "I'm sorry. I'm trying."

"You're trying?" he mimics in a high-pitched whiny tone. "Bullshit. You ran out and got high the first morning and you been out doing it every damn day since."

I'd try to defend myself, except I'm not even sure what day it is. And he's right.

"You dragged that sweet girl home with you, to do what? Sit around by herself all day waiting on your ass? Didn't she blow off work to help you?"

I swallow hard. This isn't anything I haven't been berating myself about every morning. "Yeah."

"Then pull your head out of your ass before she decides to go back to California without you."

"What are you talking about?" Oxygen's finally made its way back to my brain, and my head clears. "Where is she?"

"Out with Tally." His lips curl up, and he crosses his arms over his chest, daring me to complain.

"What do you mean, 'out with Tally?'" I ask slowly.

"You got a hearing problem?"

"When did they even meet?"

"When I introduced them."

"Why?"

"He's supervising the renovations at the house."

I jab my fingers through my hair. Tally and I grew up in the club together. His dad was the treasurer for years. Since I was busy with music, socially, we went our separate ways in high school. He's still a brother, though. He wouldn't dare hit on my girl. "What renovations?"

"Poor girl looked like she was gonna burst into tears at breakfast," my father says. As if any woman's tears have ever had an effect on him. "Took her out. Taught her how to drive stick. She's good at it. Quick learner."

"You what?"

He lifts his hands at ten and two o'clock and grips an imaginary steering wheel. "Car. You were supposed to look at it with me."

"Oh." Forgot all about that conversation.

"Yeah, *oh*. Anyway, when we came back, I sent her out with Tally to get some things for the house."

"Like what?"

He shrugs. "Furniture. Carpet. Nothing special."

"You sent her furniture shopping with Tally." I hang my head. "Jesus."

"I want you moved into the house by the end of the week. No more fucking bullshit."

"You think that house is magical, old man? It'll cure me?"

"I think you need to treat that girl with more respect, get yourself clean, and then go pay her father a visit."

All the pieces start falling into place in my drug-addled head. "They ask to see her?"

"Something like that."

"Surprised you're not sending Tally with her," I sneer.

"I will if you force me to."

"Like fuck you will." I stand and run my hands over my jeans a few times. "I know you think I'm weak and an asshole. But I *am* trying."

"Not very hard."

Fuck this shit. Why bother defending myself? Not like I plan to spill all the insane nightmares I've been having. "No more. I promise."

"Don't promise. Just do it." He slaps my back, then reaches into my pocket and takes the truck keys.

"What the fuck?" I reach for them, and he blocks me.

"Obviously, you can't handle the responsibility. From now on, you need a ride, ask your girl."

Smart move on Dad's part. He knows damn well I'd never take her on a drug run.

"And she's been told not to give you her keys, so don't think about being sneaky, either."

"Guess you two had a nice chat."

"Don't get your boxers in a wad. She tried covering for you and downplaying the situation at first. She cares about you." He coughs and mutters, "Fuck knows why."

Can't argue with him there.

He reaches for the door, then stops himself. "I'm not having this conversation with you again, Russell. Next time, I shoot you in the leg."

"Super. Great parenting."

"You're twenty-fucking-two." He pokes a finger into my

chest. "I shouldn't *need* to parent you. For fuck's sake, you had more sense when you were twelve."

Burning with humiliation, and let's face it, anger at myself, I stand there staring at him. It takes a while for the correct words to roll off my tongue. "I'm sorry."

"Do better."

I nod once.

He opens the door and grunts at me to follow him. It's a weeknight, so the clubhouse is pretty quiet. Not a lot of people around to insert themselves into our business. Honestly, I'd welcome the distraction. Anything to divert my father's attention.

Outside, he leads me over to the garage and stops at a small sedan. "This is what I got her."

"It's nice."

"Thought she was gonna hug me for a minute." Old man never did deal well with affection of any sort. "Took her to visit Record Town."

The corners of my mouth lift. Spent plenty of time there as a kid. Lots of good memories.

"Told her to get what she wanted," he continues.

"You used to make me spend my allowance money."

He tilts his head. "You need to have a cry about it?"

"Nope. Just sayin'."

"Whole big store of shit to choose from. She comes back with a fuckin' Kickstart tape."

I stop breathing for a moment.

"Get your head on straight." He slaps my cheek a few times. "Stop being a dick."

Our attention's drawn to a Ford that's seen better days rattling down the driveway, mercifully interrupting our conversation.

Tally parks and jogs around the truck to open the passenger door. Offers his hand to Mallory to help her out of the cab.

My father's arm slams into my chest as I take a step forward. "Don't you fuckin' *dare* start any shit," he warns under his breath. "I asked him to do me a favor."

"Not cool to send a brother out with another brother's old lady."

"Guess you better start treating her like your old lady, then."

"Fuck off," I growl, shaking loose.

He chuckles and follows me across the parking lot.

My eyes lock on Mallory. The sweet way she stares up at Tally and thanks him. The ways she's laughing and smiling, something she hasn't done much of lately. None of it sits well.

"How'd you do, sweetheart?" Dad calls to Mallory.

"Okay." Her voice falters when she notices me, and she looks away. Shit, that hurts.

Tally hands a neat stack of paperwork to my dad. "All the receipts are there." He lifts his chin at me. "How you been, brother?"

"All right," I grind out.

"I didn't go too crazy," Mallory says to my father, still not looking at me. "I wasn't sure how much stuff you wanted."

"Whatever will make you two comfortable. You know where the store is if you want to go back?" he asks.

My, aren't we generous.

"I think so."

"Prospects are painting through the night," Tally says. "Wanted them to get it done before the carpet's installed. Furniture will be delivered Friday."

My father slaps my back. "Good. You'll be all moved in by the weekend."

If I make it that long.

CHAPTER THIRTY-NINE

MALLORY

Whatever Chaser and his father talked about seems to have worked. Chaser hasn't disappeared on me again. Not that he could go anywhere. Stump took his truck away and warned me again that Chaser wasn't allowed to drive my car.

The club helped us move into the house.

Without the drugs, Chaser spends most of the day sleeping. Which is a relief. When he's awake, he's irritable. Instead of being stuck inside the clubhouse bedroom, we now have an entire house to ourselves, so we can avoid each other.

The car has been a blessing. And I've thanked Stump for it more than once.

Fed up, today I decided to locate the nearest library and spend the afternoon reading about addiction and withdrawal.

The fatigue and irritability seem to be normal. I still wonder if Stump's do-it-yourself approach is right for Chaser.

Maybe he needs a doctor or a counselor. A professional of some sort.

I jot down a few notes and use the phone book to compile a list of doctors.

Chaser's still sleeping when I return to the house. That's a good sign, right? His body needs the rest. I watch him for a few seconds and push his hair off his sweaty forehead. He moans in his sleep and turns over.

Downstairs, I'm about to flick the television on when someone knocks on the door. Worried the noise will wake Chaser, I hurry to answer.

"Hey, Tally." I open the door wide. "What's up?"

"Just checking in to see if you guys need anything."

I glance at the staircase. "Chaser's been...sick. He's sleeping."

"Oh, sorry," he whispers. "You want to get out of the house for a bit?"

"Actually, I was out earlier. At the library."

"The library?" He rocks back on his heels. "I've lived here my whole life, and I don't think I could find it if I had to."

"I wouldn't advertise that."

He chuckles.

I jot down a quick note for Chaser.

Not that he'll wake up and wonder where I am, but just in case.

Chaser

Out with Tally. Love, M.

I read the note a few more times. It doesn't say anything different.

How long was I asleep?

Why the fuck is she out with him again? I glance around the kitchen. My father went all out fixing up the house for us. New appliances replaced the hideous avocado green ones I grew up with. I'm not sure how long he expects us to stick around or if he wanted to fix it up because he plans to sell it after we leave. Or maybe he just needed a way to launder some dirty cash. Whatever the reason, I'm grateful the hideous gold carpet is also gone. The walls have been freshly painted some sort of cream color Mallory picked out. Most of the furniture is brand new too.

Furniture Mallory picked out with another man.

"Fuck." I scratch my hands through my hair and yawn. So fucking tired. But at least I haven't had any coke in days. Still crave it like a motherfucker. Sleep holds the cravings at bay. So I spend lots of time doing that. The shadow monsters still chase me in my nightmares, but they're less vivid and don't come for me as often.

I guess it's progress.

Headlights wash over the kitchen, and an engine rumbles in the driveway. I move to the front door and stare out the lone diamond-shaped pane of glass. Tally's truck.

Fucker.

I blow out a breath and retreat to the living room.

What the fuck are they doing out there?

Finally, Mallory's key scratches in the lock, and the door swings open. She turns and waves, a big smile on her face.

The smile vanishes when she notices me in the living room. "You're up."

"Hello to you, too."

She closes the door and flips the locks. Seems more like a stall tactic than a safety precaution. Can't imagine why, I sure have been a delight to be around lately.

"Was that Tally's truck?"

"He wanted to come in and say hi, but I told him you were sick." She shrugs and walks into the kitchen. "Are you hungry?"

Starving. If I'm not sleeping, I'm eating lately. She may not want to talk to me or even look at me, but Mallory's fed me like a king since we moved in here.

Tonight, I couldn't give a fuck about food. "Where were you?"

"Out with Tally."

"Yeah, got that. Where?"

She turns away from the refrigerator and frowns. "We went to the movies."

Not sure I heard her correctly, I cross my arms over my chest and stare at her. "You went on a date with one of my brothers?"

She blinks, and her gaze searches the kitchen as if I'd directed my question to someone else. "What are you talking about?"

"*I* haven't even taken you to a movie yet." Shit, does Mallory even like movies? Of course she does. She wants to be an actress for fuck's sake. Why haven't I taken her out on a normal date?

"We're both busy working when we're in L.A.," she says quietly. "It's not a big deal."

"I don't like you going out with other men."

"Going out with other men? Are you listening to yourself? He's been friendly to me. That's all."

"How friendly?"

"Are you kidding?" She smacks her hand against the refrigerator. "Your father made him take me shopping."

"Yeah, to punish me."

"Well, you were too busy getting high to care."

Ouch. First time she's lobbed that one at me. I deserve it. Doesn't mean I enjoy it.

"I don't want you going out with him again."

She glares at me. "Is that right?"

"You're supposed to be here helping me. Not running around with one of my brothers." Holy hell, I can't even blame those idiotic words on cocaine.

Anger glitters in her eyes, but she answers with disturbing calm. "I'm here, Chaser. I've been here every single day since we left L.A." She jabs her finger in my direction. "And you're accusing me of cheating? Are you serious?"

"I didn't accuse you of anything."

"You know what?" She drops the box of pasta in her hands on the counter. "Feed yourself. I'm going to bed."

I reach for her as she passes me, an apology burning a hole in my tongue. But she jerks her body away. "Sleep in your old room tonight."

"I'm not sleeping in there."

"Then sleep on the couch. You're not sleeping with me." Her lips flatten into a grim line, and she jogs up the stairs. A few seconds later, the bedroom door slams shut.

Sure enough, when I drag my ass upstairs later, the bedroom door's locked. It's a simple lock. I could probably pop it open with a solid thump. But I don't want to wake her and fight again.

Too tired to slog my way downstairs, I crash in my childhood bedroom.

There's something about sleeping in your old twin bed that humbles a man.

I toss and turn, trying to get comfortable on the lumpy, old mattress, wondering what fresh hell tomorrow will bring.

CHAPTER FORTY

CHASER

The thick tension in the house haunts us for a few days.

Tally doesn't stop by again. I'm not sure if Mallory told him not to or what. I don't bring him up and neither does she.

My brain cells are starting to fire again, and I pick up my guitar to strum a few notes. I haven't touched it since we've been home. Almost like I've been punishing myself.

"That's pretty." Mallory's soft voice draws my attention to the living room entrance where she's leaning against the wall. "Don't stop."

"Something I've had in my head."

"I like it."

"Come here."

She approaches slowly. Hesitant. Probably afraid I'll snap at her.

I hate what I've done to us.

When she's close enough, I reach out and grasp her fingers. She doesn't yank them back. A good sign, right?

My heart pounds. Not from drugs. Good old-fashioned stage fright. Haven't felt that in a long time.

Mallory always says she likes my voice. I close my eyes. Take a deep breath.

"When the sun goes down
And the day is done
You're my salvation
Hurting you is a sin.
This life was easier in my dreams.
I'll love you 'til they close my coffin.
Even then you'll be my salvation."

That's as far as I've gotten. When I glance up at her, she watching me with glossy eyes.

"Kinda whiny, huh?" I joke.

"Not at all. What else do you have?"

"That's it." I pat the cushion next to me.

A jolt of electricity bursts through me when she drops down, and her leg brushes against mine.

"Keep playing," she encourages.

"This life was easier in my dreams."

I stop singing, but my fingers keep moving.

Mallory opens her mouth, then closes it.

"You got something for me?" I nudge her with my elbow.

She blushes and shakes her head.

"Come on. It looks like you do." I stop teasing her and wait to see if she'll jump in. Finally, she does.

"This glittering road isn't made of gold.
One more lie that's been exposed."

Floored by her voice, I stop playing and stare at her.

"What?" She covers her mouth with her hand, like she

wants to stuff the words back in her mouth. "That was silly. Sorry."

I reach over and pull her fingers away from her lips. "You have a beautiful voice."

"Stop."

"How come you never sing in the shower for me?"

She shrugs.

I quickly jot down her two lines. Not that I could ever forget them.

She jumps up off the couch.

"Where you going?"

"I don't want to bug you."

"You're not." I wave my pen over the notebook. "You're helping."

I set the guitar down. "You know what, though? I'd like to get out of the house for a bit." I stand and stretch.

For a brief second, her hungry gaze dances over me before skittering away.

That's progress.

I approach her like she's a skittish kitten about to bolt. "Dad said he taught you to drive stick?"

A soft smile ghosts over her lips. "He was surprisingly patient with me. Although, he did make me stop on the hill—"

"Over and over until you finally did it flawlessly?"

She shakes with laughter. "Yes!"

"Want to show me?"

"No," she groans.

"Come on. Take me to Record Town."

"Oh! Okay."

I follow her outside to the car.

Except for her being in the driver's seat, things almost feel normal as she reverses out of the driveway.

Just as my father said, she has the cassette case for a

Kickstart tape in the middle console. What I'm not expecting is the Vicious Vandals' one next to it.

"Really?" I hold it up and arch a brow.

Without answering, she punches the eject button on the cassette player. "Yes, but *this* is the one I've been listening to."

She waves a copy of *Throttle Down* at me.

I grumble and stare out the window. It's weird listening to my own stuff. Or having anyone I care about listen to it in front of me. Music's always been so personal. Strange since the whole goal is to play for larger and larger audiences and sell more albums.

"The production on it was shitty." We had a crappy company mix the album, and I swear to fuck, half of it sounds like it was recorded under water. Never again.

"I like it." She pops it back in, and I groan.

All the way into town, she sings along to the radio.

Things aren't perfect yet. But at least we're getting closer.

It took more than an afternoon to fuck things up between us.

And it'll take me more than a few good moments to repair the damage.

CHAPTER FORTY-ONE

CHASER

"Fuck, I'm tired." I flop down on the couch, kick off my boots, stretch out, and close my eyes.

Warmth from Mallory's body grazes my arm. Without opening my eyes, I reach out and wrap my hand around her thigh, pulling her closer. The air between us still radiates with tension, but after a few seconds, she moves closer and runs her fingers through my hair.

I crack open one eye. "How's my girl?"

"Exhausted."

"Take a nap with me."

She waves her hand over my body. "Where? You cover the entire couch."

My mouth twists into a half-smile. "That's the point, baby. Lay your sweet body over mine."

She snorts and backs out of my grasp. "I'm going to change."

Damn, we've made a lot of progress over the last few days, but we still have these awkward moments.

Visions of her naked body drag my tired ass off the couch.

I trudge up the stairs to our room. My gaze immediately strays to the bed.

Fuck, all I want to do is sleep.

I slap my face a few times to wake myself up, and Mallory cocks her head. "You okay?"

"Tired. I'm still so fucking tired all the time."

"Your body's going through a lot."

Yeah, yeah. I'm sick of making excuses for all my dysfunctions.

Haven't made love to my girl since the disastrous limp-dick incident back in L.A. Don't think I can stand the humiliation of letting her down again.

No joke, now that I have the rest of my body under control, I'm straight-up worried my dick will never function right again. Figures I'd finally find the one girl I want to stick it in for the rest of my life, then promptly snort enough coke to put my dick in a coma.

I haven't had a line in long enough that I feel hopeful for the first time.

My head's finally clearer, but now I'm tired all the time.

Not too tired to notice how hot Mallory looks in her cute little denim cut-offs, though.

In my free moments, I've been practicing whacking off. Everything still functions.

Huge relief.

Mallory can't sit still. I don't know if she's nervous, unsure, mad at me, or bored. But she's all over the place.

Instead of changing clothes, she shakes out a fresh set of sheets to make the bed.

"Can you help me?" she asks, pointing to the opposite corner.

"Yeah, sure."

Aw, Christ, when she bends over to smooth the sheets down, I get a straight shot down her cleavage. Miss those plump tits filling my hands.

"Mallory?"

"Hmm?"

"It's time for the next phase of my recovery."

Her head snaps up at my grave tone. "What do you mean?"

Without taking my eyes off her, I stalk around to the other side of the bed and grab her by the hips. "Sexual healing."

A shaky smile plays over her lips. We've never really talked about the limp-noodle fiasco. I think she wanted to spare my manhood the embarrassment of discussing it.

"Yeah?" She slowly lifts her gaze to mine. So hesitant. Maybe it wasn't my ego she was trying to save. Maybe the whole episode made her doubt *herself*.

And that's totally unacceptable.

"Miss these sweet curves under me," I whisper. "And over me. In front of me."

Soft laughter falls from her lips. "Miss your hardness all over me." She reaches down to rub my cock, and I shift away.

"Not yet, little dove. This is all about *you* right now." Has to be. The limp-dick episode will *not* be repeated. "Need to see you come a couple times first."

She blinks up at me. "A couple, huh?"

My way of apologizing for being an asshole, for letting her down, and for lying to her. Or a way to say thank you for sticking by my side. Maybe all of the above. I can't wait to taste her, touch her, and fuck her again.

I strip down to my underwear, get in the bed, put my back

against the headboard and stretch out my legs. "Undress for me."

She immediately starts working the buttons of her shorts loose.

"No, nice and slow."

Her mouth falls open. Maybe to protest, but her nipples are poking against her top, negating any complaints.

"Come on, little dove. Show me what I've been missing."

She works her T-shirt over her head, and I let out a low whistle at the bubble-gum pink lace bra underneath. "Fuck, that's sexy."

A pretty flush races over her skin from chest to cheeks. It might seem like I said this was all about her and then asked her to do a strip tease for *me*, but I'm trying to show her she's got my full, undivided attention, and that I think she's the sexiest damn woman on the planet.

Plus, I can tell it turns her on.

"Work those shorts over your curvy hips for me. Show me your ass."

She turns and eases them down so slow, I'm hyperventilating by the time I get a glimpse of ass cheek—also covered in sexy see-through pink lace.

"Mmm, I like you in pink. When'd you buy those?"

"When I went out shopping."

"You get them for me?"

She tosses me a sexy glance over her shoulder. "Yes."

Somehow that makes me feel like both Superman and a shithead at the same time. Here, I've been neglecting her, and she's still thinking of ways to please me.

"Love you, Mallory," I rasp.

My serious tone pulls her out of the striptease. She kicks the shorts to the side. Tucking one leg under her butt, she drops down next to me on the bed.

"Why'd you stop?" I ask.

"Are you okay?"

"I'm fine." I motion her up on her knees and then over my lap. "Let me look at you."

My hands stay on her hips, squeezing for a second, before settling into the dip of her waist. "You're more beautiful than I deserve."

She presses a finger to my lips. "None of that."

Suddenly, I know exactly what I want. "You know what will shut me up?" I ask, sliding down on the bed. "Come sit on my face."

Nervous giggles spill out of her, and she glances down at me. "What?"

I grip her upper thighs, digging my fingers into her ass. "Move forward."

She shuffles on her knees way too slow for me, and I end up half-dragging her, until I'm staring up at her perfect pink cunt. I can see everything through the thin, lacy underwear and run my finger down her slit and back up, stopping to press over her clit.

Above me she trembles. From the barest touch. Can't wait to see what happens when I put my mouth on her.

"Chaser? Are you sure about this?"

"Sure about what? That I want your pussy in my face? The answer to that is always *yes*."

I slip a finger under the soaked material and rub my knuckle through her wetness.

Wait a second.

"Where'd all your pretty little blonde curls go, baby?"

She shrugs and tries to sit back, but I keep her in place with one hand on her ass.

"I don't know. Some of the girls out in L.A. said they shave everything."

Since she was doing lingerie modeling, she's always kept herself neat and pretty, but now...all smooth bare skin. "Fuck."

"You like it?"

"I fuckin' love it."

Pushing her panties out of my way some more, I rub my thumb over her slick lips. "So pretty, baby," I mumble. "Come closer. Let me taste you."

The second I touch my tongue to her, she cries out. I move my thumb to her clit, rubbing in firm circles until her hips are rocking against my face.

"Good girl. You need to come bad, don't you?"

"Uh-huh."

"Your man's been neglecting you?"

She whimpers and grinds herself against my face harder. I dive in, kissing and licking every inch of her exposed pussy. She reaches back to stroke my cock, and I grab her hand. "No. Need you to come first before we worry about me."

"Chaser," she gasps.

I slip a finger inside her, curling it to rub the spot that always makes her lose control.

"Come on my face, Mallory. Fuck, you're so hot."

"Uh," she screams and bucks, reaching back to brace herself on my thighs, so she can ride my face. I fucking love every second. She's dripping wet, and I can't wait to get her around my cock.

As she comes down from the orgasm, she peers at me with heavy-lidded eyes. "I need your cock inside me, Chaser. Now."

Has a sexier sentence ever come out of her mouth? Nope. Don't think so.

"Take it, baby." I've been so fucking hard this entire time, I think it's safe to say we won't have any issues.

She slides down, leaving a trail of desire down my chest. I

swipe my hand over my mouth and chin. "You taste so fucking good. Missed that sweet pussy."

"Chaser." She smiles as she rubs her hand over my dick and lowers my underwear. My cock springs out, happy as fuck to be hard again and thrilled to reunite with her. Dying to squeeze inside her.

She stares at my cock like it's a thing of beauty. Which, all things considered, it is right about now.

I'm way too pleased at how hard I am.

"Take it," I encourage.

She grips me and teases her tongue over my eager cock, and I groan.

"Please, baby. Need your cunt wrapped around me. I can't wait much longer," I beg.

Mallory's hot any way I can get her. But there's something about her straddling my lap. Tits bouncing free, ready for my hands. Hips in easy grabbing distance. Sexy legs pressed tight to my sides.

I reach down and give myself another pump. Still good.

Her thighs hover over me as she lowers herself. I can't stop watching as she takes all of me inside her. Every ripple of sensation echoes through my body. So damn tight as I stretch her open.

"Fuck." My head falls back, and I squeeze my eyes shut. I swear tears of joy leak from my eyes. "That's so fucking good. Don't stop, Mallory."

She barely takes a breath, before moving her hips back and forth. Fast.

"Slow down, little dove. We have all night."

"Shh."

My girl actually *shushed* me. I laugh and grip her hips tighter. "Need it?"

"So fucking bad. We're going to fuck more than once

tonight, Chaser," she warns without opening her eyes or slowing down.

Damn, my girl means business.

"I'm so mad at you." Her eyes pop open, and she drills me with a hard stare that's almost scary in its intensity, while she's riding my cock like her life depends on it.

"I'm mad at me, too."

"You stole my virginity." She thumps down hard, and I groan with pleasure. "Turned me into your cock-crazed little slut. And then took it away, you selfish ass."

Fuck me, this is the hottest sex-talk Mallory's ever engaged in. "I'm a *very* bad boy."

"The worst," she agrees.

"Fuck me harder. Punish my dick for letting you down."

She lets out these sexy little moans and grunts. Her breathing choppy, signaling she's about to come.

There's no hotter sound in the world. What the fuck was I thinking ever choosing drugs over fucking my girl?

I hang on as long as I can, letting her use me for her pleasure. But as soon as she tightens around me and moans loud enough to shake the walls, fire shoots down my spine, and I end up coming seconds after she finishes.

She collapses against me, murmuring sweet little sounds against my neck. Her hips keep moving, milking me dry.

This sobriety thing is awesome. Don't think I've ever come so hard in my life. Best high in the world.

Carefully, she lifts herself and crumples next to me. I brush my hand through her hair for a couple seconds. "You all right, little dove?"

"My heart's racing."

"Sounds promising."

She chuckles and snuggles up against me.

Her hand lazily drifts over my chest, soothing and tickling

at the same time. I capture it and kiss her fingertips. "Missed this. You know how much I love you, right?"

"I do," she whispers.

"Loved hearing you admit you're my cock-crazed little slut, too. That was hot."

She blushes and buries her face against my chest. I trace my fingers over the curve of her shoulder and down her arm. As excited as I am to be fully functioning again, it's not the sex I missed the most.

It's this.

The contentment that spreads through my body and settles my soul when she's near.

I swallow hard. "I'm so sorry, Mallory."

She peers up at me. "For?"

"Everything. Thank you for sticking with me, even though I've been such a miserable bastard."

She's quiet for a few seconds, but she restlessly rubs her fingers faster over my chest. "I went to the library to read up...I knew it was a symptom of the withdrawal." She blinks and flattens her hand over my heart. "I can't lie and say I didn't consider going back to L.A. more than once."

Shame twists my insides, but it's better than the nothing I felt before. "I wouldn't have blamed you if you did."

"Your dad seemed surprised that I stayed."

"Is that one of the things you talked about?"

She narrows her eyes. "Yes, when you were off getting high."

"What else did he say?"

She taps her chin as she tries to remember. "Oh, he thought having a baby might be a good way to get you sober."

"Jesus Christ. Seriously?"

"Uh-huh."

"While that's definitely in my future plans, now isn't the time."

"That's pretty much what I told him."

I can't help laughing, imagining my father's reaction.

Well, damn. The thought of Mallory carrying my kid gets my dick hard again. She notices, and the corner of her mouth quirks. "Already?"

"Seems so."

She kisses my chest and then sits up, arranging herself on all fours. I reach out and slap her ass. In response, she wiggles her hips and glances at me over her shoulder.

Fuck if I'm gonna turn her invitation down. I kneel up and grab her hips, barely pausing before burying my cock in her.

"Ah!" she gasps, lowering to her elbows and arching her back.

"Too much?"

"No. Harder."

"Fuck." I shove a few pillows under her hips and pound into her like the future of the entire world depends on it.

It seems like now that my dick has made a full recovery, I can't keep it out of Mallory.

CHAPTER FORTY-TWO

MALLORY

The day I've been dreading is here.

While I'm grateful Chaser's back to normal, it means we have to visit my father.

"Babe, we can't put this off any longer." Chaser's voice is gentle but determined.

"I know. I'm ready."

"I'll have Dad set it up."

I'd gone shopping again, picking up a conservative hunter-green knit dress to wear to visit my father.

Mr. Adams moves fast, because the next morning, I find myself in the passenger seat of a black and red Ford Bronco. Chaser glances over and sets his hand on my knee.

"Everything will be okay," he assures me.

Four of his club brothers ride behind us on their motorcycles. I had asked why so many people were necessary.

Chaser gave me some vague explanation about safety precautions and territory.

He glances over. "You look really nice."

"Thank you."

"That color is pretty on you."

My cheeks warm from the compliment, and I place my hand on his leg.

The drive takes a little more than two hours but still seems to be over too fast.

Even though this is a medium security federal penitentiary, we're asked to provide identification and thoroughly questioned.

"DeLova." The guard glances at my license and back to me. "Here to see your father, right?"

"Yes." I'm guessing my father's made friends all over the place and that's why the guard seems pleased my father has a visitor.

"Adams." He scrutinizes Chaser's license more thoroughly. "What business do you have here?"

Chaser's expression remains passive. "I'm here with my girlfriend for moral support," he answers.

The guard's gaze flicks between us for a few seconds before a slow smile of recognition spreads over his face. "You're Chaser Adams, right? Guitarist for Kickstart?" He glances at me again. "You're the chick from the video. I *knew* you look two looked familiar."

Oh my God. I can't afford to have news spread that my father's a notorious crime boss. The tabloids will have a field day.

Chaser seems to understand why I'm frozen in place.

"Yeah, that's us." He leans in closer to the guard. "We really need to keep this visit hush-hush, though."

The guard straightens up. "Of course. I'm a huge fan. Looking forward to the next album."

"We'll be working on it soon. It's a little different from the last one." Chaser leans in closer, as if he's including the guard in top-secret band information. "More progressive. The label let us do some experimenting."

"Totally awesome. Love 'Candy Jar.'" His gaze slides my way. "The video was perfect because of her."

Waves of possessiveness roll off Chaser, and he slips his arm around my shoulders, making it clear we're together. "Sure is. Favorite video ever. That's how we met."

I flash a hesitant smile.

Finally, the guard waves us through the metal detector. On the other side, he does a quick inspection of my small purse, before leading us into a room with a long counter in the middle. Large panes of plexiglass separate the prisoners from visitors. A mesh square in the middle allows us to speak.

"Your dad hasn't been here long, so he's still only allowed no contact visits," the guard says almost apologetically.

"Of course. I understand."

Honestly, it's probably safer that way. I doubt my father is happy with me at the moment. And I guarantee he won't be thrilled about Chaser.

Chaser pulls out a chair for me and then drags another to my side, so we're sitting as close as possible.

No mistaking that we're a couple.

"Thank you," I whisper. I don't care if it makes me weak; today, I need the safety and protection Chaser's closeness brings.

On the other side, a large, metal door swings open. My father enters the space.

I jump out of my chair at the sight of him. Chaser stands as well, more out of respect than shock, since this is the first time he's met my father and has no way of knowing how much weight he's lost since he's been inside. Also missing is the healthy glow I remember. His skin is pale, pasty and etched with new lines.

What my father has *not* lost is his air of authority. He stands tall, as if he owns the room and everyone in it.

Chaser wraps his arm around my shoulders, and my father's eyes narrow at the obvious-we're-a-couple gesture.

His gaze slides down my body and over to Chaser, before finally taking a seat. He motions for us to do the same.

"Daughter, who have you brought to our visit?" It's only now, after not hearing his voice for so long, that I notice the moderate accent coloring his words.

It's not like they can shake hello. So instead, Chaser takes my hand, lacing our fingers together. "Russell Adams, sir. Pleased to meet you. I wish it was in a better setting."

"And who are you to my daughter?" he asks with a bite to his words I've only ever heard him use with business associates who have fallen out of favor.

"Daddy, Ch—Russell is my...boyfriend."

My father's jaw tightens at the word *boyfriend*.

"You did not do as I asked," he says in the same tone that used to send terror through me as a little girl. Old Mallory shivers inside.

New Mallory sits up taller and looks her father in the eye. "No, I did not. I'm not a *thing* you can give to one of your friends. I have my own dreams for my future that I want to go after."

He drops his head, shaking it from side to side, as if I'm a simple, foolish girl.

"All I wanted was for you to be protected and taken care of."

And kept under someone's thumb. "That would mean a lot

more if your goons hadn't insisted I pay back the money I borrowed to go to California."

My father smirks. "Had you asked me, dear daughter, I would have told you it was not all mine to let you borrow."

"Well, I couldn't exactly ask you, now could I?"

"You've paid it back, yes? The family will take care of you."

"I can take care of myself."

He snorts and shoots a glare at Chaser. "Are you sure about that?"

Chaser breaks his silence. "Your man tracked her down and tried to bring her home by force. That the kind of 'care' your people offer?"

"And how exactly will your *club* treat her?" he asks, obliterating the illusion that he has no idea Chaser's part of an MC.

Chaser isn't intimidated. "My club will protect her, same as they would any member's old lady."

I've gathered from my time spent at the clubhouse that the title of "old lady" isn't used lightly, and among the brothers, it's the same as being someone's wife. But I have no idea if my father understands the term or its significance.

My father's gaze zeroes in on my left hand. "I see no ring." He waves a dismissive hand in the air. "Not one of your patches." Spitting out the last word like venom.

"We haven't been together that long," I explain. Why does everyone keep trying to rush us into marriage and babies? "But I love him and hope you'll be happy for me."

My father's face twists with annoyance. "Eh." He waves his hand in the air in a dismissive gesture. "Love."

Chaser pulls our intertwined hands forward, resting them on the counter in front of my father. He brushes his thumb over the back of my hand. "I love your daughter very much, sir. I will take care of her. Provide for her. Protect her."

A crack in my father's hard expression appears. A widening of his eyes as his head tilts in Chaser's direction. Chaser notices it too and continues his pledges. "I want to support and encourage all of Mallory's ambitions. Not turn her into a robo-wife or make her into my brood mare."

I squirm from the blunt statement, but my heart swells at the conviction in Chaser's voice.

"That's what Vasily would've expected of her, right?" Chaser continues.

Ah, he went one too far. My father's eyes harden. "You're an outsider to her world." He nods at me. "And she's an outsider to your world."

"You're not giving me the 'stick to your own kind' speech are you? Come on, it's 1989, join us in the twentieth century."

I don't think I've ever seen anyone speak to my father with such disrespect and survive. His unrelenting stare radiates hatred. "What can *you* possibly have in common with my daughter?"

"Our parents are in similar lines of work for starters," he deadpans.

My father casts a glance around the empty space and leans forward. "You think your rinky-dink motorcycle club is in my league, boy?"

Chaser drops his future-son-in-law act. "You know as well as I do, our businesses are frequently in competition." He squeezes my hand. "My father and my club have welcomed her."

"Yes, and wouldn't that be the perfect way to bend me to your club's needs?"

"Daddy—"

Chaser cuts off my outburst. "I get why you might see it that way, sir. And if I was in your shoes, I'd probably be thinking the same thing. But that's not what this is."

I finally understand what Chaser's father was trying to explain to me.

"Daddy, Chaser and I met in California."

"So I heard," my father says without taking his eyes off Chaser.

"Well, here's the part you haven't heard," Chaser says. His gaze searches the room as if he's trying to come up with a way to explain the situation. "I'm going to be completely straight with you, Mr. DeLova. I'm technically on leave with my club. Brothers in my charter always have my back if I need them, but I'm not in a position to conduct business on behalf of my club at the moment."

Now Chaser has my father's full attention. "And why is that, son?"

Chaser's mouth quirks as if he knows my father won't be impressed with the next portion of his story. "Sir, before I met your daughter, I only had two loves in my life. Music and the club. My father's been president as long as I can remember. Before that, my grandfather was in charge. So I grew up with the expectation I'd take over the club someday. I patched-in at fourteen, which you must realize isn't that common."

My father nods, making me believe he might understand motorcycle club life better than I expected.

"I had a band in high school with friends of mine. We were a fairly popular local band. Kodack isn't exactly known for its music scene, though, so when I turned eighteen, I moved to California to pursue music."

"You took off and deserted your family?" My father sneers. Clearly thinking he's figured out something significant about Chaser's character.

Chaser snorts and shakes his head. "Not at all. My father sent me with his blessing. I lost my voting privileges, but not my patch. Only money I had, came straight outta my personal piggy bank. I had to make it on my own. But I could come back to the club at any time."

"And what does this little family history lesson have to do with my daughter?" my father asks.

"Let me finish. The band I went out there with didn't last, but my friend and I met two other guys from another band and we formed a new group. We worked our asses off and finally landed a small record deal. I don't know how much you know about the music business out there, but the competition is extreme. Videos are a big deal. The label gave us some money to shoot something flashy." He chuckles and shakes his head. "Not quite what the band would have chosen."

I duck my head and laugh too, thinking of the tacky video.

My father just seems confused.

"*That's* where your daughter comes in. You had just been shipped off to this lovely facility." Chaser circles his hand in the air, indicating the prison surrounding us. "And she decided that instead of being enslaved by your minions, she wanted to pursue her own dreams and become an actress."

Cold fear at having my secret revealed to my father swirls in my gut. Knowing hell would freeze over before I gained his approval, I never shared my dream with him. Sure, I'd dabbled in the theater in high school, but that's not quite the same as running off to Hollywood.

Surprisingly, he turns to me with softer eyes. "You never told me this."

"I didn't think you'd approve."

"I wouldn't have," he answers honestly. "Continue," he says to Chaser.

"Anyway, your daughter was hired to play a part in that video." Chaser drapes his arm over the back of my chair. His hand grazes the side of my face, and he tucks some hair behind my ear in an affectionate gesture not missed by my father. "The second I saw her, I wanted her in my life."

I glance at Chaser. He knew that first day?

He notices me watching him and flashes a sincere smile, before turning back to my father.

"What I'm trying to explain to you, sir, is that I didn't pursue your daughter because I knew she was *your* daughter." He closes his eyes for a brief second and shakes his head. "She goes by a stage name. But even if she didn't, I don't think I would've known who she was. Remember, I've been out of club business for four years now." All humor vanishes from Chaser's face, and he sits up straighter, leans in closer to the plexiglass. "I didn't learn who she was until *after* Vasily attacked her."

Anger slashes across my father's face. "Attacked?"

"Yes, Father," I answer calmly. "He was not kind or gentle about his intentions."

Chaser takes my hand again. "I brought her back home to my club, because I knew she'd be safe there. My father's the one who recognized who she was." He glances over at me. "I love her. Doesn't matter to me who she's related to."

Some of this information is new to me or at least Chaser's characterization of it is, but oh, how my heart flutters when Chaser unequivocally declares his love for me in front of my father.

"You're telling me your father won't exploit this relationship for a business deal?"

"With all due respect, sir, not everything is about you." Chaser's mouth quirks. "I can't speak to my father's motivations. He's always looking out for the club, obviously. Just as I'm sure you're always protecting your interests."

Something in my father's hard demeanor finally breaks. "Honesty." My father actually smiles. "That, I respect."

"So do I, sir. I want to start our relationship out on the right foot."

"And why is that?"

Chaser pulls no punches. "I plan to be in your daughter's life for a long time, so I'm trying to be as straight with you as possible." He glances around the room. "Under the circumstances."

"Understood." My father leans forward. "Where did you say your hometown was?"

One corner of Chaser's mouth twitches upwards. "Kodack. But I've moved around a lot. Toronto, right outside Syracuse. Got family I stay with from time-to-time in twenty-five different states."

My father raises an eyebrow. Somehow, I don't think Chaser is describing a bunch of cousins scattered around the country. More likely this is some territory code.

"Toronto. It's supposed to be nice up there."

"It's a beautiful city," Chaser agrees.

"I've never been."

A cat-ate-the-canary grin spreads across Chaser's face. "Well, when you get out, maybe we'll take a big ol' family trip, and I can introduce you to some people."

I can't think of anything that sounds more unpleasant.

CHAPTER FORTY-THREE

CHASER

"I can't believe you managed to win over my father," Mallory says as we leave the prison and navigate the parking lot. "He's usually as ornery as *your* father."

Not wanting the extra attention, my brothers wait for us on the other side of the fenced-in parking lot.

"I wouldn't get too excited," I answer honestly. "I'm pretty sure he'd still gut me if he thought he could get away with it."

Mallory doesn't even blink. "But it's a start."

"Optimism, I like that." I lean down and kiss her cheek, before opening her door. "Buckle up, babe."

"I'm not a child, Chaser," she complains, but does as I ask. When she's seat belted in, I lock her door before closing it.

As I round the truck, my gaze roams over the parking lot, searching for anything out of place. We were visiting for an awfully long time. Plenty of opportunity for someone to call DeLova's crew and give them a head's up.

A pebble skittering over the pavement behind me has me ducking and turning around. Good thing too, because Vasily's fist flies past the spot where my neck was two seconds ago.

"Good to see you again too, Vasily." I smirk at him, and he grunts in frustration. I hold up my hands and back up a few steps, getting into position in case he comes at me again. "I'd rethink this if I were you. I just had a nice heart-to-heart with my future father-in-law."

"Chaser?" Mallory calls.

"Stay in the truck!" I shout without turning away from Vasily.

His dumb-as-an-ox face screws up into a frown. "What do you mean, you spoke to him?"

"Yup. Sorry you raced up here for nothing."

Confusion clouds his already vacant eyes. "I come every Wednesday afternoon."

Huh, well, fuck me. Maybe her daddy didn't approve of me after all. I shrug as if it's not a big deal, but I'm pissed DeLova never mentioned his goon might show up. Especially after Mallory told him what Vasily did to her.

"By the way, Mallory told her father how you treated her in California."

He shrugs, but a hint of fear crawls over his face. "I was told to bring her back any way necessary."

He continues glaring at me, but I'm not all that concerned. I already know he's a lousy fighter. I also know if he's planning to go inside those prison walls for a visit, he's not armed. Most importantly, four of my brothers are waiting on the other side of that fence watching this exchange.

"Besides, she was going to be my wife. I can treat her any damn way I want." He glances at the truck and snorts. "I assume she's no longer a virgin, so you don't have to worry. I'm not interested in marrying a whore."

"Motherfucker, say that again," I growl. My hands curl into fists, and I take a few steps closer.

"Do we have a problem, gentlemen?" A deep voice calls out from behind Vasily.

I glare at the asshole in front of me whose ass I'm about to kick and slowly uncurl my fists. Last thing I need is to get arrested and tossed in a cell next to Mallory's father. I let out a long, slow breath, willing my rage away.

"No, sir. Just ran into an old acquaintance and was saying hello," I answer smoothly.

"You two need to move it along. This isn't a hangout."

"Yes, sir. My girlfriend and I just finished visiting her father and are on our way home now." I back away and open my door. "Later, V." I give him a cocky wave and hop in the truck.

"What a dickhead," I grumble as I fire up the engine.

I glance over at Mallory, who has her hand pressed tight against her chest. "You okay?"

"No. He scared the shit out of me. Thank God no one else was with him."

"Yeah, let's hope we don't run into any of his pals," I mutter. Vasily watches us pull away. I'm not worried about him tracking the license plate. The truck isn't mine, and I'd love to see him show up at the owner's house unannounced.

We stop at the guard shack and sign out, before pulling onto the main road. A couple hundred feet further, my four brothers are waiting at a crescent-shaped pull off on the shoulder of the road.

"Everything all right?" Trigger asks, sauntering up to my side.

"Yeah. Had some trouble with the one guy on our way out, but he wasn't gonna make a scene there. I wanna hit the road before he decides to follow, though."

"Let's ride." He slaps the front of the truck and heads back to his bike.

"They're not in any danger, are they?" Mallory asks.

"No, babe. Everything's fine. Promise."

She makes a hmm sound of disbelief. After a few minutes of silence, she turns to me. "Our fathers want to go into business together, don't they?"

No one should ever assume Mallory's some dumb blonde. "Want probably isn't the right word. It would be *beneficial* to both of them is more accurate."

"Don't play semantics with me."

"Listen, like I said to your dad, I'm not in on all the inner club-going-ons right now. Even if I was, I couldn't discuss that stuff with you. Nor should I since it might put you in danger."

Out of the corner of my eye, I catch her shaking her head. "Chaser..." Her voice trails off when I think she realizes she has no good argument for why she needs details.

"We have access to an area your father's never been able to do business in before, okay? I assume my father's going to try to work that angle, so your dad leaves us alone."

"Like bartering for me? Some sort of gangster dowry? That's gross."

"It's better than the alternative."

"Which is?"

"They keep coming after you, and we retaliate with something stronger than hostile words." I glance over at her. "Your father doesn't have the most reasonable reputation in the criminal underworld."

She jolts at the word criminal. "I never really thought about that. I'm sorry."

"Don't be sorry." I reach over and take her hand. "Even if I'd known who you were that first day, I still would've fallen in love with you."

"Thank you for what you said to my father. About supporting my dreams and well, basically seeing me as a person, not an accessory."

"I meant every word."

"I know you did." She sighs and looks out the window. "I've messed up your life in a lot of ways since I came into it."

I definitely don't like the sound of where this conversation's going. "You've made it better, Mallory."

"Sure." She holds out her hand and lists off her alleged crimes. "I got you in trouble with your band. Cost you the European leg of Revolver's tour. You got hooked on cocaine because you were taking me to my auditions because I'm too dumb to realize that a hotel is probably not an appropriate audition venue. And now my father might try to have you killed or his associates will declare war on your club because we're together. None of those things are improvements."

Where to begin with that load? "I call bullshit on every single item on your list, Mallory." I reach over and put my hand in her face. "One, the guys and I fight all the time. Have been doing it since day one. We're guys. We fight, get drunk together and laugh it off. What Jacob tried to do to you went beyond our normal battles. He's lucky he's still breathing. Two, Revolver's an aging, has-been, cocksucking douche and I'm not one bit upset about missing that tour. Three, haven't you noticed I'm a possessive, jealous motherfucker? Arrogant as hell, too. We could've worked out some other way to make sure you were safe, but that didn't suit my ego. I made the decision to start snorting coke, Mallory. Not you. Because I had to prove that I could do everything all by myself."

She sniffles and bats my hand away. But I'm not going to be deterred by her crying, until she hears and understands what I'm explaining.

"And finally, our fathers are *criminals*, Mallory. They are *always* going to exploit a business opportunity when they see it. They're both smart enough to know they'll make more money if we work together."

"But my father's in prison. Even if he tells whoever's in charge now not to come after you, they might not—"

"Mallory, honey, I love you, but you have no idea how many criminal enterprises are run from prison. I'm pretty confident your father is still very much in charge. Why the fuck else you think Vasily is driving all the way up here once a week to visit him? It ain't out of brotherly concern, sweetheart, I assure you."

"Don't call me sweetheart."

I tickle my fingers over her shoulder and into the crook of her neck. "No? What should I call you? Darlin'? Sugar pie? Baby girl?"

"No, no, and no!" She giggles and jerks her shoulder away from my hand.

"I'm done talking about our parents for today." I stop teasing her and put my hand back on the wheel. "I'm already gonna get grilled by my dad when we get home."

"Fine." She crosses her arms over her chest. "What do you want to talk about?"

I glance over, my eyes zeroing in on that tight green sweater dress clinging to her legs and keeping everything from her shins up out of view. Reaching over, I slide the material up, revealing her thigh. "How hard I'm going to fuck you when we get home."

She tries to push my hand off, but I strengthen my grip.

"Stop, you're going to put a run in my pantyhose."

"Little dove, I've been planning to rip a big ol' hole in those things ever since I saw you wiggle your fine ass into them this morning."

"Oh, no you're not."

"Oh, yes I am." I slide my hand up farther, pushing between her tightly clenched thighs until my knuckles graze her hot center. "Gonna bend you over and rip 'em right here and then shove my dick in your tight pussy."

"Chaser," she whispers.

"Fuck," I glance down. "See how hard I am now?"

She chuckles and reaches over. "Ooo. Too bad we're still about an hour from home."

"Don't test me, woman. I got no problem pulling over on the side of the road. Be a good story for the guys to tell everyone when we get back."

She giggles and pushes my hand away. "Don't you dare."

"Yeah, you're right. Can't risk anyone getting a peek at *the* Mallory Dove getting fucked by rock star Chaser Adams."

She laughs even harder at my shitty entertainment television host voice.

"Thank you." She crosses her legs, and her skirt rises a few inches.

"You're killing me," I mutter.

CHAPTER FORTY-FOUR

CHASER

Do I get to go home and fuck my woman like I want?

No. No, I don't.

Club comes first, whether I'm an active member at the moment or not.

Mallory pouts for a second, before rising up on tiptoes. "I'll be waiting in your room wearing my stockings and nothing else," she whispers in my ear.

I groan and grab her hip, keeping her close. "What are you trying to do to me, woman?"

"Motivate you." She kisses my cheek, gives me a flirty wave and trots off down the hallway.

Behind me, Trigger whistles. I turn to find him rubbing his hand over his crotch and shaking his head.

"You better have a case of crabs and not be jerking yourself to my girlfriend." First Tally taking my girl out to the fuckin' movies, and now this asshole.

"Sorry, brother. She's a fine woman. Don't fuck that up. Lotta men would be willing to treat her right."

"Fuck you."

"You're not my type." He glances down the hall. "Now, Mallory on the other hand—"

"Don't." I hold up both hands. "Go there, brother. I will straight up gut you."

He laughs and claps me on the back.

"Don't touch me with your damn dick-rubbing hands." I jerk my shoulder out of his grasp.

The shit I'm subjected to when I come home.

Shaking my head, I follow the others into our war room.

"Sure I'm allowed in here, Pop?" I ask as I pass my dad and get a smack on the back of the head in response.

"Child abuser," I joke.

He shakes his head, but I can tell he's trying not to laugh. "Sit your ass down."

Once everyone's in their seat, my father slaps his palm on the table to get their attention.

"How'd it go with DeLova?" he starts.

"Better than I expected. He's not thrilled, but I don't think he's gonna try and off me any time soon. Kinda what we thought, he wanted to make sure she was with me willingly and that she was happy."

"Aw, ain't that precious," one of my brothers says.

"Fuck off," I growl.

My father slaps the table in front of me. "Continue."

"He wants to move into Toronto like we expected. Never been able to get into that market before."

"Yeah, because they're a bunch of bloodthirsty backstabbers," Dice shouts. "We can't be getting into business with Russians, Prez. You know this."

"We have a different relationship now. DeLova's not gonna put his daughter at risk."

"Yeah, and what about when Chaser fucks it up and Mallory dumps his sorry ass?" Trick asks. "DeLova will take it out on every one of us."

"Fuck you," I snap. "That's fucking bullshit."

"All right. Calm the fuck down." He points at Trick. "You're not the best person to be offering relationship advice. Watch yourself." He shuffles through a few papers in front of him. "Who do we have at that facility?"

"Jesus," Trigger groans. "Angelo's there."

"All right, I need you to pay him a visit. Explain he needs to make friends with DeLova. See what we can work out with their crew. We'll take care of whatever he needs."

My father glances around the table, taking yes votes from everyone. Only one brother objects, which won't stop the club from moving forward.

More delicate club business needs to be discussed, and my father sends me out of the room for that. I'm not insulted. It's the choice I made when I decided to pursue music over the club. Speaking of, I take the couple free moments to give Alvin a call.

"When the fuck you coming back?" Alvin shouts. "Shit's been crazy since you left."

"Jesus Christ, really?" I run my hand over my face. "Jacob get clean?"

"He's been trying hard." He lowers his voice. "Are *you* okay?"

"Never better, honestly. It was rough at first, but I'm feeling sane again."

"Thank fuck," he mutters. "When you coming back?"

"Next week?" I have important plans to put in motion before we head back to California.

"I sent you a copy of *LA Pulse*. You're on the cover." Even if I wanted to, I doubt I could find the weekly gossip rag in Kodack easily. Something Alvin knows. "Thanks, but why? I'm not even in L.A."

"Yeah, no shit. That's what the headline says: "Where's Chaser Adams?""

I snort. "No kidding? Didn't think I was that big a deal."

"The video has blown the fuck up. Have you bothered to turn on a television while you've been home? Andrew Lane did an interview with MTV, all about how Kickstart is his new favorite band. 'Candy Jar' has been number one on *Dial MTV* ever since."

My jaw drops as the news sinks in. The way the entertainment industry moves, that video should be old news by now. Andrew managed to breathe some life into the video Davey Revolver tried to kill. *Dial MTV?* Shit, Alvin and I used to call in to vote for videos after school all the time when we were teenagers. "Are you serious?"

"Don't let it go to your head. Most of the chatter has revolved around how hot Mallory is and whether the two of you are a 'real' couple."

"As opposed to a fake one?"

He snorts. "Yeah." In a lower voice he adds. "Jacob's not taking it well. The singer's usually the one who gets all the attention."

I roll my eyes. "What do you want me to do about it? I'm not fanning those flames. As you helpfully pointed out, I'm not even there."

"Just passing along information."

"How's Val feel about all of this?" It's been a while since I checked in with her, so it's weird I haven't gotten a "where the fuck are you" call.

He hesitates. "I don't know."

"Chaser!" my father yells. "Get your ass over here!"

"That the old man?" Alvin chuckles.

"Yeah, I gotta go. I'll call you when we're leaving."

"Make it soon. The record company's running out of patience. They want these demos finished. We've gone way over budget already." He lowers his voice. "I told them you had a family emergency and that's why you went home."

"Thanks, brother. Appreciate that."

"Tell your dad I said hi."

"Will do. Hang in there. I'll be back soon."

"Who you callin' brother?" my father asks when I hang up the phone.

"Alvin."

He smirks. "How is that kid?"

"He's the only sane one out of the four of us. He says hello, by the way."

"Think he's interested in slapping a patch on his back?" He turns and marches toward his office, expecting me to follow.

Out of my three bandmates, Alvin's the only one who could probably handle club life. "Maybe. One day."

My father closes the door behind us and points to the chair across from his desk. "Sit down."

Wary of whatever's on his mind, I take my seat. At least my odds of getting choked today should be low.

"Where you at?"

"Feel good. Better than I have in a while."

"Tell me straight now. How'd Mallory do with her dad?"

My mouth pulls into a quick smile. "She did good. I was proud of her. I don't think she's ever spoken up for herself with him before."

"She's a sassy one." He laughs. "Good for her. I'm sure DeLova was thrilled."

"He was definitely surprised."

"Where are *you* two at?"

I drum my fingers against the table, considering whether I should answer my father's question honestly. I'm really not in the mood for him to try and talk me out of my future plans.

"She's the one. I need more time sober under my belt and then I'm asking her to marry me."

He absorbs the news slowly, sitting back in his chair, but keeping his eyes on me. "You move her out of that shitty apartment yet?"

I glance away. "Not yet. The guys are right downstairs, so it's easy for us to collaborate. Mallory understands."

"Just because she understands, doesn't mean you should subject her to living in squalor. You got any idea the kind of home she probably grew up in?"

"That stuff doesn't matter to her." At least I don't think it does. "She's not materialistic at all."

"It seems fun and romantic now, but eventually, it'll wear on her." His jaw ticks. "I don't want to know how you got hooked on coke, but a change of environment now that you're clean is in your best interest."

If anyone else offered up so much advice on my living arrangements, I'd tell 'em to fuck off by now. But the old man has a point. "I'll look for a place when we get back."

"Good. Got a ring?"

Okay, not the question I expected from him. "Uh, planning to stop over at the Treasure Box before we head back to L.A. Maybe put some money down if I find the right one."

"Good. Bruce should be able to find whatever you want."

"That was my thought."

"Where you plannin' on proposing?"

I run my hands through my hair. Really wasn't expecting Dad to have so much interest in this subject, given his feelings about marriage, monogamy, and women in general. "I haven't gotten that far yet. Maybe Niagara Falls?"

Pain slashes through his features. "I took your mother there for our honeymoon."

Fuck, really? I search my brain, turning over memories I've buried for years. Did I know that? Is that what made me think it was a good idea? "I didn't realize."

"It's nice," he says absently.

"You okay?"

"I'm fine." He seems to rejoin me here in the present. "Go take care of your girl. Spend some time with her. Amazed she can still tolerate you."

So am I. "Thanks."

"You need money for the ring?" He jerks his chin at me and reaches for his wallet.

Did my father just offer me money for an engagement ring? Maybe someone needs to take his temperature or check if he's had a stroke.

"No. You've done enough for us. I appreciate it."

"Make sure you pick out a nice rock for her. Something classy."

I lift my chin and smirk at him. "You sweet on my girl, Pop?"

He snorts and waves his hand in the air. "Hard not to be. Seems to be good to you and *for* you. She deserves something nice."

Christ, maybe he's dying.

"Are you sure you're okay?"

"I'm fine," he growls. "I want my only son to be happy, so shoot me."

"Thanks." Time to go before he gets agitated. "Do me a favor and don't say anything to anyone. I don't want Doe or one of the girls to ruin the surprise."

"I'm not in the habit of gossiping with the ladies, son."

He stands, and I try to give him a hug, but he brushes me off. "Get out of here with that touchy-feely shit."

CHAPTER FORTY-FIVE

CHASER

It's dark in my room. Mallory's bright blonde hair spills over my pillows, and her soft breathing reassures me. After the morning we had, I'm sure she's exhausted. I stand there staring at her for a while. Looks like she slipped into one of my T-shirts before crawling under the covers. How the hell am I supposed to climb beneath those sheets and keep my hands off her sweet curves?

With her sleep-tousled hair and scrubbed-clean face, she looks so young, standing here drooling over her makes me feel like one hell of a creepy bastard.

I strip down to my boxers and peel the covers back. The same see-through nylon I've been dreaming about ripping holes in all day covers her legs. The shirt's all twisted around her hips, leaving her pantyhose-covered ass exposed.

"Hope you had a good nap," I mutter.

She sighs and half-turns when I slide into bed behind her.

I'm painfully hard as I pull her closer. I brush my lips over her ear. "Little dove, your man needs you."

"Does it involve an orgasm?" She shoves her face in her pillow and giggles.

Oh, game on.

"Fuck yeah, it does." I run my tongue over the line of her shoulder to her neck, and she shivers.

"Chaser."

I slide my hand under her shirt, grazing soft, warm skin, before finally cupping one of her breasts.

"Uh," she moans and tilts her head back for more kisses and licks against her neck.

"Take this off," I mutter, tugging on the shirt.

Quicker than I expected, she sits up and tosses the T-shirt to the side.

Before I can get my greedy hands on her breasts, she kneels up. "I fell asleep dreaming about you." She throws one leg over me, straddling my hips. "What took you so long?"

She doesn't wait for an answer. Nope, Mallory's feeling bold this afternoon, and I like it a hell of a lot. Her fingers trace my waistband, tugging at the boxers while I admire her bare breasts.

I reach up, brushing my thumb over her nipples, then travel lower, teasing my fingers down her belly and between her legs. "Fuck, you're soaked."

Her lips purse. "You worked me up on the ride home. Promising to take care of me. Then you abandoned me." Aw, Christ, that pouty-baby voice thing she does totally turns my crank.

"I'm here now."

"Maybe I already took care of myself." Her defiant chin lift makes me want to pin her to the mattress.

"Did you? That's fucking hot." I grab her hand and lick her fingers. "Don't taste any pussy, though."

She shrieks and yanks her hand away, laughing.

I sit up, wedging my hand more firmly between her thighs and push my fingers into the delicate material of her pantyhose, until I'm rewarded with a satisfying rip.

"Spread your legs," I demand, thrusting two fingers inside her. "You're so fucking wet."

She digs her little nails into my shoulders and throws her head back. "I told you."

"That's it," I encourage as she grinds herself against my hand. "Show me what you want."

"You," she gasps.

"Right here, little dove. What do you want from me?"

"I...I want..."

"Yeah?"

At my cocky tone, she snaps her head up and glares. She tugs at my boxers, and this time, I lift my hips, so she can slide them off. When I have her attention again, I slowly lick the fingers I'd had inside her.

She wraps her hands around my rock-hard dick and slowly strokes until I groan.

"How does it feel to be teased?" she asks.

"Really good." I give her my cocky-bastard smile and squeeze my eyes shut, so I can concentrate on her touch.

"You're the devil," she grumbles, making me laugh.

"Technically, I'm a Demon." I wink at her. "And I'm *your* sex god."

"Is that right?" She shifts, lining herself up, so she can slowly slide down my cock. "Hang on, I'm about to worship you. Hard."

"Ah, fuck," I groan and open my eyes, so I can watch her. "Fuck, little dove. You're so sexy."

A hoarse cry spills from her lips as she bottoms out. She stays there for a second, rocking back and forth. I reach down and rip the stockings even more, and she moans.

"Like my girl taking what she wants," I whisper, flicking my thumb over her clit. I'm guessing Mallory's feeling empowered from asserting herself with her father today, and fuck if I'm not reaping the rewards. "Ride my cock."

I grip her hip with one hand and press my other palm against her belly, urging her back and forth. "There you go. Want to see you come."

"I...I..." she stutters, her mouth falling open.

"Already?" Damn, she makes me feel like a king.

She grips my forearms and rides me harder, faster until her thighs tremble, and she's screaming.

Love when she can't even form a complete sentence.

She keeps riding and vocalizing the sexiest damn sounds until I can't hold off.

"Mal—" I try to warn her.

Her eyes pop open, and she stares down at me with a soft smile. That magic pussy of hers squeezes even harder, and I'm gone.

She keeps working me, slower and slower, until I finish then lowers herself, resting against my chest. She trails her lips along my jaw, kissing and licking. "I love every second with you, Chaser," she whispers against my ear, wiggling her hips to put extra emphasis on her sweet words.

I reach down and squeeze her ass, shredding what's left of her stockings. "Keep it up and I'll do it again."

Soft laughter spills from her lips. She rolls off me and snuggles up against my side, resting her hand against my chest. "Is everything okay?"

"Everything is great." I curl my arm around her and hold on tight.

Mallory

My heart's still racing. Not that I want to compare Chaser to anyone else, or God forbid want him to compare *me* to anyone else, but I'm curious.

"Chaser?"

"Hmm?"

"Is it always like this?"

He turns and stares at me for a few seconds.

"This amazing, legs shaking, heart thumping feeling," I add.

He brushes his knuckles over my cheek. "No, little dove. It's not."

"I didn't mean—"

"I know what you meant." He presses a soft kiss to my lips.

I run my hand over his chest, stopping to feel his heart thud against my palm.

"I want to find us a better apartment when we go back." Chaser's words rumble against my ear as he holds me.

"What made you think of that now?"

"You deserve a nicer place to live. I should've found us a better place months ago, but my head's been lodged up my ass."

What the hell did he and Stump discuss? "We've had a lot going on, and it made sense for you to live close to the guys."

At the mention of his band, he turns away. "My head's finally clear, and I don't want to backslide because I'm around them twenty-four seven."

I certainly want to do everything possible to support him. "I understand. Talk to the guys when we get back."

"It doesn't matter what they have to say. Either way, we're moving."

I shrug. "I wish we could afford a small house."

"Yeah, I'd like somewhere safer for you while I'm on tour."

I hate thinking about him away for three whole months.

"Hey." He cups my cheek. "What's that look?"

"Nothing. I'm excited for you."

"You know I'm going to miss you, right?"

"Yes."

"You're going to come and visit me." He sits up and groans. "I need a nap after that workout."

"Did I wear the great Chaser Adams out?" I tease.

"Yes." He turns his head to the side and checks out the clock on the nightstand. "Actually, forget the nap. I have a few errands to run. Why don't you stay here and relax?"

"How am I supposed to go back to sleep now? I'll come with you."

He hesitates and averts his eyes. My stomach drops. What does he have to do that he wants to keep a secret?

"Uh, you can't. It's something my dad asked me to do. A club thing."

I detect a lie. "Chaser?" My voice begs for the truth.

He shakes his head. "It won't take long. Honest."

After everything we've been through, so help me God, if he comes back high, I'm going to *kill* him.

CHAPTER FORTY-SIX

CHASER

A large manila envelope's jammed into our mailbox when we leave the clubhouse and return to the house later.

Where's Chaser Adams? the headline asks, just as Alvin described.

Alvin's big blocky handwriting screams, *We need you!* on a piece of paper tucked inside.

Mallory scans the article as she follows me into the house.

"Chaser Adams and his busty, blonde beauty, Mallory Dove," Mallory reads in a bubbly, entertainment newscaster voice. "Well, at least they used my name this time." She sticks her chest out and wiggles her shoulders. "I don't know. Am I really *that* busty that they need to mention my boobs *every single time?*"

"Give me that." I snatch the paper from her hands and toss it on the coffee table. "You're perfect, and if I ever meet any of the pukes who write that garbage about you, I'm going to beat the shit out of them."

"Is that your answer for everything?"

"Yes," I answer automatically.

"There are worse things they could say about me, I guess."

I glance at the clock on the living room wall and hurry over to flip on the television. "You're going to love this."

"What?" She follows me over and stares at the screen as the big-haired video deejay announces the number one video of the day.

"You guys can't get enough of this video! Kickstart with their hit, 'Candy Jar,' number one for the tenth day in a row. Amazing!"

"Oh. My. God." Mallory covers her mouth with both hands.

"Yup, according to Alvin, the video has risen from the ashes."

"That's why the tabloids are suddenly so interested in us?"

"No doubt."

She groans. "Does that mean more people are going to ask me if I banged Jacob?"

"Probably." I lean down and kiss her forehead. "I know the truth. That's all that matters."

"Chaser, you know I'm excited for you guys, right? This is huge. I don't mean to be a downer."

"I get why you're hesitant. Trust me, I feel the same way. I was hoping this video would die in the avalanche of cheesy glam metal videos produced this year, but..." I have to stop and laugh here. "Apparently, Andrew gave an interview where he raved about Kickstart so much, the video was brought back from the dead."

Finally, she loosens up and actually laughs. "After all his

crazy, obnoxious antics, he has to go and do something sweet that makes it impossible to hate him."

My girl referring to Andrew as "sweet" doesn't exactly sit well with me. "I'm sure it had more to do with getting us more exposure, so when we announce the tour, tickets will sell out."

"Of course." She rubs her hands together. "Oh, how I'd love to see the look on Davey Revolver's face. Guess he doesn't have as much influence as he thought."

"Can't overrule the will of the fans. They must've been lighting up the phone lines at MTV to do this. The nudge from Andrew certainly helped, but the rest is all the fans."

"Well," she glances around the house, "Then we should probably get back to L.A. soon."

CHAPTER FORTY-SEVEN

CHASER

Mallory and I barely set down our luggage in our apartment before I head downstairs to announce my return.

"You're back!" Alvin slams into me so hard, he almost knocks me over. "Fuck, I'm so glad to see you." He squeezes me one last time, before holding me at arm's length. "You look *much* better."

"Thanks."

"Look who the cat dragged in!" Jacob runs over and high-fives me.

"You all right?" I search his face for signs he's strung out, but he's energetic and actually seems to have put on a few pounds. "You look good."

"I'm clean, laid down my vocals, and ready to tour."

My gaze slides to Alvin who half-shrugs and nods. "Just need to finish the one song."

"All right."

Garrett joins us and also seems even.

"Should we set up a meeting with Val and see what's next?" I can't remember the last time I went so long without Val checking up on me.

"Well, about that." Jacob takes a step back and rubs his hand over the back of his neck, a sure sign he's about to say something to piss me off.

"Yeah?" I ask carefully.

Jacob glances at Garrett then Alvin, who looks away.

"We had a crisis while you were away."

"What was that?"

"We all know things weren't headed in the right direction with Val anymore." He turns his hands palm up. "Like how she couldn't get us a simple meeting with Cutter until Andrew stepped in."

"Says the guy who almost blew Cutter's offer by taking forever to record his vocals," I remind him.

"Agreed," Jacob concedes. "But a stronger manager would've seen that we were in trouble and helped steer us in the right direction."

"Are you serious right now? A month and a half ago, I was talking your drunk ass off a ledge. How exactly was Val supposed to prevent *that*?"

"After the shit she did setting Mallory up with Davey, I thought you'd be thrilled," Jacob says.

"As if you weren't a part of that grand scheme."

"Where do you think the idea came from?" he insists.

That doesn't quite have the ring of truth to it, but it's over and done with, and I don't feel like rehashing the past. "What are you trying to say?"

Garrett steps up. "We fired Val and hired Thom Woodworth."

I take a second to let the monumental shift in our career

sink in. "Without even *asking* me? Are you fucking kidding?"

Jacob shrugs. "You were away in New York. It all went down rather fast."

I drill Alvin with a look. "You didn't think to call me?"

"What was I supposed to do? I didn't want to upset you. You getting better was more important."

"What did she say?"

Jacob smirks. "She was pissed, but in the end, I think she understood."

"You're an asshole."

"You'll like Thom," Garrett says. "He's already smoothed things over with the record company for us. He's got the details of the Vicious Vandals tour ironed out too."

"You sure were busy."

Jacob has the nerve to clap my shoulder and give me a smug smile. "You were right. Everything became so much clearer once I embraced sobriety."

It's probably a mistake, but I need to pay Val a visit. I can't find her at her office. I finally track her down at her house.

"Chaser." Her posture's stiff as she opens the door wider. "I didn't expect to see you ever again."

"I didn't know what they were planning, Val."

She cocks her head and spears me with a *get serious* look.

"I didn't." I hold up my hands. "I swear. I just got back into town and found out."

"I figured." She eyes me more critically. "You look better. Healthy."

"I know it was shitty timing, but I had to go home and get cleaned up."

"Good. I was worried about you." She bites her lip. "Jacob used the opportunity to clean house too."

"I'm sorry they fired you behind my back, Val."

"It's fine." She flicks her wrist at the door. "I probably took Kickstart as far as I could anyway. You're going to be at the level where execs won't want to deal with a female manager. I would've held you back."

She worked her ass off for us for years. Took a chance on a young, unknown band when few people would take us seriously. And yet, she's probably right. "That fucking sucks, Val."

"It is what it is." She shrugs. "As much as I think Thom Woodworth's a vile snake, he has deep connections in this industry. He'll be able to open doors for Kickstart I'd need a crowbar to pry loose. You guys don't need me anymore."

I don't know about that. Jacob's always leaned toward the type of advisors who kiss his ass and tell him whatever he wants to hear. While Val did her fair share of massaging our egos, she wasn't afraid to dole out an ass-kicking when we needed it either.

"Jacob's been a handful these last few months." She pats the top of her head. "Given me my first gray hairs. I still worry about him, though. I'd definitely keep him away from Mallory."

Jacob's said and done some questionable shit, but I don't see him making a play for Mallory. "That's rich coming from the woman who tried to hand my girlfriend over to Davey Revolver."

She snorts and shakes her head. "You really think a sexist pig like Davey would talk business with me? He and Jacob cooked up that plan on their own. He told me about it, but it wasn't my idea."

I blow out a breath because, honestly, her version makes more sense than Jacob's. "Why didn't you say so at the time?"

"And throw more gasoline on that fire? No fucking way. I was afraid it would rip the band in half and you guys worked too hard to throw it all the way over—"

She stops herself and I groan. "Over a woman?"

"Well, yeah."

"Mallory wouldn't let me do that."

"I understand that, Chaser. I meant it when I said I was sorry. It was a shitty thing to do."

"It's done, Val."

"I'm glad you cleaned yourself up." She scowls. "I've heard through the grapevine Jacob and Garrett are sober too. I doubt that will last."

I can't even disagree because I have my own doubts. "I'll do what I can to help them, but I have to guard my own sobriety."

"If anyone can inspire them, it's you." She bites her lip and looks away for a second. "You're all excellent musicians, Chaser. From the first time I saw you guys live, I knew you'd be huge one day."

"I'm pretty sure that's how you introduced yourself to us." I stick my hand out and mimic an enthusiastic, younger Val. "Hi, I'm Val, and I want to make you bigger than Van Halen."

She laughs. "I was an eager little beaver, wasn't I?" More seriously she adds, "You're all special in your own way, but you're the anchor, the cornerstone of the band. Hate me for saying it all you want, but if Garrett or Alvin left, the band would probably still be able to fill their slots and soldier on. If you or Jacob leave, Kickstart's finished."

"Come on, Val."

"It's the truth."

"No one's leaving the band. I think we've all accepted that we're bound together until the end of eternity."

"Have you? You have other stuff outside the band. They don't. You told me a long time ago you always planned to go home and take over your father's motorcycle club. Music has been nothing but a fun diversion for you."

"I'm not sure how much fun it's been lately, Val. Even so, I'm still committed to the band."

"Now you have Mallory too. You don't need them as much as they need you."

As much as I know my future resides in New York at the head of the Devil Demons MC's table, I've never envisioned music *not* being a part of my life. "I'm not throwing in the towel, yet. We still have a platinum album to earn."

She smiles at the memory. One of the first things Val asked when she started working with us was to define our biggest goal. We'd easily said having an album go platinum with the eagerness of a green band with no fucking clue how the music industry works.

"You'll do it. Jacob and Garrett might be backstabbing fuckers who deserve to have their dicks rot off." She takes a breath. "But I'll always be team Kickstart. I'm rooting for you to go all the way."

CHAPTER FORTY-EIGHT

MALLORY

While Chaser catches up with the band, I listen to the fifteen or so messages from my agent and give her call.

"What's up, Marilyn?"

"Jesus, please tell me you're finally back in town?"

"Just got in." I yawn as the three-hour time difference wallops me upside the head.

"Good. Listen, *Shallow End* wants you to come in again. The casting agent was adamant that she wants *you*."

"Really?"

"Don't get too excited. It's a two-episode gig, but I have a feeling that if they like you, it might turn into a recurring role."

She gives me the details of when and where to show up. I hang onto my professionalism as long as possible but finally whoop for joy after hanging up the phone.

"What's got you so excited?" Chaser asks as he walks in the door.

Breathless, I relay everything Marilyn said.

"Seriously? The show Pamela snagged?"

I growl at the reminder. "Yes, supposedly, they specifically asked for me. It's only two episodes but—"

"That's fantastic. I'm so proud of you."

I slap his chest. "We can talk about that later. What happened?"

Chaser shares the details of his visit with Valerie. While she might not have been my favorite person in the world, I can't help but feel bad. "Poor Val. I'm proud of you, though. It took guts to go visit her."

"I wanted her to know I didn't agree to letting her go. If I'd had a problem with her representation, I would've said it to her face."

"Naturally." One thing Chaser's not afraid to do is share his opinions.

"Enough about that. What else did your agent say?"

"I need to be on set Thursday."

"Wow, that was fast."

"I know, right?" I bite my lip. "What's next for you?"

He shrugs. "As much as I don't like it, I guess I have to sit down with Thom and give the guy a fair shot."

Chaser

I'm trying hard not to be an asshole, but I can't help feeling like our new manager's a bit of a snake who slithered his way into representing the band.

"Hear him out," Alvin pleads on the sidewalk outside Thom's office. "I'm not thrilled about the way it all went down either, but he does have some good ideas for us."

"All right." I trust Alvin's opinion, and it's not like rehiring Val's an option.

Thom's a big, loud, suit-wearing type of guy who stands to shake my hand when I enter his office. "Good to finally sit down with you, Chaser."

"Nice to officially meet you." I manage to shave off enough of my sarcastic tone to almost sound professional.

"Now," he says, once we're all settled, "I just got off the phone with Cutter. He's got your demo, and he'll let us know what he thinks."

"That's it?" Alvin asked. So much for giving the guy a chance.

"Well, the record company wants to release the four songs as an EP before you start the Vicious Vandals tour."

"Fucking great." Jacob snarls and jumps out of his chair. "Are you kidding me? We bled for every one of those songs and now we're supposed to drop 'em on a half-assed EP?"

"Isn't this what we wanted? To put as much of our heart and soul into our songs and into the world?" Alvin asks.

"Yeah, but an EP is never going to sell as well as a full album," Garrett points out.

"Not necessarily true," Thom says. "It's a good way to keep your name on the minds of people who can't get to see you in concert. A little give back to the fans. Plus, you'll have more material to pull from for your set."

"That's true." Jacob finally stops his furious pacing.

As much as I don't want to agree with Thom about anything, I like his take on the matter. The fact that he seems to be able to get through to Jacob is a bonus.

"They want you to add four live tracks as well," Thom continues.

Here's where I need to add my two cents. "We don't have any decent quality live recordings."

"You'd be surprised how many 'live' albums were actually recorded in a studio." Thom skewers Jacob with a no-bullshit stare. "This needs to be done quickly. No perfectionist, drama bullshit. 'Candy Jar' needs to be one of the tracks. I'd suggest 'Hammer to the Heart' and two cover songs to round out the list. A Shooting Fences' song and a Vicious Vandals' song might be good choices, but it's up to you."

Thom finishes that "up to you" part with his eyes focused on *me*. Someone must have explained that I enjoy being told what to do as much as any man enjoys a donkey kick to the nuts.

"What about 'We Die Young?'" Alvin suggests. "That used to be our favorite Vandals song."

"That's a good one." I'd certainly played the song enough when we were younger. Still remember every note.

"Decent choice." Thom sits back and nods. "The lawyers can work out the licensing for the song, but I don't think it's going to be a problem. Shooting Fences might be harder, but there's a lot of goodwill there from the shows you did with them."

Guess they forgave us for Jacob's streaking through the hotel antics that weekend.

"Have fun with the live songs. Rough 'em up a little," Thom suggests.

"Oh!" Jacob shouts and claps his hands. "Fuck yeah. We can do a totally gritty version of 'Candy Jar.'"

"'*Let me slide my hand in your Candy Jar*' isn't sleazy enough for you?" I ask.

"Yeah, but the album version is so clean and upbeat, you have to really listen to realize the lyrics are dirty."

Garrett's practically bouncing out of his seat. "Jacob could sing in a lower register, and we could slow it down a bit, really grind it out, make it totally punk-rock."

I'm not so sure I agree with the punk-rock goal, but

anything to make that song less of a cheesefest is fine with me, since it's apparently going to haunt me until the day I die.

"All right." Thom claps his hands together and stands. "Studio time's been booked. Work on your two songs while I get the approval for the Vandals' cover. And give me a title for the Shooting Fences song, so I can work on that."

"What about 'Fire Me Up?'" I suggest. It's a classic. One of my dad's favorites. Probably one of the first songs I learned how to play. Plus, I want to decide this before leaving Thom's office, so Jacob and Garrett don't make the decision behind my back later.

"That's been done a bunch of times," Jacob complains.

"Yeah, but that's a great one to put our spin on," Garrett says. "Lots of room for interpretation. We all know it by heart."

"I'm in," Alvin adds.

"Three to one." Thom stares at Jacob with a raised eyebrow. "What do you say?"

"All right. Let's do it."

CHAPTER FORTY-NINE

MALLORY

"We did it!" Chaser announces.

"You finished?"

"Yup."

Right under the wire too. The guys are supposed to leave for their tour next month.

"Chaser!" I jump up and hug him so hard, we almost topple to the floor.

"We nailed 'Queen of the Road.' It's fucking amazing." He kisses the tip of my nose. "It will always remind me of you."

"I'm honored."

"I think that's why it took me so long. The universe wouldn't let me have the full song until you came into my life."

My heart melts at his sweet words. "You're my whole universe."

"Same, little dove."

I slide my arms around his neck and reach up to kiss him. "Do you want to celebrate?"

"Definitely. But we're meeting downstairs to try and come up with a name for the EP."

"You don't have a name, yet?"

"We have several, we just can't agree on any of them."

"You need a fifth member to be a tie-breaker."

"No, thanks. I have my hands full as it is."

We head downstairs where the loud sounds of a porno greet us. Apparently, in their quest to remain sober, Jacob and Garrett have taken up marathon viewings of adult films.

Jacob grins at us from the couch. "See, I'm doing my part to stay sober."

"Great," Chaser mutters. "Can we mute this?"

"Wait, wait." He sits up and points at the screen. "This is my favorite part. Look how hot she is when she bends over in those heels and nothing else."

"That's great, buddy." Chaser slaps Jacob's shoulder. "Are we coming up with a name or not?"

"Fuck, yeah!" Alvin shouts, slamming his hand over the off button on the television.

"At least stop the tape, so I can watch it later," Jacob mutters, crawling across the living room to punch the stop button on the VCR.

"All right. Let's do this." Jacob wiggles his fingers in the air. "Hit me with your best stuff."

Just like they did with the lyrics for 'Queen of the Road,' the guys throw a bunch of words at each other, picking them apart and adding to the ideas as they go.

"Affection for Mayhem!" Garrett shouts.

"Veto." Chaser shakes his head. "Too close to *Appetite for Destruction*."

Garrett consults the notepad on his lap. "I have a lot in this general category. I'm guessing Craving for Carnage is out too?"

"What are we a death metal band now?" Chaser asks. "Hard pass."

"Lust for Victory?"

"Boo!" Alvin jeers.

"Fuckers," Garrett mutters. "I'm out."

"Thirst for Danger?" Jacob suggests.

"Lame." Chaser gives that one two thumbs down and gets a middle finger from Jacob in return.

"Havoc and Hell?" Alvin tosses out.

"That's what we should name this apartment, not an album," Jacob says.

"Strangle the Truth," Chaser suggests.

"What are we a death metal band now?" Garrett mimics Chaser's earlier comment in a snide tone.

"No." Jacob snaps his fingers. "I like that direction. Truth and Lies..." He closes his eyes and mutters a few words. "Lies and Trust."

"*Lies and Other Promises!*" Chaser raises both fists in the air.

"Yes!" Alvin flies across the room to high-five Chaser.

"That's the one!" Jacob dances in a little circle. "Perfect. Now I feel better about putting out an album with those bullshit 'live' tracks."

"Oh, fuck yeah!" Garrett pumps his fist in the air. "Our secret FU to the label for that one."

Giddy over their accomplishment, I clap my hands and let out a happy *squee.*

"You like it, Mallory?" Jacob asks.

Afraid it's a trick question, I answer slowly. "I think it's perfect."

"It's settled!" Jacob claps his hands over his head. "*Lies and*

Other Promises is the name of our EP." He points to the door. "Let's go give Thom the good news."

"Now?" Alvin casts a look at the phone. "Shouldn't we call?"

After twenty minutes of bickering and another ten minutes spent tracking Thom down, we file downstairs. We squeeze into Alvin's car with me on Chaser's lap in the passenger seat.

"Hey!" Jacob pops his head up front. "Why couldn't I sit on Chaser's lap? My legs are longer than yours, Mallory."

"But you weigh more." Chaser twists around to place his palm over Jacob's face and shove him.

"What'd you think of that chick?" Jacob pops right back into the spot like our very own Jack-in-the-Box. "Misty Stars is the girl's name. Hot, right?"

"The porno?" Chaser asks. "Why? You planning to stalk her?"

"Maybe. She has the biggest set of tits I've ever seen on such a tiny girl." Jacob cups his own chest to demonstrate. "It's enough to make me want to be a one-girl man."

"Lucky her," I mutter.

Chaser can't keep the grin off his face. He leans down to whisper in my ear, "Fucking love when you give him shit."

Thom's brimming with energy when we arrive. He has his secretary bring us drinks and eagerly waves us into his office. I end up wedged between Chaser and the corner of the low, leather couch that lines one wall.

"We've got a title," Jacob announces.

"Finally. What'd you come up with?"

Jacob pauses and raises his hands as if he's spelling it out in neon lights. "*Lies and Other Promises.*"

Thom sits back in his cushy leather chair and nods slowly. "I like it. I've got some feelers out for artwork and should have some for you to look through in a couple of days. In the meantime, if you see anything, let me know."

The proud papa moment fades, and Thom sits forward, spearing each of the guys with a no-nonsense stare. He lingers on Jacob the longest.

"You're all set up at Sound World to mix the album. Please do *not* give Tony any grief. He squeezed you guys in as a favor to me. It should be cut and dry."

Famous last words, Thom, I want to say, but I keep my mouth shut.

He'll learn.

Warning issued, Thom relaxes his posture. "Now, for the really good news." He brandishes a piece of paper in front of him. "The nominations for the Small Screen Music Awards will be announced tomorrow, but I was able to procure a list in advance."

"Holy shit." Jacob squirms in his seat and turns to look at his bandmates. "Did we really get nominated?"

"You were nominated all right." Thom sets the paper down in front of him and mutters, "I still can't believe this."

"What?" Chaser sits forward.

"Hang onto your dicks." Thom peers over at me. "Hang onto Chaser's dick, your name's on here, too."

I'm too grossed out by the dick comment to process the rest of that.

Chaser growls a warning. "Get to it, Thom."

"All right." He winks at Alvin. "Drumroll?"

"Just read it!" Alvin shouts.

"Number one, Best Breakout Video for 'Candy Jar.' You're up against Wishing Well and some other no-names, so that should be easy."

"Ugh," Jacob moans, "I don't know how much of a compliment it is to be nominated with those assholes."

"Get over it." Thom's gaze slides to me. "Best Video Vixen for Mallory's performance in 'Candy Jar.'"

"Holy shit!" Chaser squeezes me tight and kisses my cheek. "So proud of you, baby," he whispers in my ear.

"She's up against that chick who cartwheels all over the Jaguars, so don't get your hopes up." Thom smirks.

"Fuck that," Alvin rumbles. "No contest. Mallory wins that one easily."

"Thanks, Alvin." I reach over and squeeze his arm.

Thom's gaze lands on us again. "Guitar God. Chaser Adams. You're up against Vinnie Price, so I wouldn't get your hopes up either. But it's an honor to be nominated alongside him. He must have four of those little statues by now. Danny Desmond from Wishing Well and Morgan Marvel from Bloody Revolver are nominated too."

"Damn." Garrett whistles. "Stiff competition. Chaser's still the best guitarist out of all of 'em though."

"Fuck yeah," Alvin cheers.

"Thanks." Chaser reaches over and high-fives both of them.

"Best Heavy Metal Performance Video for 'Candy Jar.' It's a new category this year. You're up against Flying Fang, Vicious Vandals, and Fuzeboys. I think you have a shot."

"Whoa," Alvin mutters.

"And finally." Thom drums his fingers on is desktop, "Video of the year. That's *all* music genres. You're up against Mitchell Howard —"

"Jesus Christ, seriously?" Jacob's wide saucer eyes are no match for my own.

"Shooting Fences, Marilynn Starr, Penny Driver—"

"Christ, I'd love to bone her thick, tap-dancing ass," Garrett mutters.

"That's it?" Jacob cranes his neck, trying to see the list in Thom's hand.

"That's not enough?" Thom throws the paper at Jacob. "I don't think any band has had this many nominations before."

"Yeah, but two of them are for Mallory and Chaser." Jacob's eyes bug out as he scans the list of nominees in every category. "*Brent* for best vocalist. Over me? What kind of bullshit is that?"

Alvin snaps the list out of Jacob's hands. "The *whole band* has three nods. That's fucking amazing. Stop being a little bitch." He scans the list and shrugs. "Andrew Lane for best drummer. Big surprise. I'm sure he'll win for the fifth year in a row." He tosses the list to Garrett.

"Best Heavy Metal Performance is new this year, so that's pretty cool." Garrett flicks his finger against the paper. "Although, Flying Fang and Fuzeboys barely qualify as metal."

"Neither does 'Candy Jar,' technically." Jacob scoffs. "Heavy Metal Performance? For 'Candy Jar?' How fucking embarrassing."

Thom points one sausage finger at him. "Work that snide attitude out of your system now. After you leave my office, every single one of you better be nothing but sunshine and humility. Everyone who's ever won gets a vote, so keep your opinions about your colleagues to yourself."

"Yeah, got it." Jacob hangs his head. "Three nominations *are* pretty fucking cool."

Garrett slaps Jacob's shoulder. "People are going to expect us to write 'Candy Jar' over and over for the rest of our fucking lives."

"It beats no one wanting you to write *anything*," Thom counters. "This is a huge deal. Breakout Video *and* Video of the year. I don't think any artist has done that before." His gaze swings to Chaser. "And Guitar God. Come on. That's—"

Chaser raises a hand to cut Thom off. "I'm stoked. No complaints here."

Thom flicks a look my way. "Video Vixen? This was your first official acting job, wasn't it?"

"Y-yes. I'm stunned but really excited. I can't believe it." Sure, I hate the video, and my nipples are probably the only reason I got the nomination, but it's still recognition.

Thom redirects his commanding sausage finger my way. "There. That's the attitude I want to see from every single one of you. Take some lessons from Mallory on grace and humbleness."

Jacob rolls his eyes at me.

"You've got time before the awards show," Thom says. "I'll work my sources to keep 'Candy Jar' playing."

Oh, goodie.

"You stay out of trouble." Thom's stern dad attitude returns. "We clear?"

Everyone answers with some sort of affirmative noise, while I try to ignore what I think is jealousy glinting in Jacob's eyes.

CHAPTER FIFTY

MALLORY

"Congratulations!" Pamela's voice coos out of our answering machine. "Call me!"

"You better call her back, it's probably about the show," Chaser says.

"You don't think it's about the award nominations?"

"Thom said it won't be officially announced until tomorrow."

As if she won't know about Andrew's nomination. But instead of arguing about it, I just call Pamela back and get it over with.

"Hello, Miss Video Vixen," she answers.

I point to the phone and mouth, "She knows" at Chaser, who laughs and shrugs.

"You already heard, huh?" I say to Pamela.

"Duh, Andrew's dick manager woke us up with his news this morning. Are you excited?"

"Yeah, I'm shocked too."

"So was I."

Gee, thanks.

"I wouldn't tell anyone on the set if you can help it. Video Vixen isn't really all that impressive to serious actors, you know?"

Couldn't let me enjoy it for a few minutes, could you?

"I wasn't planning to."

"Anyway, I called to see if you want me to pick you up in the morning?"

Chaser and I haven't really discussed my transportation needs since we returned. Even though he says otherwise, I can't help feeling like some of the blame for his addiction falls on me. I can't depend on him to drive me to work every day. "That would be great. Are you sure I'm not out of your way?"

"Everything's out of the way in Hollywood. It's fine. I'll pick you up at seven, okay?"

"See you then."

"Who are you seeing when?" Chaser asks.

"Pamela's picking me up at seven."

His mouth turns down. "I wanted to drop you off tomorrow."

"I'm not a little kid going to my first day of school, Chaser." I wave my hands at him. "Don't you need to be in the studio mixing the album or whatever?"

"Yeah. Somehow I don't think it'll be as easy as Thom thinks."

"No kidding." I tap his chest. "Watch out for Jacob. His wounded pride isn't going to let the snub from the music awards slide for long."

"Christ. It's not like it's the VMAs or the Grammy's."

I press my hand over his lips. "Humility and grace," I remind him in a bad imitation of Thom's stern manager voice.

322

He chuckles and kisses my palm, before tugging it away from his mouth. "I'd only say that to *you*."

"Pamela told me not to mention it on the set. As if I was going to go in wearing a *Video Vixen* sash across my chest the first day. I'm so nervous, I'll be lucky if I don't pee my pants."

He loosely wraps his arms around my waist. "You sure you wouldn't rather have me take you? She'll probably make you even more anxious."

"Maybe. But it'll be nice to have a friend on the set, you know?"

"Some friend," he mutters.

I poke him in the gut. "Hey, this is *your* fault for being best buds with Andrew."

"Actually," he teases, drawing out the word, "*You* met Pamela first. So technically, *you* brought them into our lives."

"Oh my God." I cover my mouth with both hands. "You're right."

He tickles his fingers over my ribs. "You're going to be awesome tomorrow. Don't let Pamela rattle you."

I should've taken Chaser's warning more seriously.

"Is *that* what you're wearing?" Pamela asks after I'm situated in the passenger seat of her shiny, black Porsche. "It doesn't matter. You'll be in a bathing suit and bathrobe most of the day, anyway."

I glance down at my white denim skirt and pink T-shirt, not sure what's so offensive about it.

We both have to produce ID to be allowed onto the set. Even Pamela, which helps me feel less like an outsider.

She zips into a spot in front of a long, narrow building and turns to grab her bag. "Ready?"

"I think so."

She leaves me in the hands of one of the show's assistants. I'm taken to wardrobe, fitted with a bright yellow bathing suit cut low in the front and high on the hips, then dropped off at makeup, where I finally see a friendly face.

"Cindy! How are you?"

"Nervous as heck." She lowers her voice. "It's my first day too."

"It's meant to be. We're going to do all our Hollywood firsts together." I laugh and hug her.

"I sort of let it slip that I'd worked with you before." Cindy drops her gaze. "I hope you don't mind."

"Oh my God, of course not. I'm so excited you're here!" Even though I haven't seen her since the disastrous Blue Alien Incident, it's like we're old friends.

We catch up while she spackles makeup over my face and chest. Finally, I'm presentable and sent onto the set.

Even though I don't have a lot of lines, I'm in the background a lot and need to be present all day. For a show about lifeguards, it seems like we spend an awful lot of time taking showers.

But who cares? I'm on a real television show!

By the end of the day, I'm tired but still buzzing with excitement from my first day.

"How do you feel?" Pamela asks me on our way to the dressing room.

"Good. It was fun."

"That'll wear off," she promises. "I need to speak to Steve. I'll meet you out by the car?"

"Okay." I watch her walk off in the direction of the director's office, before continuing down the hall. I'm inches from stepping inside the wardrobe room when I catch my name.

"We should probably burn Mallory's swimsuit." Laughter follows the comment. "Bet she's riddled with STDs from dating that loser rock star."

"And probably blowing the producer," another female voice whines. "I'm sure she's just as slutty as her bestie, Pam."

More laughter.

The sting of humiliation washes over me. This is how people see me? Because I'm friends with Pamela and date a musician? They don't even know me.

"That's not true." Cindy's timid voice perks my ears up. Knowing she's new to the show makes me appreciate her defending me even more. "Mallory's not like that. We worked on a movie together. Skylar Mars hit on her, and she told him off. Her boyfriend punched him out. It was in all the papers."

"That guy is *so* gross," the first one says. They move on to discussing different directors and sets they've worked on, thankfully forgetting all about me.

Cindy steps out of the room, knocking into me. "I'm sorry!" Her guilty eyes ping between me and the room she just left.

I reach out and touch her shoulder. "Thank you for defending me."

Her lips quiver. "I couldn't let that slide. I'm sorry you overheard it, though."

"Better I know early on what I'm in for, right?" I try to give her a reassuring smile, but inside, I'm dying to get home to the one person who cares about me.

CHAPTER FIFTY-ONE

CHASER

So much for mixing the album in a day.

The "live" tracks will be polished by another team, and we won't have much say over how they turn out. We nailed our gritty version of 'Candy Jar,' and I hope to fuck no one messes with it. 'Hammer to the Heart' ended up being acoustic, something we've never tried before, so that was fun. The two cover songs were cool, and we did our best to put a unique spin on each of them, but they're not as exciting as our four brand new tracks.

We're almost finished mixing those songs. Watching the whole process was a lot of fun and having Mallory join me in the evenings was even better.

Our sound engineer Tony manually works the board, making adjustments every time one of us has a suggestion. He has to do each song in one take, flicking knobs and faders while the music plays. The guy's a genius. An absolute machine the way he expertly manages to have his fingers in four places at once, depending on what aspect of our sound he's tweaking.

Maybe because we're all so attached to it, "Queen of the Road" has been the hardest song to nail down. Every one of us seems to have a different vision for the final sound.

Garrett's version was straight up ridiculous. All you could hear was the bass and Jacob's screams. Alvin's drumming and my playing were barely background noise.

We redid it several times.

And it's finally *perfect*.

We all sit around the studio to listen to the full version of "Queen of the Road" one last time, before calling it finished.

It's flawless. Every note. Every element is there. The perfect song to close out a short album that includes some of the best performances we've ever recorded.

"This is my favorite." I bump Mallory's shoulder.

She lets out a sigh and leans against me. "I'm so...*proud* of you guys. I can't believe I watched you take it from that little riff...to what it is now. It's incredible."

"No, no." Jacob starts pacing as soon as the song's finished. "It still needs something more."

We've abused Tony quite a bit throughout this process. But today, he seems ready to take the long walk up to the roof and dive right the fuck off the edge.

"He's right," Garrett adds. "The bridge needs some element we're missing."

"More drama!" Jacob snaps his fingers.

"Okay," I answer slowly. "What do you suggest?"

"The song drips sleaze and sex. It needs something extra filthy—"

"So, what do you want?" Tony's exasperation comes through clearly. Thom's probably going to get a full-length report of all the grief we caused him the last couple days. "You want to go beat off in the live room and have me record it?"

"Yes!" Jacob and Garrett clap their hands together.

"No." Alvin and I say at the same time.

"Well, not *me*." Jacob's face takes on a sinister shade I don't trust. And I really don't care for him aiming that evil expression at my girl. "Mallory. We all know how...*ahem* vocal you get at *certain* pleasurable moments."

I push up off the counter I'd been leaning on, prepared to beat the shit out of Jacob. "Watch yourself."

Mallory's wide eyes dart between Jacob and me. I'm sure she's regretting coming down here today. "I'm not a singer."

"No, but you're a screamer." Jacob rubs his hands together like he's appointed himself the band's official evil genius. "You two go in the live room. We'll light some candles. Get you in the mood and then record her orgasmic screams. Layer it over the bridge..."

His voice trails off in the now dead-silent room.

"Are you out of your fucking mind?" Alvin finally asks.

"What?" Jacob shrugs. "It'll sound so cool. It's exactly what that song needs. Our candy girl can forever be immortalized on one of our records."

I can't tell if he sincerely thinks he's paying Mallory a compliment, or he's risen to new levels off assholery. Either way, I'm not entertaining this discussion.

Mallory's scared eyes meet mine. "I can't do that, Chaser," she whispers.

Of course she can't. Nor would I ever ask her to.

Jacob turns his talk-to-your-woman eyes my way. "Chaser. Come on."

"Absolutely fucking not."

"We need to break through this squeaky, clean, glitter metal image that video gave us." Jacob hooks his arm around Garrett's shoulders. "You know me and G are gutter rats."

"You're from Canoga Park," Alvin says.

"Doesn't matter." Jacob jabs his finger in my direction. "Here's the problem. You think you're too sophisticated to be associated with something like that but that's what this band was all about when we started. It's exactly what we need to reclaim our street cred."

"Sophisticated?" There's something I've never been accused of before.

"Back in the day, you would've been in there, dick in hand, slick and ready to fuck your girl. Out of all of us, *you* were the biggest gutter rat."

Even at the dirtiest points of my life, I don't think I would've been eager to record myself in the act and slap it on an album. "Let me guess, you're fucking high. Again."

The room's silent. It's the first time I've had to call Jacob out in front of everyone since we got sober.

"Don't act all saintly now that *you're* squeaky clean. All our heroes were high when they created their masterpieces."

"It would create buzz for the EP." Garrett seems to be putting as much enthusiasm into his voice as humanly possible in an effort to stop Jacob and I from coming to blows. "We're already worried sales will be slow because it's not a full-length record. We can plant the rumor that 'Queen of the Road' has live orgasms mixed in. Everyone will buy a copy to find out if it's true. Think about all the publicity you two have already gotten. People will go nuts when they find out they can listen to Mallory Dove's orgasm noises."

Somewhere in the middle of the conversation, Mallory's moved behind me, her fingers curled into my belt loops, hanging on tight.

Jacob peers around my side. "What's the big deal, Mal?

We're not, like, gonna watch or anything. We'll all leave if it makes you more—"

This has gone on long enough. I slap my hand against his chest, pushing him back. "Don't talk to her."

"Why so shy now? We've all heard you two go at it like animals for months."

I curl my fists, ready to knock Jacob the fuck out.

"Come on, Jacob. That's enough. Drop it," Alvin says. "This isn't cool."

"Guys, this EP is killer," Tony says, dipping his toes back into the conversation. "And EPs sell. Bloody Revolver's last one entered the charts at number five. What you guys did here is better than anything they've ever recorded. You won't need some cheap rumor to sell it."

"It's not cheap," Jacob argues. "It's bold and artistic."

"Oh-kay." Tony rolls his eyes and strolls out of the room.

Poor bastard. This isn't what he signed up for. How did things snowball out of control so fast?

"Let's do it now." Jacob jumps up and claps his hands. "We can have it done and ready to—"

"No. I'm not discussing this further."

"Fine!" Jacob throws his hands in the air. "I'll find someone else to do it, but it won't have the same emotional meaning to it that Mallory would give."

What the fuck ever that's supposed to mean.

"The song's fine without any theatrics. Let's leave it alone," Alvin pleads.

"Sure." Jacob's gaze skips to the now-dark live room, and I don't exactly trust him when he says, "Then it's a wrap."

CHAPTER FIFTY-TWO

MALLORY

A coating of ickiness lingers on my skin after leaving the studio.

Outside on the sidewalk, Chaser rests his hands on my shoulders. "I'm so sorry, little dove. You know I'd never ask you to do something like that."

"I don't understand why Jacob would think I'd want to."

"He's been watching too much porn, I guess."

"I may not be an expert, but the song already sounded so good. I can't imagine adding some moaning and groaning will *elevate* it."

"It won't. I don't even know where he came up with such a stupid idea."

"Hey," Alvin calls out, jogging down the sidewalk to catch up to us. "Andrew called looking for us. He wants to meet up at Pogo's Deli to celebrate. You up for it?"

Chaser raises an eyebrow at me, and I shrug. "Why not."

After the deli, we somehow end up back at our place with Andrew in tow.

He bops around our apartment, checking out everything from our bathroom to my bedroom closet. "Oh, man, this reminds me so much of my first place. You guys are way neater though."

"Go, sit." I shoo him out of our bedroom. "Chaser has something for you to listen to." And I don't want to leave him alone anywhere near my underwear drawer.

The phone rings, and I hurry to answer, pulling it into the kitchen to blunt the noise the guys are making out in the living room.

"Mallory?" Audrey's weak voice has me pressing the phone to my ear harder.

"Audrey? What's wrong?"

"I'm at...I'm at the hospital. Can you come pick me up?"

"Are you okay?"

"Not really." She gives me the address. Unfortunately, I have no idea where it is and no way to get there, but I promise to pick her up and ask her to wait for me.

After hanging up, I poke my head out of the kitchen. "Chaser?"

I motion for him to join me. For some reason, Andrew follows.

Too eager to get to Audrey, I don't bother telling Andrew to leave when they both join me in the kitchen.

"Uh, Audrey's in the hospital."

"Is she okay?" Chaser asks.

"I don't know. She didn't tell me much."

"Who's Audrey?" Andrew asks.

By now, I know he's impervious to my scowls, so I do the easier thing and answer, "My friend." My gaze returns to Chaser. "She asked if we can come pick her up."

"Yeah, I'll get Garrett's car."

"I'll take you," Andrew offers. "My truck's right downstairs."

I'm torn. Do I want to subject Audrey to an obnoxious man-child when she's hurt or waste time tracking down Garrett to get his car keys?

"Are you sure you don't mind?" I ask.

Andrew pulls his keys out of his pocket and waves them at me. "Nope. Let's go."

It turns out Andrew was a good choice because he knows his way to the hospital. "Kyle got drunk and totaled his car right after our first album dropped. Spent a lot of time here," he says almost solemnly.

"I remember reading about that," Chaser says.

"Yeah, it was totally fucked up."

He pulls up in front of the Emergency Room, and I hop out. It's dark, so I don't notice Audrey sitting on the bench right outside the doors at first.

"Mallory."

My jaw drops as soon as my gaze lands on her black eye and split lip. "Audrey! What happened?"

She shakes her head, drawing my attention to the angry bruises around her neck. "I can't. Please."

"Come here." I pull her close and gently wrap my arms around her. "Are you okay?"

"No," she whispers.

"Everything all right?" Chaser's concerned tone breaks through my confusion.

Audrey pulls away and wipes her cheeks.

"Jesus," Chaser breathes out. "What happened?"

"Nothing."

"Audrey?" he insists.

She glances at the hospital doors. "Not now, okay. Please. I need to get out of here."

"Yeah, all right. Come on. Let's get you home."

Chaser helps her into the narrow backseat, and I squeeze in next to her.

"Oh shit, were you in an accident?" Andrew asks, watching us from the rearview mirror.

Audrey aims a who-the-fuck-is-this expression my way.

"Audrey, this is our friend, Andrew. He offered to drive..." My voice trails off, it really doesn't matter.

"Thank you, Andrew," Audrey whispers.

"No problem." He glances at Chaser. "Where we headed?"

Chaser turns to speak to Audrey. "You want to go home?"

"Please."

Chaser gives him the address, which turns out, isn't far from Andrew's place.

Once we're on the move, Audrey leans her head on my shoulder and quietly sobs. I wrap her up in my arms, trying not to squeeze her too tight. "Please tell me what happened," I whisper. "Did Doug—"

"No." Her sharp whisper prompts Chaser to glance over his shoulder, but he doesn't speak. "Please. I don't want him to know."

"Okay but what happened?"

"A client. A regular. He's always been...rough. But never like this." She sniffles, and I don't have anything to wipe the tears off her cheeks but my T-shirt. She winces at the contact and pushes my hand away "I only met with him because the agency insisted I tell him I was quitting in person. And he just *lost* it."

"I'm sorry." I'm so choked up from the resignation and pain in her voice I don't know what else to say.

We pull into her driveway, and I help her into the house,

depositing her on the couch. "Do you want me to make some tea?"

She nods.

Andrew and Chaser followed us into the house. I'm trying to think of a tactful way to ask Andrew to wait outside. Having a stranger in her home after whatever happened to Audrey can't be helping. Thankfully, he's quiet for once, observing everything from a darkened corner of the living room.

"Audrey, I couldn't overhear everything you guys were talking about," Chaser says.

"Good. You weren't supposed to." She pulls a blanket around her, up to her chin.

From the kitchen, I watch Chaser shifting from foot to foot. Agitated but trying to be calm. I fill her tea kettle and set it on the stove.

"Chaser," I call.

Ignoring me, he squats down in front of Audrey and takes her hand. "Please tell me what happened."

"Why? So you can tell me it's my own fault?"

He ignores her defensiveness and keeps his voice gentle. "Did someone do this to you?"

She glares at him. "No, I walked into a wall. Several of them."

"Who?"

"It doesn't matter." She turns her head away from his pleading eyes.

I return to the living room and pull one of the chairs closer to the couch. "Did you talk to the police?"

She snorts, then winces. "Whores can't be victims."

Chaser's jaw tightens.

"Audrey." I squeeze her hand. "Let's talk to someone else then. I'll go with you."

"It won't matter. It never does."

"Audrey," Chaser says, "Where did this happen?"

"At the Palm. A worker heard me screaming and... interrupted. Otherwise, I'd probably be dead." She coughs, and her face contorts with pain. "Poor guy probably got fired for his troubles," she wheezes.

"Why?" I ask.

"This client's well connected." She hisses. "Strong for such an old fucker, too."

Chaser flicks his gaze at me, but I'm not sure what he's asking.

Andrew steps forward. "Which room?"

Audrey slowly slides her gaze his way. "Thank you for the ride, but why are you still here?"

"Do you want us to call Doug for you?" Chaser asks, drawing Audrey's attention back to him.

"No!" Audrey sits up and sucks in a pained breath. "Please. I don't want him to know."

"Audrey, he cares about you. He'll want to know," Chaser insists.

"He's out of town, so it won't matter." She glares at him. "He *knows*, so if you think you owe him some man favor by telling him what his whore girlfriend was up to, don't bother."

Chaser grits his teeth. "That's not why I want to call him, Audrey."

"Sure, it is. I know what you're thinking; I got exactly what I deserve."

"Jesus Christ, Audrey. Really?" Chaser pinches the bridge of his nose. "I'm fucking worried about *you*."

"Right." Audrey's inner wounded animal isn't finished lashing out yet. "That's why you were such a jerk about Mallory and I being friends."

"Audrey," I say but Chaser's not letting her comment slide.

"Yes, I was an asshole back then and I'm sorry. Now, please let me help you."

She blinks at him. "How can you help me?"

"Give me the guy's name and the room number."

"Fuck yeah," Andrew mutters.

"Are you crazy?" She sits up, tossing the blanket aside.

The tea kettle blows, startling me out of my chair. I hurry into the kitchen to pour tea for Audrey, swirling in a generous amount of honey.

When I return, she accepts the cup and takes a tentative sip.

"What kind of *connected* are we talking about, Audrey?" Chaser asks after she sets the mug on the coffee table. "Mafia? Hollywood? What?"

I raise an eyebrow at mafia because that hadn't occurred to me.

"Mafia?" Audrey shakes her head. "What can you do if he is?"

"A slightly different plan." He curls his fingers in a hurry up gesture. "Tell me."

"He's a big-name actor, Chaser. You can't go after him."

"Give me his name."

I actually gasp when she finally whispers the name because I recognize it well. He'd been one of my mother's favorite actors.

Chaser nods. "Can I borrow your phone?"

Audrey points to the counter.

We watch in silence as Chaser picks it up and dials a number, pulling out the antenna of the cordless phone and walking down the hallway. "Torrin, it's Chaser Adams. I need a favor..." His voice trails off as he closes a door behind him.

Audrey pulls the blanket around her again and shoots a

glare at me. "I don't appreciate being bullied by your boyfriend."

"I know. I'm sorry."

"There's nothing he can do," she insists.

I'm busy watching Andrew pace the hallway, waiting for Chaser to emerge. When he does, they share a few quick words.

"Let's go!" Andrew slams his fist against his palm. "I got a bat and a tire iron in the truck."

Chaser nods.

"Wait. Where are you going?" I hurry over to Chaser.

He hands me the phone and lifts his chin at Audrey. "What room?"

"Chaser, this is nuts. What are you going to do?"

"What needs to be done," he answers as if it should be obvious.

She squeezes her eyes shut and slowly pulls herself off the couch. "You can't."

"Where else are you hurt?" he asks.

"What?"

Chaser points to his eye and his mouth. "Where did he hurt you that I can't see?"

"It doesn't matter," she whispers.

Chaser's a dog with a bone now that he's gotten some answers from Audrey, but there's still sympathy in his voice when he runs his hand over his side and asks, "Ribs?"

She drops her gaze to the floor. "Two cracked."

He opens his mouth then stops himself. "Okay."

"Chaser," I plead. While I appreciate his need to avenge my friend, I'm scared. "I can't have you getting hurt or arrested."

"I got lawyers on retainer and plenty of bail money," Andrew answers.

My hands ball into fists at my side. "That's not helpful, Andrew," I spit out.

"Sure, it is," Chaser says. "Room number, Audrey?"

"He's not in the main part of the hotel. One of the bungalows out back. For 'privacy,' you know?" She scoffs.

"Excellent." Andrew rubs his hands together and grins like a maniac. "I know that place like the back of my hand."

Audrey lifts her gaze and glares at Andrew. "You don't even know me."

He points to her face. "I know enough to know no man should ever do *that* to a woman."

"Andrew!" I snap.

He shrugs. "What?"

"Will he still be there?" Chaser asks. "Or will he have left after the commotion?"

"There was no 'commotion,'" Audrey says. "The hotel discreetly called an ambulance for me. I spoke to the cops at the hospital. From their attitude, I doubt they bothered going out there to talk to him."

"Which bungalow?" Chaser asks.

"Twenty-two."

I stare at Audrey, and she shrugs. "He's going to badger me until I tell him, and I want to go to bed."

Chaser nods, almost apologetically. "Does he have anyone with him? Security? Anything like that?"

"Not when he goes there," Audrey answers. "We met in the bar to 'talk,' and he lured me back to the bungalow to give me a 'present.' I never saw anyone else with him."

"Does he know where you live?"

Audrey's eyes widen, and she slowly shakes her head. "No...the agency is very careful about not giving out information like that. I don't even use my real name."

"That's a detail I needed," Chaser growls. "What name?"

"Belle."

"Anything else?" Chaser asks.

She shakes her head.

"Let's go." Andrew waves his hand at the door.

Chaser settles his hands on my shoulders and pulls me closer. "Stay here with Audrey."

"Chaser, you don't have to do this."

"Someone has to." He presses his palms to my cheeks. "I'll be fine. I've dealt with scum like this before."

"What if you get arrested? Or he recognizes you guys." I throw my hand in Andrew's direction. "You two don't exactly blend into the general population."

Andrew grins at me. "I can be quite stealthy when I need to be."

"You wouldn't know stealthy if it bit you on your right ass cheek," I shoot back. I'm ready to strangle him for feeding into Chaser's madness.

"You're so cute when you're mad." Andrew bops me on the nose, and I lunge at him.

Chaser hooks an arm around my waist, holding me in place. "We'll be fine." He kisses my cheek. "Stay here and take care of Audrey. We won't be gone long."

Audrey watches the guys go and shakes her head. "Who's your crazy friend?"

"Andrew. He's a drummer."

Her eyes widen as recognition settles in. "Andrew Lane. From Vicious Vandals? Why does he care so much?"

I honestly can't explain why Andrew seemed so invested, so I shrug. "He and Chaser have a love/hate friendship thing."

"Must be a lot of love to have his back like that."

She tosses the blanket on the couch and shuffles closer to me. "Will you help me? I need a shower in the worst way."

"Of course."

A few minutes later, the coward in me wishes I'd said no. The welts and bruises from her shoulder blades to the back of her knees are enough to make me bite my lip to keep from crying.

"There's Epsom salt under the sink. Can you grab it?" she asks.

"Sure."

When the water's warm enough, I hold her steady, while she climbs the three steps leading up to the large circular tub.

"I'm so sorry, Mallory," Audrey whispers.

"Why?"

"I didn't know who else to call."

"It's okay."

It seems to take hours to get her bundled up and settled into bed.

And Chaser still hasn't returned.

Exhausted and scared, I grab a poker from the fireplace and prop it up against the nightstand before crawling into bed with Audrey.

"Do you need anything?" I ask.

"To forget this whole night." She turns, so she's facing me. "Tell me about your big T.V. show. Are you loving it?"

"You don't want to talk about that now."

"Yes, I do. Please?"

I blow out a breath. "*Love's* probably not the right word. It's *intimidating*." I regale her with some other stories but leave out the part about how the wardrobe girls hate my guts. It seems like a ridiculous thing to whine about after what happened to Audrey tonight. Besides, I haven't even confided in Chaser about it yet.

"Thank you," she finally whispers, her eyelids drooping. "For helping me forget."

I roll over and turn off the beside lamp.

"Thank you for staying."

I laugh softly in the darkness. "They didn't leave me much choice."

"I mean staying in *here*. Thanks for not leaving me alone."

I reach out and brush my fingers over her hand. "I'm right here, Audrey."

CHAPTER FIFTY-THREE

CHASER

"You don't have to do this, Andrew."

Torrin, the president of the Devil Demons MC's SoCal charter, did a quick check for me and determined that the multi-Oscar winning actor Audrey named was, to his knowledge, not connected to anyone who would be seeking payback or protected by anyone. He also offered to send help. An offer I accepted because I'm not sure how far into this I want to drag Andrew.

"I'm in, bro."

"You can drop me off at my place. I'm meeting a few people to go with me."

The Palm was actually halfway between Audrey's place and the closest Devil Demons MC charter. It had taken so long to pry the info out of Audrey, I'm worried the brothers sent to assist are waiting on me.

"Chaser, dude. You can't go buzzing on into the Palm on

your Harley. Not gonna happen. They'll call the cops before you make it anywhere near the bungalows. And you ain't parking outside and hiking in. You need me. I know the security guys at the gate, and my truck's big enough to haul us in and out."

He's got a point.

"You can wait in the truck."

"Fuck that. I'm gonna crack that motherfucker's ribs then jam that tire iron up his ass."

"You're awfully bloodthirsty."

"Bro, I watched my mom get knocked around by fucking assholes my whole life. As soon as I was big enough, I put an end to that shit." He glances over and smirks. "My therapist is always trying to tell me you can't solve violence with violence. And in some cases, I actually agree with her."

"But?"

"This isn't one of those cases."

"Your therapist, huh?"

"Oh, yeah. I'm totally fucked in the head, dude."

No shit. "I don't want to get you in trouble. You've got a tour coming up. You don't need the bad press."

"*We've* got a tour coming up. Besides, now that I'm off coke, I need to do something to keep myself entertained."

"Even more reason I shouldn't drag you into this."

"You're not dragging me into anything. This girl a friend of yours?"

"She's Mallory's friend, and she's been good to her."

"You fuck her?"

"Jesus Christ, what is it with you? No. Fuck no."

"Just trying to assess the situation."

"Not every decision I make has to do with my dick."

"So wrong, young grasshopper. All of life's decisions are made by the dick."

"Maybe for you," I mutter. "You don't get it, but when you find the right woman, you will."

"I don't need the right woman. I need the *right now* woman." He takes one hand off the steering wheel and grabs his junk. "I need to come—hard, fast, and often."

Why am I even bothering with this conversation? "When you're with the right person, it's better than—"

"Bro, what's better than an orgasm?"

"You've never really been in sync with someone so much that giving them pleasure, heightens your own? There's more to being intimate than rutting like a fucking dog."

"Intimate?" Andrew scratches his head like it's the first time he's ever heard of the concept. "Who wants intimacy? Getting needy with a chick is like handing them a knife to carve out your insides."

Ah, finally a piece of the Andrew insanity puzzle.

"It shouldn't feel needy. Just because you've been hurt once—"

"Who said anything about being hurt?"

"The whole knife thing?"

"Whatever." He waves me off.

"Pull in there." I gesture to a gas station up ahead, eager for this conversation to be over. "That's where I'm meeting them."

He guides the truck into the parking lot, and a few minutes later, two bikers rumble in.

I step out and wave. Torrin wasn't fucking around. He sent his SAA and another brother who easily weighs as much as Andrew and I combined.

"Dude," Andrew mutters under his breath. "These are biker-bikers. Like *outlaw* bikers. How do you know them?"

"Don't worry about it."

It's not that I'm ashamed of my MC roots. No, my desire to keep my family ties to myself stems from a need to *protect* my

MC brothers from outsiders. Andrew has a big mouth and blabs everything to everyone. So, no, I'm not eager to tell him about my club family.

"You can still back out," I remind him.

"No way, bro. I'm all in."

"Chaser, long time." Freak walks over to us slowly. His expression remains blank, but his eyes never stop moving. Assessing everything around us, especially Andrew. His extreme caution is how he landed in the role of Sergeant-at-Arms for the Devil Demons. "Who's your friend?"

"This is Andrew. The facility's tricky to get access to. Andrew can help us with that."

Andrew sticks his hand out. Both Freak and Frisco give it a withering look before Andrew withdraws. "Okay. No handshakes. That's cool."

Freak snorts like a bull. "You trust this guy, Chaser?"

I glance over at Andrew. Jesus Christ, do I really want to put my life and reputation on the line with my club by vouching for this clown?

"Yeah, he's cool."

Instead of discussing the details out in the open, the four of us pile into the truck. Apparently terrified of my biker brothers, Andrew miraculously keeps his mouth shut the entire time.

Mallory

"Mallory, I'm back." Chaser's soft whisper pulls me from sleep.

"Chaser?" I roll over and barely make out his shadowy form in the dark. "Are you okay?"

"Shh, don't wake her. Go back to sleep."

How am I supposed to sleep now?

Carefully, I ease out of bed. Audrey moans softly, and I

pause, waiting to see if she needs anything. When she doesn't make another noise, I tiptoe out of the bedroom.

Chaser's on the couch with the television on low but doesn't seem to be watching anything. "Why are you up, little dove?" he whispers.

"What happened?"

"Nothing you need to worry about."

I move closer, studying him. He's changed his clothes, so he must have stopped home. "Where's Andrew?"

"Home. He dropped me off at the apartment, so I could change and get my bike."

"What happened?"

He sighs and drops his head, running his hands over the back of his neck. "The less you know the better."

My gaze zeroes in on his battered knuckles. "Chaser," I whisper, sitting next to him, taking one of his hands in mine. "What did you do?"

"Nothing he didn't have coming."

Frustrated with his lack of answers, I let go.

Another sigh and he wraps his arm around me, pulling me closer. "Remember how you didn't ask questions when we were home and I went on a run?"

"This is different. It's not club business. And I'm involved."

"No, you're not. And that's the way I want it to stay."

"Chaser—"

"Don't ask for more answers than you can handle, Mallory." He taps my temple. "You've seen enough ugliness tonight. I won't put anymore in your head."

"Did anyone see you?"

"No."

"Is the guy alive?"

The long pause he takes before answering flips my stomach

upside down. "Unfortunately, yes." His gaze strays to the hallway. "Is she okay?"

"I think so."

"Are *you* okay?"

"I'm still scared."

"Nothing's gonna happen to me, little dove." He kisses the top of my head. "And even if it does, at least I did the right thing."

"That's not reassuring."

"It's the best I've got."

"Is Andrew okay?"

He considers that question too long for my liking. "No, he's totally fucking insane."

I tap his chest. "You know what I mean."

"He may seem like a big goofball, but he's hardcore."

I'm not sure what to make of that. "He has a big mouth. Do you trust him not to say anything?"

"He won't say a word."

After a while, we fall silent, and my eyelids start to droop.

"Hey." Chaser hugs me to him. "Let me tuck you back into bed. She shouldn't wake up alone, and you need more sleep."

"What about you?"

He pats the arm of the couch. "I'll sleep out here. I'll be fine."

Reluctantly, I return to the bedroom and settle in next to Audrey.

It only seems like minutes later but has to be hours, voices from the living room wake me.

Audrey rolls over. "Who is that?"

"Chaser stayed over."

She cocks her head and listens. "That's *Doug*. Did Chaser call him?"

"I...I don't know."

"Oh my God." She whips the covers back, but a short scream stops her movements. "Fuck."

"Easy."

"Easy nothing. I'm going to kill your boyfriend."

Chaser

Maybe it was shitty of me to call Doug after Audrey begged me not to. But if the guy's going to be a coward who cuts and run, isn't it better she finds out now?

Turns out, Doug's a decent guy. Ditched his meeting and came straight to the house when I told him Audrey had been hurt.

I gave him a vague outline of the night—Audrey can fill in the details later if she wants—but let him know the guy had been taken care of and wouldn't be bothering Audrey again.

"I don't know how to thank you for taking care of her," he says. "And how you handled...I wouldn't have been able to do what you did. I wouldn't even know who to ask."

He almost seems embarrassed, but he shouldn't. He's a square, squeaky clean guy. Exactly what Audrey needs and what I'll never pretend to be. "I'd do the same for any friend."

"I don't know what to do." His gaze strays toward the bedroom. "I've begged her to give up the life. Promised to take her anywhere in the world she wants to go."

"From what I gathered, she was trying to make a clean break. It's not her fault this guy was a psycho."

"I don't know."

"You love her, Doug?"

"I do, but—"

"No buts. If you love her, don't give up on her. If you do, it'll just reinforce everything bad she thinks about herself and what she deserves."

He seems to turn that over in his head. "I wanted to marry her."

Not liking the past tense he uses, I try again. "She *expects* you to leave her over this. Don't prove her right."

"You know I'm so naive I really thought I was hiring a date for this stupid event I had to attend." He shakes his head. "It took a few dates to realize...and it was too late by then."

"I don't know if that's you being naive or the universe helping two people who need each other get together."

He stares at me. "You're quite a poet. I need to buy one of your albums."

I chuckle and slap his shoulder. "Get her out of this toxic city. At least until she's feeling stronger."

"I have properties all over the world."

"Good. Take her someplace nice. Get her mind off of this phase of her life and focused on the next."

"Thank you." He holds out his hand, and we shake. "Now, let me do something for you."

I raise an eyebrow. "I don't need anything from you."

He tips his head toward the house. "Move in here. It's furnished—"

"I can't take a *house* from you, Doug."

"I'm not handing over the deed." He chuckles. "But you and Mallory move in and make it yours for now."

I doubt I can afford the normal rent he gets for this place but I have to give him something. "We'll pay you rent."

"I don't need your rent." He holds up his hand to stop me from protesting. "You'll save me the trouble of finding a tenant and the cost of having someone check up on the tenant and maintenance."

"You want us to be caretakers?"

"Exactly." He glances around the living room. "You made a good point. I want to focus on Audrey and what she needs right now. I can't afford the distraction of worrying if I rented the house to some crazy person who's going to destroy it, right?"

Doug might not be a fighter, but he's a skilled negotiator.

"Deal." I hold out my hand, and we shake again. "Thank you."

"Damn you, Chaser." Audrey's angry voice rasps from the shadows. "I told you—"

Doug takes a few steps toward the hallway. "I'm glad he called. You think I wouldn't want to know about this?"

"It wasn't your place, Chaser," she says without acknowledging Doug.

A shadow of doubt falls over me. But what's done is done. "I hope you'll forgive me one day, Audrey."

"Chaser?" Mallory's disappointed voice pricks at what's left of my conscience.

"Let's go," I answer. "These two have some talking to do."

Doug sucks in a breath when Audrey finally steps out of the hallway. "Jesus Christ, Audrey." His head swivels between Audrey and me. "Where is this—"

"It's handled, Doug. Just take care of your girl."

"What happened?" He cradles the side of her face not covered in bruises.

Mallory tiptoes around the couple, but Audrey's hand shoots out, pulling Mallory back. "Thank you," she whispers.

"Of course."

"Are you okay?" Doug asks.

"I'll live."

"Pack your stuff."

Audrey takes a step back. "You're kicking me out?"

"What? No. I'm done waiting for you to make a decision. We're going to Paris like we talked about. End of discussion."

"That a boy, Doug," I encourage.

Mallory socks me in the gut and glares at me.

I take her hand. "We're leaving. If you need anything, call us."

"I'll have the keys messengered over to your place when the house is ready," Doug promises.

"What's he talking about?" Mallory asks.

I lean down and kiss her temple, stopping to inhale her clean scent.

"Big changes coming soon, little dove," I say against her ear.

At my bike, I stop and pull her into my arms. Holding onto her for a few seconds. Needing her close to wash away last night's ugliness.

CHAPTER FIFTY-FOUR

MALLORY

Doug moved fast. Within days, he and Audrey are on a private jet to Paris.

Chaser and I move into the house shortly after.

Alvin takes our move out of the apartment the hardest. He does assume our lease upstairs. So at least he has a less chaotic place to sleep now.

My part on *Shallow End* has expanded into a recurring role, so Pamela and I are still driving to work together on the days we're both filming. At least now that we live closer, I don't feel as bad about her picking me up every morning.

"Chaser's in rehearsal all afternoon, right?" Pamela asks after we finish filming for the day.

"Yes." I planned to ask her to drop me off at the rehearsal studio, but she obviously has other ideas in mind.

"Let's go dress shopping! You're up for Video Vixen. So, you need something extra-hot for the awards show."

"I have time to find the right dress." Honestly, I've been so consumed with the new job, moving into the house, and worrying about Chaser leaving for tour, that I haven't given the awards show a lot of thought.

"If you wait too long, you'll be left with bedsheets for a dress." She curls her arm around mine and marches me out to her car. "We'll have fun. Promise."

"Okay." Not that another answer seems to be an option here. "My agent said a few people contacted her about loaning me a dress."

"Pssh," she waves off my comment. "I know people too."

"Is Andrew excited about his nomination?"

She frowns at me for a second before answering. "He's already won like twenty times. It's more of an excuse to show off at this point. It's a bigger deal for Chaser." She squeezes her eyes shut tight for a few seconds. "And I really hope he kicks Vinnie's ass."

"I think he was just excited to be nominated with Vinnie."

"You don't always have to be so diplomatic, Mallory."

"I'm not."

She starts the car and reverses out of the parking spot. "How can you be dating a rock star for this long and still be such a good girl?"

"I don't know about that." I snort-laugh. "Chaser's worked *that* out of me."

"Mallory! I'm shocked." She hesitates for a second. "Wait a minute. How many other boyfriends have you had?"

My cheeks warm. I hate when people ask personal questions. "He's my first."

"Wait. First official boyfriend? First long-term boyfriend? First live-in? What kind of first are we talking about?"

"Everything."

She slams on the brake, whipping my body forward.

"Get out of here," she says in a low, dramatic voice.

I glance out the window over the studio parking lot. We're blocking the flow of traffic, but Pamela doesn't seem to notice or care.

"Pamela," I plead. "Let's go."

"Sorry." She shakes her head fast and steps on the gas. "How is that possible?"

"I don't know. I wasn't allowed to date back home."

"Neither was I. Still lost my virginity at fourteen. That's what sneaking out is for."

"Trust me, there was no *sneaking out* of my father's house."

"What is he, like a warden or something?"

I cough into my fist. "Not at all." Spilling my love life to her is bad enough, there's no way I'll tell her how my father makes his living.

"Damn. And Chaser's not wigged out by that?"

"By what?"

"Oh, God, is he one of those freaks with a virgin fetish?"

"No," I snap, annoyed she'd suggest that.

"Sorry. Some men are obsessed with shit like that."

Our weird conversation is mercifully cut short when she pulls into a dress shop parking lot. "This is it!"

Every dress Pamela picks out looks more like lingerie than something I'd wear to an awards show.

"It's the Small Screen Music Awards. You're *supposed* to wear something daring and edgy," she says.

"Then, won't it be daring to show up in an evening gown?"

She screws up her pretty face into a frown at my logic. "No."

The dress she ends up choosing is a mix of see-through nylon and leather. I gravitate toward a floor-length, metallic gold beaded gown in the back.

"Who are you, Melanie Griffith on her wedding day?"

Pamela plucks at one thin, off-the-shoulder cap sleeve. "This isn't the Oscars, Mallory. Far from it."

"But it's so pretty."

"You'll look like something between Scarlett O'Hara and a gold disco ball."

"I'm pretty sure one of my Barbies had this exact same dress when I was little." I press it to my chest and twirl around, ignoring Pamela's exasperation.

"It's very old Hollywood glamour," the shop owner assures me.

"You're supposed to help me talk her *out* of it," Pamela complains.

"Nope," I smile at her, "This is the one."

CHAPTER FIFTY-FIVE

CHASER

There's one important shopping trip I need to take before leaving for tour.

Unfortunately, the most annoying person in the world joins me.

"Dude, you're buying her a Honda?" Andrew runs his calloused fingers over the shiny green paint. "Mallory's classy. Strikes me as a BMW or Porsche kinda girl."

"Yeah, well, I don't have BMW or Porsche money yet." I glance at the car I picked out for Mallory. It's brand new, so several steps up from the car my father got her for back home, which she claimed to love. It's small, so she can zip in and out of the ridiculous traffic around here. I spent time researching exactly what to get her that would be both reliable and in our budget. Andrew's begging for a beating if he keeps running his mouth.

"You want me to loan you the cash?" he asks.

That's a big hell-fucking-no. "I don't need your money to buy my girl a car."

"I bought Pammy's Porsche." He squeezes his eyes shut and a filthy smile curls his lips.

"Don't," I warn.

"What?"

"Whatever disgusting car sex story you're about to share. Just keep it to yourself."

He grins. "Busted." He takes another look at the car. "It's nice. Cool color. She'll look good in it."

"Thanks for your blessing," I grumble.

After ironing out the details with the dealer and signing some papers, I'm ready to go.

"You psyched for the tour?" Andrew slips on his sunglasses outside and searches the parking lot.

More like a mixture of excited about the tour and bummed I'm leaving Mallory. Not sure what sort of spell I'm under, but I actually *like* the routine we've settled into since moving into the house. No point in explaining that to Andrew, though.

"Can't wait."

"Mallory going to visit you on the road?"

"As often as she can." Already bought her first ticket to join me in Texas for a weekend. A few weeks later, she'll meet me in New York and stay on tour with us until our last show. At least that's what we're planning.

"Cool." He jumps into the driver's side of his truck and unlocks my door. "Pammy will join us in New York. *Lots* of fun to be had before then."

"Uh-huh."

"Seriously?" He hangs his head and turns the key in the ignition. "Chaser, I don't think you understand the *quality* of women who turn up at our shows."

I blow out a long breath, while counting back from ten.

"And I don't think *you* understand, this isn't a conversation I want to have."

"We still meeting the guys at Pogo's?"

"Yup."

Thom and a short, skinny guy I don't recognize, are waiting for us in a back, corner booth of Pogo's. As soon as his gaze lands on Andrew, Thom jumps out of his seat to introduce himself.

"I'm just here as Chaser's ride, man, but nice to meet you," Andrew says.

"Sure, sure." Thom seems to remember who his actual client is and reaches out to shake my hand. He motions for the skinny guy to get up and join us. "This is Pete, he's going to be your tour manager."

"What now?"

Behind Thom's back, Jacob curls his fists together in front of his face and shakes hard—like he's choking a chicken. A snort of laughter escapes me, and I avert my eyes.

"He'll handle the logistics and call me if there are any issues," Thom explains.

Super. Another person I didn't hire drawing a salary off the band. "We've never needed a tour manager before. Val went to the U.K. with us."

"Yeah, and look how that turned out," Thom reminds me.

"Big fan, Chaser," Pete interrupts. "Really excited to work with you guys."

"Thanks."

"Here's my number. You need anything before we leave, just let me know." He passes me a card, and I give it a quick glance, before shoving it in my pocket.

"The guys can fill you in, but we have a date for the EP's release, and Cutter's agreed to work with you," Thom says.

"Fuck yeah," Andrew says under his breath.

"You should've started there, Thom." I shift and run my hand through my hair. "When?"

"As soon as the tour finishes. Pete will set up time for you to work on some of the new material while you're on the road."

When none of us object, Thom claps his hands together. "All right. We're leaving. Oh, and limo's all set up for the SMA's."

"You're the man, Thom." Jacob stands and points two finger guns at Thom.

Andrew throws himself into the booth next to Jacob and signals the waitress to bring us menus.

I'd hesitate to discuss band business in front of Andrew, except he inserts himself into my business all the time. Maybe in this case, he can actually be useful.

"Did you know about this, Jacob?"

"About Pete? Fuck no. Thom sprung him on us today."

"Not the worst thing," Garrett says. "Be nice to have someone to be our gopher."

"Do you have a tour manager?" Alvin asks Andrew.

"Yeah, we've been through a few of 'em. Kyle has his own guy." Andrew snort-laughs. "Fuck, half the time, we do all our talking *through* our managers. It's out of control ridiculous."

"We don't need anyone to do our talking for us." Jacob's lips curve into a sly grin. "None of us are afraid to call each other out on our bullshit."

"Ain't that the fuckin' truth," I mutter.

"Don't let go of that," Andrew says. "Work shit out with each other. Don't let it fester until you can't all stand to be in the same room together."

Well, that's a conversation downer.

The waitress stops by to take our order, and Andrew orders corned beef sandwiches for all of us.

"So, what happened in the UK?" Andrew asks.

I shoot a glare at Jacob that I hope he interprets as *shut your fool mouth.*

"Eh." Alvin waves his hand in the air. "We toured with Bloody Revolver, and they—"

"Aww, fuck that douche!" Andrew shouts.

Heads turn, and Andrew lifts two middle fingers in the air.

"Fucking Davey Revolver." Andrew's normal happy-go-lucky-puppy demeanor morphs into the vicious monster I witnessed the night we handled the guy who hurt Audrey. "I'd love to kick his motherfucking ass."

"Chaser did." Alvin cackles.

I tilt my head and stare him down. *Really?*

He gives me an apologetic shrug.

"He hit on Mallory?" Andrew asks. "Am I right?"

"Something like that."

"Yeah, I wish I'd known you guys, then. I coulda warned you. He's a total piece of shit."

Finally, we agree on something.

Mallory

After dress shopping, Pamela drops me off at the house.

I'm in the kitchen figuring out what to make for dinner when Chaser slams the door and announces, "Honey, I'm home," as he's done every day since we moved in.

Today he adds, "And I have good news."

"What's that?" I rush over to hug him, well aware that our time together is precious. Soon, I'll be saying goodbye for three months.

"Cutter agreed to produce our album."

"Oh my God!" I squeeze my eyes shut, saying a quick 'thank you' to the universe for making this happen for Chaser. "That's amazing."

"And we have a release date for the EP."

"Even better!" I can't help bouncing up and down and clapping my hands.

"Yup. Second week of the tour, so we can promote it and let the fans get to know the new material."

"Perfect timing." I hesitate, not wanting to steal any of his excitement. "I have good news too. I found a dress for the SMAs."

"Awesome." He pauses. "Where is it?"

"It's still at the shop." I give him a quick description.

"I can't wait to see it."

His brows pinch together, and he glances at the clock. "Thom hired a tour manager for us."

"You don't sound happy about it."

"Got a weasel vibe from him." He shrugs. "Nothing specific."

"Try to give him a chance." I poke him in the stomach. "But trust your instincts too."

"Have I mentioned you're the best thing that's ever happened to me?"

"Once or twice, but I don't mind hearing it again."

We're interrupted by a rattling in our driveway followed by a knock at the door.

Chaser jumps up with a grin on his face. "They're early."

"Who?" I ask, following him.

He checks the peephole before opening the door.

"Mr. Adams?"

"Yup."

"Need you to sign this." The burly stranger on our front step thrusts a clipboard at Chaser.

"Let me take a look at it first."

He shrugs and steps back.

"Come here, I have a surprise for you," Chaser says, taking

my hand.

"For me?"

"Close your eyes."

He takes my hand, leading me outside, but when I stumble on the sidewalk, he swoops me up into his arms. "Chaser! What are you doing?"

"Shh, eyes closed, little dove."

I squeeze my eyes shut and hang on. A few seconds later, he gently sets me down.

"Okay, open."

Shiny, pearlescent blue-green paint. My gaze scans the length of the little Honda CRX hatchback sitting in our driveway. "Chaser?"

He turns to the man with the clipboard and scribbles his signature at the bottom. The man hands him keys and a copy of the paperwork. "Enjoy."

"Chaser, what is this?"

He turns to me. "You need a car while I'm gone. You can't depend on Pamela all the time."

"But?" Words, where are my words? "I can't."

"What did you tell me? We're in this together for the long haul." He nods to the little Honda. "This is an investment in our future, so you can get to the set on time."

"Chaser!" I press my palms against his cheeks and lean up to kiss him. "Thank you. I love it so much. How'd you know?"

"I'd love to buy you a fancy BMW or—"

"Absolutely not. I *love* this. This is exactly what I would've picked out."

He glances down. "I know your dad probably gave you much nicer..."

"What are you talking about? My father taught me how to drive in his precious Mercedes, long enough to get my license, then never let me touch another vehicle again." My mouth quirks. "Well, until he got arrested, then I drove that little beauty all over."

"Fuck, I love you." He picks me up, squeezing me tight.

"I'm going to miss you so much," I whisper against his neck.

"I know, baby. Me too."

I sniffle and use a handful of Chaser's T-shirt to dry my cheeks before he sets me down.

"Keys." Chaser sets the keys in my palm.

I stare at the car. "Can we afford this?"

"Yes. I put a chunk of my advance down and the payments are low." He glances at the house. "Our living expenses took a dramatic decrease. I got a phone call from Mitchell Howard the other day. He invited me to come down to his studio and play on two songs for his next album."

I blink at him as I absorb the enormity of what he just said. "Mitchell Howard? He's all contemporary pop music. Why does he want a heavy metal guitarist?"

"He's done some stuff with heavier riffs in the past. I think he wants to continue in that direction." He shrugs as if it's no big deal. "He heard about the Guitar God nomination."

"That's..." I can't even form the right words. "Incredible."

"I haven't said anything to the guys yet. Alvin and Garrett won't care. As much as I'd enjoy bruising Jacob's ego, I can't afford to do it right before we leave for a tour."

"What are you going to do?"

"Try and lay down the tracks before we leave. Thom's supposed to get something in writing."

I reach up and hug him. "I'm so proud of you."

He snorts. "Mitchell's offering more than our last advance for two songs. So, yes, we can afford the car."

"Holy crap."

"Yup."

Things are finally looking up for us.

CHAPTER FIFTY-SIX

Mallory

As PAMELA so cheerfully keeps reminding me in the days leading up to the awards show, it's not the Oscars.

I'm still having trouble containing my excitement as our limo pulls up to the red carpet. Gold ropes keep fans at bay, and photographers jostle one another for the best position.

An entire roll of boob tape seems to be keeping my dress in place so far. I'm still nervous about accidentally flashing someone when I climb out of the limo.

Chaser squeezes my hand and drops his gaze to where my fingers are pressed against my chest. "I got you, babe," he whispers.

"Go on," he says to Jacob and the others. "Singer should go first."

Naturally, Jacob doesn't disagree. He scoots out and raises his hands over his head, waving to the crowd. Garrett follows.

Alvin stops in front of us and pats my leg. "All my money's on you, Mallory."

A huff of laughter escapes me, chasing my anxiety away. "Thanks."

After he steps out, Chaser and I are alone.

I run my hand over his black pinstriped trousers. "You look sexy." He'd paired the pants with a plain black T-shirt and a pair of black Converse sneakers, assuring me that was as dressy as he was getting.

He leans in and kisses my forehead. "No matter what, you'll always be my favorite Video Vixen."

I'm too emotional to respond, and someone knocks on the window, signaling that we need to hurry anyway.

Chaser steps out and turns his back to the crowd, blocking their view while I do a quick check to be sure my boobs don't try to escape.

"Ready?" he asks.

"Ready." I tuck my gold clutch under my arm.

He takes my hand and together we face the red carpet.

"Chaser, over here!"

"Chaser, can we grab a photo?"

"Mallory, will you win Video Vixen?"

I wave at the reporter. "We'll see!"

Chaser stops in front of a different reporter and answers a few questions. Someone else comes up on my side.

"How badly do you want to win Video Vixen, Mallory?" he asks.

"Oh, I'm just thrilled to be nominated." I smile brightly, even though I'm already tired of the question.

Chaser answers questions and stops for pictures while continuing to move us forward.

Inside, we're herded into a room with a bar and tables overflowing with snacks and desserts.

"You want something?" Chaser asks.

"I'm too nervous." I smooth my hand over my dress.

"Let me get you some water."

I tighten my grip on his arm and lean up on my tiptoes. "No water. I don't think I can unlace this dress on my own, so I don't want to have to pee later."

He closes his eyes and snort-laughs at my predicament.

"It's not funny."

"If you're this nervous here, how are you going to survive when you get nominated for an Oscar?" he asks.

"I'll already have practice from going to these things with *you*."

"Hey, lovebirds," Jacob calls out. "Think you can cool it for a minute?"

"Aw, they're so cute," Vickie coos. I'm not sure if she's Jacob's or Garrett's date tonight, but she joined us at the last minute.

"Chaser!" Andrew bellows behind us.

"Christ," Chaser mutters under his breath.

Andrew embraces both of us before I have a chance to take in his outfit.

"Are you wearing...*zebra stripes*?" I ask when I pull away.

"Yeah, isn't it rad?" He holds his arms out and turns in a semi-circle to show off the black and white vest with nothing else under it and skin-tight leather pants. "Pammy picked it out."

"It's...something," I say.

"Come on. I made sure we're all sitting together." He waves for us to follow.

Chaser briefly closes his eyes. "Three months of this," he says low enough that only I can hear him. "Three months."

"Maybe he'll let you borrow his spiffy vest," I whisper.

He pinches my butt and kisses my cheek. "Careful," I warn. "I'm wearing about a pound of makeup."

"You're beautiful." He signals to the guys that we're going to find our seats, and we head down the aisle.

The show starts with Best Breakout Video.

"Shit," Jacob mutters.

The guys are all tense while each nominee is announced and a brief clip of the video plays. Chaser's holding my hand so tight, I have to give it a shake, so he loosens up.

"And the winner is...Wishing Well for 'Fear Nothing!'" the announcer shouts.

Chaser sits back. Disappointed or relieved, I can't tell.

Alvin mutters, "Fuck," under his breath.

"What a dick," Andrew says loud enough to be heard by half the theater.

I glance over at him, and he flashes his middle finger to Brent from Wishing Well. Pamela covers her mouth and giggles.

Chaser stares straight ahead at the stage, ignoring the spectacle next to us. I lean against him. "I guess Andrew's manager didn't give him the *gracious and humble* speech."

Chaser cracks a smile. "Guess not."

I don't have time to catch my breath from the excitement of Kickstart's first nomination.

"And now the nominees for Best Video Vixen!"

Blood roars through my ears. Of course, they choose the scene from 'Candy Jar' where I'm getting hosed down. I cringe and close my eyes.

"Fuck yeah!" Andrew whoops.

"Mallory Dove for 'Candy Jar' by Kickstart!" the announcer screams into the microphone.

My ears buzz. They did *not* just call my name.

"Mallory." Chaser tugs on my hand.

We both stand, and I'm frozen in place. "Chaser, please come with me," I whisper.

"No way, babe. This is all yours."

Everyone's staring at me now. The instrumental version of 'Candy Jar' thunders through the theater, calling me to the stage. "I'm afraid I'll trip going up those stairs," I admit.

Concern darkens his eyes, and he gently guides me out of the row and to the edge of the stage. I stare at the steps. I never ever expected to win, so I didn't put a lot of thought into things like tripping over my four-inch stilettos and landing flat on my face in front of five thousand people. Chaser doesn't release me, though. I gather the long skirt of my dress in my free hand, and he slowly leads me up the stairs.

"Go on," he whispers when we reach the top. "This is your moment." He presses a kiss on my forehead.

There's a collective "Aww" from the audience and heat stings my cheeks.

Projecting as much confidence as I can, I cross the stage to the podium. The long, heavy skirt of my gown swirls and swishes around my ankles. The presenter holds out a stubby silver statue, and I accept.

"Congratulations, Mallory." She leans in and kisses my cheek.

"Thank you."

What little girl, who wants to be an actress when she grows up, hasn't stared into the mirror and thanked the academy, her parents and God himself for recognizing her talent? None of that prepared me for this moment. Sure, it's not an award for my acting skills. And I hate the video. But it's still an honor and something I never expected.

I lean down next to the microphone. "I'm really not sure what to say." Well, that's an understatement. I crane my neck and glance at the screen behind me with the list of the other nominees. "I never expected to win tonight. There were so many other talented ladies...I never thought..." My voice falters. "Thank you so much." My gaze searches the crowd, landing on Alvin who flashes me two thumbs up and shouts my name. "Thank you to Kickstart for giving an unknown, new-to-Hollywood girl a chance." Garrett and Jacob let out shrill whistles. My gaze shifts to the left, where Chaser's waiting at the edge of the stage, with his hands clasped in front of him. "Thank you to Chaser Adams, whose support means everything." Behind me, the announcer clears her throat, signaling I need to wrap up my speech. "I also need to thank my agent Marilyn Stewart, Valerie Malone, and oh my gosh, I know I'm forgetting someone. But thank you!"

My heart hammers so hard, I'm afraid it'll jump out of my chest and run away. Music blasts over the speakers, and I resist the urge to flee from the stage. Carefully, I step back from the podium and off to my left, where I've watched every other winner disappear tonight. Chaser meets me halfway, and I'm still so nervous, I fling myself against him, forgetting we're in view of everyone.

"You did great," he says against my ear. "So proud of you."

I pull away, and he wraps an arm around my waist, guiding me behind heavy red velvet curtains.

Backstage is chaos.

"Congratulations, Mallory!"

Flashbulbs momentarily blind me, but serve as a reminder to play my part.

Look happy.

Act grateful.

Smile.

"Mallory, can we get a picture?"

"Chaser are you upset your girlfriend won while Kickstart lost Breakout Video?"

"Absolutely not." Chaser's terse answer sends the reporter scurrying away.

"Congratulations!" Andrew's dopey smile swoops in fast, as he grabs me in a big hug and spins me around. "You know I voted for you, right?" he whispers against my ear.

"You did?" I laugh.

"Fuck yeah, I did." He sets me down but doesn't let go. "They sent us tapes of all the nominees. Watching the videos back to back, there was no question who the hottest chick was."

Chaser clears his throat and drops his gaze to where Andrew's hands are resting on my waist. Andrew snatches them away, as if my hips suddenly turned into flames. "Proud of your girl?" he asks.

"Always," Chaser says.

One of the show's assistants rushes over to us. "You have to get back out there. Guitar God is coming up." She glances at Andrew. "You're not supposed to be back here."

"I'm Andrew Lane. I can be wherever I want, sweetheart."

She blushes. "I...know who you are, Mr. Lane. Your category is up soon."

"Gotcha." He winks at her, and I swear the girl almost swoons out of her heels.

When she comes to her senses, she glances at me. "I'll take your statue. We have a table you can pick it up at later."

"Thanks."

Chaser holds out his arm to me. "Ready?"

Chaser

This night is insane.

We barely make it back to our seats before the Guitar God category is called. Still excited over Mallory's win, I barely listen to the names as they're called out. I lean over when Vinnie's name is mentioned and shake his hand.

Because I thoroughly expect Vinnie or even Danny Desmond to win, I'm not prepared to hear my name, and, at first, assume it's a mistake.

Alvin, Garrett, and Jacob jump out of their seats, fists in the air, shouting for me to get my ass up. Vinnie even puts his hands together and stands.

"Fuck yeah, Chaser!" Andrew shouts, which is awkward as fuck, since the guitarist for his own band lost to me.

I reach for Mallory, and she squeezes my hand. "Get up there."

"Come with me."

"No way. I'm not going up there again."

I lean down. "I need you."

The Guitar God category apparently isn't limited to music videos. Footage from one of our shows with Shooting Fences plays over the screen. Do I really look that serious when I'm playing? I drop my gaze and laugh. *What a dick.*

I shake a few hands as we head up to the stage. Mallory stops, probably assuming I'll leave her to wait where I stood earlier. But no. I want her right next to me. Truth is, without her, I'd probably be rolling around in the gutter high out of my mind, instead of accepting this award.

The microphone's low, and I have to lean over to speak. "Guitar God. Wow. I never..." I stop and shake my head. "Thank you to our fans for making this happen. Every single one of you means so much to me and every member of Kickstart. Thanks to my father who always hated my music, but encouraged me to play it anyway." I glance at the small, silver trophy, suddenly feeling choked up. There has to be someone else I'm supposed to thank? No one comes to mind. "Alvin, Garrett, Jacob, thanks for sharing this dream with me.

Andrew, thanks for being so *rad*." I smirk into the camera, and Andrew's cheer can be heard over all the other noise.

I stop and glance behind me where Mallory's standing and reach back to grab her hand, tugging her forward. "Finally, I need to thank Mallory. If I'm a guitar god, it's only because I'm blessed to have this goddess in my life. Thank you."

My mind's blank except for my need to touch Mallory. Forgetting about the lights, the cameras that are taping every moment to play on television after, and the fact that we're on a stage in front of a huge audience, I pull her closer and slam my mouth over hers. At first, her body's stiff. Then she melts into me, sliding her arms around my neck.

"Best. Night. Ever," I whisper against her lips.

Mallory

Three down.

Two to go.

Jacob's tense, and I really hope the guys win one of the next two categories.

"Best Heavy Metal Performance Video goes to Vicious Vandals for 'Sinner's Breath'!"

"Woo!" Andrew jumps out of his seat and pumps his fists in the air. All four members of his band follow him up there, but Andrew's the only one who seems excited.

Pamela leans over Andrew's vacant chair. "It really should've been Kickstart."

I shrug and clap as the guys walk off with their trophies.

We sit through several more categories. Andrew picks up another statue for Best Drummer.

Video of the Year is saved for last, and I close my eyes. There's no way. We'd all talked about it. It's too broad a category with too many big-name artists with years in the music industry for a relatively unknown band to win.

"Kickstart for 'Candy Jar!'"

"Holy shit!" Jacob shouts.

"Fuck me!" Alvin stares at Chaser with a wide-eyed, wild expression for a few seconds before they bear hug each other.

This time, I shake my head when Chaser tries to pull me out of the aisle with him. "Go," I urge.

He races up with his bandmates, and I remain standing with the rest of the crowd, clapping my hands until they sting.

"Mallory, are you crying?" Andrew shouts.

"I'm really happy for them." I swipe at my cheeks but can't stop laughing and crying.

Chaser's right. Best night ever.

CHAPTER FIFTY-SEVEN

CHASER

"Chaser, bro, wake up."

Jacob's needy tone pulls me from a deep sleep.

"What?" I mumble.

Sleep's been a rare commodity on this tour. I'm so annoyed at the intrusion, I don't bother opening my eyes. Maybe he'll go away, and I can go back to dreaming about Mallory.

Unfortunately, I'm surrounded by a pack of unneutered dogs determined to fuck any woman willing to step on our tour bus.

Jacob's the biggest hound, but thankfully, he spends a lot of his time on Andrew's bus.

"Help. Please, you've gotta look at this."

This morning he seems bound and determined to annoy the fuck out of me.

"What now?" I crack open one eyelid and find a hairy, wrinkly ball sack dangling in my face. "What the fuck?" I jolt upright, nearly smacking my head into the bunk above me and shove him away.

Somehow, I went from best night ever and winning awards to waking up with my singer's balls in my face. Not exactly living my best rock star life at the moment.

"Chaser, I'm serious," he whines.

"I don't want to look at your sack first thing in the morning. Or *ever*." I push the curtain to my bunk all the way open. Where the fuck's the "tour manager" Thom sent on the road with us? With the money we're paying the useless asshole, he's the one who should have to look at Jacob's nut sack first thing in the morning.

"Not my balls," he pleads. "Look. There. What is that?"

Carefully, I lift my gaze to see where he's pointing. A patch of red bumps above his groin.

"Do I look like a fucking doctor to you?"

"Is it AIDS? Did I catch AIDS? Garrett and I read that *Time* magazine article, and I swear in one of the photos some dude had lesions just like this."

"Jesus Christ, you're a sex ed fail." I glance over again, studying the redness. "I don't know. It's probably a simple rash."

"Remember that little junkie stripper I fucked in Salt Lake City? I bet it's her fault."

"Really? I bet it's the fault of the dude who sticks his unwrapped dick in anything that moves."

"Not cool, bro."

"Forgive me." I scrub my hands over my face, if only I could burn the image of Jacob's nuts from my eyeballs as easily. "I'm a bit grumpy from waking up with someone's diseased dick in my face."

What city are we even in today? After a while, all the cities we visit seem to blend together.

The tour's been amazing, but one of the most fast-paced we've ever been on. Turns out great for me. Keeps me focused and disciplined. The other guys took it seriously for a while too. Even Vicious Vandals, a notorious party band if ever there was one, clung to their sobriety for the first few weeks. That slowly slipped away until the band had divided themselves onto two separate buses. One sober bus and one party bus. Jacob and Garrett eventually gravitated to the party bus, which didn't bother me as much as it should have. Less of their bullshit to tolerate.

Until today's balls-in-my-face episode.

When I open my eyes again, Jacob's still grumbling, but thankfully, zipping up his jeans. "Fuck you. If I die, you're going to feel bad for being mean to me."

I crawl out of my bunk, stand and stretch, listening to my vertebrae snap, crackle, and pop. Next time we tour, we better be able to afford more frequent hotel stays.

I slap Jacob on the shoulder. "Dude, if you die, I'll definitely feel bad, but it won't be because of that."

His mouth twists, and he reaches down to scratch his balls. "Shit, this hurts all over. I think it's spreading."

"Get your ass to a doctor before your dick falls off."

"That's not funny." He duck-walks down the aisle toward the front of the bus.

Maybe I'm an asshole, but I can't stop laughing. "Karma comes for you when you least expect it!" I shout after him.

He throws up his middle finger.

Unfortunately, he returns fifteen minutes later. At least this time, he keeps his pants on. "I found a clinic not too far. Will you come with me?"

"Where's Garrett?"

"Fucking that chick we picked up in Santa Fe. I don't want

to interrupt his flow. What else do you have to do but sit around moping about Mallory?"

"*That's* how you want to convince me to come with you?"

"Come on, please? I don't want to be alone if it's bad news."

"Fine." Fuck knows the asshole's liable to get lost trying to score drugs, and we need to be on stage at seven p.m. He's been cutting it closer and closer every night.

I grab my leather jacket and follow him outside. We flag down a cab, and Jacob gives him the address.

The driver keeps eyeing us in the mirror, until I ask him if he has a problem. Maybe he recognizes us. Maybe he knows where he's dropping us off and he's afraid we're infecting his seats. Who knows.

The area the clinic's located in is downright nasty. I peer out the window. The grungy building has no sign or indication that it's a medical facility.

"This is it," the driver announces.

Jacob tosses him some cash, and we slide out of the car. The guy can't speed away fast enough.

Jacob and I stand there staring up at the building.

"What is this? The saddest dick clinic in the world?"

"I don't know." He shrugs. "The ad in the phonebook said free, confidential clinic."

Reluctantly, I follow him upstairs. I don't see any rats, but it definitely has the vibe of a place rats would find cozy.

A nurse in a white outfit greets us inside the office.

"Holdin McGroin," Jacob announces. "I called earlier."

The woman rolls her eyes and hands him a clipboard. "Fill that out, Mr. *Mah-Groin*." Her gaze shifts to me. "You too?"

"Nope. Just here for moral support."

"You don't have to be so gleeful about it," Jacob bitches.

We drop into two chairs, and I glance around at the crusty medical office. "Bro, keep your boxers on and don't lay down anywhere. If you do, fifty to one says you're leaving here with crabs in addition to whatever else you've got going on down there."

"I hate you." He flips through the papers on the clipboard. "Garrett would've been more supportive."

"He's an enabler. You're in need of tough love."

He waves off my assessment. "Bro, don't you miss strange pussy?"

I glance at him and arch an eyebrow at our surroundings. "Not even a little."

"Shit!" He laughs and slaps my leg. "Do you remember when we all caught crabs from Patricia after the Clover show?"

"Jesus Christ." I sit up and run my hands through my hair. "That was fucking horrible."

"Remember how pissed Alvin was when we didn't warn him?"

"We didn't *know*."

"And we kept calling her Crabby Patty until she tried to run me over with her car?"

"We were assholes."

"What are you talking about? That was fucking hilarious. I wonder what she's up to now? She was a fireball in the sack."

"Yeah, and a crotch fire after."

We're stopped from our disgusting stroll down degenerate memory lane by the nurse calling several times for "Holdin."

I nudge him with my elbow. "I'll wait here."

Jacob stops and stares at me. "You're really making me do this by myself?"

"You already played your *dick in my face card* for the year." I shrug and hold up my hands. "Sorry, buddy. Nothing I can do."

"Asshole."

I tap my fingers against my leg and pull out the small

notepad and pen I keep stashed in my jacket pocket. Despite my less than sterling surroundings, I miss Mallory. No matter where I am, my need for her is a tireless throbbing inside my chest. Writing has helped channel all my pent-up desire. I use my time alone to jot down some lyrics. The need to finish my latest song about her has turned into a never-ending beat against my ribcage.

The band's supposed to go from the tour into the studio to record our next album with Cutter, and I want to have plenty of material.

About forty-five minutes later, Jacob returns with a readjusted attitude and a bottle of pills.

"Do we need to burn the bus to the ground?" God damn do I enjoy being an asshole to Jacob as frequently as possible. "Throw all your pants into a bonfire?"

"Shut up."

"You're not going to tell me? You can't keep me in suspense after I dragged myself down to the bowels of hell to hold your hand."

"It's nothing some antibiotics won't cure."

He pays the nurse, and she calls a cab for us.

Downstairs, Jacob glances at the building then hunches over and pulls something out of his jacket pocket. "I relieved them of some of these." He giggles like a little kid.

I stare at the hypodermics in his hand. "I thought you kicked that shit back in L.A.? What the fuck do you need needles for?"

"I don't want to share with Vinnie. He's been fucking everything with a pulse. God only knows what he has."

I squeeze my eyes shut and tip my head back. This tour gets worse every day. "Is *that* what you and Garrett are up to? Speedballs with Vinnie?"

"Vinnie's a generous dude. You should come party on their bus with us more often."

"No thanks."

I nod to the hypodermics he's stuffing inside his coat. What the fuck am I going to do about this? "We could've, you know, stopped at a drug store or something. You didn't need to steal from the free clinic."

"The opportunity presented itself, so I took them." He shrugs. "No biggie."

"Yeah, sure."

As much as Jacob pisses me off, this new development kills me. But I have no idea how to handle it without making things worse.

What can I do to stop my friend and bandmate from taking this long, casual stroll into the abyss?

CHAPTER FIFTY-EIGHT

MALLORY

"Cut!" The director yells.

My assistant tosses a robe my way, and I hurry to wrap it over my skimpy swimsuit.

Please let this be it for the day.

"Jesus," Pamela mutters. "That had to be the longest shoot in history."

"I know." I sneak a look at the clock. "I'm hoping we're done."

"Big plans?"

The question's full of the usual snark I've come to expect from Pamela. Working on the same show, our boyfriends both out on tour together, you'd think we'd be friends. But she's treated me more like a competitor since the day the producers announced I'd now have a recurring role in the series. I don't know why. She's still the star. My face isn't even shown in the credits.

"I'm flying out to see Chaser," I answer without looking at her. I'd learned the first week the guys were out on tour she didn't want to talk about anything related to Vicious Vandals.

"How cute. God only knows what you'll walk in on."

Chaser and I are way past the stage in our relationship where I'm insecure about what he's doing out on the road. Despite the expense, he calls me every night after a show. On his days off, we're able to talk longer, and he's filled me in on everything.

"I'm sure it'll be chaos." I shrug and turn to leave for my dressing room. I have a flight to catch.

After several delays, my plane finally lands in Houston. I can't push my way through the throng of people to find Chaser fast enough.

"Are you really finally here or am I dreaming?" he asks as I throw myself against him.

"I thought I'd never get here. Have you been waiting the whole time?"

"Baby, I'd wait for you forever." He cups my face, tilting my head to the side. "How are you even more beautiful than when I left?"

The chance to answer is stolen when he leans down and presses his lips to mine for a deep, unhurried kiss.

When he releases me, I sway on my feet. All around us, people have stopped to stare. Whether it's from our melting-hot reunion kiss or because they recognize him, I'm not sure. Chaser easily slides back into his give-no-fucks persona, ignoring the gawkers.

"Any bags?" he asks.

I hold up my one lone duffel. "Nope. I didn't want to waste

any time. I hope you'll forgive the lack of makeup and dressy clothes this weekend."

His lips curl. "You didn't need to bring any clothes at all, little dove."

Outside, he's more serious. "I borrowed Darren's car. It's disgusting."

"I don't care."

"And we have to sleep on the bus tonight. Actually, it's rolling out at midnight." He stops to check his watch.

"Chaser, I'll sleep on the side of the highway as long as I'm with you."

We arrive at the stadium parking lot quicker than I expected. Except for a few scattered cars, groups of random people loitering around, and three large tour buses, the lot is empty.

"How was the show?" Guilt that I'd missed another one of Kickstart's performances gnaws at me.

"Incredible. The crowd was amazing. Most of them already had the new songs memorized. It was wild."

"I'm so happy."

He grins at me. "I can't wait to play you some of the new things I've been working on."

"Hopefully, we'll have a little time tomorrow?"

We stop next to the red and black painted bus. Their top-hat wearing skull logo stares down at us with a sinister smile. When I saw the bus back in L.A., it had seemed huge. Now, that I'm planning to spend the next couple of nights on it, not so much.

Chaser's guitar tech Darren holds out his hands for the keys. "Hey, Mallory," he greets in a low voice. "We were starting to worry you weren't coming back," he says to Chaser.

"Her flight got delayed a couple times."

"We'll probably roll out in twenty. Drive straight through and find somewhere for breakfast."

"Sounds good."

The bus is mostly dark and quiet as we climb aboard.

"Wow." I glance at the bunk beds near the back of the bus. Two on each side, separated by a narrow aisle. "You can reach out and high-five each other."

"We do, frequently." Jacob pokes his head out from behind his curtain. "How you doing, Mallory?"

"Hey, Jacob."

Something taps my head, and I glance up to find Garrett leaning out of his bunk. "Welcome to the madhouse."

"Seems tame tonight."

The two of them grin at each other, and Jacob answers, "Don't worry. That can always change."

They disappear into their bunks, and I glance at Chaser. "That's not ominous," I whisper.

"Ignore them."

"What are the chances of me taking a shower before bed? I reek of delays and desperation."

"Desperation?"

"To get to you." I tap his chest.

"Oh, puke!" Jacob moans from behind his curtain. "Can you two go do that romantic shit somewhere else?"

Female giggles from both upper bunks follow Jacob's demand. Chaser lifts his middle fingers in the air and jerks his head toward the back of the bus.

He slides a small door open, revealing what passes for a bathroom. "We're not the neatest."

His apologetic tone prods me to try not to wrinkle my nose in disgust.

He places his hands on my waist, sliding them up, until he's cupping my breasts. I glance down the hallway, but no one's paying attention to us.

"Everyone's busy." He kisses my neck while nudging me into the bathroom.

Inside, there's just enough room for me to perch on the edge of the sink if we're both going to occupy the tiny space.

The heat of the bus and our close proximity heightens his unique, masculine scent. I rest my head against his chest for a moment, inhaling him. "I love the way you smell."

He chuckles softly, his hot breath grazing my shoulder.

"Tomorrow," Chaser mutters in between kisses. "We'll check into a nice hotel, and I'll worship you properly."

"All I want is you. Any way I can have you. Anywhere."

He kisses the crook of my neck, nuzzling and rubbing his bristly cheek over my skin. "Let's take this off." He slips his hands under my shirt, lifting it out of the way and tossing it over the shower door.

He sucks in a slow, deep breath as I work his jeans loose. "Going right for it, huh?" He winks, then groans when I stroke my hand over his cock.

"You have no idea how much I want you inside me."

"Let me see you first." He unhooks my bra and drops it in the sink. "You're so pretty," he murmurs, gazing at my breasts. He strokes rough fingers over my nipples then lowers his head to flick his tongue over the tips.

"Oh!" I gasp when he sucks one nipple is his mouth and pulls hard. He gives my other breast the same love. I rake my fingers through the soft strands of his hair, holding him in place. He pulls back and blows a breath over my damp nipples, gazing up at me with smoldering eyes.

His mouth finds mine again, hot and wet. I wrap my arms around his neck, holding on while he works my pants and underwear down my legs.

He growls when they get stuck on my sneakers. "That's good enough." I part my knees, unable to wait another second. "Come here."

He slides his hands down my back, holding me still as he rolls his hips, brushing his thick erection against me.

"Don't tease." Desire fires through me, leaving me hot all over.

He pushes my thighs wider and rubs his fingers through my wetness. "You want it bad, don't you?"

"Chaser." Instead of the stern tone I was aiming for, my voice quivers as a flood of heat rushes between my thighs. "Please."

Finally, he thrusts inside me slowly, hissing with pleasure. "Fuck, you feel good. I missed you so much."

"Me too." I pull him down for another kiss. "But please fuck me harder."

He lets out a strangled groan. "I don't want to hurt you."

"You won't." Sweat glistens on his chest, highlighting his beautiful ink and muscles. He throbs inside me, so hard and thick. I don't mean to, but my nails dig into his shoulders, struggling to draw him closer.

His quick, measured drives tighten my body.

"So good." My back bows, and I slam my palm against the wall to hold myself up. "I love how you feel inside me."

He kisses me again, his hands clutching my hips, as he finds a steady rhythmic pace. I gasp and moan, not really caring if the whole bus can hear me as I tighten around him.

"There." I shiver with pleasure, climaxing with gasping, shuddering breaths.

"That's it," he coaxes. "Fuck, you're so beautiful."

His pace quickens and turns erratic. He throws his head back, squeezing his eyes shut when his orgasm hits. I watch every beautiful second. His large, powerful frame trembles as he groans my name.

He releases his bruising hold on my hips and nuzzles his sweat-slicked forehead against mine.

"I can't feel my legs," I whisper.

Slowly, he returns to himself. "Sorry that was so quick."

"I loved every second."

No matter how skilled we are at sharing tight spaces, there's no way for both of us to fit in the shower. We take turns cleaning up under the weak spray. Chaser wraps me in a towel, he swears is clean, and leaves for a minute, returning with one of his shirts. "Wear this for me?"

I hold the shirt up against my body. "It'll be a nightgown on me."

"I want it to smell like you, so when you go home..." His soft, dark eyes watch as I slip on the shirt. "I'm going to stuff it in my pillow and pretend you're still here."

"Chaser." That is both the sweetest and saddest thing he's ever said to me. How am I supposed to leave him to go back to L.A. in a few days?

"What can I say?" He shrugs. "Your junkyard dog needs the scent of his woman on the road."

"Please don't talk about leaving," I whisper. "I just got here."

"You're right." He holds out his hand. "Ready for bed?"

The fatigue hits, leaving me yawning and nodding at the same time.

"Come on."

We step out of the bathroom into the mostly darkened bus. I try not to speculate what sticky substances my feet come into contact with on the way to Chaser's bunk. Something crinkles and crunches under my toes. A half-eaten bag of chips?

Finally, we reach the bunks. He pulls his curtain back, and I peer into the darkness.

Sensing my hesitation, he unhooks a miniature flashlight from a hook on the wall and shines it into the space. "It's safe," he assures me.

"You're all set up like a boy scout here, huh?" I nod to the flashlight.

"Nah." He shines the light under his chin. "Alvin and I were telling ghost stories the other night."

Not sure if he's kidding or not, I crawl into bed.

"Hey, Mallory," Alvin calls out from across the way. "Welcome home."

"Aw. Thank you, Alvin," I whisper back.

"Home away from home," Garrett mumbles from above us.

"Home is wherever you are," I whisper in Chaser's ear, when he settles in next to me.

"Same."

Chaser

"Where's Chaser? I got a present for him." Andrew's sneaky voice floats down the center of the bus, jarring me out of sleep. Female giggles follow.

Why the fuck is he on our bus at this hour?

We're not moving anymore, but it still has to be pretty early.

"I wouldn't man," Alvin says. "Hey, hon. How you doing?"

"Hi, Alvin," the girl coos.

"Come on, I thought you wanted to meet Chaser?" Andrew persists.

"He's sleeping," Alvin warns.

"That's the problem." Andrew's version of a whisper is

bound to wake up the whole bus any minute now. "He hasn't had any fun on this tour. I'm worried about him."

"He's fine. I'm warning you, man. He won't appreciate it."

"What's going on?" Mallory whispers.

"Nothing. Go back to sleep. It's still early." My body coils, ready to strike the second someone invades our space.

"Chaser," Andrew sings. "Where you hiding, bro? I've got a surprise for youuu."

This bullshit's gone on long enough. Two or three times a week, he sends some random, unsuspecting groupie onto the bus in search of me. I've either sent them away in tears, because Andrew assured them I was a sure thing, or one of the other guys eases her disappointment. Andrew pulling this stunt when Mallory's here is too much.

Time to put an end to his childish antics.

Stealthy as a panther, I reach up and unlock the secret compartment above my bunk. Mallory was partially right earlier. It was the biker in me, not the boy scout, who fitted out my space with whatever I might need on this tour.

The weight of the revolver in my hand is like reuniting with a faithful friend.

The screech of the curtain above us being pulled back is punctuated by a squeal and Garrett's hostile, "What the fuck?"

"Sorry, looking for Chaser. Howdy, my lady." Andrew giggles like a little kid.

One...two...three...

Our curtain whooshes open, revealing Andrew's maniacal grin. "Ha! Found ya, motherfucker—"

I point the revolver dead center to Andrew's forehead, digging the metal into his skin. His gleeful expression morphs into shock. "What the fuck, bro!?"

"I tried to warn you." Alvin doesn't even bother to hide the glee in his voice.

The half-naked girl at Andrew's side shrieks and runs for the front of the bus.

"What did I tell you about bringing girls to my bunk, Andrew?" I ask, slowly sitting up, but keeping the gun pointed at him.

"To stop doing it." He backs up into the bunks on the other side and puts his hands in the air.

"Knock it off," Jacob mutters.

"Then why are you here?" I ask.

"I was worried about you, bro. You gotta be lonely by now."

"Andrew, have I given you the impression I can't take care of myself?"

He scratches the side of his head. "Huh?"

"Chaser?" Mallory's soft voice dials my rage back to a simmer.

"Oh, shit. Hey, Mallory. Didn't realize you were here." Andrew cranes his neck to peer into the bunk. "Could you ask your boyfriend to stop pointing his gun at me? It's making me nervous."

Mallory chuckles. "What'd you do to piss him off?"

"Get the fuck off our bus." I take a step toward him, and he backs away, hands still in the air. "Your band's got two fucking buses full of all the entertainment you need. No reason for you to be over here."

"Okay. Okay. It's cool, Chaser. Everything's cool. We're cool."

He backs all the way down the aisle and stumbles off the steps, hitting the pavement ass first.

The girl he brought cuddles up to Alvin and runs her fingers through his hair.

Alvin flashes me a thumb's up.

Our driver's crashed out in his captain's chair and snorts in his sleep. Apparently, he missed the entertainment.

Shaking my head, I tuck the gun in my waistband. Garrett thrusts his hand out of his bunk, and I slap it as I walk by.

"Nice job, Chaser."

"I've had it with that overgrown fucking toddler," I grumble. Jesus Christ, my MC brothers love playing pranks on each other. Did all sorts of deranged shit to me when I was prospecting for the club. I still never put up with the sort of bullshit Andrew comes up with almost every single night.

I throw myself into my bunk and tuck the revolver back into its hiding spot.

"Chaser, what was that all about?" she whispers.

"Nothing, little dove. Andrew thinks he's a prankster." I hold out my arm for her to snuggle against me.

"Does he bring...women to you when I'm not here?"

"Every chance he gets."

"Why?"

I turn my head, but with the curtain closed, it's hard to make out her face in the darkness.

"I told you a long time ago, most guys fuck around out on the road. Apparently, it annoys him that I don't participate."

"He cheats on Pamela?"

"I don't want to talk about them."

She pinches my nipple.

"Watch yourself, woman." I lean down and growl against her throat, making her laugh.

There's some truth to that old saying; be careful what you wish for.

I can't wait for this tour to finish.

CHAPTER FIFTY-NINE

Mallory

The buses pull up to an all-you-can-eat breakfast buffet a few hours later.

"Morning!" Andrew greets us at the front door. He holds his hands in the air. "I'm unarmed, don't shoot me, Chaser!"

"Heard you pulled a gun on him last night." Vinnie walks up and hugs Chaser from behind. "Been wanting to blow a hole in him for years myself."

"You fucking love me, asshole," Andrew shouts.

Everyone in the restaurant is staring at us now.

Peter runs up to us. I've only met Kickstart's tour manager once, but he's a nervous guy who doesn't seem to be a fan of mine. "Please tell me you didn't pull a gun on Andrew Lane. He's been telling everyone you went Dirty Harry on him last night."

Chaser shrugs, casually, as if he threatens to shoot people

on a regular basis. "It was the middle of the night. I thought he was a burglar."

Pete's beady eyes land on me, and his nuclear expression threatens to melt me into a puddle. "Do you need to cause trouble everywhere you go?"

"I didn't do anything." I hold one hand up to the heavens. "I was asleep."

"Watch it, Pete," Chaser warns. "I'm still feeling trigger happy this morning."

He chuckles as Peter flails his arms in the air and stomps away.

"Are you going to get in trouble?" I whisper.

"Nah." He waves off my concern.

"What if Andrew files a police report?"

"As dumb as he is, he's not a snitch." He rubs his knuckles over my cheek. "The gun's legal."

Somehow, I doubt that.

We make our way over to the buffet. I scoop a pile of soggy eggs and bacon onto my plate, grab a glass of orange juice and scan the room for an empty table.

"Mallory!" Andrew waves his arms and pats the seat next to him. "Chaser!"

Chaser grumbles under his breath but pulls out a chair across from Andrew for me and then takes the one next to me.

"When'd you get in, Mallory?" Andrew rests his chin in his hands and leans forward.

"Late. My flight got canceled twice."

"Chaser didn't say you were coming to visit."

I raise an eyebrow. "Is that your excuse for bringing a girl over for him?"

He flicks his gaze toward Chaser. "Just fucking with you, bro. I didn't think you'd get so pissed."

Chaser shrugs. "Now you know."

Still unsettled from last night, I can't stomach the lukewarm food and end up pushing my plate away.

"You want me to grab you something else?" Chaser asks.

"No, it all looked pretty bad."

"You pregnant?" Andrew asks.

Chaser closes his eyes and inhales a long, slow breath. I rest my hand over his in an attempt to keep him from blowing up.

"Not that I know of, Andrew." I force a sweet smile. "But if I am, I promise you'll be the first to know."

Next to me, Chaser chuckles.

"Cool. Can I be the godfather?"

"No," Chaser answers without looking up from his plate.

"Why not?"

"Probably because you keep trying to get him to cheat on Mallory." Alvin taps his cheek. "I mean off the top of my head, that's my first guess."

"Nah, her man's passed with flying colors. She should be thanking me. Right, Mallory?"

"Oh, absolutely, Andrew. Thank you *so* much."

He grins, either oblivious to the sarcasm or willfully ignoring it.

How the hell did this strange and childish man manage to become so successful?

"Guys!" Peter stops at the end of our table. "I need a word with you. Now."

Chaser leans over and kisses my cheek. "Hotel tonight. Let's try to check in early."

I'm too excited about not sleeping on the bus to question whether we have the money for a hotel. "Okay."

He kisses my forehead. "Go pack up your stuff. I'll meet you outside the bus as soon as we're done."

"What'd Pammy say when you told her you were coming to visit?" Andrew asks after the guys leave.

"Not much." I shrug and keep pushing the food around on my plate.

Andrew's big, tattooed hand comes into my field of vision, pushing my plate aside. He drops an apple on the table in its place.

"Where'd you find that?" Actual fruit had been absent from the buffet.

"I swiped it from the front desk at our hotel." He lifts his chin. "You can have it. My apology apple."

This is why it's hard to stay mad at Andrew for long. I pick up a knife and slice the apple in half, then quarters. "I'll share."

He scoops up one of the slices and chomps down. "Rest is yours," he mumbles around the mouthful.

"Thanks." I glance around the dining room but all the servers seem to be afraid to approach our section. Can't blame them.

"What's wrong?" Andrew asks.

"I was going to ask if they had any peanut butter."

He stands and slaps the table. "Be right back."

I nibble on one of the apple slices and search the room, hoping Peter isn't yelling at the guys over something stupid.

"Here you go." A heavy tub lands on the table in front of me.

"What the?" I scan the industrial label on the side. *Extra Creamy Peanut Butter.* "Oh my God! Where did you steal that from?"

"I borrowed it from the kitchen." Andrew grins and hands me another apple.

I can't stop laughing. "Thank you."

A seriously annoyed man in an apron walks up behind Andrew and taps him on the shoulder. "Excuse me, sir. You can't just—"

"Shhh." Andrew places one finger over his mouth and

reaches into his pocket, pulling out a fistful of crumpled money and shoves it at the man. "Go. Just go, dude."

Still laughing, I shake my head and peel the lid off the container. "You're nuts." I take a clean spoon and scoop out a hefty amount of peanut butter and drop it into an empty bowl.

"Thank you, sir." Andrew sticks the cover on the tub and pushes it over to the man in the apron. "That'll be all."

The man leaves, grumbling all the way.

"That's so sweet, Andrew. Can't wait until Chaser hears. Maybe he'll actually blow your brains out this time," Kyle yells across the room.

Andrew raises his hand and flips him off, without taking his eyes off me.

Ignoring Kyle, I spread some peanut butter on one of the apple slices and hand it to Andrew. I prepare another one and offer it to Vinnie.

"Thanks, hon."

"Do you ever," Andrew stops and swipes his tongue over his fingers, "Like, let Chaser lick stuff off your body?"

I close my eyes and sigh.

"What? It's just a question."

I point my butter knife at him. "You had to ruin the nice thing you did."

"That's his modus operandi," Vinnie says. "In case you haven't noticed."

"Oh, I noticed."

"It's a tricky thing," Andrew continues. "You have to make sure you get it all; otherwise, you have food smeared in places that get uncomfortable. And it's all sticky."

"Thanks for the tip."

"Ah-ha! That means you've never tried it."

I finish eating and grab a cup of coffee before heading

outside to the bus. Andrew catches up to me, slinging his arm around my shoulders and steering me toward his band's bus.

"What are you doing? I need to grab my stuff."

"I have a present for you."

He sighs and gives me the wounded puppy expression when I refuse to get on the bus with him. "I'll wait right here." I promise, firmly planting my feet on the asphalt.

A few minutes later, he returns with a black T-shirt. "I just got a new order of these in and wanted you to have one."

"Oh, thank you." I unfold it and chuckle at the Vicious Vandals cartoon on the front. Andrew's happy face, smack dab in the middle. "Did you draw this?"

"Yeah. Someone else did the shading and had them printed up for me, though."

"You're multi-talented, huh?"

He points to the right side of his head. "Yeah, but only left-brain stuff, you know?"

I bite down on my lip, trying not to laugh. "I know."

"Will you wear it to the show tonight?" His mouth stretches into a slow smile. "Please?"

He has done an awful lot to help Kickstart out. Wearing his shirt for one night seems like a simple way to say thank you. "Maybe."

Chaser

Peter's lengthy meeting to warn us not to fuck up our *Rolling Stone* interview this afternoon doesn't improve my mood.

Rolling fucking Stone wants to put Kickstart on the cover. How the fuck did that happen?

"They want to talk to Mallory, too. That won't be a problem, will it?" Peter asks.

"Nope."

"Just steer clear of any questions about Bloody Revolver. We don't want that to become an issue again." Peter was so scandalized when he found out I'd beaten Davey Revolver bloody in England, he can't stop bringing it up. Apparently, he's a big Bloody Revolver fanboy. One more reason I hate this dude.

"Why?" Alvin asks. "The world should know what a sleaze bucket he is."

Peter glares at him.

"Oh, that's right, Alvin," I drawl. "Then we'd have to explain that our singer is just as sleazy."

"I thought we'd moved past this?" Jacob says.

I shrug. "Peter started it." I shoot a glare his way. "Why the fuck would I ever bring up that fiasco?"

"It may be a respectable magazine, but they still want to dig for dirt." He huffs and flips through the papers in his lap. "Talk up the tour with Vicious Vandals. Your friendship with Andrew and the guys. Fans love hearing that their favorite bands are friends and hang out behind the scenes, so talk up that angle." He flips through a few more pages.

"Anything else?" I'm not thrilled about leaving Mallory alone with Andrew on the loose.

"Please don't fuck up this interview. It's a big fucking deal." He casts his murderous manager face at Jacob. "Do *not* show up drunk or high. There are enough rumors about your addictions swirling around without you confirming any of them."

Jacob has the nerve to act insulted. "I never drink before I go on stage. Well, anymore." He rubs his hand over his throat. "I can't do much talking at the interview anyway. I need to preserve these babies."

"I'm sure they'll pick up your slack." He nods to Garrett, Alvin, and me.

Once we're set free, I hunt Mallory down and find her stretched out in my bunk on the bus, reading a book. "Ready to blow this cage?" I ask.

"Thank goodness, I was starting to wonder if Peter locked you up before the show."

"He can try." I drop down on the sliver of mattress available and run my hand over Mallory's legs up to her shoulders. "Would you like to go somewhere we have some privacy?"

She closes the book and rolls to her side. "More than anything. I'm all packed."

I pick up her duffel bag, find my own and stuff a few things inside, then take her hand. "Peter arranged early check-ins for us."

Outside, Mallory stretches her arms toward the sky. "I'm looking forward to a real bed."

"Me too." Not even for carnal purposes. I've got so many kinks in my neck and back from being jammed into the tiny bunk for so many nights, I'm not sure I'll ever walk straight again. "Andrew behave himself after I left?"

She snort-laughs. "He's crazy. He gave me his apple, and when I mentioned I wanted peanut butter to go with it, he stole a giant tub of it from the kitchen."

Not sure I like any man—but especially Andrew—feeding my woman, I simply nod. "That's nice."

"I think it was his way of apologizing for last night."

"Sure."

"This has been a good tour for Kickstart, right?"

There's no denying we've gained a lot of new fans. Robbie has been manning our merch booth and swears we sold more T-shirts than Vicious Vandals the other night. A big deal for the opening act. "Yeah, it's been good."

"I'm so happy you've found the success you deserve."

"Ahhh." I take her hand and spin her around the parking lot a few times until she's laughing uncontrollably. "Success can never be owned, little dove. We only rent it. If we want to hang on to success, the rent's due every day."

"Wow." She thumps into my chest and stares up at me. "That's deep, Chaser."

I lean down and whisper in her ear, "I'm going to pin your ankles to your ears when we get to our hotel room and show you the meaning of *deep*."

She slicks her tongue over her bottom lip and darts a look at the tour bus. Good to know she wants me as bad as I want her, but I need a bed this time.

"Come on."

We race across the hotel's parking lot and into their front lobby.

The hotel's desk clerk seems less than thrilled to have a bunch of dirty rock stars invading the place. Given some of the guys' antics that have been reported in the papers on this tour, I can't blame him.

"Hey." I lower my voice and lean in. "Any chance you can put us on a different floor from the rest of my 'em?" I glance at Mallory. "We'd like some quiet."

He hums and flips through his giant book. "I can put you on the seventh floor. The rest of your party is on five."

"Perfect. One more thing. Promise me you won't give our room number out to anyone? No matter who asks. I don't have any sisters or brothers. And my dad's all the way in New York."

"Yes, Mr. Adams." He sighs as if he's dealing with an idiot. "It's against hotel policy to give out the room numbers or names of our guests."

"Yeah, I get that, but some people are pretty persuasive."

"I'll make a note, you're not to be disturbed."

"Thank you."

He hands me two keys. I sign some paper, and we head upstairs.

"What was that all about?" Mallory asks.

"I don't want Andrew to call the desk clerk and say he's my long-lost brother or some shit, so he can barge in on us to show off his collection of leather thongs."

On this tour, I'd learned he owns enough tiny cock hammocks to be considered an actual *collection.* And on hot nights, that's *all* he wears on stage. All this time I'd thought that was a rumor. But, nope one-hundred percent true.

"Oh. Good call."

Finally alone in our room, I slide all the locks home and turn to face her. She's closer than I expected and reaches up to brush her fingers against my jaw and cup my face. "I'm so happy we're finally alone."

"You have no idea." I lean down and press my lips to hers, slowly licking her lip.

She moans, angling her head, seeking more. I press forward, gripping her hips and yanking her closer. I thoroughly tease her with soft nuzzling strokes of my tongue.

"More," she whispers against my mouth.

I shift both hands lower to grab her ass, pulling her closer with a demanding grip.

Except for traffic noises from outside and our heavy breathing, the room is silent.

"Missed you." I pull back and study her face. "I'm thrilled the show gave you the recurring role, but I can't stand us being away from each other for so long."

"I hate it too."

"We'll have to figure out a plan. So the next time I'm on tour, you can come see me more often." Even as I say the words, I don't know how that's ever going to work. She can't dictate the production schedule any more than I can decide the touring schedule.

"We'll be off for the summer...Marilyn says there's a movie audition. The director really wants me to read for it, but I'd be in Canada all summer then."

"Fuck." I look past her, staring out the window at the gray sky. Summer's prime touring season. "We'll work it out. I want you to nail that audition."

She nods, but I see the hesitation in her eyes. "I mean it, Mallory. We'll be fine. You'll fly out to see me when you can, and I'll fly to see you on our days off."

"Okay."

I glance at the clock. "We need to get downstairs and over to the arena. There's a reporter from *Rolling Stone* who wants to interview us."

"Us, you and me? Or *us* Kickstart?"

"All of the above."

"Do I have time to change?" she asks.

"Only if I can watch."

I'm stopped from following her to the bedroom by the phone ringing.

"I asked not to be disturbed," I answer.

"Sorry, sir. There's an Andrew—"

"Give me that," someone mutters in the background. "Chaser! Brother, where are you?" Andrew yells into the phone.

"We'll be down in a few minutes."

"What room are you in?"

"Thirteen-oh-one." Like most hotels, this one doesn't have a thirteenth floor, so that should keep Andrew busy for a while.

"On my way!" He hangs up, without saying anything else.

I'm still laughing to myself, picturing Andrew running

around looking for the thirteenth floor, when Mallory shouts, "Ready!"

I glance up and take in her outfit, slowly absorbing every beautiful detail.

Black suede boots, tiny denim skirt, bracelets laddered up her arms.

My breath stutters.

A Vicious Vandals T-shirt.

No. Nope. No way.

A cartoon version of Andrew's goofy face sits smack between her tits.

Hell-to-the-fucking-no.

The frown on my face must be working overtime. Mallory blinks up at me. "What? Andrew gave me the shirt and asked me to wear it tonight."

I bet he did.

"I thought it would be a nice gesture for the interview... both bands support each other...the way Andrew's gone on MTV and the tour..." Her voice trails off as the *fuck no* expression on my face doesn't soften.

Despite the tornado brewing inside me, I gently set my hands on Mallory's shoulders and lean down so we're eye-to-eye. "Baby, I love you so much. That was a very sweet idea. And you know I'd never be some controlling asshole who tells you what you can and cannot wear. You're so fucking sexy in everything you put on your body." I stop and take a breath. "But you absolutely can*not* wear that tonight."

Or ever. But I'll deal with that later.

She plucks at the material and stares down at the design. "It's just a shirt."

If she were any other woman in the world, I'd assume she was deliberately trying to provoke me. But this is Mallory and she'd never do that. She really doesn't see the harm. "It will make me fucking insane to see that motherfucker's band logo splashed across your tits all fucking night." I was aiming for calm, but a few more fucks than I planned on slip into my explanation.

Her fingers curl in the hem. "You're friends. You don't want me to support your friend?"

At the moment, my friendship with Andrew is debatable at best. And after the shit he pulled last night, she shouldn't want to show him any damn support.

Besides all of that, I'm ninety-nine percent positive what she's wearing is the same shirt he hands out to groupies he's fucked or girls he wants to fuck, so his security guard knows who to bring backstage after a show. "You're *my* girl. I'm asking you, don't—"

"Okay." She lifts the shirt, revealing a sexy as fuck see-through black lace bra. "Give me a minute to find something else." She tosses the shirt on the couch. I'm tempted to burn it and shove the ashes down Andrew's throat as soon as I see the sneaky prick.

"Here." She returns and holds up two black tank tops. One with the Harley Davidson logo and the other with Kickstart's top-hat wearing skull and two guitars on the front.

"Either one."

She tosses the Harley one on the couch and slips the other one over her head. Her gaze lingers on the discarded Vandals shirt. "I'm sorry."

I press my palms to her cheeks and kiss her forehead. "Don't apologize. Not your fault you've got a possessive motherfucker for a boyfriend."

Jealousy's the explanation I'm going with. Not to protect Andrew. Fuck that asshole. To protect Mallory. I can't even imagine how much it would hurt her feelings to find out he tried to embarrass her in front of a stadium full of people tonight.

Guess I'll have to figure out some other plausible explanation for why I'm going to knock the fucker out the second I see him.

CHAPTER SIXTY

MALLORY

Peter's spitting fire when we finally arrive at the arena.

"Don't you two fuck enough? I warned you to be on time for this—"

"Ease up." Chaser levels a withering stare at his tour manager. "We had a hard time getting into the place. Maybe you should've mentioned we needed passes even at this hour."

"Oh." He gives us a sheepish look and pulls two laminated passes on black lanyards out for us. "You were on the list. The other guys got in without an issue."

Chaser shrugs and hands me my pass.

"Chaser! You fucker! There is no thirteenth floor." Andrew's booming voice makes all three of us turn his way.

Chaser glares at him.

"Aww, Mallory, you didn't wear my shirt." His childish pout is almost cute, but I still feel bad I ever considered wearing the stupid shirt tonight. Of course I shouldn't be running around at one of Chaser's shows wearing another band's shirt.

Chaser hasn't stopped his death glare and even growls low in his throat.

As usual, Andrew's oblivious.

Peter's freaked out eyes dance between the two musicians. "Chaser. Let's go. They're waiting for you." Peter shoves us into a dressing room that has Kickstart's name on the door. I quickly point it out to Chaser while we rush by.

Inside, there's another door to a lounge area, where the band and interviewer are chatting.

"Sorry we're late. Had trouble getting into the arena." Chaser's earlier menace evaporates as he pastes on a professional smile.

"No problem. We were catching up about the tour."

"Uh." I tap Chaser's shoulder. "I need to run to the bathroom," I whisper.

Clearly torn, he glances at the door.

"I'll be fine." I hold up my pass. "I'm all legal now. No one will harass me."

The interviewer flicks her gaze at me. "We don't need you for a little while, Mallory."

I don't know why she needs me at all. I'm not part of the band. Either way, it doesn't matter. I need to pee.

I poke my head out of the room, searching for a familiar face to point the way to the nearest bathroom.

Tons of people litter the large backstage area. Photographers. Fans. Family. Road crew. I wave to a few who call my name as I wander down the corridor, searching for the ladies' room.

Ah, finally. I push inside and take care of business.

At the sink, I dig a small brush out of my purse and fix my hair. Two girls burst into the bathroom giggling. I watch them with envy brewing in my chest. None of the guys have significant others I can hang out with when the band's busy. The girls they hook up with rarely want to talk to me—that's *if* the guys let them stick around after they've served their purpose.

I thought maybe Pamela and I would develop a friendship since our boyfriends are so close. It's probably a blessing she didn't join me on this trip, though.

"Hi," one of the girls says. "You look familiar. Have you— oh my God! You're Mallory Dove! The 'Candy Jar' girl. Hey!"

"Hi." I stick out my hand and project a friendly smile. "That's me."

"That's so cool you're here." The first girl shakes my hand enthusiastically. "I'm Kim, this is Pearl."

"Oh, what a pretty name."

"Thanks."

The two girls share a look. I can already sense what they're going to ask.

"So, is Alvin traveling with anyone?" Kim asks.

"Or Garrett," Pearl adds.

How about that? Usually girls ask about Jacob. I'm oddly pleased the groupies are starting to notice Alvin, since he'll treat them a lot nicer than the other two will.

"Not that I know of." My gaze drops to Kim's shirt and slides over to Pearl's almost identical one. "Oh." I laugh feeling silly. "I have the same shirt."

The girls glance at each other. "But you're with Chaser," Kim says.

"Well, the guys are friends, so they hang out a lot." I shrug. "Andrew gave me one this morning."

"Oh, honey." They share another weird look that I can't interpret. Kim taps her chest. "Andrew hands these out to girls he's...*you know*...hooked up with in different cities. Usually asks us to wear it, so his bodyguard can easily pick us out and bring us backstage. Each guy has one that's slightly different."

"Mine's from Vinnie," Pearl adds, pointing to the cartoon of Vinnie's face in the middle of her shirt.

No wonder Chaser's head almost exploded when I came out of the bedroom wearing Andrew's shirt. If he's been on tour with them all this time, he has to be aware of its significance. I would've been walking around all night completely unaware I was announcing to the world that I'd fucked Andrew *and* made Chaser look like a fool.

"Excuse me." I push out of the bathroom and storm down the hallway, searching for the Vandal's dressing room.

A-ha. Benny's big body sticks out, and I make a beeline for the door he's guarding. I'm smaller and quicker on my feet than Andrew's burly bodyguard. I duck under one of his tree-trunk sized arms and manage to fling open the door before he even knows what's happening.

Mouth open, I stop and stare at the scene in front of me. Andrew with a girl who definitely isn't Pamela bent over a chair. Both of them naked from the waist down. Fully engaged.

"Shit." I gasp. "Oh shit."

"You planning to stay and watch, Mal?" Andrew thrusts his hips, and the girl moans. "I don't mind an audience but close the door before some fucker takes a picture."

His casual attitude cuts through my shock, reigniting my fury. "You asshole!" Tears burn my eyelids, but I'll be dammed if I'm going to cry in front of them.

Embarrassed and disgusted I back out of the room.

"Mallory, wait!" Andrew calls out behind me. I'm so furious I keep power-walking down the corridor. We're attracting enough attention to make people turn and stare.

A heavy hand lands on my shoulder, spinning me around. "Get off me!"

"Shhh, don't cause a scene," Andrew pleads.

"Cause a scene?" My jaw drops as I lower my gaze to his unzipped, barely-hanging-onto-his-narrow-hips black leather pants. "You're the one running around like a jackass with your pants about to fall off."

"Shhh, come here." He guides me into an empty room and flicks on the lights. But before he closes the door, Chaser yells my name. Andrew tries to slam the door, but it flies open, smacking him in the elbow.

"Ow fuck!"

"What the fuck are you doing?" Chaser roars. "Get your fucking hands off her!"

"Jesus Christ. Calm down." Andrew shakes his arm and stumbles back a few steps. "Fuck, that hurts!"

"What's going on?" Chaser's murderous expression softens as he comes closer to me. "I thought you were coming right back?"

"I met some girls in the bathroom." I throw a glare at Andrew. "They told me the significance of the T-shirt Andrew gave me. I stopped by his dressing room to give him my opinion on the matter, but he was busy with someone, who *wasn't* Pamela, so I left, and he followed."

Chaser closes his eyes for a second, and I swear he's either praying or trying not to laugh.

"You knew, didn't you?" I sock Chaser in the gut.

"I suspected," he clarifies, wrapping his hand around my fist and tugging me closer.

"It's just a shirt," Andrew grumbles. "I knew Chaser wouldn't let you wear it. I was just fucking around. We always play pranks on the opening band."

"Smear some Vaseline on Jacob's mic or dump confetti on them during the last song." God, I wish I had something to smack him with right now. "Don't humiliate *me*."

Andrew squints and scratches the side of his head. "Fucking me is humiliating?"

Chaser takes a step forward, but I wrap myself around one of his arms and use all my weight to hold him back.

Andrew holds up his hands. "You know what I mean."

"And you know what *I* meant," I snap.

"Okay, okay. I'm sorry." He holds out his arms, preparing to embrace both of us. "I love you guys. You're like my favorite people. Don't be pissed. Please?"

When neither of us respond, Andrew drops his arms. "Okay, not ready to hug it out. That's cool."

"I need to finish that interview," Chaser says to me.

I slip my hand into his and he opens the door.

"Mallory, wait." Andrew touches my shoulder.

"Get your filthy fucking hand off her." Chaser reaches past me and slaps his palm against Andrew's chest, shoving him away.

"Fine." Andrew sticks his hands in the air but holds my gaze. "Don't say anything to Pammy. She knows, but she doesn't want to *know*. You feel me?"

"Whatever, Andrew."

Quite a crowd has gathered outside the room. Chaser throws his arm around my shoulders, keeping me close, as we push our way through.

"Chaser, did you and Andrew have a fight?"

"Were you fighting over Mallory?"

"Is it true you pulled a gun on Andrew?"

"Mallory, are you sleeping with Andrew Lane?"

I whirl around seeking the person who asked that question, but Chaser pulls me forward. "Ignore it."

We work our way into Kickstart's dressing room, and Chaser shuts the door. "Are you okay?" he asks in a hushed tone.

I glance toward the door where the band was being interviewed, but it's still closed. "Did you know?"

He sighs. "Listen, I'm not lodged so far up Andrew's ass that I know the details, but I strongly suspected it was the same shirt. I wouldn't have wanted you to wear it no matter what. But I definitely couldn't have you wearing it if I was right."

"Why didn't you explain it to me?"

"I was hoping you'd never find out." He shakes his head. "I didn't want your feelings hurt."

"Did you know he cheats on Pamela?"

He rolls his eyes. "Who *doesn't* know?"

"Dammit, Chaser. I work with her."

"I'm not sticking my nose in their business." He scowls at the door. "Although, after the last two nights, I'm tempted."

I rest the back of my hand against his cheek. "Forget about Andrew. You need to calm down and finish that interview."

He takes a long deep breath.

"*Rolling Stone* is here to interview Kickstart." I raise my fists in the air and let out a hushed cheer. "Yay!"

Finally, he cracks a smile.

We enter the interview room, and the woman stands. "Everything okay?"

"Everything's fine," Chaser answers with perfect calm.

He must sense that's I'm still rattled and pulls me over to the couch and into his lap when he takes his place in the corner.

"So, Chaser, rumor has it you've been asked to play on a few songs for legendary pop singer, Mitchell Howard's new album. How'd that happen?"

Jacob casts a look Chaser's way.

Why hello cat, guess you're leaving the bag now.

"Uh, he called me out of the blue. Said he dug my playing

and asked if I'd come down to the studio and try a few things. Nothing's written in stone yet," Chaser explains.

"That's great." She eyes the rest of the band. "Anyone else have any side projects they're working on?"

"Nah, we're all too committed to this tour and recording Kickstart's next album as soon as we get off the road," Jacob answers for everyone.

As if Chaser isn't committed.

Chaser wouldn't have time to entertain Michell's offer if he didn't have to sit around waiting for Jacob to pull himself together with alarming frequency. How badly I want to blab about all the wasted studio and rehearsal time the band's endured because of Jacob.

Instead, I sit there, smile pretty, and when I'm asked, gush about how excited I am for tonight's show.

CHAPTER SIXTY-ONE

CHASER

Wild's the only way to describe tonight's show. The electric energy sparking from the crowd fuels my performance and burns my irritation from the earlier events away.

Why can't every night be like this one? My girl watching from side stage. All four of us in sync and in peak performance. The crowd enraptured by our performance.

So flawless I'm tempted to pinch myself.

Not even watching Andrew come up behind Mallory and lean in to speak to her dulls my enthusiasm for the show.

Jacob announces, "Candy Jar," and the crowd loses their minds. On this tour, we've been giving it the same gritty treatment as the EP version. Tonight, during my solo, Jacob runs off stage.

Not unusual. I'm too wrapped up in playing to pay much attention. A collective gasp and screams from the crowd draw my attention to the side. Where Jacob's leading Mallory on stage.

The fuck?

"Our official 'Candy Jar' girl's visiting us tonight!" Jacob shouts. "Give it up for Mallory!"

For a second, she gets that doe-staring-down-the-barrel-of-a-shotgun fear in her eyes, but she shakes it off and waves to the crowd.

Jacob picks up the last few lines of the song, and we finish to thunderous applause.

I grab Mallory around the waist, lifting her in the air and carrying her backstage. "Sorry about that," I say in between kisses.

"I was shocked. I thought he didn't want me on stage ever again."

I glance over, but Jacob's gone. "Who knows what's going on in his head."

"You were amazing," she murmurs, leaning in for another kiss. "Do you have any idea how sexy you are when you're on stage?"

"Why don't you show me?"

"You gonna watch us tonight?" Andrew yells from about three feet away.

Mallory and I both groan.

"I'm still not speaking to you," she says without looking at him.

I choke on a laugh and bury my head against her shoulder.

"I said I was sorry."

"A grown-ass man whining is a sad sight." Alvin slaps Andrew's arm. "Have some dignity, bro."

"Where'd Jacob go?" I set Mallory down and face Alvin.

"He wasn't feeling great," Garrett says.

"Shit, I hope he's not sick." As the words leave my mouth, I spot Jacob way down the hallway, arguing with Vinnie.

"The fuck are they doing?" I jerk my chin in their direction.

"Vinnie swore he had a hookup in town, but the guy never showed." Andrew shrugs. "I'll go help him look after our show."

"Jesus Fucking Christ," I growl. "Are you fucking kidding me?" The last thing we need is the three of them trolling the city in search of coke, heroin, or whatever the fuck they're shooting these days.

Mallory searches the backstage area. "There are plenty of girls here for him to hook up with."

"Not that kind of hookup." I lean down and kiss her cheek.

"Oh." Her eyes widen. "Shit."

"I haven't slipped up," I assure her.

She runs her fingers over my cheek. "I know you haven't."

I tip my head and brush my lips over her inner wrist. "Thank you."

The roadies finish moving our set out of the way. Vinnie joins us but doesn't say much. My fingers itch to wrap around his damn throat for getting Jacob hooked after he'd been clean for months. Then again, I don't know that it didn't happen the other way around.

"You've never seen us live, right?" Andrew asks Mallory.

"No."

"So stay and watch," he pleads.

"Chaser and I have other plans."

I smirk and shrug at him.

"Go bang in your dressing room, then come back and watch."

We don't bother replying. Instead, I take Mallory around and introduce her to different people. Fans waiting in the hallway to talk to us rush forward, and I sign a few autographs.

The noise from the crowd out in the arena intensifies. "Do you want to watch them?" I ask Mallory.

"I'm curious, but still mad."

"So, we won't watch the whole show."

We wander back to the spot that will give us the best view of the stage.

"Awe-*some*," Andrew says. "You're gonna watch?"

Mallory crosses her arms over her chest. Unfortunately, instead of stern, it just makes her sexier. "Not for *you*."

"How about now?" He whips off his white shorts and tosses them aside, leaving him in one of his famous leather cock hammocks. Tonight, it's red leather. Not an improvement.

"Jesus Christ," I mutter.

"It's hot." He angles both his hands, palm up, toward his dick. "Besides, it showcases my goods."

Mallory blinks and stares. "It's not as flattering as you think it is."

"What are you talking about?" He waves her off and starts jumping around, pumping himself up for their show.

A grown man jumping around in nothing but leather underwear is disturbing as fuck to witness.

"Aren't you glad I always keep my pants on?" Alvin jokes.

"Yes."

The lights over the audience go down, and the screams intensify. Andrew runs out first, climbing up behind his massive drum kit.

"He really is amazing to watch," Alvin says.

"*You're* amazing to watch." Mallory pats his shoulder. "No one could ever replace you as my favorite drummer."

"Aw, thanks, Mal."

Her gaze scans the hallway, landing on two girls in Vicious Vandals T-shirts. "You know, the pretty dark-haired one asked me about you earlier."

Alvin follows her line of sight. "Pass. Saw her deep-throat Andrew last night."

Mallory wrinkles her nose.

"Nice try," I whisper in her ear.

A steady thumping comes from the stage. Vinnie hurries past us, followed by Kyle and Boner, who've barely spoken a word to us this whole tour.

In between songs, Andrew's tour manager approaches us. "They want you guys to join them for 'We Die Young' tonight. That cool?"

"Really?" I search the area for Darren and motion for him to bring my guitar. "Yeah, of course."

Sure enough, a few songs later, Kyle calls us out on stage.

Mallory bounces up and down and hugs me.

Garrett strolls up and shakes his head when I ask where Jacob is. "His throat's bothering him."

"Sure."

The crowd goes nuts when we join Vicious Vandals on stage. Vinnie and I riff out a dueling guitar solo completely off the cuff. Excitement pounds through my veins. Talk about a rush. Vinnie launches into "We Die Young," and I try to follow his lead, without stepping on his toes. Behind me, Alvin bangs a tambourine around. Garrett seems to be as overloaded as I am. He keeps missing notes, and I know damn well he has this song memorized.

Finally, the song closes. The lights go down. The crowd keeps chanting.

Vinnie high-fives me. Kyle actually shakes my hand and thanks me for coming out.

"That was rad!" Alvin laughs, as he catches up to me.

"Don't start that *rad* shit with me." I shove him, and he laughs harder.

"That was so good!" Mallory hugs both of us, after Darren

takes my guitar again. "Is that the first time you've gone on stage with them?"

"Yup," Alvin answers. "Guess that's why Andrew kept asking us to stick around."

Mallory lifts her gaze to mine. "Now I can't even be mad at him."

"Sure you can." I sling my arm over her shoulder.

Yeah, Andrew tried to do a nice thing, but I'm sick and tired of the back and forth with him. One minute he's a dick, the next he's our benevolent benefactor.

Makes it hard to decide if I want to shake his hand.

Or murder him.

CHAPTER SIXTY-TWO

MALLORY

Where the heck is Chaser? After a brief celebration with the guys, we came back to our room. As we were falling asleep, Jacob called with some emergency.

Chaser gave me a quick kiss and told me to go back to sleep.

As if I could sleep.

I glance over at the clock. He's been gone for hours.

As much as I can't stand Peter, I call down to his room. "Peter, have you heard from the guys?"

"Christ, Mallory. It's two in the morning. They probably found some groupies."

Gee, thanks.

By eight o'clock, I'm beyond worried.

Nine o'clock.

Ten o'clock.

The phone rings, and I hurry to answer it.

"Hello?"

The line crackles. "Mallory, it's Pamela."

"Pamela! What's going on? Where are you?"

"In L.A. Are you still with the guys?"

"Yes, we're in Texas." While it's not unusual for her to call me, she's the last person I expected to hear from this morning. I'm too jittery for social niceties "What's up?"

"What's *up?*" she parrots back. "Are you fucking kidding?"

"What are you talking about?"

"Were you there when it happened?"

My anxiety over Chaser's absence shoots through the roof. "There, when *what* happened?"

"It's all over the news about Andrew."

A boulder of dread settles in my stomach. "What news?"

"Someone *shot* him."

"What? Oh my God. Where?" The phone beeps. Desperate for information about Chaser, I click over to the incoming call, without saying goodbye to Pamela.

"Mallory?" Chaser's strained voice crackles over the line.

"Chaser! Where are you? Oh my God. Are you okay?" Was he with Andrew? Was he hurt, too?

In a low, desperate voice, he says, "Mallory, I need you to call my dad for me."

"What? Are you okay?"

"I'm fine."

"Where are you? Pamela called and said someone *shot* Andrew. That's crazy." A hollow laugh escapes me as I reach for the remote to switch on the television.

The line's silent, and I'm afraid he hung up. "Chaser?"

"I'm at the county jail."

"Jail? What happened?"

"Mallory, I can't talk long. I need you to call my father. You and I won't have enough to cover the bail. *If* they give me bail."

A thousand memories of my father calling me after the FBI

426

took him into custody pummel me in the chest. "Chaser, what are you talking about?"

My scared mind can't connect the dots fast enough.

"Have him wire the money."

"What money? Chaser, what's going on?" Terror claws through my insides.

"He'll know how to get a hold of an attorney for me too. Are you listening, Mallory? I don't have much longer."

"Yes." Tears run down my cheeks. "What's going on?" I whisper.

I saw the news about Andrew. Pamela's words echo in my mind a second before Chaser responds.

"Someone shot Andrew. And the cops think it was me."

Mallory and Chaser's journey concludes in
Wheels of Fire.

READING ORDER

I'm frequently asked where the standalones fit into the Lost Kings MC Series. Although the *Kickstart Trilogy* is not technically part of the Lost Kings MC series, there are some crossover characters. If you're so inclined, you could read my books in the *chronological* order in which they happen in the Lost Kings MC world. It goes something like this:

Kickstart My Heart
Blow My Fuse
Wheels of Fire
Cards of Love: Knight of Swords
Slow Burn (Lost Kings MC #1)
Corrupting Cinderella (Lost Kings MC #2)
Three Kings, One Night (Lost Kings MC #2.5)
Strength From Loyalty (Lost Kings MC #3)
Tattered on My Sleeve (Lost Kings MC #4)
White Heat (Lost Kings MC #5)
Between Embers (Lost Kings MC #5.5)
Bullets & Bonfires

More Than Miles (Lost Kings MC #6)
Unhinged (Iron Bulls MC #5) by Phoenyx Slaughter
Warnings & Wildfires
White Knuckles (Lost Kings MC #7)
Beyond Reckless (Lost Kings MC #8)
Beyond Reason (Lost Kings MC #9)
One Empire Night (Lost Kings MC #9.5)
After Burn (Lost Kings MC #10)
After Glow (Lost Kings MC #11)
Zero Hour (Lost Kings MC #11.5)
Zero Tolerance (Lost Kings MC #12)
Zero Regret (Lost Kings MC #13)
Zero Apologies (Lost Kings MC #14)
Swagger and Sass (A Lost Kings MC Novella)
White Lies (Lost Kings MC #15)
Rhythm of the Road (Lost Kings MC #16)
Lyrics on the Wind (Lost Kings MC #17)
Crown of Ghosts (Lost Kings MC #18)

And many more to come...

ABOUT THE AUTHOR

Autumn Jones Lake is the *USA Today* and *Wall Street Journal* bestselling author of over twenty novels, including the popular Lost Kings MC series. She believes true love stories never end.

Her past lives include baking cookies, bagging groceries, selling cheap shoes, and practicing law. Playing with her imaginary friends all day is by far her favorite job yet!

Autumn lives in upstate New York with her own alpha hero.

www.autumnjoneslake.com

facebook.com/autumnjoneslake

goodreads.com/autumnjoneslake

pinterest.com/autumnjoneslake

www.ingramcontent.com/pod-product-compliance
Lightning Source LLC
Chambersburg PA
CBHW031142050726
47495CB00018B/362